PENGUIN BOOKS

When They Find Her

Lia Middleton is a barrister who specializes in crime and offender management. She graduated in Drama and Theatre Studies before transferring to a legal career, which she practises alongside her lifelong love for writing.

Lia lives with her husband and two young children in Buckinghamshire.

When They Find Her is her first novel.

You can find Lia on:
Twitter @liamiddleton
Instagram @liamiddletonauthor
www.liamiddleton.com

When They Find Her

LIA MIDDLETON

PENGUIN BOOKS

PENGUIN BOOKS

UK | USA | Canada | Ireland | Australia
India | New Zealand | South Africa

Penguin Books is part of the Penguin Random House group of companies
whose addresses can be found at global.penguinrandomhouse.com

First published by Michael Joseph 2021
Published in Penguin Books 2021

002

Copyright © Lia Middleton, 2021

The moral right of the author has been asserted

Typeset by Jouve (UK), Milton Keynes
Printed and bound in Great Britain by Clays Ltd, Elcograf S.p.A.

The authorized representative in the EEA is Penguin Random House Ireland,
Morrison Chambers, 32 Nassau Street, Dublin D02 YH68

A CIP catalogue record for this book is available from the British Library

ISBN: 978-1-405-94821-0

For my mum and dad – Anna and Panayiotis Yiacoumi.
The parents every child deserves.

Freya was sleeping. Her warm breath, fast and shallow, fluttered rhythmically against my skin as I clutched her to my chest. That's just how babies breathe, the midwives told me.

'You ready?'

Aiden's hand rested on the small of my back and I nodded up at him in response. He lifted her out of my arms and strapped her into her seat. I was shocked by the instant keen sting of her absence. We walked through the ward, shuffling along at my slow pace until we finally emerged into the harsh white of outside. I tilted my neck, the back of my head pressing against the nape, and looked up at the expanse of world hanging heavily above us. It was too big. A butterfly leaving the suffocating safety of its cocoon.

Was I ready?

I blinked rapidly, pulling Freya that much closer, and looked down at my shoes. One foot in front of the other. One step at a time.

On the long drive home, I sat in the back of the car – in the middle seat, closest to her. I watched her, as the city disappeared and the countryside emerged, rolling out its green carpet to guide us to the horizon, and home. Fields whizzed by, dappled in sunlight. Trees hung over the road, kissed by the vibrant greens of summer. Animals grazed in paddocks. Soon we would be at the farm and we could finally start our life together. My little family. The three of us against the world.

She shifted in her seat, eyes opening slightly to take in the world before closing again.

I love you so much, I thought. I promise I'll look after you. I promise I'll never hurt you.

A foolish promise to make.

Sometimes we hurt people by accident.

PART ONE

I

Four years later . . .
November

They should be here soon.

The grandfather clock that ticks loudly in the hall seems to have slowed down. Each second feels an hour, and with each swing of the pendulum, the tingle of anxiety increases. Kneeling on the soft blue cushion of the window seat, I strain my neck to look out of the porthole window at the long stony drive: a dark grey ribbon under the overcast sky.

I paced the hall for half an hour before taking up my position in the window. A sentry, watching and waiting. I just have to make sure that he doesn't see me peer out through the glass. I need to be calm when he arrives.

I glance at my watch. He'd said they would be here by ten . . .

I wish she didn't live so far away. Aiden has sworn they won't move further than London. But it still feels too distant.

My hands are clammy. I wipe them on my jeans and shake my head, trying to force myself to savour the excitement, which is peeking timidly out from behind my fear. I wasn't sure when or whether this day would come. Now that it has, it needs to be perfect.

I glance down at my hands where my engagement and wedding rings still nestle against each other, comfortable in the pale white groove of my skin. Aiden has asked me to take them off, but the rings are stuck beneath the knuckle of my permanently swollen fingers – one of many side-effects of motherhood.

Gravel shifts on the drive and I stretch up again to see Aiden's car manoeuvring in front of the house, taking up the position where it used to park permanently. I scramble off the seat, run to the door and pull it open. The old iron hinges creak and a gust of freezing air whistles into the house.

The door on the driver's side swings open and my toes curl on the cold tiles. Aiden groans as he holds on to the rim of the door to pull himself out, his knees straining under the weight of his body. I can't hear them, but they'll have clicked – a remnant of his younger days when he used to play rugby. What a ridiculous car for a man so tall. He moves around to the back passenger seat and I push forwards on to my tiptoes, trying to catch a glimpse of her. A slam, and then –

There she is: running towards me, a huge smile plastered to her face, a large piece of paper flapping in her hands.

'Freya!' I shriek, my voice high with excitement.

My darling girl.

Freya Grace Williams. Four years old. Born on 16 August weighing seven pounds and two ounces. Twenty inches long; ten fingers; ten toes; green eyes like her father; raven-black hair like mine.

She slows down as she reaches the house, her feet scuffing and sending gravel skittering in all directions as she stops just short of the front door. She looks up at me, a small smile on her round face, the chubby cheeks she had as a baby yet to disappear. Her long, wavy dark hair is partially pulled back, so that it doesn't fall into her eyes, and in the sunlight they almost look gold.

I crouch and pull her to me.

'Mummy!' she says, her breath tickling my ear as she turns her head to kiss my cheek.

Aiden approaches and stands behind Freya, grasping her shoulder. She breaks away from me and turns her head to look up at him. He smiles down at her, the skin around his eyes crinkling. It was his eyes I noticed the first time I saw him all those years ago. He had approached me and my friends, full of confidence. A heatwave had rolled over London and the rooftop bar was buzzing in the afternoon sun, but as I looked up from my drink, my thoughts interrupted by his 'Excuse me?', all I could see was him. The light shimmered brilliantly on the Thames behind him, but I was transfixed.

'Show Mummy what you made her.' His voice sounds husky, like it does when he hasn't slept very well.

I smile, and she holds out the piece of paper at arms' length.

'Did you draw this?'

A nod of confirmation as her cheeks flush and she looks down at her feet.

I take the piece of paper. On it is a horizontal, slightly wonky green line, shaded in. Through that expanse of green: a curvy blue wave. Brown trunks are topped with swirls of another shade of green and dotted with red spheres. Above that, a scratchy sea of blue. And, last, two figures: one small, with green dots for eyes; one tall with brown dots, holding hands, both with U-shaped smiles in pink.

Our farm.

Us.

I look up at Freya and her face is furrowed. I grin at her. 'I love it, darling.' My voice cracks and I cough to clear it. 'It's perfect.'

Her face relaxes and she beams back at me.

'Thanks, Freya.' I lean forward and kiss her forehead. She smells fresh and clean, and I'm transported back to lying on the sofa with her on my chest. Soft skin underneath my fingers. Breathing in that new-born scent.

As I stand up, Aiden holds out her pink backpack, and our hands brush as I take it from him. My fingers flinch as if I've been stung. He meets my eye, his eyebrows raised. I smile and the tight cord of tension between us breaks. In return, he crosses his arms and steps back, away from the threshold of the door.

I turn my attention back to Freya, who is waiting at my side, but I can feel Aiden watching me through narrowed eyes. I look back up to his face and he holds my gaze. He wants to break me open so that he can understand me better. So that he can expose my insides and see exactly what is in my heart, pumping through my veins.

'Okay, Freya.' I break the silence, tearing my eyes away from Aiden to smile down at her. 'Say goodbye to Daddy and then you can go inside, if you like – there's a surprise for you in the snug.'

'Books?' she asks.

'Maybe,' I say, shrugging my shoulders playfully.

She grins at me, then rushes into Aiden's arms. He kisses her on the side of the head and whispers something in her ear. She nods in response, shouts a final goodbye, scooting past me into the house. Sitting down on the stairs – the second step up – she pulls off her shoes, flinging them onto the floor below her, then runs towards the kitchen and through to the snug.

Holding onto the door, I turn back to Aiden, whose arms are still crossed – a barrier between us. I wait for him to say something else – goodbye, see you tomorrow, anything to end this awkward interaction – but he just stands there watching me.

'Well . . . Thank you for letting me have her.'

He scoffs.

I force my face to remain friendly, passive, but at my side, my hand clenches into a fist. 'I really do appreciate it,' I say.

'Well, just make sure you look after her.'

'Of course.' I take care with my words, but they're clipped. Dull.

'You know what I mean, Naomi. You haven't had her overnight for a reason. Remember?'

I bristle. 'I know that. And it's been a long time.'

He doesn't respond and I can feel him assessing me in the silence. He wants to say something – I can feel it waiting in the space between us.

'What is it?'

'Promise me you're not still taking those pills.'

'I already have. But yes . . . I promise.'

He watches my face carefully, then glances into the hall behind me as Freya skids across the stone floor on her way to the kitchen.

'You know what? Maybe I'll just take her home. I'm not sure I'm ready –'

'You won't take her anywhere,' I snap, as anger instantly bubbles in my stomach. 'You agreed I could have her tonight. You promised. Remember?' I echo his condescending word back at him.

His chin drops to his chest and he nods. 'Just look after her. Okay?'

'I'll look after her, Aiden. I *am* her mother.'

He glares at me, shakes his head and opens his mouth, taking a deep breath in as if he is going to say something but then, for some reason, he doesn't. He simply shakes his head again, decisively this time, and walks off without looking back.

As he drives away, I'm struck by a familiar pang deep in my stomach. Seeing him leave never seems to get easier. But then a small hand tugs on the hem of my cardigan, and I look down to find Freya, clutching a book in her small hands.

'Mummy, can we read in the snug?'

'Of course, darling.' She trots off towards the back of the house, and I push the door firmly shut.

Freya beams up at me as we fill the bath with hot, foamy water. She's poured in almost half of the bottle and squeals with delight as the bubbles multiply.

Leaving the tap running, we go across the landing to her bedroom. Even when she isn't with me, and I float around the empty house, I occasionally go into her room. For so long, it was a relic of the time before, the time when we were a family. I couldn't bear to change a single thing. The cot stood empty in the centre of the room, the mobile above it hanging aimlessly from the ceiling, and the nursing chair – where I'd cradled her for hours – gathered dust. But I suddenly realized that staying in the past won't bring my family home. This summer, I painted the walls lilac for her fourth birthday. With each paint-stroke I imagined her playing in her room, reading. Falling asleep. When she came over for her birthday visit, she ran into it, squealing and spinning around in small circles. I sold the cot she'd slept in from six months old at a charity sale and replaced it with what she calls a 'big-girl bed' – white posts and a canopy covered with clouds. A tall bookshelf stands proudly in the corner of the room. It is bursting with books, new and old, some of which belonged to me when I was a little girl. The walls are adorned with framed quotes and pages from her favourite book: the tale of a little girl who followed a White Rabbit and fell down a hole to Wonderland. She even asked me once if she could change her name to Alice.

I've perfected her room, curating it in the hope that one day she might finally be able to come home. The space is bursting with toys she hardly ever gets to play with. A bed she has never slept in. Until now.

She's standing in front of the bookshelf, where the copy of *Alice in Wonderland* I had as a child stands in pride of place in the middle of the centre shelf. Its cover is worn, the edges of the pages curling from countless readings. She loves it, just as I did. She always places it so carefully on the shelf, standing it in front of the other books, gazing up at it in awe. And she is staring at it now, already distracted from her excitement for a bath.

I reach quickly into the back pocket of my jeans and wriggle my phone out.

Snap. Snap, snap.

She undresses clumsily, then we pad past the staircase and my parents' old room, and cross the landing to the bathroom. I lift her into the bath, the sides still too high for her small frame. As I do so, my phone vibrates.

It's Rupert.

I hope it's going well. Thinking of you xxx

My stomach flips with a rush of guilt. He had wanted to be here, but I said no. That it needed to be just me and her. The two of us, alone.

Thank you. All good, just about to have a bath and then bedtime.

I promise you'll meet her soon x

I balance the phone on the edge of the washbasin, but it 'brates again and tumbles to the floor. I pick it up – the screen still intact – and his message flashes in front of my background photo: baby Freya, in a mint green Babygro, smiling for the first time.

I can't wait. Have you told her she's going to be a big sister? xxx

I look up from my phone and Freya is still watching me over the edge of the bath. Her eyes fall to my stomach before returning to the bubbles. Can she tell already?

I place my hand on my tummy. It is still flat, slightly concave where my hip bones jut outwards. There is nothing yet: it's only been a few weeks. My imagination sometimes runs away with me.

I put the phone on the closed lid of the toilet, ignoring his message, and watch Freya in the bath, the water up to her chest, each hand laden with a pile of bubbles.

'Freya . . . do you like staying at Mummy's house?' I bite down on my lip, hard. I shouldn't ask her questions like that.

She continues to play with the bubbles in her hands, but after a moment, she nods, almost imperceptibly.

I breathe out quickly, the breath I was holding coming out in a loud exhale. I shouldn't ask her any more: I shouldn't put any more pressure on her.

But I can't help myself.

'Would you like to stay with Mummy more often?' I smile at her, soften my tone. I want to be reassuring, to make her feel loved. As if, no matter what answer she gives, it will be all right. That she won't upset me. Guilt is the worst emotion, especially for a child. 'We could ask Daddy when he comes to collect you tomorrow, if you'd like?'

She stops playing and repeats the motion. The slightest nod.

'Okay. We'll ask him.' Aiden will hate it – he'll say I'm trying to manipulate him. That I'm using Freya as a weapo

But that isn't true. I would never do that. She needs me, just as much as she needs him. More, even. Every child needs their mother.

Kneeling over the bath and scooping up a huge pile of bubbles in my arms, I breathe in and expel all of the air quickly and powerfully out of my lungs, sending the bubbles flying towards her. She laughs uncontrollably as they blow into her hair and onto her face. And she continues to laugh, all the way from her tummy: the kind of laugh where you can't quite catch your breath, the kind that almost hurts. And I laugh right along with her.

After some time splashing about, I take care as I wash her hair and rinse it, making sure not to get shampoo in her eyes. When we still lived here as a family, she used to hate having her hair washed – terrified that the water would sting her eyes. She would shout, 'Ow!' before I even began to pour the water onto her head.

I wish I could make her less afraid.

I lift her out, and she stands on the bathmat as I wrap a fluffy white towel around her and pull her into a hug. Her wet hair drips on my shoulder.

'Come on, let's go and get you dry.'

We walk hand in hand, and giggle together when I trip up the step into her room. 'Silly Mummy,' she says.

I help her into her favourite pyjamas – unicorn ones – which I had already laid out on the bed. But when I plug in the hair-dryer and turn it on, she jumps, presses her hands to her ears and shrinks away from me.

'Don't you like the hair-dryer, darling?'

This is new.

'No! Please turn it off!' she shouts, over the noise. I turn it off abruptly. The only sound that fills the room is her fast breathing, her bare chest heaving up and down.

I kneel so that we're face to face. 'It's just a hair-dryer. It won't hurt you.' I stroke her face, pushing her hair away, and her lip quivers.

'I don't like it. The noise is scary.'

'That's all right. We'll just dry your hair with the towel, okay?'

'That's what Helen does.'

My hand jolts at the sound of her name, and my fingers catch in a knot in Freya's hair.

'Ouch, Mummy.'

'Sorry. I'm sorry. It was an accident.' I chew the inside of my cheek and concentrate on rubbing the towel rhythmically over her hair.

She's just a child – she doesn't understand. She didn't mean to hurt me. 'Would you like to read to me while I dry your hair, then?'

'Yes, please,' she whispers.

I retrieve her school reading book from her backpack, which is lying by her wardrobe. It's a simple picture book: one short sentence to a page and big bright illustrations. It takes almost fifteen minutes to towel-dry her hair, but she doesn't care: her little chest puffs with pride as she sounds out the words.

Once her hair is dry, she climbs into bed and I tuck her in tightly, the duvet all the way up to her chin.

'Is your bed comfy?' I ask.

She nods happily.

'Here's Mouse,' I say, and she pulls her arms up to reach for her favourite toy. She can't sleep without him.

'Do you want me to read to you again, darling?'

'Yes, please.'

'What would you like? Any book you want.'

She grins. '*Alice*!'

'Again?' I gasp, feigning shock. 'Shall we read from where we left off? To the finish?'

She nods, her eyes gleaming with excitement.

I clamber onto the bed next to her, lean against the headboard and begin to read. I read all the way to the end, as I promised her I would.

'. . . "Lastly, she pictured to herself how this same little sister of hers would, in the after-time, be herself a grown woman; and how she would keep, through all her riper years, the simple and loving heart of her childhood: and how she would gather about her other little children, and make *their* eyes bright and eager with many a strange tale, perhaps even with the dream of Wonderland of long ago: and how she would feel with all their simple sorrows, and find a pleasure in all their simple joys, remembering her own child-life, and the happy summer days."'

I sneak a sideways look at Freya – her eyes have closed and her long dark eyelashes flutter against her cheeks.

I ease myself off the bed, not wanting the shift of my weight to wake her, then turn back to kiss her cheek.

'Goodnight. I love you, Freya.'

I tiptoe across the room and out of the door. As I pull it closed, not quite shutting it completely, her small voice emerges from the darkness.

'I love you too, Mummy.'

'Night-night.'

I click the door shut as tears fill my eyes. I lean against it and exhale, letting go of the years of waiting. She's home. She's finally home. And this is just the beginning: from now on this will be normal. Freya, asleep in her bedroom, at home with me where she belongs.

I get dressed for bed, then curl up on the sofa in the snug with a pile of marking, occasionally looking out of the French windows to the vast star-filled sky suspended above the trees, which stand, invisible in the dark, at the foot of the garden. Time ticks forward and the fire crackles loudly as its embers die out.

When the last spark has gone, the grate empty and black, I climb the stairs to the bathroom and brush my teeth, trying to be as quiet as possible, even though she won't be able to hear me from the other side of the house. I wash my face, then open the cupboard under the basin, my hand instinctively reaching for the plain white box.

My fingers pause, just for a moment, but then I pull out the packet and push a turquoise pill into my hand.

I love you too, Mummy.

Her words swim in my mind as I meet my gaze in the mirror, place the pill on my tongue and swallow.

My girl is safe. My girl is home.

My eyes strain open to the sound of crying. I blink rapidly in the dark, trying to catch up with the present. Whenever I wake up, it takes several moments to collect all of the small fragments of my life, and piece myself back together. The adjustment is sometimes hard to bear.

What's that sound?

I cover my eyes with my hand and focus, trying to identify the noise that is ringing out in the darkness.

Crying.

It's Freya.

But it can't be: this wail is high and shrill, like a new-born. But it is familiar. Like a cry from the past.

I sit up and my head swims with the sudden motion, but as I close my eyes again, the sound grows louder.

There's a baby crying. And it's her cry.

Freya.

I shake my head from side to side, trying to force the noise out of my mind, faster and faster, but as I do the black infinity behind my eyes explodes with bursts of light and colour.

Stop.

Silence. The crying has stopped.

Maybe it's the pill. The mornings are always the hardest: in the minutes after waking, its effects hang over me like a fog. I shouldn't have taken one. Not now, with Freya here.

I reach out for my phone and press the button. The time illuminates the silent room: 7:35 a.m.

Maybe Freya's awake. I should check – she'd be scared to come and find me in the dark.

I swing my legs off the bed but stumble forward as I stand up. Steadying myself on my dresser, I straighten and shake my head again, as if that will expel the grogginess.

The darkness of the landing is lit only by a faint stream of daylight that is falling onto the stairs through the large window that overlooks the drive. I squint across to her bedroom.

The door is wide open.

I definitely pulled it shut last night . . . Maybe it creaked open on its own. Or maybe she got up to go to the toilet and didn't close it again – she isn't a baby any more, after all.

My head spins, the house swirling as if I'm looking through a kaleidoscope.

Just breathe.

As I step off the carpet and onto the floor of the landing, the stone is cold under my feet. The corridor seems to lengthen in front of me – each of my cautious steps taking me no further towards her room – and the door begins to rotate until it is hanging from the ceiling: a topsy-turvy world.

I stop and stare at my feet, my eyes blinking rapidly. But

my gaze is drawn to the smile-shaped light falling on the stairs. The Cheshire Cat: its teeth gleaming.

We're all mad here.

The world is no longer upside down and I am standing directly in front of her open door. My eyes adjust to the dark of her room and lock onto her bed.

It is empty.

I burst into the room and click on the light.

She isn't here.

The room is empty.

'Freya?'

I clear my throat.

'Freya – where are you?'

Gentle fingers of fear begin to creep up my neck and my hand flies up to the base of my skull. I scratch them away.

Maybe she's hiding.

Striding across the room to her wardrobe, I throw open the doors. But she isn't there. Just hangers dressed in barely worn clothes.

I spin around and scan the room.

Where is she?

Those fingers return and curl coldly around my neck. Squeeze.

I press my lips together and breathe in slowly.

You're dreaming. Nothing has happened to Freya.

I step out of her room and listen intently for any sign of her presence. But the house is silent and dark.

Inching across the corridor towards the stairs, my breath quickens.

Stop it.

She woke up early and went downstairs.

But my heart is racing.

Calm down, Naomi.

'Freya?' I call again, and her name echoes in my ears.

I approach the stairs but hesitate to look over. My heart slams against my chest.

Just look.

She's going to be sitting there, on the second step up, like always: playing with her soft toys, a book at her side.

I move forward and reach for the banister. My hands are shaking but I curl them around the wooden rail, searching for some comfort in the solid foundations of my home. Ignoring the tight knot of panic that is forming in the centre of my ribcage, I take a deep breath and look down to the entrance hall below.

My brain stalls and, for the smallest fraction of a second, it doesn't comprehend what it is seeing.

Freya is lying at the foot of the stairs: eyes unblinking, her hair fanned around her head, like a halo. So still, she could be sleeping.

2

When I first saw Freya – when the midwife, who looked as exhausted as I was, finally placed her on my chest, skin to skin – I watched her rise and fall, my breathing moving her up and down, up and down. She looked like she was from another world – one different from mine. Her eyes were too large, her mouth so small, and she was covered from head to toe with a soft, downy fuzz. The hair fell out within a few days, and my beautiful daughter emerged from beneath it, but my overwhelming memory from the birth was my bemusement at her appearance.

That, and the blood. It was mottled dark brown and bright red, coating her new pink skin, slick like oil. Now, her skin is pale.

Look away. Look away, look away, look away.

I freeze, swept up for a moment in the serene eye of the storm, paralysed by the shock. But my eyes are drawn back to where my daughter lies motionless.

The grip that was holding me to the spot releases, and I fly down the stairs, tripping over my feet on the bottom step, and tumbling to the floor, my knees smacking hard and my arms flailing outwards.

I lift my head. Freya's face is only inches away and I raise my fingers to her cheek.

'Freya?'

No response.

This has to be a dream . . .

'Freya?' I shout – my voice ricocheting against the silence.

I brace my hands against the unyielding floor and push myself up to lean over her, my ear just a hair's wisp away from her mouth – like I used to when she was a baby and I was scared she'd stop breathing in the night.

'Freya?'

The air is completely still. There is no warm, shaky breath, blowing softly against my face. There is nothing.

Nothing at all.

Wake up, Naomi.

Hot tears begin to fall down my face and I choke on phlegm that is beginning to block the back of my throat. I reach out my hand and take her wrist, pushing my index and middle fingers into the soft flesh.

Nothing. No pulse.

Wake up, wake up, wake up. It's just a nightmare. Wake up.

The sobs burst out of me without warning. As I gawp open-mouthed at her, she gazes lifelessly upwards. There is a stain of fear in her eyes.

What did she see?

I stretch out my arm and take hold of her hand. It is cold.

How long has she been here? How has this happened? And how can I bring her back? Surely, if I close my eyes, hold my breath, make a wish, she'll wake up. Or I will.

You're dreaming. All you have to do is wake up.

Letting go of her hand, I pinch the sensitive skin on the inside of my elbow – hard.

Wake up, Naomi!

I close my eyes, wait a few moments as I try to calm my breath, then open them.

I'm not back in my bed, eyes flying open with relief. I'm still kneeling on the floor of my silent hall. And Freya is . . .

The scream comes from my very core: a noise I've never made before.

I look frantically around, searching for a clue of what happened, searching for a sign that this is a dream, just a nightmare but –

What's that?

Lying at the far end of the hall, almost touching the front door, is a small, grey object, slumped over itself as if it has been discarded.

I narrow my eyes, trying to distinguish the shape, trying to focus, although my vision is shifting, the room swinging violently from side to side.

What is that? What is –

It's Mouse. Freya's mouse.

She must have brought it down with her. It must have flown out of her arms as she . . .

No.

I look back down and Freya is still there. Still unmoving.

How did this happen? How did she fall? Did she try to wake me? Did she try to sneak across the long, uneven corridor to my room? Or to the toilet? Had she needed something? Did she try to go downstairs on her own? In the dark?

Wake up, Freya. Wake up, wake up, wake up.

Somebody help me.

Please.

I shake my head and press my fingers into my temples, willing myself to think but panic is rising inside me.

Think, Naomi. Think. Try to remember. Did she attempt to wake you?

I frantically search the corners of my mind, but I can't remember anything. Once I take my tablet, I disappear from the world. As if in a coma. As if I will never wake up again. And sometimes whole chunks of time disintegrate into fragmented pieces in my mind. Sometimes they disappear completely and I'm left with just a vast, gaping black hole where my memory should be.

I need time to think.

If I hadn't taken that pill, I would have been able to help her. What if she called and I didn't hear her? What if she needed me?

I open my eyes and her face comes into focus.

Why did she try to go downstairs in the dark? Why did she leave her room? Why did she do that? Why?

Out of all the questions, one repeatedly rushes to the fore-front of my mind and clings. Of all the questions asking why, one refuses to be pushed away or go unanswered.

How am I going to tell Aiden?

My hand moves to my stomach, my vision blurring.

When I found out I was pregnant, just a week or so ago, those two faint lines on the test meant one thing – a second chance. Hope.

After everything we've been through . . . how am I going to tell him?

And when I do . . . what will happen to the baby?

3

Five years earlier . . .
November

Clutching the pregnancy test, I slowly opened the bedroom door and crossed the narrow landing of the flat to the bathroom.

'Naomi?' Aiden shouted from the living room. 'You okay, love?'

'Yes, I'm fine. I'll just be a minute!' My voice sounded strange. It had gone high and overly cheery, like I'd inhaled a balloon full of helium.

'You sure?' Concern bled into his words.

I pushed my voice down into its lower register. 'Yeah.'

Closing the bathroom door behind me, I pulled my jeans down and sat on the edge of the toilet seat, awkwardly aiming the test into the bowl, trying to avoid weeing on my hands. I waited, thinking that nothing was going to happen but then there it was, a fast stream gushing directly onto the stick. And my hands.

I clicked the test's cover into place and balanced it, face down, on the edge of the basin. Standing up, I washed my hands, then paced back and forth in the small space.

How long has it been?

I looked at the timer on my phone – forty-five seconds had passed. Three minutes would feel like an eternity.

I sat down on the edge of the bath and leaned my forehead against the sink for a moment, then jumped up at the soun of the door clicking open, revealing Aiden's astonished face as he took in the test on the sink.

'I think I might be pregnant,' I whispered, gesturing at the test. 'Obviously.'

Aiden stood stock-still in the doorway, his eyes still focused on the test. 'Really?'

I nodded. A small, shocked smile played across his mouth. He crossed the bathroom, plopping himself down beside me on the ledge of the bath, and held out his hand. I latched onto it. Glancing sideways at him, I tried to gauge his reaction. We hadn't been trying for long.

He caught my eye. 'I'm so excited,' he whispered, grinning.

'Me too.'

We smiled at each other, then stared straight ahead, watching the test as it lay there, readying itself to predict our future.

'It's time,' I whispered.

We stood and inched our way towards it, still clutching each other's hands. I reached out slowly.

'Ready?' I asked. He was staring down at my outstretched fingers, chewing his bottom lip. As he nodded, he gave my hand a squeeze but never took his eyes off the test.

I hesitated – then flipped the test over.

Two solid lines.

'Holy fuck, we're going to be parents!' Aiden said, holding his hand to his forehead.

I looked up at Aiden, his eyes large and round, his smile so wide it could have broken his face in two. 'We're going to be parents,' I repeated. He laughed and reached out, scooping me into his arms – my feet lifting off the floor, my heart brimming over. I threw my head back and laughed too, high and happy.

I sighed as he placed me back on my feet and kissed me, his hands cupping my chin.

He was my family now. Him. And our baby.

4

'Hello?'

I've been pacing the hall, back and forth, over and over, but I halt abruptly at the sound of his voice. I feel as if I'm standing on a cliff edge, and if I leap forward, I will fall away from my life and nothing will remain of it, or me, when I hit the ground.

The sound of blood rushing in my ears fills the silence, and an icy chill runs down my back.

'Hello? Naomi? Are you there?'

My eyes flicker to the large clock that hangs by the front door. It's almost a quarter past eight. Aiden is an early riser so he'll be awake, but he won't have showered or dressed yet. Instead, he'll have gone downstairs and sat at the kitchen table cradling a large cup of coffee: black, no sugar. I expect she'll still be asleep.

I press my head against the wall, my forehead pushed into the exposed bricks, and adrenalin courses around my body. My breath is uneven, anxious. I try to get it under control, but a familiar feeling of panic rises up from my stomach.

She fell. It wasn't your fault.

But he will never understand. He doesn't trust me – and I pushed him to let me have her overnight. He'll blame me.

'Hello?'

I lied about the pills. I promised him I don't take them any more. Just like before . . .

Say something, Naomi.

'Something's happened to Freya,' I whisper into the

phone, and tears begin to spill from my eyes and into my mouth. I taste salt.

'Naomi? What did you say about Freya?' Aiden replies. 'What's happened?'

This can't be real . . .

I breathe in through my nose, deep into my lungs, knowing that my voice will come out in a quiver. My throat begins to close. Panic stretches its fingers around my head, tightening the vice that is gripping my temples, and I spread my fingers on the wall. It blurs.

Freya has fallen.

I urge myself to say the words but the pressure in my head is so intense I can't think.

Freya is dead.

The whole room begins to spin.

It was an accident.

Just say it.

Freya is dead.

A black curtain descends before my eyes and I picture flashing blue lights. Paramedics kneeling at the foot of the stairs. Police standing to one side, watching. The sound of a zip on a white bag. *We're sorry for your loss.*

They will take away the baby, too. They will take away Freya. Both of my children – gone. My home will be filled with people in uniform who will carry her away to some cold, sterile place –

'Aiden, did you come and get Freya without telling me?'

My voice sounds strange, like I'm hearing it from far away.

I open my eyes, and the world has stopped swaying. Aiden hasn't spoken. I can see him sitting at his table, his hair falling into his eyes, not quite understanding the question.

I don't understand the question.

'Naomi? What on earth are you talking about?'

I need to backtrack. Right now. Tell him that something terrible has happened but it wasn't anyone's fault and I'm sorry.

I'm so sorry.

Say it.

'I can't find Freya. We were outside and I came in to make her some food and now she isn't here. Didn't you come and get her?' My voice breaks. He will think it is concern.

'Why were you outside?'

'She got up early . . . She wanted to play –'

'Naomi, is this some twisted joke?'

The lie fills my mouth like sick: thick, full of undigested truths. I want to spit the foul-tasting stuff out of my mouth, but it sticks between my teeth and coats my tongue.

Tell him the truth. Just tell him the truth.

But it's too late. I've already lied. How can I take back what I just said? How can I speak the truth and make him believe that it wasn't my fault?

Just tell him.

But he won't believe me.

'I can't find her. She's not here any more.'

'Have you called the police?'

'No, not yet –'

'Call the fucking police, Naomi. I'm leaving now. I'll be there as soon as I can.'

The phone goes dead. I stand in the hallway with it pressed to my ear, blaring out its dull, relentless tone.

What have I done?

I have to call the police before he arrives. Otherwise he'll want to know why I didn't do it straight away. But once I make that phone call, the lie will have to become my truth. There will be no recovery from this horrendous betrayal of my daughter, of her memory – her bright eyes and little laugh.

But if I tell the truth now, after lying, who will believe me?

I poise my finger over the 9 –

No. I need to call Rupert.

Rupert will help me. He loves me. More than anything. *I'd do anything for you* – isn't that what he always says?

But will he do this?

Just call him.

I dial his number and wait. One ring – and he answers, the line clicking open. Like always.

'Rupert?' I blurt, before he even has time to say hello.

'Naomi? What's wrong?' he says. 'You sound strange.'

'Can you come here, please?' I try to keep my voice steady, but it wavers – a flimsy dinghy on violent waters.

'Where are you? What's happened?'

'I need you. I need . . . I need your help.'

'Naomi, tell me what's happened.'

I bite down on my lip – hard. Wincing, I wipe my mouth with the back of my hand. Blood.

If anyone would understand – if anyone would help me – it would be Rupert. Kind, sweet, horrifyingly dedicated Rupert.

'Freya is . . .'

You can't tell him.

No, I can't. Telling him would mean telling him everything. Laying myself bare for him to look at me, naked. And he doesn't know anything. Nothing about the separation. Or before.

And what kind of monster would help me then? Rupert loves me, I know he does. But he's no monster. I close my eyes.

'Freya is missing. I can't find her.'

'What?'

I bite down even harder and my lip stings as it splits towards the inner corner, the delicate skin tearing, like wafer-thin paper.

Shit.

He's going to race round here – he's only around the corner. He'll be here in ten minutes.

'Rupert, I –'

'I'll be there as soon as I can, okay? It's going to take me nearly two hours to drive back.'

'Two hours?'

'I'm in Bristol, remember? I came to see my sister.'

I stifle a shaky breath of relief.

Bristol. Of course. When I told him I wasn't ready for him to meet Freya – that I didn't want him at the house for her visit – he'd decided to go to Bristol to see his sister. She's been asking him for months.

'Okay. Well, get here as quickly as you can, please,' I say.

'I will. I'm leaving now,' he says. I can hear him moving about the house, the sound of items rustling as they're shoved hurriedly into his bag.

'And drive safely.'

'I will. I love you.'

'Love you too.'

I hang up the phone with a stab of my finger. There's only one call left to make . . .

I tap my phone and it lights up, still on the call screen. I place my finger on the bottom right number.

Don't do this, Naomi.

I push the 9 –

You will regret this for the rest of your life.

9 –

You'll never forgive yourself –

9.

The phone is ringing, three long trills and –

'Emergency services – which service do you require?'

Hang up the phone.

'Police, please – my daughter is missing.'

5

After I've hung up, the lie takes over. I can feel it spreading like an infection, obliterating any remnants of what might have been the truth.

'The police will be here soon,' I whisper, as I kneel next to Freya. 'I can't let them take you . . . I have to move you. I'm so sorry.'

I stroke her hair, my tears dripping onto her face, and as they come to rest on her skin, it looks like she is crying too. I hold her hand between mine. She always had warm little hands. And chubby, when she was a baby. None of that warmth remains. The heat of life has disappeared completely.

Eight thirty-five.

I need to hurry.

'I'm so sorry,' I say, my whisper breathing against her cheek. 'I'm so, so sorry. I just need to keep you with me. Just for a little bit longer. I won't let anyone take you away – I'm going to take you somewhere safe.'

Mouse . . . She can't be without him.

I clamber up from the floor and run to the door where Mouse is lying, almost tripping over the mat in my rush to get back to her.

'Here's Mouse, darling,' I whisper, as I kneel beside her, tucking him under her arm.

I slide my hands under Freya and –

Stop.

The rug.

I need to hide the rug. What if there's something on it? Something I can't see – a glaring beacon for police to find. It needs to go.

I shuffle my hands under it. It takes all of my effort to lift both her and the rug, but I hoist them up and carry her, like a baby, to the back door in the kitchen. I slip on a pair of shoes from the haphazard pile on the mat and try to turn the key in the lock. But it won't move. I can't twist the key and hold her and the rug in my arms at the same time.

I kick the door, which rattles in its frame.

I can't carry it all. I'll have to come back for the rug.

Be quick.

I place her and the rug on the floor, then push against the door and turn the key simultaneously. The lock clicks open. I grab the large set of keys and pull the door towards me.

It swings open and cold November air creeps into the house. I still only have my flannel pyjamas on. A red and blue tartan pair that Aiden bought me four Christmases ago. Our last Christmas together. I shiver. It's freezing: the kind of cold that stiffens your back against the chill. I pick Freya up and kiss her forehead.

My eyes adjust to the outside. Everything is changed. It looks different, as if I'm emerging into another world. And perhaps that's it – perhaps this is only a nightmare.

I cling to the thought, and the woods in the distance sparkle in the rising sun, glittering in frost.

I crunch quickly along the gravel path that leads away from the house down to the orchard. Dead grass scratches at my bare ankles as I cut through it towards the river, dodging the apples that fell from the trees in the summer and have decomposed to mulch. The orchard used to be perfectly manicured, the branches heavy with fruit. Now a smell of rot hangs in the air.

I reach the far side and follow the fence line south-east to where a small bridge crosses the narrowest point of the river. By the willow tree. I open the gate, my breath loud, my shoes clacking on the wooden slats as I cross the water. The skin on my neck prickles and I pause. Is someone watching me?

But no one is here. No one overlooks the farm, and no one will be able to see what I'm doing. No one is watching me.

Keep going.

I dash across the short stretch of land and disappear into the thick copse of silver trees. The woods surround the area to the south of the farmhouse on all three sides, but those to the south-east are special. They will give me time, while I decide what to do.

Keep going, Naomi. Soon you'll wake up.

The trees lean over, bearing witness. A gust of frigid wind hits the side of my face, and I look up at the frozen branches. They are familiar. I've reached the spot – this is definitely it. I place Freya on the uneven ground and am struck by the same feeling. Someone is watching me. What if the police or Aiden have already arrived and followed me? I glance over my shoulder, my heart pounding, breath shallow.

I am alone.

I shift the blanket of decomposed leaves until I reach the freezing dirt and begin to search through the frozen soil with my hands. My fingers are red and stiff, and my movements become more frantic as they start to turn numb. But I am sweating: the exertion and stress bleeding out of my skin.

I keep digging and then – my fingers flinch against tarnished metal.

The door.

The trapdoor had been my discovery as a child. These woods were my playground. I climbed the trees and straddled the branches, my legs dangling either side. One day, the noise I made as I jumped off sounded heavy, as if the ground below me was made of something denser than leaves and earth. I spent ages staring down at the leaves beneath my feet, trying to make sense of that sound. I knew something wasn't right, but I simply couldn't figure out what it was. When my dad arrived home from his delivery to the village market, I ran out onto the drive and threw myself into his arms.

'I found something in the woods!' I yelled.

'What have you found?' he gasped mockingly.

'I don't know!' I started running around the side of the house, knowing it would be faster than navigating my way through. 'Come with me, Dad! I need to show you!'

He caught up with me and I jumped on the spot where I had landed. He raised his eyebrows at me, his lips moving in a wry smile, and bent down. I copied him and together we began to move the leaves. He laughed as I gasped at the sight of metal.

It felt as if I had revealed a magic entrance. A door to another world. My own little Wonderland out there in the woods.

A bunker. My great-grandfather had been an officer in the army during the war and my great-grandmother had volunteered to have children to stay at the farmhouse to protect them from the dangers of London. So they'd built this, one of many forgotten bunkers, hidden around the country, the memory of them lost to time. It was built to be undetectable. A box buried in the ground – reinforced concrete and steel.

About a year after I discovered the bunker, I slipped on the ladder and broke my leg. My mum was furious. Dad replaced the cover and buried it. I pleaded with him to uncover it but he refused.

His voice echoes in my mind.

We don't tell lies, do we, Naomi? We must always be honest and kind.

I'm so sorry, Dad.

Don't think about him. Not now.

I heave at the metal ring of the door and grit my teeth against the weight.

I never told Aiden about the bunker. I never told anyone. I have shut away my memories of Dad, locking them inside where only I can reach them.

Finally, it opens. I stand, panting, with my hands on my hips, and look down at the place that, once upon a time, had been so magical to me as a child.

She'll be safe here.

I walk back to Freya. The morning sun is colouring the clouds with a reddish hue and falls on her through the gaps in the canopy of trees, her unicorn pyjamas shining jauntily against the dull ground. I carry her over to where the trap-door is waiting, uncovered.

I lift her head to my face and rest my cheek against her forehead as I begin to climb down the ladder. As I reach the last rung, I lower myself to my knees and cradle her across my lap. I can see what she looked like as a baby – the round, soft curve of her face, the small, pouting lips. But I can also see her as a woman: long dark hair and Aiden's cheekbones.

I lay her gently on the concrete floor, lowering her head until she comes finally to rest.

'You'll be safe here,' I whisper, my bottom lip quivering. 'No one will find you, and you can stay nice and warm. No one will find you, no one will take you away . . .'

I could just drag the trapdoor back into place, sealing us both down here for ever. What is left for me without her? Who is left to miss me? I could stay down here with her, until I too closed my eyes and never woke up.

You can't . . .

The baby.

'I'll come back for you. I won't leave you here, I promise. I love you.'

As soon as the police have gone, I'll come back for her.

I crawl over to the door and pull myself out of the hole, dragging myself across the leaves, which are frozen solid to the ground.

I stand panting, and pause to catch my breath –

Keep going: they could be here any second.

I sprint back through the woods, across the land to the bridge and through the orchard to the back door. A searing pain shoots through my side as I bend down to roll up the rug, and I gasp as I try to fill my lungs with oxygen. I hoist the rug onto my shoulder and turn back to the woods but a sob escapes through my closed lips and my heaving breaths turn into agonized moans.

Just one more return journey.

Do it.

I make my way back to the bunker and pull the rug down the ladder. I place it over Freya, up to her chin, like a blanket. 'I'll come back for you,' I promise.

It's only a nightmare. Soon you will be back together.

I climb out of the bunker and slam the door. The sound of metal hitting metal thunders its way up to the trees and through the canopy to the open sky.

With the door back in place, I retrieve the rag I stuffed down the front of my pyjama bottoms and rub at the metal. Summoning all of my energy, I heave the displaced dirt and leaves back into place. The door shrinks, becoming smaller and smaller, until it disappears.

I back away, but my shoulder thuds into someone tall and solid. I fling myself around, unable to breathe.

It's just a tree.

I run. I run as fast as my weary legs will go, the lights shining out from the house guiding me home: a lighthouse in a storm.

Running inside, I turn the hot tap all the way to the right, grab random cleaning products from under the sink, and dart into the hallway as hot water sputters, then gushes out. I stand over the area where the rug had been, then drop to all fours to inspect the large slabs of stone.

I can't see anything. There's no sign that she was ever here at all.

My body doubles forward, pain coursing upwards through my body.

Keep going.

I run back into the kitchen. I throw everything into the cupboard, then stoop over the sink and wash my hands, scrubbing at my fingers and palms. I want them to bleed.

My foot lashes out. I kick and kick and kick at the cupboard, my rage rising up from my stomach and into my throat, and I let out a guttural cry.

You are a monster.

Grabbing a towel from the counter, I bend down and clean the dirt off the cupboard. The wood has splintered upwards, the grains tearing away from each other.

I take off my shoes and chuck them back on top of the messy pile, reaching for the cardigan that's hanging by the door, then tug it on as I run into the hallway to the large silver mirror that leans against the wall. But the mess of a woman staring back at me is not me. That woman standing there, her hair in a bun falling down onto her shoulders, the ankles of her pyjamas covered with mud, a sheen of sweat and tears on her pallid face, and eyes that are alive with sorrow, is not me. She is a ghost — the reflection that used to gaze back at me when loss was a lingering spectre that hovered just behind me wherever I went.

I thought I told you not to come back.

I jump at the sound of a growling engine. My ears strain. There it is: the sound of people walking on gravel.

Breathe, Naomi.

I stare at the solid mass of the wooden front door. I imagine them standing on the other side, looking up at the farmhouse, and the house looking back at them. Watching. If only I could lock myself in and shut the world out. But I can't.

A moment of silence before the inevitable –

There it is.

Three sharp knocks.

6

'Naomi Williams?'

Three police officers are at the door, wearing fixed masks of concern. A man and a woman both in uniform, and a second man dressed in regular clothes. He will be the one in charge.

'Yes, that's me.'

My eyes switch from one face to another, then to the sky behind them. I try to make my eyes focus on one face – on one person – but I can't. The sun is rising higher and higher, and its fingers of red and orange streak across the sky.

'I am Detective Sergeant Michael Jenning, and these are my colleagues, Police Constables Denver and Callaghan. You called us about your daughter?'

Open the door. Why are you looking at them through a two-inch gap?

I yank it open, exposing myself to the gaze of the outside world.

'Yes, yes. Please come in.' I step aside, and they enter in single file, their mouths breaking into small smiles as they move past me.

I close the door and turn to face them, wringing my hands.

Are they waiting for me to speak first?

My eyes wander to the spot at the bottom of the stairs, where less than an hour ago, Freya was lying. I bite down on my trembling lip, hard.

Maybe I'm still dreaming. Maybe I'm in the deepest kind of sleep, the kind where your eyes are so heavy, they're impossible to open. The kind where it feels as if you're falling.

One of the other officers, whose name I have already forgotten, clears his throat and I jump.

'Um, sorry. Do you want to come through to the lounge?'

They glance at each other and Jenning smiles in a way that I'm sure he means to be reassuring but, instead, just looks sad.

'Wherever you are more comfortable, Mrs Williams. Is the child's father here?'

'He doesn't live here,' I say, my words clipped. 'We aren't together any more.'

His eyes dart sideways to the others. 'What's his name?'

'Aiden Williams.'

'So, Williams is your married name?'

I nod. I need to maintain control of my face, to remain passive at the mention of Aiden, but I can feel my expression beginning to crack. A fracture in a china plate. One misstep and I'll smash into pieces.

After he left Aiden filed for divorce, quoting irreconcilable differences. Several months later, I wandered aimlessly to the letterbox, not expecting any communication from the outside world, but there it was. I ripped the envelope untidily, the paper tearing open, like a wound. I can still remember that it felt as if it was resisting, unwilling to leave the confines of the envelope, when really it was me who was resisting, knowing what would be written on the pages inside. And I didn't want to see the words in black and white, typed across a page, so final in their formality: *Decree absolute.*

That was it: just like that, we were divorced.

But I still haven't been able to bring myself to change my name.

'I'm sorry, yes. It's my married name. Aiden's actually on his way. He should be here any minute.'

'And how long ago did you separate?'

'A few years.'

'And where does he live?'

'In London.'

'And your daughter lives here with you?'

'No. She lives with her dad and his wife.'

'And what's her name?'

'Sorry?'

Please don't make me say it.

'Mr Williams's wife. What's her name?'

The betrayal binds my lips together. I have spent all this time refusing to say her name out loud. Instead she is simply *her, that woman, Aiden's wife*. But I have to say it.

Just say it, Naomi.

'Helen.'

He shifts his weight to the other leg and places his hands on his hips.

'Sorry to bombard you with questions, but it's easier to ask them as they arise.'

'No, it's fine. Do you want to come and sit down?'

I cross the hall, leading them to the lounge without waiting for their answer. They follow me, their boots thumping on the stone floor.

I go in but Jenning has come to a standstill at the door and held out his hand – stopping the other two stepping inside. 'Would you like us to take our shoes off?' He nods towards the thick cream carpet.

'No, no.' I wave them in. 'Please.'

They traipse in and sit together on the deep seats of the grey sofa facing the fireplace. I sit down in the armchair to their right, my hands clasped together as I lean towards them.

'Do you live here alone?' he asks, a friendly lilt in his voice. He is trying to form a relationship. To make me open up.

'Yes. I do now.'

'It's beautiful.'

'Thank you. I grew up here.'

'Is it a running farm? Or do you work elsewhere?'

'No, not any more.'

'The farm, or the work?'

'Pardon?'

He shuffles forward in his seat. 'Is it the farm that isn't running any more or do you not work any more?'

'The farm. But it just wasn't for me . . . And work – I used to teach full-time, but I stopped when my daughter was born. Now I'm a supply teacher.'

'What do you teach?'

'English literature.'

He nods politely, his closed lips stretched across his face.

'Now, I'm just going to ask you some questions about what's happened, if that's all right?'

'Yes, that's fine.'

'I'll take a few notes and the officers will turn on their body-worn cameras so that we have an accurate record of your account. Is that okay with you?'

I nod. What I say now is going to be recorded.

Be careful, Naomi.

'What is your daughter's full name?' He smiles again, and his face is approachable, friendly. The kind of detective you can open up to. Is that natural or intentional?

'Freya Grace Williams.'

'And how old is she?'

'She's four.'

'Before you and your husband separated, did you all live here?'

'Yes.'

'And did Freya live here until you separated?'

'Yes. We moved here just a couple of months before we had her.'

'Why did you move here?'

I glance into the hall. I can almost see Dad standing there, his eyes sparkling, his voice croaky with pride.

You'll come back one day, mark my words.

'It was just a lifestyle choice,' I whisper, as I blink Dad away.

It was Aiden's idea. He did it for me. For Freya.

And then it all went wrong.

'Okay. I know this is a very scary and difficult time for you but can you tell us what has happened this morning?'

I nod, squeezing my palms together, my knuckles turning white. They look quite comical, really, all three of them trying to appear as professional and serious as possible, while attempting not to sink further and further into the depths of the plush sofa. In any other situation, I would have laughed. I begin to click my fingers, one by one, waiting to hear the crack of air escaping before moving onto the next. I manipulate each knuckle while they watch me. They are waiting for me to start.

Crack, crack, crack, crack, crack.

Pause.

Crack, crack, crack, crack, crack.

I don't know how to begin.

Just start talking.

'Well, I woke up this morning and Freya . . .'

Freya was gone. But I can't tell them that. I can't even tell them that I woke up and she was missing. There's no evidence that someone broke into the house. Why didn't I plan what I was going to say? As soon as they search and find nothing, they'll know I'm lying.

'Yes?'

'Freya woke up at around . . . six thirty.' My voice is quiet, just louder than a whisper. 'And we went downstairs and had breakfast.'

He nods, his gaze unfaltering.

'Then what happened?'

'After that she asked to go and play outside. I told her it was too dark and she had to get dressed first but she kept on asking. She doesn't live with me, so I guess I spoil her sometimes. I put on her coat and let her outside to play.'

'What time was that?'

'Around seven thirty.'

'Did you go outside with her?'

'For a while. But I went inside to make us a snack. She was hungry again but wanted to carry on playing, so I went into the kitchen.'

'How long were you gone?'

'Ten minutes? Maybe slightly more.'

'Then what did you do?'

'I don't know . . . It's all jumbled up.'

I can't think. I don't want to lie.

'I'm sorry,' I mutter.

'It's okay.' Jenning continues to look at me, the same gentle, reassuring smile playing across his face. 'I know that everything is probably a blur right now and you're worried about your daughter, but if you could walk us through exactly what happened in as much detail as possible, that would really help us.'

'Okay.'

Keep talking.

'I went back outside and she wasn't there. I couldn't see her anywhere.'

'What time was it when you noticed she was missing?'

'Um . . . Just before eight.'

Jenning moves forward again, so that he is perched on the very edge of the sofa.

'So, then what did you do?' he says, his voice assertive for the first time – commanding me to continue.

I do not want to tell this story. But I will. Just a few more minutes. Then they will have what they need and they will leave. And I can work out what to do.

'I came back inside. I thought she might have come in and I didn't notice. I called her name but she didn't answer. She loves playing in her room, so I went up there to check first. I checked everywhere upstairs . . . She wasn't there.'

'Did you check downstairs?'

The image of Freya lying at the bottom of the stairs hits me hard: a slap you should expect but don't see coming.

'Ms Williams?'

They are waiting patiently, watching me while I sit here with empty eyes. I can't see them. They are just shadows lurking behind Freya lying like a broken doll – limbs bent and limp.

'What happened then?'

'Then I . . . I came downstairs and searched everywhere. In here, in the kitchen, the snug, the dining room, the loo. Then I went back around the whole house again and looked in all of her hiding places . . .'

Jenning frowns slightly, a flash of confusion appearing on his face. He doesn't have children.

'She likes to hide. Children like to hide.'

'So . . . you looked everywhere and couldn't find her.'

'Yes.'

'Did you go back outside? We noticed there are woods out the back. Did you look there?'

The woods. Freya's arm, which hung limply, swinging violently, hitting against my leg. Her wide eyes staring up at the sky.

The acrid taste of sick coats the inside of my mouth.

'No.' I swallow, but my mouth refills with saliva. 'I only went as far as the river. I was scared that she might have fallen in. But she wouldn't go to the woods on her own.'

'And could she have fallen into the river?'

'She wasn't there.'

'Could it have carried her downstream?'

'Inside the fenceline it's very shallow. Less than ankle-deep. And I don't think she could get past the fence. But she wouldn't go to the river anyway. Or the woods.'

'Are you sure?'

'She's very timid. She's scared of everything and she hates those woods.' My voice breaks, my throat tightening as grief swells in my chest. 'She doesn't even like to go in there with me.'

'Okay. So, then what did you do?'

'I called Aiden and asked him if he had come to get her from –'

'Is that something he would do?' Jenning interrupts, sitting up straight.

His voice has changed.

'I – I don't understand the question.'

'Is coming to your house and taking your daughter without you knowing something Mr Williams would do?'

'No . . . He's never done that or anything like it, but I . . . I was just trying to think of a possible explanation for where she had gone. We didn't agree a time for him to collect her, so I thought that maybe he'd come to get her and she'd heard his car. Run around the front or something.'

'And what did Mr Williams say?'

'He said no. Then he told me he was on his way and to call the police. I called you as soon as we hung up.'

'And is there anyone else in the family – partners, grandparents – who would come and take Freya?'

46

'No,' I whisper. 'No one would just take her without telling me.'

He looks down intently at his notebook, writes a few lines, then returns his gaze. His face is instantly more relaxed, his brow unfurrowing, as if the very process of writing down the information he gathers relieves some of the weight of responsibility.

'How easy would it be for someone to gain access to your property, Naomi?'

'Very.'

He doesn't say anything but continues to watch me. He wants me to elaborate.

'Well, from the road to the house there are no gates or barriers and there's nothing to stop someone coming onto the drive and around the side to the back.'

'And could someone come from the back rather than the front?'

'Yes.'

'How many acres is the farm?'

'It's fairly small. Twenty-one hectares. Just over fifty acres.'

'And are there any fences or anything?'

'Only around the periphery. And there's quite a few public footpaths that run straight through.'

He turns his focus to his notebook again.

I trace a scratch on my arm, which stings as my finger glides over it. The skin is raised and raw. I pull the sleeves of my cardigan down to cover my arms and hug the material closer to my body, wrapping my arms across my shoulders: I'm so cold. There is a small scrap of skin flaking away from the side of my thumbnail. I bring my hand up to my mouth and try to chew it off, but it won't come away.

'Okay. I'm going to send constables Callaghan and Denver to cordon off the land, if that's okay?'

A creeping panic runs down my arms, the skin turning cold.

They aren't going to leave.

But I need time: I need to figure out what to do, how to get back to her and fix what's happened. Make sure I can keep her safe. But I'm trapped in here. And Freya is out there.

'That's fine,' I say, my voice breaking.

'And then we'll do a thorough search of the house and a larger team will search the land and the woods.'

The woods.

The remaining heat in my face drains away. Can they see?

In just a few short hours, the lands surrounding the farm – the fields, the orchard, the barns and the woods – will be teeming with police officers, their sole purpose to search for Freya. To search for a child they think has gone missing. To search for a child who will never be found alive.

I have to tell them.

I've done something terrible.

Just say it.

There's something I need to tell you.

'Shall I let you out of the front or the back?'

I hear the words as they fall from my lips, but my voice sounds like it doesn't belong to me.

'Either is fine,' the woman answers.

'Be careful where you're walking,' Jenning says. They nod in response to his firm command.

My body moves automatically across the hall to lead them into the kitchen. Opening the back door, I stand aside to let them past.

You can never tell them the truth now.

No one will ever understand. Maybe they might have if I'd told the truth from the beginning. But no one will understand the lie. Especially if they start looking into my past. They will take both my babies away.

And I can't let anyone take my babies away. I won't allow it.

I shake my head, tugging myself out of my thoughts. Jenning is walking around the kitchen, each step purposeful as he takes everything in, from ceiling to floor.

I go to the sink and yank open the cupboard. I reach behind the pile of cleaning products and feel around until my hand grasps a half-empty packet of paracetamol. Turning the tap on, I wait a few seconds, allowing the stream of water to run cold, before I collect water in my cupped hand and swallow two tablets. The beginning of a migraine is pounding dully at the front of my head, and it will intensify quickly until all I can do is lie in my bedroom with the curtains closed, eye mask on. A side-effect of the sleeping pills. I close my eyes and lean my forehead against the cupboard next to the sink.

Why are you doing this, darling?

I flinch at the sound of Mum's voice. I look up but no one is there.

She sounded so real but she's been gone for so long.

Every so often it's as if I can still hear her voice, as if she is still here, tucking my long hair behind my ear and telling me that everything will be okay. 'Tell me what's wrong,' she used to say. She always knew, even when I tried to hide it. 'You can tell me anything, sweetheart.'

Anything . . .

If she was still alive, could I have told her everything? If she was still alive, would I be here now?

No . . . Never. I would've been a better mother if she'd still been around. She was perfect, a natural. She would have known what to do.

Please, Mum. Tell me what to do.

Jenning sniffs. I look over and he is standing on the other side of the island, near to where the large orange Aga is radiating heat. Freya's drawing is pinned proudly to the extractor fan, held in place with a magnet. Our imperfect stick figure family.

My head throbs. 'Sorry, I'm starting to get a migraine.'

'It's okay. Please, don't apologize, Ms Williams. I know that this is difficult. Do whatever you need to do. This is your home.' He breaks eye contact. 'What happened there?' he asks, pointing down to my right.

Shit. I completely forgot about the cupboard.

No more than half an hour ago, I kicked the cupboard under the sink with the full strength of my grief. But as I opened it to get the paracetamol, I didn't absorb the fact that the door was sticking, wood scraping roughly on wood. It used to open smoothly before I kicked the life out of it.

'I'm sorry.' There's that word again. 'When I couldn't find her . . . I lost my temper.'

'What happened to the cupboard?'

'I kicked it. Quite a few times. I just can't understand what's happened. How have I lost her?' My lip quivers and my hands fly up to my face, covering my eyes. 'My frustration took over and I kicked it.'

Jenning approaches me and places his hand carefully on my shoulder. He smells like cigarettes, stale smoke. What a vice. But we all have them.

'I'm so sorry this is happening to you, Ms Williams, but we're going to do everything we can to find your daughter. Okay?'

I move my hand away from my eyes, holding it less than a centimetre from my mouth – my shaky breath, hot on my palm.

'Okay,' I parrot back.

We are interrupted by a heavy knock on the door.

My heart leaps. Freya. Maybe someone has found Freya. Wandering in the next farm's fields, or playing on the lane, alternating between eating and pocketing the blackberries that grow in the thickets on the side of the thin track road –

I stall. For just a moment there, my body acted on instinct – fooled by my own stories – and believed.

But still I sprint frantically the rest of the way to the front door. The police are here. I am being watched. If she was really missing, I would run.

Standing on the doorstep – his eyes bloodshot – is Aiden. He is wearing the faded grey tracksuit bottoms that he normally reserves for lazing around the house or decorating. And a flannel shirt only, no jacket – its buttons done up incorrectly from where he must have pulled it on in a hurry, so the whole collar sits askew. He wears the panic of the last hour like a heavy coat, his shoulders stooped.

The blurred landscape of the morning shifts sharply back into focus. This isn't a nightmare. It isn't a dream at all.

7

'Is she here?' he croaks. Aiden's words usually boom around whatever space he's in but now he sounds small. Tired.

I meet his eye and, paralysed, I shake my head.

He hangs his head and begins to cry. I had expected shouting, an outpouring of rage, but there is none. This is far worse.

'I thought . . . I thought you might have found her already.'

I stare down at the grouting between the stones at my feet, not wanting to look him in the eye. He isn't angry yet, but it can only be a matter of time, mere moments. It is his immediate horror that is stopping his anger surging outwards and knocking me off my feet. He didn't want to leave her here, he will say. I convinced him to relinquish control. He knew that I still couldn't be trusted.

'What happened, Naomi? How has this happened?'

'I –'

'Mr Williams?' Jenning appears at my side.

'Yes?'

Jenning steps backwards into the house, away from the door, gesturing for Aiden to come inside. I step backwards also, my eyes still trained on the grouting, as if those curved lines will reveal all of the world's secrets, if only I focus hard enough. Aiden crosses the threshold, his eyes darting about uncomfortably. He closes the door behind him, and it slams at us, angrily.

The house knows what I've done.

The three of us stand in silence, waiting for someone to speak.

'So, Mr Williams –'

'It's Aiden, Detective.'

'Aiden. I'm Detective Sergeant Jenning. I'm leading the search for your daughter.'

Aiden covers his eyes with his hand and his shiny new wedding ring flashes in the sunlight. He whispers something, though I can't make it out.

'Pardon?' Jenning tilts his head. 'Aiden, did you say something?'

Aiden tries to clear his throat with a guttural cough, but his words still come out barbed – his sadness, choking him. 'I said, I can't believe this is happening.' He lowers his hand, revealing dark eyelashes clumped together with tears. 'I'd do anything to have her back. Please,' he rasps. 'Please.'

My fingers flex at my side and graze against my leg. I want to reach out and hold his hand. I want to comfort him – pull him to me and sob in his arms. But I can't. He isn't mine, and I am no longer his wife. He has a new one now. A shiny new woman to offer him comfort. One without my flaws, which had so often frustrated him – like blurry stains on a glass table that you can never quite wipe clean.

'Ms Williams?'

Jenning is watching me again. Always watching. Did he talk to me? Did he ask me a question? He must have done because Aiden is looking at me as well, his head cocked.

'I'm sorry,' I whisper. 'I didn't hear what you said.'

'I was telling Aiden that you can both stay in one of the rooms while we search the house.'

My heart is thudding. Thump, thump, thump. Almost in sync with the swinging pendulum of the grandfather clock, ticking its way slowly through time. Tick, tick, tick. It's as if the ticking is slowing down and getting louder, each swing extending from seconds to minutes to hours, until both

Aiden and Jenning are frozen images, juddering back and forth – my life at a standstill. Maybe if it slows down even further, time will begin to reverse: back through the horror of this morning, past Freya's fall, over the darkness of the night when mother and daughter slept soundly, and back to last night, to the second when those pills were in my hand.

I promise I'll never take another pill again. Just give her back to me. Please. Please, please, please.

'Ms Williams?' Jenning grips my shoulder, jolting me back into the moment. Time has resumed its normal pace.

'Sorry . . . How long will the search take? Of the house?'

'It shouldn't be too long.'

I nod robotically. Aiden inhales – a breath so deep that it's audible – and presses his lips together before he exhales. He wants to ask something. I can always tell. It's like he is processing the question and possible answer before it even happens. Buffering.

'My wife is waiting in the car,' he says. 'Is it okay if she comes in?'

His wife.

He has brought her here. To our house. My house.

Jenning scratches his chin, his eyes darting in my direction. 'Yes, there's no problem with that from our perspective. Ms Williams?'

Aiden did this on purpose. He asked if she could come inside in front of Jenning so I can't make a fuss. Can't refuse to let her in. Even if I did – even if I threw myself on the floor like a child and screamed that she wasn't welcome – would anyone blame me? Would Jenning even react?

'Of course,' I say, in a monotone. 'She can't just sit in the car.'

The air between us is infected with awkwardness. I can feel it. So can they. Jenning scratches once again at his chin.

'Rupert is on his way as well. Is that okay?' I interrupt the silence, my gaze fixed like a laser on Aiden, waiting for a reaction. Anything.

'Who's Rupert?'

'He's –'

'Rupert is her boyfriend,' Aiden interrupts.

There it is.

'That's not a problem,' Jenning says.

Aiden looks up at the ceiling, his eyes glassy in the light. He wipes them with the back of his hand and looks down at me, an angry rim of red surrounding each green iris.

'Before I go, there's just a few more things I need,' Jenning says, breaking the tense silence that has been building itself around us, like a wall. 'Aiden, there are two officers outside securing the area, and the Detective Chief Inspector, who will be the senior investigating officer, is at the station briefing a team. Okay?'

Aiden nods.

'We'll need a photo of Freya. And details of what she was wearing,' he says, his mouth turning down in an apologetic grimace.

His question is a stab to the chest, and it pierces my lungs, making it impossible to breathe. No matter who sees Freya's photo or knows what she was wearing, they won't be able to save her. It will make no difference. Because of what I have done.

Aiden pats his pockets. 'Shit, I left my phone in the car – I'll run and get it.'

'Don't worry,' I say. 'I've got one right here.'

I walk to the console table where several silver frames sit scattered in front of the mirror. This entire hall used to be filled with hundreds of photos. Happy, beaming faces shone down from every spare inch of wall: my parents, me with my friends, Aiden. Images of a smiling, content family who loved each other. A family who would stay together. Parents who could never die. A husband who would never leave. But all of those are gone now. Only photos of Freya remain.

I pick up one frame and look down at it, dumbfounded. There she is, smiling up at me from behind the glass as she runs towards the camera in the long grass of the orchard, the curve of the river gleaming in the background, her hair bouncing out from underneath her bobble hat and flying around her shoulders, her eyes wide and happy. Her beloved Mouse dangling from her hand. I took that photo only a few weeks ago. It was such a beautiful October day, and we played hide and seek outside, wrapped up in our coats, hats and gloves, breathing heavily, our bodies seizing up with the giggles.

And here I am now: playing hide and seek again.

I open the back of the frame, pull out the photo and walk back to Jenning, holding it out in front of me. It trembles in my shaking hand.

'This is the most recent photo I have of her. It's from a couple of weeks ago.'

'Thank you.' He looks at it, and a smile lights his eyes. 'She's beautiful.'

Aiden gazes at the photo, his mouth downturned, his eyes wide. 'Where's Mouse?' he whispers, his voice almost inaudible.

'I . . .'

'She needs her toy,' Aiden continues, his words racing. 'I want Mouse, Naomi. I need that toy – she needs it –'

'She had it with her outside.'

The explanation falls gently from my lips. Aiden covers his mouth, his fast breaths rattling through his fingers.

'She had it with her?'

'Yes.' I turn to Jenning. 'I'm sorry I forgot to tell you.'

Jenning pauses. 'It's okay. I can't quite make it out in the photo. What did this toy look like?'

'He's medium-sized. Grey material. He's really soft, has a long light grey tail and black eyes. She took him everywhere.'

Everywhere.

'And she had him with her outside?'

'Yes. She took him outside to play.'

'And you couldn't see it when you searched?'

I shake my head.

'Okay . . .' He pulls out his notebook and writes, jabbing his pen at the paper in a full stop. 'And what was Freya wearing?'

'She was wearing pyjamas. Red ones. With fluorescent unicorns. She loved them.'

'Loved,' I said instead of 'loves'. Did they notice? Did they hear my unconscious slip into the past tense? But, no – Jenning is scrawling the details in his notebook again, and Aiden is staring at the floor, his eyes glazed.

'And her coat?'

My eyes flash to the hallway where, in the cupboard under the stairs, Freya's coat is hanging exactly where she left it.

Will they find it? Will they know?

Aiden will.

'She was wearing a pink coat with grey fur around the trim,' I say. Another lie.

Aiden looks up from the floor. 'Didn't I bring her in her cream one?'

'I bought her a new one. She saw it and wanted to wear it.'

Does he know? Does he know I'm lying?

His eyes drift away from mine. He returns to staring at nothing.

Jenning stops writing and slips the photo into an evidence bag that he pulls out of his large pocket. 'I'm also going to need a piece of Freya's clothing, something she was wearing yesterday.'

'Um, okay. Should I get it now?' I ask.

He nods. 'If you wouldn't mind. A dog unit is on its way – we let the dogs search first so that any scent doesn't get contaminated by lots of police officers marching around.'

I climb the stairs, my mind ticking as it whirs into action. Dogs. They're going to use dogs. Will her scent lead them straight to the bunker? Is it deep enough that they won't be able to detect her? These are trained animals, creatures whose very existence is to track, to find their target.

What have I done?

I need them gone. I need them out of the house, out of the woods, so I can think.

I reach the threshold of her room and hesitate. The last time I saw her alive, she was in her room. I was putting her to bed and telling her I loved her. And she told me she loved me.

I step into the room and wait. Wait for something to wash over me – some sign that she's still here. Somehow. But there is no feeling left. Not a single ounce of her remains in this room. No buzz in the air of her energy. She is gone.

I plunge my hand into her washing basket and retrieve the top she was wearing before I changed her into her pyjamas. I bring it up to my face and breathe in. Her fresh, clean scent. The very same way she smelt when she was a baby. If I were to close my eyes, she could be standing directly in front of me. My head spins. I will never smell her like that again. I will never be able to pull her to me and bury my nose in her hair, hug her tightly and have her little arms grip me back.

I breathe her in one last time, then drop the top back into

the basket. Walking over to her wardrobe, I look over my shoulder at the door before pulling out one of the tops that is folded in a neat pile of freshly washed clothes. I crumple it in my hands and turn it inside out.

I make my way towards the door but my foot becomes tangled in something on the floor. My arm instinctively flies out to prevent myself falling and I grip the edge of Freya's bed, wincing as my elbow smacks against the wrought-iron bar. I glance down and frown at the item that caught my footing.

Freya's backpack.

I pick it up slowly and trace the soft material, before placing it on the bed. My vision blurs. I shake my head and turn away, taking several large strides until I'm out of her room.

Jenning is alone waiting for me in the hallway. Aiden must have gone to get her. Both disgust and relief churn in my stomach – he is with his wife, but at least he isn't here: he might have asked why Freya was wearing a different top from the one she was dressed in when he dropped her off.

'Here you go.'

'Thank you,' he says, taking it from me with now gloved hands, and pushing the material down into another clear bag. He retrieves a black marker and writes on the outside of the bag. Marking those clothes as evidence. When, really, they are evidence of nothing – except another lie.

'We can all go into the snug to get out of your way when Rupert arrives. He shouldn't be long now. Will that be okay?'

'Wherever you're most comfortable. I'm just going to speak to the other two officers. The team should be here soon. Then, please, feel free to ask me if you have any questions. Anything at all.'

'I will. Thank you.'

He strides to the front door, making the distance in just a few long steps. I can see the two others through the window, and they face him as he approaches them. But as he comes to a standstill, he glances over his shoulder into the house.

I turn and walk to the toilet, although I want to run – hide. I close the door and my back slams against it.

Something isn't right. Something about her room wasn't right. There was something there, lingering in the air. Something sinister. Like that feeling you get in a place where something bad happened.

Is there anyone who would take her? That's what Jenning asked me. Because that's the situation he's dealing with. A taken child. But if he knew the truth, what questions would he ask then? Would the police have just made the assumption that she had fallen? Or would they dig deeper?

My knees fold beneath me, like paper being crushed by an invisible hand, and I crouch with my head against my knees and my arms wrapped around my legs. My heartbeat is thrumming in my ears. It's so loud – wave after wave crashing overhead – and my throat tightens with each pounding beat.

I try to inhale but the oxygen lingers in my chest, failing to reach my lungs. I gasp again, but nothing is happening. No relief from the unrelenting pressure building in my chest.

I can't breathe.

I throw my head backwards, my hands reaching up to pull my top away from my neck. I suck in air through pursed lips, forcing myself to think of nothing else, nothing but the breath flowing through my mouth and into my lungs.

Not the police.

Breathe.

Not the dogs.

Breathe.

Not Aiden.

Breathe.

But Freya . . .

A low cry bursts out of me and the pressure breaks, like air rushing into a vacuum. I lift my hands up to my mouth, which is wide open – no longer making noise after that one animalistic cry, but instead frozen – my lips set in a silent scream.

I stay there for several minutes, until the shaking and tears subside, and I hear voices in the hall.

I grip the edge of the washbasin and pull myself to standing. My reflection looks back at me, from the mirror that hangs wonkily above the basin. My eyes are small and red, my skin patchy and tear-stained.

I can't go out there like this.

But of course I can. My reflection shows a grieving mother. That isn't a lie.

I unlock the door and plod out into the hall, pulling my oversized cardigan around me, so that it is wrapped around my body, even though a damp slick of sweat has settled on the skin at the back of my neck. But as I look up from the floor, I catch a glimpse of an icy gaze – someone has let a blizzard inside.

Aiden is standing by the foot of the stairs, almost exactly where I found Freya. But his back is to me, his arm wrapped around her waist in a tight hug, his head turned in towards her neck, like he used to do when he held me, and her blue eyes pierce mine from over his shoulder.

Aiden's wife – Helen Williams.

Although, when she was my best friend, she was Helen Steele.

8

Four years earlier . . .
March

Helen raised her glass of champagne, her eyes twinkling slightly from the half-bottle of wine she had already consumed over our starters.

'I want to make a toast,' she said, her face wide open with a cheek-to-cheek smile. The type of smile she rarely gave because it brought out the laughter lines around her eyes. She hated them. I thought they only made her more beautiful.

It was Helen who had organized the meal: a celebration for the first baby of our group. She had decorated the table with balloons shouting 'Congratulations', and scattered those little sprinkles that take for ever to tidy up. She had made sure everyone was at the restaurant early so that I would be surprised – we so rarely managed to get together – and had filled a huge hamper with gorgeous gifts: baby clothes and muslins and personalized artwork for the nursery, even though the baby wasn't due for months. It was perfect.

'Naomi, we're all here because we love you and are so happy to be celebrating the growing-ever-closer arrival of the first baby of our group. And even though you will disappear into your cocoon with Aiden, even more than you already have, we –'

'Don't be stupid – no, I haven't,' I said, as I looked down the table at my friends, all leaning in closely, giggling loudly.

'Yes, you have!' said Gemma, as she pinched my arm, jostling my glass filled with Coke. A little bit of caffeine won't harm the baby, I thought. 'We hardly ever get to do this any more – all of us together.'

'Yeah,' shouted Sophia, from the opposite side of the table. 'We know Aiden's fit and everything –'

'Sophia!' said Lucy.

'What? He is –'

'But you don't need to say –'

'All kidding aside, I do actually want to make a toast,' interrupted Helen. 'To our Naomi, who is going to be the best mum in the world.'

'To our Naomi!'

We raised our glasses, all six of us in tandem, and the sound of them chinking together made my heart soar. They were all so happy for me, so excited. We had grown up together. Together we had experienced first boyfriends, first periods, first heartbreaks. Now three marriages. And a baby on the way. They had always guessed that I would be the first to have a baby. I was the mummy of the group. The one who had always taken care of the others. The one who absolutely loved children. The one who had always wanted to be a mother.

Helen sat next to me, her arm resting against mine, my skin seeming even paler next to hers.

'Topped up your tan in Saudi?'

'You know what it's like.' She smirked.

'No, I don't, actually. Not much room for tanning in a classroom.'

'Well, there's got to be some kind of bonus for all that travelling back and forth.'

'Oh, you love it.' I laughed. 'Anyway . . . Thank you so much for all of this. It's perfect, Helly.'

'You're so welcome,' she whispered, her cheeks flushed with alcohol. 'I know you said you didn't want anything but I just wanted to do something special for you to celebrate.'

'I know and I love it. Really.'

'Good.' She smiled, sweeping away the hair that had clung to her lip-gloss, then taking another glug of wine. She put down her glass and her lips settled into a grin. 'Maybe once you've had the baby, we can have another party to celebrate you not being fat any more.'

'Helen!' I said, my eyes stinging.

'Oh, my God, I'm so sorry,' she said, reaching her arm around the back of my chair to force me into a hug. 'I didn't mean that. It was meant to be a joke.'

'I'm not fat, I'm pregnant.'

'I know, sweetie. And you haven't even put on that much weight. You look beautiful. I'm so sorry, you know I love you.'

'But you can be so brutal sometimes.'

'I know.'

'Don't do that to a pregnant woman.'

'I promise I won't. Never again.' She laid her hand on her chest and pouted, and I couldn't help but laugh. She was such a nightmare, but she was my best friend.

Our mains arrived and I breathed in the smell of chips as my plate was put in front of me.

'How are you feeling about it all, Naomi?' said Margot, as she hacked away at her meat and placed a hunk of steak in her mouth, closing her eyes in indulgence. 'Mm, that's so good.'

I tried not to gag. My pregnancy had made me go off meat – even the smell made me feel sick.

'Great. I'm feeling great. I've been nauseous but that's finally starting to go away.'

'I can't think of anything worse. It's like having a parasite inside –'

'Sophia!' interrupted Margot. Sophia had always made her views on having children abundantly clear. We were polar opposites.

'What?' She giggled. 'Doesn't mean I'm not over the moon for Naomi. You know that, right?' Her face dropped, her eyes streaking with concern.

'Yes, I do. No offence taken.' I smiled back at her.

'Well, it's good that you're not feeling ill any more,' said Margot. 'But I meant . . . how are you feeling about being a mum?'

All eyes turned away from the food, the wine, the other girls, and locked onto me with laser-focus.

My gaze wandered, making eye contact with each girl before darting to the next. My friends. My most trusted confidantes. 'I'm so excited. It's what I've always wanted. But . . .'

'But what?' Lucy leaned in from my right, her red hair falling into her eyes as she stretched across Gemma to squeeze my arm. The other carer of the group.

'I'm just a bit . . . worried. Scared. I don't know what I'm doing. And without Mum I just . . .'

'How long has that been now?' Sophia asked.

I tried to swallow but my mouth was too dry.

'It's been . . .' I trailed away, unable to declare the number of years out loud.

'Ten years. We were all eighteen, remember,' said Helen, making the declaration for me. Part of me was grateful, but the other was annoyed, frustrated with her for answering the question on my behalf. It was my decade of loss. My mum.

'What if . . .' I said '. . . what if I'm not good enough?'

A barrage of responses ploughed into me, my friends' overlapping voices thick with reassurance.

'Don't be silly!'

'You've got us – we'll help you!'

'We know it'll be hard without your mum, but you'll be amazing . . .'

Helen wrapped her arm around my shoulders again, rubbing her thumb back and forth over my hand. 'You've got nothing to be scared of,' she said. 'You'll be a natural.'

'Really?'

'I've never been more certain of anything in my life.' She looks around at the others. 'When we were little, Naomi used to drag a doll with us everywhere, in a toy pram, even in the woods. It drove me absolutely mad but she insisted – she couldn't leave her baby alone.' She cradles my chin in her hands. 'You were born to be a mum.'

I smiled at her. She was right, of course she was. This is what I was meant to do all along.

'How's your dad? He still really excited?' Margot asked.

'Oh, yes. He can't wait. He's bought loads of clothes and toys – he's over the moon.'

'He'll be a great granddad,' Helen said.

'He really will.'

'And you'll be a great mum,' Lucy said.

I nodded.

'Say it, repeat after me: I'll be a great mum,' she said.

I cleared my throat. 'I'll be a great mum.'

They all cheered, raising their glasses, and toasted me again.

I repeated the words in my mind as I watched them, and with each repetition, my worries became smaller, shrinking until I could no longer feel them.

I was going to be fine. I was going to be a natural. I had my friends. I had Dad. I had Aiden.

And soon I would have my baby.

9

'Naomi,' Helen says, as she extracts herself from Aiden's arms. 'I'm so sorry.'

Her voice says my name with all the familiarity of a long-standing friendship, a cadence created by saying the name hundreds of times over so many years. If I concentrate enough, I can still hear the way she said it as a child, high and shrill, and always hanging onto the final syllable. My name, said by her, echoing through the woods as we played hide and seek. My name whispered in the dark as we shared a bed. She was *my* Helen. She was my best friend.

Until she wasn't.

She walks towards me and I resist the urge to back away. I mustn't retreat. This is my house. I can't shrink any further and allow her to take over another inch of my life. I straighten my slumped shoulders. Lift my chin.

Her eyes are red and an inky stain of mascara dulls the skin below her thick lower lashes.

I nod at her in response. What can I say? What words would suffice? I don't know what to say or how to broach the chasm that seems to expand the small distance between us. I glance in Aiden's direction but he is hanging back, seemingly giving us space.

Say something, Naomi.

'I know. I'm sorry too,' I mutter, the words almost imperceptible, but she takes the smallest step towards me, closing the distance between us. Her eyes water and she brings up her hands to shield them, sniffing loudly before flicking her tears away with the tip of her manicured finger.

'I know it isn't good between us . . . And I know I'm the last person you'll want to turn to for help, but . . .' her voice cracks under the grip of emotion as more tears stream down her tanned cheeks '. . . if you need anything,' she continues, 'I'll be here. I'm so sorry.'

She lifts her arms like she used to, slightly away from her body, only inches forward: her indication for a hug.

Aiden approaches Helen and lays his hand on her shoulder. She grasps it instinctively, their fingers linking.

I wish I could be the bigger person – the better person – and accept it. Step into her arms. Tell her that I'm here for her too, that I know she loves Freya and we can all get through this together, but I can't. She isn't my friend any more.

'I should wait outside,' I say. 'I need to make sure Rupert can get past the cordon.'

Her mouth falls open slightly as she steps to the side. I march past them but hear him whisper to her as I pull open the front door.

'I'm going outside to see what they're doing,' he says. 'You stay in here. It's freezing.'

I walk out of the door onto the drive, and try to focus on the sound of the frosty gravel crunching beneath my feet. But all I can hear is his footsteps behind me.

Why did he have to follow? I can feel his glare boring into the back of my head, and my cheeks burn in the frigid winter air. I don't want to talk to him or acknowledge his presence – I can't – so I tip my head backwards and look up at the sky. It has clouded over, the pressure low and intense. Something wet and cold falls on my face and I hold out my hand.

Snow. It's starting to snow.

I shiver and wrap my arms around myself, tucking my hands inside my cardigan. I turn back to the house. I guess I could go back inside . . . But she's there, her face backlit in the porthole window.

I'd rather face the cold.

Rupert should be here any minute. Is there anyone else I should call?

No . . . There is no one. The worst thing ever to happen to me – the worst thing that could ever happen to anyone – and there's only one person I can think of to turn to.

What does that say about me?

The two officers who arrived with Jenning – I already can't remember their names – are trying to make themselves invisible. As if it isn't glaringly evident that there are strangers in the house, as if I can't feel their presence in my bones. They have begun searching upstairs. I don't know what they're looking for, but I imagine them fingering through my belongings. What if they find my tablets?

My stomach drops. What if they find my journal?

My breath quickens as I imagine someone else's fingers riffling through it, reading the words I've poured into the pages. That can't happen. I can't let them find it.

I need to hide it.

I turn back towards the front door but Jenning is standing halfway up the stairs, speaking to two other officers.

Will they let me up there? Will they ask what I need?

No. It's too risky.

I spin around and look back down the drive. As I lift my face to the falling snow, I hear a crunch of footsteps and the shape of Aiden moves into my peripheral vision. He stands beside me and sighs, his breath expelling outwards in a cloud of frustration.

'Are you going to stay here? In Royston?' Did I speak?

Words escaped without me forming them, as unconsciously as my breath billowing from my mouth, like fog. I turn to face him and cross my arms – a barrier to protect myself.

'Yes.'

'Where will you stay?'

'At the Queen's Arms.'

I flinch and he meets my eye, his already pink cheeks flushing. 'I'm sorry, I didn't mean to –'

'It's fine,' I mutter.

The Queen's Arms: a pub in the village, around a mile from the house, a few rooms tucked into its first floor. The place we stayed the night Aiden met Dad. The place where he first whispered that he loved me. The place he proposed. And the place where everything fell apart.

I blow on my hands – it's so cold. I look sideways at Aiden. When we were together, if I was cold, he would clasp my hands between his and rub them. If I close my eyes, his hands are around mine, his warmth the perfect antidote to the burning chill. He always wanted to be my protector.

And he tried.

A silver four-by-four turns onto the drive, slowly crunching its way around the three cones one of the officers has placed in an attempt to block the way, and makes for the house.

Rupert.

We met last year. The night Aiden told me about him and Helen. Aiden had called me to a pub in Montham, and after he left, I sat at a table on my own and slowly consumed a bottle of wine. Rupert approached and asked if he could join me. The first thing I liked about him was his voice. It was soft. Gentle. So different from what you'd expect in this giant of a man, with his broad shoulders and stubble-flecked jawline. And so different from Aiden's authoritative tone. His confidence. The voice that drowned everyone else's.

I wasn't looking to find anyone – I wasn't looking to be anything but alone – but he blundered into my life, clumsily, in his own charming way.

And there he stayed.

Aiden shifts his weight from foot to foot next to me, and I freeze to the spot, rigid. I always planned that they would never meet. There was no need, not then, and definitely not until Rupert had met Freya.

My stomach tumbles. Rupert never met Freya. He had wanted to come over last night. If I had said yes, instead of refusing him so bluntly, would Freya still be alive?

He drops from the car, his bear-like body heavy as it lands. He walks quickly towards me, almost running, and opens his arms. Aiden coughs.

Rupert pulls me towards him as he reaches me, wrapping his arms around my neck, but mine hang lifeless at my sides.

'I'm so sorry,' he whispers, his mouth in my hair. 'I'm so, so sorry.' He grasps my shoulders and leans back to look me in the eye. 'But they will find her, okay – the police are going to find her.'

I nod but I've switched off by the time his arms envelop me again. Over his shoulder, a row of yellow-and-blue-striped police cars are crawling up to the farm, their engines growling.

They're here. And in no time at all, they will begin methodically to comb my home, looking for any clue as to what has happened to her. They will search everywhere – house, garden, orchard and woods – to try to bring her home.

Rupert's right. They will find her. And what will happen when they do?

I begin to weep into his shoulder, and he holds me closer as I wrap my arms around him. He tells me it's going to be okay. Over and over. It's going to be okay. It's going to be okay. It's going to be okay. And every time he says it, I cry harder and he holds me tighter and says it again.

Breathing heavily, I remove myself from his arms.

'Let's go inside,' he says, and kisses my forehead. But as he does so, he looks over to Aiden and takes a step towards him. Confident but cautious. Always polite. Always considerate. 'Aiden?' he says. 'I'm so sorry for what's happening. And I'm so sorry to meet you like this. I'm Rupert.' He holds out his hand.

Time seems to stand still as Aiden assesses Rupert, a quick flick of the eyes from his head to his feet and back up again. He reaches out, grasps Rupert's hand and shakes it firmly.

'Rupert.' Aiden nods at him, just once. They shake hands for too long, but when they let go, Aiden's hand curls into a fist.

Rupert steps back and places his hand on my shoulder. A sudden urge to shrug it off tingles on my back, but I resist and clasp his fingers. Poor Rupert. In any other situation, he would have stood happily and allowed a smile to spread from ear to ear while he found a way, any route in, to spark a conversation with Aiden. I've never met anyone so at ease in the company of strangers, and who can make them feel so comfortable in return. How would Aiden have reacted if they were meeting in better circumstances? But I've never allowed that to happen. I have manically avoided the situation, cancelling on mutual friends at the last minute, even telling Rupert that he hadn't been invited in the first place. Anything to avoid the two of them coming face to face: the two men of my life; the exponentially different poles at opposite axes of my world.

I turn my head towards the house and Helen is still at the window, but she moves away as she sees me looking, pulling her blonde hair forward over her shoulder. I scuff my boo through the gravel and watch how the different-coloured pebbles tumble away. One simple action is creating a reaction that shifts the ground below me, like a stone thrown into a lake sending growing ripples outwards. Bigger and bigger, until they're so large they're no longer visible.

'Let's go in,' Rupert says, and I look up at him and nod. Aiden moves purposefully ahead of us as Rupert wraps his arm around my shoulders. He reaches the front door first, and goes to push it open, then steps to one side, and lowers his eyes. It isn't his house any more.

I walk forward and open the door with a shove, but immediately step back from the image that greets me. Two dogs, spaniels, are being led around the hall, the sound of their sniffing noses amplified.

A shiver runs down the length of my back. What are they looking for? What are they trained to do?

'Naomi, if you could all go to the snug now, that would be really helpful,' Jenning says, from his position on the bottom step.

'Okay,' I mutter, unable to look away from the dog nearest the foot of the stairs. Its keen eyes. Its wet pointed nose.

Jenning ushers us out of the hall in single file, and through the kitchen into the snug, keeping as close to the wall as possible.

'We did in here first,' he says. 'You don't have to worry about disturbing anything.'

Rupert and I nod at him.

'Apologies, I didn't introduce myself. I'm Detective Sergeant Jenning.'

'Not a problem, sir. I'm Rupert. Burton-Wells.' He adds his surname compliantly. He comes from another army family – for Rupert, figures of authority are to be respected. I know he won't sit down until someone tells him to or

Jenning leaves the room. But Aiden and Helen have already sat, sinking down next to each other on the sofa in the window, lost in quiet conversation.

'Naomi, before I go back, I just wanted to ask a couple more questions.'

'Of course.' I lean my head back to look up at Rupert. 'You can go and sit down, if you like.'

'Sure?'

I nod. He extends his hand to Jenning, who shakes it absent-mindedly, then sits down on the other sofa, the one facing the window. The one with the view of the dense woods in the distance.

'How can I help?'

He is grasping his notebook in his right hand, the pen pressed between the thumb and index finger on his left. Left-handed. Like Aiden.

'Is there anything else you can tell us about the land before we begin the search outside?' he asks. 'We're getting the official documents from the Land Registry, but until they arrive, any information you could give us would be really useful.'

The bunker.

'Um . . .' My mind scrambles: all words and thoughts and memories amalgamating.

'Entrance and exit points?'

'Um, there's an exit with a gate that leads onto a public footpath at the end of the furthest field. There's the same in the woods.'

The bunker.

'Anything else?'

There is a Second World War bunker in the woods.

'There are quite a few outbuildings. A barn, stables . . . I looked in all of them and called her name. But I don't think Freya would go out there on her own.'

He doesn't ask another question, so I wait as he continues to write quickly, almost scribbling in his notebook. 'Thank you,' he says. 'An officer will be back to let you know when the search of the house has finished. It shouldn't be long. We just need to do a sweep.'

'Thank you.'

He leaves the room, pulling the door behind him, but it doesn't close completely. Best to leave it ajar. I might be able to hear them searching the kitchen. Unless they've already done that. I'm not worried about the dogs until they go outside – into the woods. Freya's smell will be everywhere in this house.

But the searching, forensic eyes of a human might find something. Did I hide the bunker properly? Will they be able to tell that the ground was recently dug up? That the leaves haven't fallen into place naturally? Will the dogs lead them to it?

Questions continue to swirl around my head, my mind now a soupy whirlpool, and I stagger over to the sofa, trying to maintain my composure in front of Helen, but I stumble slightly on the lip of the rug that lies under the coffee-table.

'Are you okay?' Rupert asks, putting out his hand protectively.

'I just tripped,' I say.

'You're shaking,' he says, his eyes filled with concern.

'I can't do this,' I whisper.

'You can. I'm here for you. And they're going to find her.'

A choking sound erupts from my mouth and I bury my head in my hands.

I'm running out of time. What happened last night? Try to remember something. Anything.

I begin to turn my wedding ring in circles around my finger. Round and round. Round and round. The metal catching in the light.

'It's okay to cry, Naomi,' Helen says. 'If you need some –'

'Please, Helen, not now,' I snap.

I look up from my hands and meet her eye. She stares back, her mouth twitching. She's never been one for self-restraint. But she stays quiet, shrinking back into Aiden's arms.

I sit up and rest my head on the back of the sofa. Sniffing loudly, I let out a slow rattle of breath.

Rupert puts his arm around the back of the sofa, but I inch slightly away from him. I can't help it. How can I be normal, sit here with his arm around me, when my daughter is gone? When my husband – ex-husband – and his wife are sitting six feet away from me, like some kind of perverse afternoon-tea party?

We remain silent. Rupert is rubbing my back, his palm firmly pushing down the length of my spine before his fingers trace small circles at the base, then begin the return journey to my neck. This should be comforting, but Aiden is leaning forward, his elbows propped on his knees, his head in his hands, and Helen is stroking the back of his neck.

Rupert fidgets, and I can tell he is readying himself to speak, to break the tension permeating the air. 'I'm sorry we're meeting in these circumstances,' he says, shuffling forward on the sofa but keeping his hand on my back.

'Me too,' Helen says. She picks at the end of a long tendril of hair, then plays with a loose strand that has come away between her fingers, before flicking it off with her nail. It floats gently to the floor. I want to pick it up, to throw it into the bin – better yet, just open the window and let a gust of wind carry it away. Once she is gone, I want no part of her left in this house.

Aiden leans back in the sofa but doesn't look up from his point of fixation on the rug.

'But I'm glad we can all be together for Freya – even in

these circumstances some people wouldn't want to do it,' Rupert continues.

'Yes, when was the last time we were together? It was the wedding, wasn't it?' Helen says.

Heat rises up the back of my neck.

'Helen –' Aiden says, finally looking up from the floor.

'Oh, I didn't realize you went to the wedding, Naomi. That's good,' Rupert says, but his worried eyes bely his calm, measured tone. Not so naive, after all.

'It was just for a little bit. I didn't stay.' My breath is shallow, caught in my chest, like a bird in too-small a cage.

'Yes. It was just for a bit,' Helen repeats. 'But it was good of Naomi to come.' She flashes a brief smile at Rupert, and he smiles politely back, then kisses the side of my head, ending the conversation.

Aiden diverts his glance away from Helen and catches my eye, fixing me with his gaze. The old, familiar look – like he's staring directly into my soul.

He's the only person in the entire world who knows everything about me, everything about my past, and he's watching me closely, his eyes still set on mine.

He was there when it all went wrong. What is he thinking?

Does he suspect I'm lying?

Rupert's hand curls around my shoulders, and I allow myself to be drawn into the gap under his arm and rest my head on his wide chest.

But I don't look away from Aiden.

10

Four years earlier . . .
April

'Well, happy anniversary for yesterday, darling,' Dad said, a smile taking over his sun-weathered face.

'Thanks, Dad,' I said.

'And thank you for coming to see me on your special weekend. You didn't have to do –'

'Dad, as if we'd come out here and not visit.'

'I know but I saw you last week –'

'I wanted to see you, Dad.'

'Well, I'm always happy to see that bump.'

I placed my hands on my stomach. 'I'm getting big, aren't I?'

'You're beautiful. I'm so proud of you, darling. And Aiden will be a fantastic father.'

'He will. He's so excited.'

'Are your friends excited? What does Helen think?'

'You know Helen. She's thrilled for me, but children aren't really her thing.'

'How is she? I haven't seen her in a while.'

'She's good. She's away a lot for work but she's happy.' I sighed, but as I glanced sideways, a photograph on the wall caught my eye: Mum's warm face, her smile beaming out at me. 'Dad . . . Do you . . . Do you think Mum would be happy?'

'Happy?'

'With how my life has turned out. I don't know . . . Would she be proud? Is this what she wanted for me?'

Dad's expressive face stilled and his eyes flickered down, noticing his empty wine glass. He stood up, turning to the sideboard for the bottle – busying himself away from the question. He filled his glass, deep in thought and sat down.

Then, leaning across the table, he reached for my hand, holding it tightly, and whispered, 'She'd be over the moon. This life you've made – your career, Aiden, a baby . . . Your life is exactly what she wanted for you.'

'I miss her.'

'I know, love.' He sat down again, his hand still clutching mine. 'Me too.'

'What have I missed?' Aiden said, stalling as he entered the room, sensing a change of atmosphere.

'We were just talking about Mum,' I said, as he sat down and snaked his arm around my shoulders, shuffling his chair towards me so that he was only centimetres away.

He kissed the side of my head. 'You okay?' he whispered.

I turned to him and nodded, my eyes fixed on his lips, then kissed his cheek, feeling warm in his embrace.

God, I love him.

I had been sitting in that very chair the night I realized I was in love with Aiden. The night he'd met Dad for the first time. The thought had been lingering in the back of my mind, slowly creeping forward, but that night I finally knew it was true. I loved him. I wanted no one – nothing – but him.

And nothing had changed. I loved him just as keenly as I did then. He was everything.

Aiden raised his glass. 'To Charlotte,' he said.

Dad and I mirrored his action, lifting our glasses high into the centre of the table, chinking them together, the sound ringing like a bell.

'To Charlotte.'

'To Mum.'

'And to the newest member of our family,' Dad said. 'I can't wait.'

A couple of hours later, after Dad and Aiden had drunk several more glasses of wine and I'd eaten a pudding smothered with cream, we said goodbye at the door, Dad's hand on Aiden's shoulder.

'Are you sure you don't want to stay? There's plenty of room.'

'I know, Dad, but I booked the Queen's Arms for our anniversary. We'll stay next time, I promise.'

'You two and that place.' He smiled. 'It's wonderful there, isn't it?'

'Gorgeous,' Aiden said. 'I love it.'

'I keep telling Naomi that London just doesn't compare.'

'All right, Dad.' I chuckled, rolling my eyes.

'You'll come back one day, mark my words,' he says, winking at me.

Dad held out his hand and Aiden did the same, both of them grinning as they shook.

'Are you sure you don't want me to drive you?'

'We can walk. It's a beautiful night.'

I stepped forward. Dad enveloped me in his arms and, just like that, I was a little girl again – happy and proud. Safe.

'I love you, Dad.'

'I love you too, sweetheart. See you soon.'

Hours of silence have passed when a police officer finally knocks on the door and tells us that they have finished searching the house. I peer out of the window – the sun is beginning to set.

'Can I ask . . . ?' Aiden says. 'Why did you search the house when Naomi told you she went missing from outside? And why did it take so long? Hasn't this been a waste of time? Couldn't you have been searching outside? There's so much land to cover.'

'I know,' the officer responds, 'and I'm sorry it took longer than expected but it's a large property. A team has begun to search outside, but it's standard procedure for the property to be searched when a person goes missing, even if that person went missing from the garden, rather than the house itself. It's our job to gather as much evidence as we can, even if that's by eliminating possibilities.'

'Eliminating possibilities? So, basically, confirming what the mother of the child already told you?'

'Aiden!' Helen and I say at the same time. She glances at me and places her hand on his chest.

'Well, it's a bloody joke –'

'Leave it. They're doing their job.'

'I know it's frustrating, sir,' the officer says, his tone apologetic yet firm, 'but there are procedures we have to follow. And people are searching.'

'Fine. I need a drink,' Aiden mutters, stalking past the

officer into the kitchen. The man retreats, with further muttered apologies.

Aiden crosses the kitchen, instinctively reaching up to the cupboard to the left of the sink and retrieves a tumbler. He turns on the tap, allowing it to run for a few seconds before filling the glass and gulping thirstily, then refilling it.

He splashes some on his face and wipes his mouth with the back of his hand.

'Sorry,' he says, to no one in particular. 'It's just . . . I don't know how to handle this. Would anyone else like some water?'

'Yes, you should drink something, love,' Rupert says, giving my shoulder a gentle nudge.

I rush forward to grab a glass of my own before he says any more. No one else needs to know about the baby. Especially the people in this room.

I move to stand next to Aiden and fill my glass from the still-running tap. I can feel him glancing down at me. How many times did we stand like this? Side by side at the kitchen sink, like every other married couple. The very picture of marital life.

'Can I have some too?' Helen appears at Aiden's side. He doesn't respond, but gets her a glass, placing it under the running water.

'I feel so useless not doing anything. We should be out looking for her,' he mutters.

'It'll be dark soon,' Rupert says, walking around the kitchen island towards the three of us. 'Maybe you can help search tomorrow. It's probably best if we all try to get some rest.'

'Rupert's right,' Helen says softly. 'We can come back early tomorrow morning and help.'

'No, I want to stay,' he says, in the same harsh tone.

'What do you want to do?' Rupert asks, as he reaches me. 'We could go and stay at mine if you'd rather be elsewhere?'

The image of Rupert's house ripples into focus. The first time I saw it, I thought it was so quaint and picturesque, with its cream-painted stone, chipping with age, flowers outgrowing the plant pots under the windows, and ivy curling all the way up to the grey slate roof. I had laughed at the notion of a man his height living in a period cottage. But he said it was love at first sight and he was willing to compromise for something he loved. I remember smiling – so taken by his words. This is a man who will love me no matter what, I thought. That night we had sex for the first time and I fell asleep on his chest, his arm around my waist. I felt content. Safe.

But neither Rupert nor his home can offer me safety or comfort now. I need to be here. I need to know what's happening – what the police are doing.

And when I can go back to Freya.

'No, I need to stay here,' I whisper. My eyes shift past him into the hall – it is finally empty. 'I'm a bit cold . . . I'm just going upstairs to get a warmer jumper.'

'I'll come with you –'

'No, you stay here. I'll be two minutes.'

I leave the kitchen and run up the stairs to my room, not looking behind me to see Rupert alone with Aiden and Helen. As I enter, I swing the door shut and the lock clicks into place.

The room spins.

I dart to my dressing-table, which sits under the window, overlooking the woods. The sky is dark and grey, heavy snowflakes still falling. I pull open the bottom drawer and plunge my hand into the depths of mismatched socks and underwear, my fingers grasping around the leather cover.

My journal. From when Freya was born.

Did they find it? Surely, they didn't go riffling through my drawers. And even if they did find it, would they even care to look at it?

My nails scratch over the etchings of my embossed initials on the front. I thumb quickly through its pages, scrawls of writing flashing before my eyes – and something drops to the floor. Three faces beam up at me.

The photograph. The one from the day before he left.

That morning three years ago, Aiden had come downstairs, dressed and ready for his work trip, looking handsome in his three-piece suit. He wrapped his arms around me, roughly kissing the side of my head and Freya toddled towards him. She threw herself at his legs and his throaty laugh had filled the kitchen as he lifted her into his arms. Seeing her gaze up at him in adulation, I had pulled out my phone to take a photograph and held it at arm's length, leaning in so it would capture all three of us. After he left me, I had it printed and spent hours and hours, day after day, staring at it, trying to rewind time inside my head so I could live it again: Aiden smiling down at me, the sound of Freya's giggle as she waved her arms in excitement, the touch of his hand on my waist.

I retrieve the photo from the floor and place it carefully between the pages.

I need to hide it.

I walk to the top of my bed and drop to my knees. Grasping the bottom of the headboard, I pull firmly but slowly, conscious of the sound rumbling through the floor. I jam my shoulder into the gap and push, inching backwards until I've created enough space to open the door that is hidden behind. When we were little, Helen and I played a game of hide and seek and I hid inside – it took her for ever to find me. It's small – half my height – and conceals a space in the eaves: the perfect hiding place.

I crawl into the gap and push my journal as far into one of the dark corners as I can reach, then come out, close the door and push the bed back into place.

Another secret.

'Are you sure you want to stay?'

I look up at Rupert as we stand in the hallway, and his eyebrows are raised in a question. I begin to nod but the pressure in my head is building as I think of all the watchful eyes – the questioning gazes. I want to tell them all to get out, that this is a huge mistake, and to leave me the hell alone. To admit what I've done. To admit the lie.

But I can't. I can never tell anyone. They would take her away and she would be all alone, with strangers examining her. Examining my past. And I will be blamed. I'll lose them both.

I would give anything to sprint to the woods, fling open the steel hatch with superhuman strength and carry my baby home. When the police have searched the woods – when they have ruled out that she is somehow still within the farm's land – I'll move her.

Unless they find her . . . They could discover the bunker at any moment. But fat snowflakes are falling quickly, already covering the drive with a layer of pristine white. Maybe it will hide the recently dug ground, or any footsteps I left behind. Maybe the snow will hide what I've done.

'Call me as soon as anything happens, Naomi,' Aiden says, and I snap back to reality as he and Helen walk out of the front door and shelter from the snow under the porch.

'I will,' I say.

'Promise me –'

'Aiden. I will.'

He sighs, glancing at Helen as she pulls on his arm.

'I really don't want to go,' he whispers to her.

'Jenning said there's nothing we can do today. Let's go to the hotel and get some rest,' she says, cocking her head towards the car.

He hesitates, but as his eyes shift away from her, he meets my gaze. The back of my neck tingles as we stare for a moment too long.

My cheeks flush as he turns away.

He strides to the car, three paces ahead of Helen, and when he reaches it, he lowers himself in clumsily. Less than twenty-four hours ago, I laughed at exactly the same sight.

I dig my nails into the crook of my elbow. I should be in the car with Aiden. We would go to the Queen's Arms and console each other, our shared grief bonding us. But instead he is going there with her.

Aiden's car begins to roll down the drive, past a group of officers and a dog straining at its lead. I crane my neck to watch as it turns left out of the farm and –

And there she is.

Freya.

She is standing at the bottom of the drive in her pyjamas, her hair ruffled like a baby bird, looking up at the front door. She rubs sleep out of her eyes, the way she has done since she was a baby, her little hand clenched in a tight fist.

I squeeze my eyes shut.

I wait, and then blink, long and slow, preparing myself for her image to have disappeared.

But she's still there and now she's walking towards the house, her stare fixing me in a question. *Why did you leave me?*

'Rupert?' I push against his arm. He is beginning to close the front door, and his brow furrows at the exclamation in my voice. 'Open the door.'

He lets the door swing open and I walk out of the cover of

the porch and into the snow, my bare feet stinging in the cold as I ready myself to run straight to her –

She isn't there.

She was never there.

She is gone, and the loss rises up and over my head again.

I turn back to the house, which looms over me. It has stood here for hundreds of years, witnessing all the colours and seasons of our lives: the celebrations; the failures; the day-to-day mundaneness; the once-in-a-blue-moon joys; and the all-too-often stings of sorrow. And now – the irrecoverable loss of a child. The unforgivable lie of a mother.

I walk into the house and slam the door behind me.

12

I stare out of the French windows at the early evening sky suspended above the woods. It is heavy with clouds, but the moon is bright, almost full, the shadows on its surface faintly visible. Freya used to ask about the man in the moon. What was he doing up there? How did he get there? Isn't he lonely?

I wish that I believed in something. I wish I had the kind of faith that would reassure me that Freya is now happy, with people who love her. And she will never feel lonely or scared again.

But I have no faith. Freya isn't anywhere. She is gone.

In the quiet of the snug, I turn the same questions over in my mind. What happened to her? What happened last night? I keep picturing her falling, the same imagined scenario playing out over and over again, but the picture is blurred, the details unclear.

I should have woken up. I should have been there for her. She would have called out to me – she would have shouted or cried. She needed me. And I wasn't there.

Unless I did wake up, and I don't remember? Is that possible? There have been times – too many times – when the pills make me forget. I find myself trying to remember but am faced with nothing but blank space.

Did I hear her? Did she come to me?

'Naomi?'

Rupert shifts on the sofa. He gestures for me to sit down but I'm stuck on the spot, a puppet with no strings. I can't move.

'Sit down, Naomi. You need to rest.'

I shuffle across the room and collapse into the armchair, my head dangling over the arm so I'm looking at the world turned on its head. The sky is below me and the ground rises upwards and I'm tumbling over myself, over and over, until I don't know which way is up.

What happened to my daughter? Will I ever know?

Do you want to know?

The room spins. I lift my head and rest it on the back of the armchair.

I need to know what happened to her. How can I not know? She was in this house, where she should be safe. How did she fall? Did she call for me? Or was it instant? Like a switch being turned off: light one moment; dark the next.

Hours pass. Rupert cooks but I do not eat. I just sit and watch him. He tries to talk through my silences. My phone rings and I run to grab it, but it's someone asking if I've been in an accident recently. I hang up without saying a word.

After a while, Rupert's eyes close and his head drops backwards, heavy with exhaustion, his breathing deep and slow. I ease myself off the sofa and tiptoe upstairs to my bathroom.

I catch my reflection in the mirror and that tired, fragile woman is looking back at me. But, unlike this morning, her eyes are dull. There is nothing beyond them, no emotion. Nothing.

I open the door of the bathroom cabinet and retrieve my packet of pills.

No . . . I'll never take one again.

But you need them. And the doctor said that one a day wouldn't harm the baby.

But they harmed Freya. This all began with just one little pill.

Did the police find them? Do they know?

I throw the pills back into the cabinet as a scream rushes up through my chest. I turn away from the mirror and force myself down the stairs, though my feet feel heavy, each step requiring exponentially more effort.

Rupert opens his eyes as I walk back into the snug. 'Are you okay?' he whispers.

'Fine. I just needed the toilet.'

'Shall we go up to bed?'

'No,' I say, as I crawl onto the sofa, curling my body around his and resting my head on his chest. 'Let's stay here.'

He has never slept in our bed.

My bed. It isn't Aiden's any more.

'Are you sure?'

'Yes. I like the fire.'

'Okay,' he whispers, as he kisses the top of my head. 'They'll find her soon. I promise. Try to get some rest.'

He rests his chin on the spot where his kiss lingers but his words scald me. I feel him wait for a response, but when I give him none, he rests his head back, his arm around my shoulders, and we both lie awake in the light of the crackling fire.

Maybe I'll go to sleep and tomorrow I'll wake up in my bed, and I'll run across the hallway to Freya's room, and when I throw open the door, she'll be there, rubbing the sleep from her eyes, her sweet smile spreading from ear to ear.

Rupert's breathing changes, now slow and steady, his eyes closed.

My phone buzzes and I reach across to grab it from the side table.

New message: Helen

I hold the phone, barely gripping it, my fingers just grazing the edges. It rests menacingly on the palm of my upturned hand.

The screen turns black.

I click the circular button, just to make sure that it's actually there – that I didn't just imagine it.

And there it is: new message. Helen.

I sit up carefully and Rupert's eyes remain closed. I swipe up and my home-screen appears. The little green message symbol in the bottom right corner, with a '1' hanging perilously next to it in red. My shoulders inch up to my ears. My breathing is shallow and tight.

I tap on the notification.

Hey. Naomi, I know you hate me for what's happened and it's impossible for us to be friends again but I can't stop thinking about Freya and what you must be going through. I'm so sorry. They'll find her, I just know it. X

She hasn't messaged in years. Even after Aiden told me about them, she never explained or apologized. Our friendship – which had foundations buried deep in the earth – was demolished, and I was left standing alone in the rubble, wondering how and why it had collapsed around me.

So I made myself forget. That was the only way to survive it. She was no longer a person I had ever been friends with. She was just *her*. That woman.

I open Instagram.

Don't do it.

My finger lingers over the search bar. I tap it and type her name.

Her profile loads and I see their faces. Her picture shows them pressed cheek to cheek in a tuxedo and wedding dress, and their wide smiles look like sneers, plastered on especially for me. I scrape my thumb upwards on the screen, over and over again, as fast as I can, and the pictures scroll in a frenzy. Images fly past too quickly for me to focus but I catch glimpses of her blonde hair, of Aiden's fair skin, Freya's green eyes. I keep on scrolling, scrolling, scrolling downwards, the past flashing in front of my eyes in a blur of colour, and then I stab my thumb at the screen and it freezes.

It's us. Seven years ago, lying next to each other on colourful towels placed on white sand, our heads close together, hair entwined. Dark and light together.

I tap on her profile picture and the black-and-white photo of them at their wedding magnifies. I take in every detail. The wrinkles by his eyes from his cheek-breaking smile. Her dress, beautiful in its simplicity, a single flower tucked into the side of her low bun. His lips touching her forehead.

She was maid of honour at my wedding. She helped me plan every minute detail. She whooped as we ended our first dance and he kissed me, holding the back of my neck, just so.

But then it all went so wrong. She helped him through it all, or so I've heard. And, six years after that first dance, he married her. He kissed her the same way. And I watched.

I wasn't invited.

But I was there.

I had watched as the doors of the church opened and guests flooded the courtyard. My mother- and father-in-law shouted directions at everyone, their faces breaking open with happiness. They had been my family – now they were hers. Elated cheers erupted as Aiden and Helen emerged and, with a rainfall of confetti falling down into their hair and onto their shoulders, they stopped to kiss. I craned forward as far as I could, my desperation to see outweighing my self-preservation. She brought her arms up to wrap around his shoulders and leaned back. His hand reached around her head to cup her neck under her hair.

I turned the key in the ignition, still watching them, when a flash of blue caught my eye.

Freya.

Her hair was flying behind her as she played, her vivid blue dress shining in the sun. She shrieked with delight, then ran haphazardly across the courtyard and into Helen's open arms.

My foot jolted and the car stalled, the engine growling.

I look again at the photo of them that day, and pause – disappearing into the memory.

Stop it, Naomi.

I fling my phone out of my hand and it falls to the floor with a thud. Rupert shifts but his eyes remain closed, his breathing slow.

I stare out of the window to the woods. Freya is out there. She's all alone and I can't get to her. I promised her I would go back. I need to go to her. But I can't: there are people everywhere, watching me. Tears fill my eyes and I blink them away but, in the blur, the trees inch towards me.

I press my fists into the sockets and rub, clearing my vision.

The tree-line is still, the moonlight reflecting on the snow-covered branches. But they've moved closer.

I shake my head. That isn't possible. It must be the angle and the darkness of night that is making it appear as if the trees are creeping towards the river.

I climb off the sofa, and pull a blanket and cushion from the armchair before lying down directly in front of the fire. I force my eyes shut and try to slow my breathing, counting slowly up to five and back down again. But they spring open, no matter how many times I try, my body fighting the urge to rest.

I won't sleep tonight. Not without my daughter. Not without my pill.

I watch as the flames flicker and dance, and time seems to stretch itself out into the darkness: seconds morphing into minutes, minutes into hours as I count down the moments until morning. At my lowest, I have reminded myself that days are relatively short periods of time, filled with only twenty-four hours. One thousand four hundred and forty minutes. No more than twelve hours of daylight. Some days pass us by and there are no happenings that have any lasting effect on our emotions, or burn themselves into memory. We go to sleep, and when we wake up, the previous day could simply not have existed – it just disappears into nothingness.

These are the lost days.

But then there are days like this one. Days where your world is shaken by a seismic shift. The pieces of your life begin to move away from each other and you try not to fall between the gaps.

Life is irrevocably changed.

I've had days like this before. The birth of a child, the death of a parent, the betrayal of a spouse, a careless accident. After the tremors cease and the earth settles, you manage to convince yourself that you will never have one again. That nothing else could possibly change your life so fundamentally.

Yet here I am, trapped inside another. And every day going forward will be like this. Life will never return to any semblance of normality without her. After what I have done.

What have I done?

13

I am falling.

My body hurtles over itself, head over feet, over and over again, waiting to hit whatever lies at the bottom. I gasp as the roof of the farmhouse hurtles towards me and hold my arms up to my face. The roof is only feet away and I scream, the sound rocketing through the open sky, my lungs filling – balloons ready to burst. I brace myself for the impact but as I hit the roof I continue to fall, and there is no searing pain, no breaking bones as my body plummets through the tiles. The house is collapsing, flashes of black and red scattering around me, stencilled faces blurring, and the canopy of the woods rises up to meet me. I tumble through the trees, branches scratching my face and scraping at my body. The door of the bunker opens, its gaping mouth ready to consume me, and I brace myself, ready to smash into the concrete floor.

My eyes fly open and the beams that criss-cross the ceiling of the snug come into focus.

It was a dream. It was just a dream. Everything is okay.

Except –

Freya.

She is gone. Grief and fury blossom in my chest, and I want to scream. I just want her back.

I bolt upright and squint out of the doors to the land beyond. It's still dark – it must be early. The fire died out overnight, but the windows are steamed up where the frigid air of outside meets the warmth of the house. But even through the mist, my eyes are drawn to the trees. Their branches reach out to me as they slowly surround the house.

You're just imagining it. The woods are just trees – they don't know what you've –

I freeze as my thoughts slam to a halt at the sound of a knock on the glass.

What was that?

I force my gaze to the outside.

I don't want to look out there, I don't want to see the woods, I don't want –

No . . .

Someone is standing on the other side. Their features are blurred but there's no mistaking the shape of her face, the slight tilt of her head as she moves even closer. Her breath billows against the glass. I can see the green of her eyes.

Freya.

I pull the blanket up and over my face, my breath fast and hot against the thick material.

That isn't her. It isn't her, it isn't her –

'Mummy,' her voice whispers in my ear.

I wail into my hands, which are clasped across my mouth, and sit up.

The room is empty. She isn't here. But she is trying to tell me something.

'What's wrong? What's happened?'

I jump at the sound of Rupert's voice as he dashes into the snug, his clothes crumpled from his night on the sofa. I forgot he was here. Even as he crouches to sit beside me, his legs crossing awkwardly, he seems unreal, as if I'm imagining his presence. Another ghost.

'Just a bad dream . . .' I whisper.

'Did you get much sleep?' he asks, as he kisses my forehead.

'Not really,' I reply. Sleep had come to me in waves: washing over me briefly before pulling away again in an endless tide. 'I'm going to shower.'

'Shall I make you something to eat?'

I can't bear the thought of food but I have to eat. For my baby: I can't lose this one, too. 'Just some toast, please,' I say.

I head to the bathroom upstairs but avoid the mirror. I can't look at myself. Instead I brush my teeth staring down into the basin, forcing the brush onto my gums, harder and harder, and watch the water as it swirls down the plughole. It is tinged with blood.

By daylight, the farm is teeming with people. The boundary is cordoned off with crime-scene tape, which shines brightly, its fluorescent blue glaring garishly against the bright white of the snow-covered ground and dull grey sky.

'Are you sure you don't want me to stay?' Rupert says, tucking a strand of hair behind my ear. 'You might want some company . . . I can't bear the thought of you on your own, worrying.'

'I think I'd like to be alone,' I say, staring ahead, distracted by the sight out of my front door: my home is flooded with strangers. Strangers who are searching for Freya. 'Sorry . . .' I turn my head to look him in the eye. 'I didn't sleep well. I should try to sleep if I can.'

'It's fine. Don't apologize. I'm on the farm – if you need me, just call.'

'I will.'

He steps into the space separating us and kisses me, but I pull away after only a moment.

'I'll call you later.' I follow him out of the front door but I don't watch as he climbs into his car and drives away.

Aiden and Helen are here.

He is pacing to the left of the drive and she is leaning on the brick façade, her eyes trailing him as he moves back and forth in front of her. There are police everywhere – some uniformed, some in their own clothes, but all talking under their breath. Their eyes shift towards me, then slide away as I pass them.

I turn away from Aiden and Helen to follow the sound of a distinctive voice. Jenning is standing at the side of the house where the river makes its tightest bend before heading back across the land to the woods. I walk towards him cautiously and my feet crunch through the now thick layer of snow, my breath visible in the frigid air, shallow and fast.

Aiden and Helen approach us and come to a standstill beside me. Aiden is almost close enough to touch. My hand flexes at my side.

'Naomi.' He nods at me.

'Aiden.' I nod back.

So formal – like strangers.

'Hi, Naomi,' Helen whispers, her usually golden face pink from the cold.

'Have you found anything?' Aiden asks Jenning, before I can respond to Helen. He looks exactly how I imagine I do: like he didn't sleep for a single moment last night, but instead lay wide awake, eyes fixed on the ceiling, thinking of Freya. But his thoughts would have been of his lost little girl, taken from him, his body shaking with the urgent need for any small scrap of news.

'As you know we searched the house,' Jenning responds, as he gestures to the swarming officers around him. 'We began the search with the dogs, and today we're going to continue into the woods.'

We nod, our movements out of rhythm, like those nodding

dogs you used to see in the back windscreens of cars. Passive, the movement completely out of our control, jostled by the shifting ground beneath us.

'Did you see the appeal made by the Chief Inspector on the news last night?' Jenning asks.

Aiden and Helen nod immediately but Jenning catches my brief hesitation.

'She made an appeal last night on every major news channel. They showed Freya's photo and gave details of when she went missing. Hopefully, we'll get some useful information from that.'

'Can we help with the search?' Aiden says.

'In these scenarios, it's always best if the police are left to do their jobs for the initial search – contamination of evidence, you understand.' He smiles at us like you would at a child, one who has asked to do something that is clearly not allowed, but who has been naive enough to ask.

Ask a question, Naomi.

'What should we do now?'

'I know this isn't what you want to hear, but what you need to do now is wait. We'll contact you as soon as we know or find anything.' He beckons at someone behind us and we both turn. A woman dressed in jeans and a black T-shirt makes her way over to us, dodging police officers who cross her path. 'Naomi, Aiden, Helen – this is Detective Constable Kate Bracken. Your family liaison officer.'

'Please – call me Kate.' She holds out her hand to each of us in turn. I shake it, offer her a slight upturn of my lips. I don't want to look at her but I force myself to meet her eye. She has a kind face. Understanding eyes. If I hadn't lied, would she be with another family this very second? A different family who truly need her?

'As the FLO, it's Kate's job to keep you up to date with

everything that's happening with the investigation. I know it's incredibly distressing and frustrating to feel as if you're not doing anything to help, but you'll know anything as soon as we know.'

'You can call me, any time, day or night. I'm here for you both,' she says. She has a soft Irish accent – warm and reassuring.

Guilt shudders through me and I dig my nails into the flesh at my wrist.

'Do you mind if I speak to my wife for a second?' Aiden asks.

'No, of course not,' Jenning responds. 'We'll be here if you need anything.'

'Thank you, both,' I say, watching them as they retreat to the other side of the drive.

'Yes, thank you,' Aiden calls after them, then turns to Helen, who is looking up at him expectantly. 'Helen,' Aiden says, his voice lowered, 'can you go to the car for a second while I talk to Naomi?'

'What?' she says, her eyebrows raised, her blue eyes round with disbelief. 'Why?'

'I just think it would be better if I discuss things with Naomi alone.'

'But why?'

They are talking in whispers, their voices hushed and intimate, even in a disagreement. I force myself to lower my gaze. I shouldn't get involved. It isn't my place.

'I just think, given our situation, that's what would be best. Please, don't make this more difficult than it already is.'

'There's no need for you to talk to her alone. I don't get it. I'm Freya's family too.'

Don't get involved.

'I know you are, of course you are, but I just –'

'Helen,' I shout, 'just for once can you try not to be so selfish?'

They turn to face me.

'Selfish?' Helen says, her mouth remaining open in disbelief. 'I've been trying to help you. I've reached out to you. And I'm selfish?'

'Naomi, please . . . ' Aiden says, his eyes fixed on me as he wills me to not say another word. Begging me for my silence.

'Yes, selfish. She's our daughter. Mine and Aiden's, not yours. If he wants to speak to me alone, who are you to say no to that?'

She scoffs and her breath billows in the cold air. 'Who am I? I know you hate it – I know it kills you – but I'm Freya's stepmother. She lives with me. It's me she sees every day. It's me she wakes up to, it's me who takes her to school, it's me who cooks for her, and draws with her, and tells her stories, and plays games. You might be her mother but it's me who loves her every day. And not from a distance. Up close. So don't you dare act like this has nothing to do with me. She's my child too.'

The cold wind is harsh against my back but the air in the space between us falls completely still.

'Leave.'

Her gaze does not shift – she doesn't even move to wipe away the angry, heartbroken tears that are flooding her face.

'I want you to leave,' I repeat. 'Now.'

'Just go to the car, Helen,' Aiden whispers, squeezing her shoulder.

She shrugs away from his grasp and stalks back to the car, slamming the door as she throws herself into the passenger seat.

'Why did you have to do that?' Aiden whispers. 'Why couldn't you just stay out of it?'

I shrug and look at the ground. I can hear his teeth grinding against each other, the picture of seething self-control.

'I just don't . . .'

I glance up at him. 'You don't what?'

'Nothing.'

'No, what were you going to say?' I ask – desperate to know what thought crossed his mind that he feels unable to speak out loud. 'Aiden – what were you going to say?'

'It's nothing,' he says, avoiding the eyes of the police officers mingling around us.

'Do you blame me?' I whisper.

The muscles in Aiden's jaw twitch. I can feel the tension between us, taut like a steel cable. The white noise of the commotion around us roars above our heads, like the brief pause before a wave spills over.

'Yes,' he mutters, the wave crashing down. 'I do blame you.' He gestures around him, arms wide open. 'I blame you for all of this. I trusted you.'

His words settle and he watches me, waiting for my defence, for my retaliation. But I have nothing.

Relief. Of all the emotions to feel in this moment, I feel relieved. I deserve the blame – just not in the way Aiden imagines.

'You can blame me.' My heavy breaths escape in clouds of condensation. 'I blame myself.'

'How did I let this happen?' He raises his shoulders, stretching his arms out, as if he can pull answers from inside me. 'How did this happen?'

'I don't know.' I shake my head. 'It was an accident. I didn't mean for this to happen. I'm sorry.'

'You're always sorry,' he cries. 'I stood by you, Naomi. I always looked after you. And you threw it all away. And now this?' His voice breaks and he looks up at the sky. 'This can't be real life. This isn't happening.'

'Aiden . . .' I reach out to touch his arm, but he thrusts his shoulder upwards, throwing my hand off.

'Don't touch me.' He stops, his body becoming completely still as our eyes meet. There is anger in them, and sorrow, but something else too. Suspicion? He knows me – the real me – inside and out. Can he see what I've done?

He bites down on his bottom lip. I want to run to him. I want to disappear into his arms and tell him I'm sorry, I wish he hadn't left, that I'd do anything to take it all back.

'I'm leaving,' he whispers, blinking away the connection between us. 'I've got to go . . . I can't do this. I can't be here.'

And within seconds he is gone, his car screeching down the drive, police officers moving sharply out of the way. I watch him leave, unable to move – to do or say anything. What can I say?

Jenning and Kate walk towards me, but I lower myself to the ground. The truth of his words has always been there, but they are now too heavy. Too much of a burden to continue carrying. I place my bare hands on the cold earth and spread them out, making imprints in the snow.

Freya loved snow.

Snot runs from my nose and I wipe at it with the sleeve of my coat, but it smears across my face.

Somebody tugs on my arm. Kate has crouched next to me, her face screwed up in concern. 'Come on, Naomi,' she says. 'Let's go inside and I'll make you a tea.'

I let her tug me onto my knees, then to my feet. It takes all the effort I can muster.

We go inside and I sit at the table while she potters around the kitchen, riffling through the drawers and cupboards, looking for the right utensils. I could help her, but I stay silent, unable to summon the energy. Exhaustion and grief have wrapped themselves around me, weighing me down.

The gentle scrape of china draws my attention to where Kate is retrieving mugs from the cupboard. She has reached behind mine for the almost pint-sized one that hides at the back, never to be used. It is pale blue and handmade, and the rim is slightly chipped from the time he knocked it against the sink. I told him not to carry on drinking from it, but he insisted.

Dad's mug.

I watch her pour boiling water into both mugs, but it's as if I'm looking at her through a thick fog: her movements distort and judder as the past blurs with the present.

'Sugar, love? I can't remember if you still take it.' Dad's voice echoes out through the haze, and suddenly my vision is clear. He's standing by the kettle, his arm poised over the sugar jar, his eyebrows raised in a question.

'N-no,' I stutter. 'Not any more, Dad.'

'Sweet enough already,' he says, then laughs at his own joke. He smiles at me as he retrieves the milk from the fridge.

'How is your new job going?'

'New job?'

'Yes, your teaching. Are you enjoying it?'

'Yes,' I whisper.

'I'm proud of you, Naomi.'

The mug seems to slam into the table and I jump –

Dad is gone.

Kate has sat down opposite me and pushes the steaming tea towards me. I wrap my hands around it. It is scalding but I grasp it even tighter, relishing the feeling as the tips of my fingers burn.

'I'm sorry,' I mutter. 'What did you say?'

'Is everything okay with Aiden?'

I take a sip and concentrate on the liquid burning my tongue and the delicate skin on the roof of my mouth. 'I'm sorry about that. All of us arguing. And Aiden and I –'

'It's okay –'

'No, it isn't. But the three of us . . . It's complicated.'

'Really, it's okay. Please don't worry about it. Believe me, I've seen far worse.'

I try to smile. 'Thank you.'

'You're welcome. Is there anything you'd like to ask me?' Her red hair falls in front of her face as she leans forward on her elbows, minimizing the space between us. I already know that this woman is a Rupert of the world. Kind. Empathetic. So very good at making people feel comfortable. Making people like her without having to try.

'I don't know what to ask,' I say.

And I don't – I can't tell any more lies. So there is nothing left. My lies are a house of cards, one stacked on top of the other, always a split second away from collapsing.

'How old is Freya?'

Poor woman. She must already know this detail; she'll already have been briefed, but she wants to make conversation with me, to forge some kind of relationship.

'Four.'

'When was her birthday?'

'In August.'

'Did you have a party?'

'Her dad did. We celebrate her birthdays separately.'

I saw the photos. She had asked for a unicorn party. I suggested doing it at the farm, imagining all her little friends travelling out to spend the summer day in the orchard, which I would decorate with pastel streamers. I would borrow some of the ponies from the stables at the end of the lane. We would play games and I would march out of the house, singing 'Happy Birthday', clutching a cake complete with fondant horn, and four iridescent sparklers.

At first, Aiden agreed. But then he said he had hired a hall in London, and we should carry on with our usual arrangement for special events. In other words – celebrate them separately. I'm sure that was down to her. Helen. Why else would he change his mind?

'What did you do for her birthday?'

'I took her riding. She didn't like it.'

She was terrified. She cried the whole way around the field, even though the pony was small and going no faster than a brisk walk. I begged Aiden to allow her to stay over – it was our birthday celebration after all – but he said no. He wasn't ready.

'I'm sorry,' I say, uncurling one hand from around my mug to wipe a stray tear from my cheek. 'I'm just going to the toilet.'

She nods, her eyes brimming with sympathy. I walk out into the hall and stop by the stairs. I can't talk about Freya any more. Any question Kate asks will raise memories, and every memory chips away at my ability to carry on without her. And I have to carry on without her.

The house is so quiet. It feels empty. Even emptier than it did on all of those endless days I spent here without them. Without Freya. Without Aiden. But now the house is completely still. Its soul has ascended out through the rafters. It is lifeless.

The front door is ajar. I walk over to it and tug on the iron handle.

Jenning is standing on the gravel holding Freya's top in his outstretched hand. He signals at someone to come forward. A muscular policeman strides to him with two dogs at his side, a German Shepherd and a Labrador. They sniff at the material. But there are three other dogs who aren't given their turn to smell the piece of clothing, even though they're straining on their leads. It can't be their job to track the scent of a person who is alive. No . . . These are the ones you hear about on the news, in famous cases of children who have been missing for years.

Cadaver dogs.

They already believe Freya might be dead.

I back away from the open door, the creeping cold stretching its fingers into the house. My lungs feel like they're about to burst. I want to scream so loudly that it will echo up, up, up, crack through the roof and blast open the huge expanse of sky.

'Naomi?'

I swing around. Kate has emerged from the kitchen.

'Are you okay? Would you like to talk?' Her eyes are wrinkled around the edges, like she's someone who spends a lot of time smiling. Laughing.

'I think I might go upstairs and lie down.'

'Okay.' She places her hand on my arm. 'Like I said, any time, day or night – I'm here.'

'And same to you,' I say. 'If you find something, please tell me straight away.'

'I promise I will.'

'Thank you.'

I watch her slip out of the open door, her hand reaching back to close it behind her, barricading out the cold. I climb the stairs but my feet are weighted, each step heavier than the last.

I'll never get her back. I'll never hold her close to me and feel her small hands stroking my hair, her head resting against my shoulder. I'll never hear her voice. Never again will she read to me or ask me to play or tell me she loves me.

Worst of all, I'll never know what really happened.

I rest my hands on my stomach. If I wasn't pregnant, I would give up now. I would tell them everything. But then what would happen to me?

I have to go on for the baby.

My baby.

I enter my bedroom and the scrawled words covering the pages of my journal scroll before my eyes. I glance at my bed. There is no sign that it has moved position, that the police found my hiding space. If they found it, they would have questions. Questions I don't want to answer.

I walk to the window and see my reflection in the glass. My haunted face, ghostly pale. But as my eyes shift to focus on the outside world, my mouth drops open. The snow-covered fields are dotted with the black-and-white uniforms of police, moving systematically in a straight line across the land, making their way steadily towards the woods.

I want to let out a cry, expel a scream, but there is nothing there. No emotion. I am numb.

I close my eyes and block out the black-and-white film rolling on the other side of the glass. But I can still almost hear the stomp of their boots as they trudge across the snow. The shout of Jenning's commands. And the rhythmic panting of dogs.

PART TWO

14

My feet pound across the floor as I run to the toilet. I throw myself to my knees and my stomach turns. I push my hair away from my face, my back aching, my eyes watering, until finally my body settles. I lean back against the wall. Breathing heavily, I close my eyes and place my trembling hands on my stomach.

I haven't forgotten you, little one. I haven't forgotten either of you.

I slam my head backwards and my ears ring as the back of my skull hits the wall. My vision blurs. I pinch the bridge of my nose and shake my head, but the room continues to swim about me. I am unanchored – my feet pedalling as I try to stay afloat.

'Mummy?'

Her voice echoes, like something out of a dream. I look out to the hall but it is empty. A low murmur of voices is coming from outside the house but inside –

No. Inside there is nothing. I am alone.

Completely alone.

'Mummy?'

I jump, drawing my knees up to my chest.

That was Freya. And not like something from a dream . . . It was real. Her voice was clear and sweet. It was her voice. It was her.

She isn't here. She's gone.

I grip the side of the washbasin and pull myself to my feet. I inhale deeply and spread my feet on the floor, trying desperately to ground myself, but I feel sea-sick. As if the whole world is moving and I am forced to move with it.

I creep into the hallway and stand at the foot of the stairs. I wait, listening, waiting. But as I wait, my eyes are drawn to the floor beneath my feet.

This is where I found her.

'Mummy?'

Her room. It's coming from her room.

I run as fast as I can up the stairs, my feet slipping out from under me as I reach the top. I push myself off my hands, dash across the landing and through her door.

The room is empty.

The woods beckon to me through her window under a heavy grey sky. I can see them from almost every window in the house.

'Freya?' I whisper. 'Are you here?'

Nothing.

'I'll read *Alice*, if you like? I'll read it cover to cover every day.'

Still nothing.

'What are you trying to tell me?'

I survey the room, slowly, methodically, taking in every detail of my daughter's last moments. She left her room and went out into the dark on her own. But that's so unlike her. So unlike my little girl with all of her fears.

I've tried so hard to recollect the events of that night. To remember anything: a shout in the dark, her calling my name. It was only two nights ago but it could have been a lifetime. I took my tablet and then –

Nothing. There's nothing except darkness.

My fingers trace the delicate fabric of her bed, the covers rumpled and unmade. Her backpack is lying forlornly at the foot. It is empty. Only a pair of socks remains, tucked into the side pocket.

Why can't I remember anything? I can't even remember getting into bed. That used to happen more often, when the time between taking my tablets and falling asleep faded away and failed to commit itself to memory, but that was when I took two —

Panic storms my body and I run out of her room and into the bathroom, my hands scrabbling to open the cabinet. I grab my pills, but as I fumble with the box, the words on the packet shift in and out of focus. I narrow my eyes, trying to still my mind, but as I do, two words become sharp and clear.

Take me.

I close my eyes. That isn't what it says. It doesn't say, 'Take me.'

My eyes open and the world settles into place. I look down at the box in my hands and slowly read the words on its side.

Take only when required but no more than one in 24 hours.

With shaking hands, I pull out the pill packets. The day I found out I was pregnant, I marked them up, day by day, to force myself to take no more than one. Taking two had become a bad habit, a gnawing need for sleep pushing me to break the rules, to ignore my doctor's instructions. But I can't do that now, not while I'm pregnant. Not with so much to lose.

But what if I took more by accident? What if instinct took over and I popped two into my mouth and swallowed them, not even realizing what I'd done?

What if I've forgotten what happened?

I turn the packet over and check the days.

There are no days missing. Last night's tablet is still there, and every day after that.

I haven't forgotten. She didn't call out to me. She woke up, needed something and must have got disoriented. And then she . . .

She fell.

The grief twists suddenly, a knife to the stomach that leaves me breathless. I hold onto the edge of the cabinet and sink to my knees. My head is heavy and my chin drops to my chest, my shoulders rising up to my ears as the tension within me builds.

There is no mystery. She's not trying to tell me anything. She's gone. And now she's out there and I can't get her back.

I lost her while I was sleeping.

I swore this would never happen again.

15

Four years earlier . . .
April

My phone buzzed, the sound muffled. I opened my eyes and squinted, reorienting myself: our room at the Queen's Arms was already growing bright in the morning sun. After the walk back from the farmhouse we had sat in the bar by the fireplace until I began to drift off, my head resting on Aiden's chest, his arm hugging me to him. My head spun: I was exhausted.

Aiden rolled onto his side and eased his arm around my waist, his fingers slowly dancing down my thigh.

'Aiden, wait.' I laughed, my nerves tingling.

The phone stopped.

I reached out to the bedside table. The phone wasn't there. I began to move my hand to the floor, my fingers searching for it, but closed my eyes as Aiden began to kiss my neck.

'Do you remember when you first told me you loved me? Right here, in this bed?' he said, breathing into my hair.

'You said it first.' I giggled.

My fingers grasped my phone, which was hidden under Aiden's T-shirt, and I sat up, still giggling as he reached for me again.

Missed Call: Dad, 3:44 a.m.
Missed Call: Dad, 3:45 a.m.
Missed Call: Dad, 3:47 a.m.

Missed Call: Dad, 3:48 a.m.
Missed Call: John Bishop, 8:27 a.m.

'Aiden . . .'

My stomach fell, my fingers fumbling to unlock the screen, but before I could manage it, the phone vibrated again in my hand.

John Bishop calling . . .

'John?'

'Naomi –'

'What's happened? Is everything okay? I've had missed calls from my dad.'

The line crackled, but I could hear John's breathing. It was uneven. And too fast.

'John?'

'Naomi, I'm so sorry to do this . . . you're pregnant –'

'Just tell me what's wrong.'

'You need to get here. We think your dad's had a heart attack –'

'What?'

Aiden sat bolt upright at the tone of my voice.

'Naomi, what's wrong?' he said.

'Ssh.' I pressed the phone against my ear. 'John?'

'He didn't deliver the milk at the usual time so we thought it was strange and went around to the house. He's collapsed. You need to get –'

'I'm coming right now.'

I threw my phone to one side and scrambled out of bed, pulling on my clothes, which were scattered on the floor.

'Naomi, what's happened?'

'My dad's collapsed. The farmer next door thinks he's had a heart attack. Shit. I missed his calls. He tried to reach me!'

'Naomi, try to stay calm, the baby –'

'He's been on his own for hours.'

'It's not your fault –'

'We should have stayed there –'

'Naomi –'

'I've got to go.'

'Naomi –'

I ran out of the room, not turning back to see if Aiden was following. Not seeing anything, not thinking of anything but Dad.

I need to get to Dad. Please . . . I can't lose him. Please.

My car flew down the lane to the farm, my thoughts galloping wildly, veering manically from hope to horror. I turned onto the drive and –

No, no, no, no, no, no, no.

An ambulance was obstructing my view of the door, parked at an angle, as if it had stopped in a hurry. Its blue lights flashed silently. A police car was parked beside it.

My body flew forward as I slammed my foot on the brake. I threw myself out, the sound of my feet pelting through the gravel mirroring my heartbeat. I ran past John, who was standing on the drive, waiting for me, his eyes small and red.

'Naomi!' he called.

The front door was ajar. I burst through it. 'Dad?' I shouted. My heart stopped.

A policeman was standing near the door to the kitchen. One paramedic was kneeling at the foot of the stairs, while another began to cross the hallway towards me. As he moved, he revealed the sight of my dad lying on the floor, his face turned towards me, his skin pale, his eyes closed.

'Dad!' I screamed, running towards him.

The paramedic reached me, holding onto my shoulders. 'Are you Naomi?' he said, as I fought against him.

'That's my dad!'

'Naomi, I'm sorry –'

'You need to help him!'

'There's nothing we can do. He had already passed away when we got here. We're so sorry for your loss.'

My knees buckled. The paramedic caught me by the elbows and lowered me to the floor.

'Do you want to be alone before we have to take him?' The question echoed towards me.

'Take him? Take him where?'

'We have to take him to the coroner's office.'

I stared at the paramedic. He looked sad. How many deaths has he seen? I wondered. How many family members has he had to offer condolences to? Does he go home and hold his family even closer? Does it make any difference?

'Yes, please,' I whispered. My body tingled for a moment as I stood, but by the time I reached my dad, it was numb. Shock infiltrated my system, like a hacker breaking into a computer. I gazed down at him. He was gone – and so was I.

I don't know how long I sat there with him. I just wanted to appreciate those last few moments with my father, the man who had taught me to be kind, and hard-working, and curious. The man who had looked after me when we lost Mum, who had stayed so strong for me when he might have crumbled. The man who had been there to welcome me into the world. It was my turn to give him his last goodbye.

My breath shook as I moved my face towards his, and his hair ruffled as I pressed my lips to his forehead for one final kiss.

'I love you. Oh, God, I love you.' My voice wavered. 'I'll miss you. Say hello to Mum. I'm so sorry.'

The door behind me opened and Aiden ran in, followed by the paramedics pushing a stretcher.

'Naomi!' He knelt beside me and hugged me to him but my arms hung limply by my sides.

'I could have saved him,' I cried.

'You couldn't, Naomi. You can't think like that.'

'He called me four times and I didn't help him. He needed my help –'

'It's not your fault. You were sleeping. I didn't hear it either.'

'He never asked me for anything, and the one time he needed me, I didn't help him. I should have been here. I . . .'

I collapsed forward, my head on Aiden's chest, my body shaking. Closing my eyes, I allowed myself to be consumed by the darkness, ignoring the noises of the paramedics as they wheeled the stretcher past me and lifted Dad's body.

But there was one noise I couldn't ignore.

The sound of a zip as the body-bag closed.

16

A solitary chair separates Aiden and me as we sit in the claustrophobic room. Aiden is scrolling robotically through his phone, his face blank, every so often glancing in my direction then averting his eyes quickly. The sound of my clicking fingers is the only noise other than the quietly ticking clock. I know it must be driving Aiden insane – he always hated it when I cracked my knuckles.

My eyes are drawn to the window and I peer at the grey landscape of the outside world. Snowflakes are falling again, heavy and fast, swirling across the ground in a heavy wind. Each day it snows, the bunker is hidden more and more, inch by inch.

Aiden's phone rings and we both jump – the bright, happy ring-tone sounding ominously out of place in the small room. He looks at me out of the corner of his eye and stands up, turning his back on me as my eyes follow him out of the room. He pulls the door closed behind him but thankfully the lock doesn't click into place and it swings back on itself, leaving an inch of space for his voice to float through.

'Hello?' His whisper is hoarse – cracking from the worry and pressure of the past forty-eight hours. I inch sideways on my chair, moving as close as possible to the gap in the door.

It must be Helen. When I arrived, I expected her to climb out of the car, but he slammed his door and locked it behind him. Did he tell her not to come? Or did she choose not to?

He stays silent and I can hear the faint babble of her words. I turn my head to peek through the gap – he is leaning against the wall, scuffing his foot on the dull grey carpet as he listens, bleary-eyed, shoulders slumped.

'I'm fine, I promise. I'm just very tired.' He pauses again, leans his head back against the wall and closes his eyes. 'No . . . No, I really don't think that's a very good idea.'

I move even closer to the door, slowly so he won't hear me.

'I know . . . No, I know you want to be here for me, and for Freya, and I appreciate that, I really do, but . . . It's just very sensitive, especially at the moment. You get that. Right?'

He told her not to come.

He stops speaking, and as she continues to witter on at him, he opens his eyes and looks right at me, his gaze burning. 'Okay, I've got to go. Yes . . . No, I really have to go. No. Don't come.' He hangs up the phone without saying goodbye.

He pushes open the door and sits down again but this time in the chair next to mine. The closeness is unnerving – being in his presence alone is unnerving. I am still Naomi and he is still Aiden. Everything we once were – everything we once had – vibrates in the hair's breadth between us.

'Everything okay?' I ask, as he squirms in the uncomfortable plastic chair.

'Yeah, as okay as . . .' His voice trails away, his sentence left unfinished.

'Where's Helen? Did she come separately?'

I know I shouldn't ask but I can't help myself.

'I told her not to come,' he says.

I turn in my seat to face him. 'Why?'

'Because even though you really pissed me off, the way you acted with Helen yesterday, I know how hard this must be for you,' he says, still looking at the floor. 'How hard it has all been for you. Not just all this. But everything. Helen. How you found out.'

How I found out.

He called me one morning last December and asked if I'd meet him in Montham. It's important, he said. I had pushed the phone against my face so hard that when I put it down a red rectangle, hot to the touch, radiated against my skin – a visual reminder of his words.

I need to see you. Please.

I sat at a corner table in the village pub, the table with the best view of the large double doors. Every time they were pushed open, I envisaged how the evening would play out. He hadn't asked to see me alone before, and that word – *need* – launched my heart out of my chest and into the sky. This is it, I thought, what I've been waiting for. He wants to come home.

As I watched the door, the stem of my glass squeezed between my fingers, I could picture him walking towards me in the faces of the milling strangers, imagine his hesitant smile, almost feel his kiss on my cheek. The last time I had seen him, to visit Freya, he had hugged me goodbye and I shrank into his arms, absorbing myself into him. Dissolved. Like paper submerged into water.

I missed him so much.

The door creaked as it swung forward and I craned my neck to see past the people who had sat at the table in front of me. And then I was no longer imagining it. It was him.

I took a moment to watch him, secretly take him in, before he spotted me. He moved past the crowds of people with such ease: a gentle hand on a shoulder as he tried to squeeze past, a friendly 'Excuse me' to a large group of young farmers who were blocking one side of the bar. He was dressed in a suit but had pulled off the tie, its tip poking out of his front pocket. His collar was loose around his neck, and the memory of the hundreds of times I had buried my face in that very spot kicked me in the stomach.

'Naomi,' he said, his voice calling to me, and the other conversations, all of the jeers and laughter halted, as if someone had pressed a mute button on everything except him.

He made his way from the other side of the bar to my table, a smile on his face. A half-smile, where only one side of his mouth turned upwards. I should have known from that smile alone that he wasn't there to give me good news — to tell me he still loved me and wanted to come home. He only smiles like that when he feels uncomfortable or awkward. It's a smile of defence. Of disarmament.

I tried to compose myself as he approached. How should we begin our lives together again? Should I stand? I wondered. Greet him? But how? With a kiss on the cheek? A hug? I wondered how we could climb down from the mile-high towering wall of knowing each other intimately on one side, and being strangers on the other. Aiden is still the man I have always known, I thought, warm, funny, affectionate, brutally honest. He is the man I met on the river; the man who held my hair back as I threw up every morning during the first five months of pregnancy; the man who sang karaoke with me, very badly, even though he hates singing. The man who looked after me with no thought for his own needs when I couldn't take care of myself. He is still the man I married.

But he is also the man who left.

'Hi,' he said, leaning down towards me, planting a friendly kiss on my cheek, the part closest to my ear, furthest away from my mouth. 'How are you?'

'Fine,' I said, tugging my hair forward over my shoulder. 'How are you?'

'I'm good, I'm good . . .' His voice trailed away, his eyes darting about the pub, avoiding mine. I remember thinking that he was nervous too. I thought it was a good sign.

'Thanks for meeting me,' he continued.

I smiled. 'You're welcome. I got you a drink.'

He picked up the beer and took a sip, his eyes finally meeting mine over its rim. 'Thanks.'

'You're welcome.' I waited for him to begin, to say something – launch into his grand-gesture speech. But he said nothing. He just took a large gulp from his glass, awkwardness settling on both of our shoulders.

'So, what did you need to talk to me about?'

He set his glass on the table. It sounded heavy – and it was. It marked the beginning of the onslaught. The guillotine as it thudded down.

'I need to tell you something,' he said, meeting my gaze. His fingers were centimetres from my own, and I watched as they grazed the wood of the table, which was stained with countless circular markings, years' worth of glasses placed down, of congratulations and commiserations. Of conversations like ours. His fingers stopped moving and he stretched them forward so that they rested on the tips of my own. 'You're not going to like it. I don't want to hurt you, but you deserve to hear this from me. In person.'

I curled my fingers away from his, my hand making a fist. 'Just say it,' I whispered, still feeling as if the world around us was silenced, although my voice was probably swallowed in the shouts and laughter.

'I'm with someone. I have been for a while now.'

Everything slowed down, his mouth moving in slow motion as he said my name and a buzzing filled my ears.

'Who is she?'

He paused, his eyes dancing over my face. That brief hesitation sent chills down my spine. This woman was not a stranger. I knew it then.

'It's Helen.'

His words were swift in their delivery. Brutal. A sharp slice of the blade, then nothing.

'Helen?' I asked, her name faltering out of my mouth in a stammer. 'My Helen?'

'Yes. I'm sorry.'

I wish I'd responded maturely, with dignity, or even better that I'd given him a piece of my mind. Shown him my anger. The betrayal. Either end of the spectrum would have been better than how I sat there, not saying a single word. I ceased to exist.

He tried to get me to speak. 'Say something –' he whispered '– anything.' But I couldn't.

'I'm sorry,' he said. 'I'm not doing this to hurt you. My relationship with her isn't to hurt you.'

Then he left.

I sat for several minutes until the world came back into sharp focus. I scrabbled in my bag for my phone and went to my most recent phone calls. Her name was there as it always was. I tapped it carefully, as if it might bite, and held the speaker to my ear. It rang and rang – then voicemail. I pressed her name again but this time it rang only once. She rejected my call. Apparently all she owed me – all I deserved – was the automated cadence of that robotic voice telling me to leave a message after the tone.

A blaring noise echoes in my ears and I shake my head to escape the memory.

'I also want to apologize for what happened yesterday,' he says.

'Yesterday?'

He chews the fullness of his bottom lip. 'I jumped down your throat. I didn't mean to. I just . . .' He rubs his hand across his forehead, where stress lines seem to have been etched into the skin. 'I need someone to blame. And it would be easy to blame you.'

The guilt squeezes my heart. 'I know . . . Maybe you should.'

He reaches across my lap and grips my hand. The shock of his hand on mine sends a flush all over my body. He hasn't touched me since . . .

It's been too long.

'Don't say that.' His thumb is rubbing the back of my hand. 'You didn't do anything wrong.'

I stare at him, searching for suspicion in his eyes. Does he really believe I'm telling the truth? 'Why don't you blame me?' I whisper. 'How can't you blame me after everything that's happened?'

He looks down at our hands, knotted together on my lap, the engagement ring he gave me rubbing against the wedding ring she chose for him.

'I know it might not seem like much after . . . everything but . . . You're a good mum. I know how much you love her. I know you wouldn't hurt her.'

My lip quivers and for a few moments neither of us speaks.

'Aiden?'

'What's wrong?' he says, his brow furrowed at the concern in my voice.

I look over my shoulder at the door.

We're still alone.

'Have you told them?' I whisper. 'About what happened? About . . . me?'

He stares at me, his eyebrows raised and mouth open. I pause, not breathing, waiting for him to show some indication of what he's done.

Please say he hasn't told them.

He shakes his head and I exhale, my vision spinning.

'No,' he whispers, his eyes flicking to the door over my head. 'I haven't told them. And I won't.'

I nod quickly, gratefully, unable to believe what I'm hearing.

'I know we've been through a whole ton of shit, but I'll always care about you. You know that, right?' He tilts his head. 'I would never willingly do something to hurt you.'

'Yes.'

We sit in comfortable quiet, like finding a lost pair of pyjamas at the back of the wardrobe that still slip on effortlessly. I would give anything to stay like this in this comfortable, confusing, excruciating silence.

She's not here.

And he's still holding my hand.

'Excuse me, Aiden, Naomi?' Kate opens the door and Aiden and I jump apart, my hand balling into a fist. It stings with the separation.

I like Kate. It's easy to see why she works in this kind of job: a job so full of emotion, a job you take home at the end of the day, a job where no amount of self-care or personal joy will scrub away the stain of someone else's sorrow. She's kind and instantly trustworthy. She chooses her words carefully. She . . . cares. I'm sorry I've made her care about a façade. A falsity. And me. I'm sorry I've made her care about me.

'I'm sorry for interrupting, but we're ready.' Her eyes fly back and forth between us. 'Are you both okay? Are you ready to do this? Remember, you don't have to. DS Jenning can speak on his own.'

Aiden frowns. 'No, we want to do it. We need to do it. He said it would help.'

She lays a hand on his shoulder. 'Well, people connect

with a case a lot more when they hear from the parents, rather than just a police officer.'

'Yes. We want to do it.' He looks back at me, his mouth set in a determined grimace. 'We're ready.'

I nod obediently and we stand, the moment slipping away.

A press conference. Those traumatic things you see on television that you wish you could turn over but you just can't tear your eyes away from the horror of the parents sobbing into their laps while the police give details about the child, and ask for anyone with information please to come forward.

And now that's us. Those parents are Aiden and me.

Whenever I see missing children's cases in the news, I analyse the parents' behaviour, their body language, the way they speak. And, like so many other people, I always wonder the same questions. I try not to ... Those poor parents sit there suffering the worst pain they will ever experience in their lives, and we judge them, wondering what they're capable of. Do they know something? Are they somehow involved? What do they know?

Now someone else will study me as I look out at them through their screen, as they sit comfortably on their sofas. They will ask themselves those same questions.

We walk closely, following Kate out of the room and down a long corridor. Our arms graze as we walk side by side and that same frisson of energy runs up to my shoulder, then tingles down my back. I feel closer to him now than since before we separated. He feels it too.

I shudder. If he knew the truth . . .

But what is the truth?

I inhale sharply as Kate holds open the door and allows us to walk through. A wall of noise and intensity hits us. The room is packed, chairs lined wall to wall, photographers kneeling before the front row, primed to capture the perfect picture. Clamouring to be the ones to write the hardest-hitting headline, to unearth the secrets, to expose me for what I am. Isn't that what journalists want? They don't actually care about us. They just care about the story. But as Aiden and I make our way into the room, silence surges outwards from us, the noise and commotion halting progressively in a wave towards the back of the room. A table has been set up on a low stage, behind which stand three chairs: one for Jenning, one for Aiden, and the last for me. The photo I gave the police of Freya has been blown up into two posters, which have been erected on either side of the table. My vision blurs at the sight of her. But Kate steps in front of it and I refocus on her smiling at us, nodding encouragement. I step up onto the platform and into the blinding light that illuminates us and our grief: the dark circles; the gaunt, sallow faces; the round, dead eyes.

The three of us sit down, synchronized in our movements, and I cross my legs.

I look out into the sea of people. Are they analysing my every move? Will someone watch this footage and dissect my body language, my hand gestures, my facial expressions? I turn my head, searching for Kate and her comforting smile, but looming large behind her is an even more comforting presence: Rupert. He smiles at me, nodding.

'You can do this,' he mouths.

I nod and place my arms on the table. My hands move to start their well-practised routine of click, click, click, but I stop myself. Instead, I turn my rings around my finger, one band rubbing against the other, and concentrate on my breathing.

In – then out. In – then out.

For just a moment, in the silence before anyone speaks,

dozens of pairs of eyes are fixed on me and Aiden. The police hope that the press will be an army of dogs: highly efficient hounds who will sniff out the truth. But I see a pack of wolves – growling and baring their shiny white teeth. They'll rip me to pieces.

Kate steps forward, in front of the stage.

'Thank you all for coming.' Her usually projected voice is being swallowed into the void. 'Detective Sergeant Jenning will be available for questions but the parents will not be answering any today.' Her mouth is downturned at the corners, and the bags under her eyes are dark and grey. I don't think she's slept since she arrived at the farm.

Beside me, Jenning begins to speak.

'I am Detective Sergeant Michael Jenning, one of the officers investigating the disappearance of Freya Williams. Freya is four years old and lives with her father, Aiden Williams, in London. However, she was last seen by her mother, Naomi Williams, on the morning of the twentieth of November, at her home near Royston.' He pauses, and several flashes light the dark space in front of the stage. 'We have begun a thorough search of the house and surrounding lands and are gathering forensic evidence to assist with our investigation. However, we need the assistance of the public. You are our most effective tool.' He looks directly into the lens of the news cameras, and gestures at the poster of Freya. 'Look at her face: have you seen this child in the last forty-eight hours? Spread her image on social media, keep your eyes open, and if you have any information about her, please call the dedicated police line, which is on-screen. Now her parents would like to say a few words.'

Jenning sits down and Aiden raises his eyebrows at me. I move my head slightly from left to right, the movement almost imperceptible. He nods in understanding and looks out to the sea of journalists. Cameras flash, like firings from an automatic weapon.

'Naomi and I would like to thank all of the police officers who are currently combing the countryside for our daughter.' He looks at me and I smile benignly. I don't know what to do with my face. Every tiny movement feels accentuated, as if someone is looking at me under a microscope. Every blink, wince, wrinkle of the nose, lowering of the eyebrows: I am painfully aware of them all. I try to relax my face, making it completely and utterly blank.

But what if my face is too blank? What if I appear devoid of emotion? Like a monster? Or will people think I'm just numb?

Stop it, Naomi.

'We would like to thank every single person in Easthampton and the surrounding areas who has rallied around us in the past forty-eight hours to support us and support the search for Freya.' He stops, his eyes trained on the huge posters of the photograph of Freya hanging to either side of us. He breathes in deeply then, with his mouth set in the shape of an O, breathes out slowly before looking back out to the crowd. Cameras flash.

'Our daughter is Freya Grace Williams. She was four on the sixteenth of August. She is quite small for her age, petite, and was dressed in unicorn pyjamas and a pink coat with a grey trim when she went missing. She's a beautiful little girl. Happy, kind, intelligent . . . She's very timid and she doesn't like to speak to or be spoken to by strangers. So, if you think you see her, try to keep her in sight and call the police. Please.' He coughs. 'But the reason we fear the worst is because . . . we know that Freya would not wander away from the house. Nothing would compel her to do that. So, please. If you know where Freya is, if you have her or know who has her, please help us get her safely home, back to us, her parents. We love her so much. We don't know what we'll do without her.'

I have been unable to look at Aiden, unable to watch him as he poured his grief so openly into the world. But now I risk a glance at him, and see that a steady stream of tears is trickling down his face. I reach out and grip his arm, unable to resist my instinct to comfort him. Is it inappropriate? Helen wouldn't like it. He looks at my hand on his arm, hesitating only for a second before he reaches across and covers it with his. And there it is: the image of the perfect, fractured family. There is the image that I will see on every news channel, on the front of every newspaper with the headlines: 'Desperate Parents Beg for the Return of Their Missing Daughter'.

There is their cover story.

'Please. Come forward, do the right thing, and bring her back to us. We can't understand why anyone would do this. But all we care about is getting her back. That's what matters now. I don't care about why, I just want her back, unharmed. Please. Please do not hurt her. Just bring her back. Bring her home.'

I start to shake. My hands are clammy, and I can't breathe properly, no matter how many times I repeat my mantra: in – then out. I don't want to hyperventilate or faint but at least that would get me out of having to speak.

'Naomi, are you okay?' Aiden's eyes are wide with worry.

I can't do this.

Please don't make me do this.

But everyone's watching me, waiting for me to speak. Waiting for the mother to take her turn, her sorrow fully lit under the glare of the blazing lights. And Aiden is still watching me, his brow furrowed, my face flushing under the heat of his gaze.

Don't tell any more lies. But say something.

'I . . . I don't know what to say,' I whisper, the microphone taped to the front of the table amplifying my voice around the room. It sounds strange – like someone else. 'Normally, people can't get me to stop talking but now . . .' My breath is quickening and I can feel a manic smile beginning to transform my face.

'I have no words,' I continue. 'Words . . . words fail.'

Breathe, Naomi.

Breathe.

'Less than seventy-two hours ago, I was reading my daughter a bedtime story and tucking her into bed. Wishing her goodnight. Kissing her forehead and breathing her in. My baby. And now I'm sitting here, in front of you all, and she's gone. How is that possible? I don't understand. I can't understand it. I left her alone and she was gone. Just like that. Disappeared. Vanished . . . My Freya. I just want her back. Please. I want her back. Bring my daughter back to me. Please, bring my daughter back to me. I'm begging you. Bring her back to me.' I look up at the ceiling. 'Bring her back.'

I look down as I finish speaking. There is silence. Then, as I lift my face, a rapid gasp of air. And the cameras begin to flash.

17

The press are already stationed at the bottom of the drive, lined up along the fluorescent tape, their backs hunched against the falling snow, but as they see the car turning in, they surge forward in a wave towards us, their mouths moving, their eyes wide and eager. Their voices are muffled through the glass of the car windows, but they are calling my name. Baying for a story, for some explanation.

'Are you sure you don't want me to take you back to my house?' Rupert says, as he parks the car directly outside the front door.

I place my hand in his lap and he intertwines his fingers with mine.

'I'm sure,' I say. 'I just need some time on my own.'

'I just . . . I don't like the idea of you being here on your own. The stress . . . It could harm the baby.'

'Please don't. I won't be any less stressed, or any less upset if I'm somewhere else.' I bring his fingers up to my lips and kiss the back of his hand.

'I know. I could just stay with you?'

His eyes are so worried, filled with so much pleading that I almost give in. I so desperately want to love him the way he wants to be loved. To let him in. No walls or boundaries. But I can't. I can't even begin to let him in.

'I really do need to be alone.'

And that is the truth. Or at least a shade of the truth. I don't want anyone around me, asking me questions, wondering how I'm feeling – what I'm thinking. I want to shut myself away until this is over. One way or another.

He moves towards me. I kiss him and he lifts his hands to my face, his fingers tangled in my hair. I rest my head on his forehead and from this close I can see something else in his eyes. Not worry or sympathy. Fear. He's scared. Scared that if I'm left alone, I might do something stupid.

I kiss him again. 'I love you, Rupert,' I whisper.

He nods and pulls me into a hug, his large arms tensing as he squeezes me close. 'I'll see you later,' he says. 'I love you.'

I open the car door, and as I do, I hear Kate getting out of the car behind us. 'Are you okay, Naomi?' she asks.

'I'm fine,' I answer, but as I hear the shouts of the press, my face turns clammy and I feel the colour fade away.

'We can't prevent them from standing at the bottom of the drive – it's public land – but if anything happens, if any of them come past the cordon or around the back, call an officer straight away, okay?'

I walk backwards towards the front door. I need to get away from their voices, from their prying, enquiring eyes.

'I'll speak to you later,' she says, rubbing the top of my arm.

'Thanks for everything today,' I say, the words coming out in a rush as I push the key into the lock, step into the house and throw her one last grateful look before closing the door. Shutting them out. All of them. Everyone.

I shiver and turn onto my side on the sofa in the living room to face the fire, which is no longer warming my back. It has died down, its embers glowing a warm orange, the flames no longer pummelling out their heat. I never come into this room, always preferring the snug, but when I came down this morning and settled into the armchair to gaze out of the

French windows, the woods were staring back at me. The trees lined up, like the journalists at the front of the house, shoulder to shoulder, their thick branches extending towards the house, gnarly fingers pointing at me. Those woods know my secret. They know the truth. And those people outside want the truth.

I am surrounded.

And Freya is out there. She's so close but I can't reach her . . . When are they all going to leave? I thought they'd be gone by now. I thought I'd be able to go back to her. But they're still here, searching. Watching.

I roll off the sofa, but as I stand, a fresh dose of nausea pounds through me.

'It's okay, baby,' I whisper, resting my hand on my stomach. 'Mummy's here.' I breathe in deeply several times, and the urge to heave disappears from the back of my throat. But a pain is throbbing at the front of my head, similar to one of my migraines. I haven't taken a pill in days. Is this withdrawal? Is this my body retaliating against my refusal to take them? I wish I could call my doctor. I need help. But what if my call makes her question or suspect me? Would she be obliged to tell the police everything that happened? What if she's already spoken to them? I lift my hand to my temples, but my fingers tremble.

The basket that sits at the side of the fireplace is empty. I want to curl up on the sofa, in front of the fire, and not leave it until I carry myself off to bed, the imprint of my body left behind in its impressionable material. But I need more logs.

I shove my feet into the slippers that dropped off as I lay on the sofa and shuffle out into the hall. As I pass the front door, there is the faint sound of knocking on wood.

Is somebody at the door?

I flatten my back against it and wait.

There it is again – a very gentle knock, tapped out in a jaunty rhythm that I recognize. An old friend used to knock just like that. Always the same set of raps of their knuckles. But it can't be . . .

Biting my lip, I turn my head, so my ear is resting against the wood. I can hear hushed whispers – more than one person – but can't distinguish either voice. I creep along to the window, but as I do a face appears, her brown eyes flashing with surprise as we come face to face.

Sophia.

'Lucy, she's here,' she says, gesturing at the person standing to her right.

Lucy appears at the window. She has cut her hair since I last saw her, the chin-length bob accentuating her almond eyes, her heart-shaped face.

'Can we come in?' she asks, with a timid, curious smile.

I nod through the glass and step sideways out of their view.

A wave of heat flushes across my face and chest. What are they doing here? And how can I get them to leave, to go away? They're going to ask questions . . . What if they can see right through me? Right through my lie? My hands shake as I reach up to the door handle and dread squeezes my chest as my fingers hover in mid-air, unwilling to let the outside world in. I knew it was Sophia from the sound of that knock. I should have stayed hidden – they would have retreated, given up, eventually.

I open the door and there is a pause, full of history, as we stand and assess each other. I know I could invite them in, smile at them, open my arms, but I can't – all I can do is stand and stare. I haven't seen them in years and here they are, at my door.

'Hi,' Sophia says, fiddling with the pom-poms at the end

of her scarf. 'I know this is really weird, but can we come in? It's freezing.'

I shuffle backwards, allowing them enough space to step into the house. Sophia was always more forthcoming than Lucy. If Sophia hadn't been there, Lucy and I would have remained at a standstill, neither of us knowing how to begin, how to break the barrier dividing old friends and strangers.

But as Lucy steps inside, she turns to look over her shoulder, and another person emerges from behind the door.

Helen.

'What is she doing here?' I ask, glaring at Lucy.

'I just want to talk to you,' Helen says. 'You didn't answer my message and then we argued –'

'Exactly, so why on earth would I want you in my house?'

'Naomi,' Sophia interjects. 'Come on, she's trying.'

I turn my head, assessing each of them in turn. These girls used to be my whole world. When I was growing up they were my lifeline. Always there when I needed them most. But then they disappeared.

When Helen was still my friend, even a knock was unnecessary. I would just hear her key as it was pushed inside the lock, and wait for her beaming face to appear around the door. That was when it really hit me our friendship was over: not when Aiden told me he was with Helen; not when she ignored my phone calls; not even when I saw her waiting in the car when he dropped Freya off. It was when her key dropped through the letterbox, and she could no longer let herself into my home. She was locked out and I was locked in, alone.

Let them in.

'Fine. Come in.'

'Thank you,' Helen says.

She steps inside and Lucy smiles at me encouragingly. I click my knuckles, the loud crack filling the silence.

'Sorry to just turn up but Lucy and I saw you on the news and wanted to see how you were doing,' Sophia says.

'Yes, we're so sorry, Naomi.' Lucy pulls off her woolly hat, which she then crumples in her hands, the material protruding from between her fingers. 'We got you these.' She holds out a large bouquet of flowers.

'Thanks,' I whisper, taking them from her. 'Would you like a drink?'

'If that's okay,' Lucy says. 'We don't want to bother you too much, just wanted to make sure you're all right.'

'It's fine. Follow me,' I say, wincing at the words. *Follow me*, as if they haven't been to this house hundreds of times. As if they hadn't helped themselves to things from the kitchen or slept in the spare bedrooms. As if Helen wasn't here her entire childhood.

'What would you like? I can make a hot drink?'

'That would be great,' Sophia responds. 'Tea, please.'

Lucy nods in agreement, smiling at me sadly.

'Helen?'

'I'm okay,' she says, shaking her head.

'I can make you a drink,' I say.

Helen looks at Lucy and Sophia, and Lucy raises her eyebrows, willing her to accept my gesture.

'A tea would be nice.'

I leave the flowers on the worktop and stay quiet as I make the tea. I want to ask Lucy and Sophia why they are really here. Why they chose today of all days to show their faces when years have passed – years of loneliness, years of no friendship. And Helen.

I let out a shaky breath as I stir in milk for Sophia and Helen, leaving Lucy's black.

'Shall we sit down?' I ask, placing each mug on a tray.

Sophia steps away from the kitchen table and walks towards

the door behind her. 'Can we sit in the snug? I always loved it in there.'

'Um –'

'Oh, yes, it's so cosy.' Lucy beams.

'Sure,' I say. My hands begin to shake, and the spoon, still in my mug, rattles against the china. Anger is bubbling in my stomach and I can feel it rising into my chest. We were friends our whole lives, but they've been gone for years. How quickly should that familiarity return? Not straight away. Not like this.

I follow them into the room, keeping my eyes fixed on the table and away from the doors. I place each of their mugs on the side of the table closest to the sofa, and mine on the side closest to the armchair, so I can sit with my back to the woods. Luckily, they follow my signals and sit beside each other, all three in a row on the sofa, their shoulders touching. Lucy leans forward, still clasping her hat, and Helen is sitting upright, her back poker-straight, but Sophia tucks her foot beneath her body and settles into the sofa. Relaxed. My stomach simmers.

I need to get them out of here. Soon the questions will begin. What if they ask me something and I hesitate or stumble? What if they can still read me as well as they always could? The pain in my head thrums. They know this place so well. My eyes dart around the room, searching for clues, signs that something has changed – for evidence of my lie.

What if they realize I'm not telling the truth?

'We're so sorry about Freya,' Sophia says, breaking the silence. She sucks in her bottom lip, which disappears behind her front teeth.

'We couldn't believe it when we heard,' Lucy mutters, her eyes fixed on the steam rising off her tea.

'I guess Helen told you?' I ask, although I know the

answer. They didn't just find out from watching the television or reading the papers.

Sophia's eyes slide sideways to Lucy, who looks down at her lap. Neither of them answers the question.

'Yes, I told them,' Helen says. 'I told them the day it happened.'

'If you've known since it happened, why didn't you reach out to me? A message, a phone call? Why have you just turned up after years of not talking?'

They gawp at me in shock.

I don't want to do this, I don't want to get angry, to let all of these years' worth of feelings spill out of me and knock them off their feet, but I can't push them down to where they can be controlled. And, with the anger, panic is brewing inside me: a dangerous concoction.

'We – we . . .' Lucy stutters '. . . we were worried about you. I know we haven't been friends, but we still care about you, Naomi.'

'Care about me?' I say, wanting to snort with laughter. 'Care about me? You haven't cared about me since Aiden left. You didn't care about me when I didn't have Freya any more, you didn't care about me when he married *her* – you don't care about me!'

'Hey!' Sophia barks, interrupting my rolling rampage. 'We always cared about you. Always. We were your friends. After what happened . . . after Aiden left, we wanted to help you. All we did was try to look after you, to make sure you didn't do anything stupid, but you refused to accept you needed help. You just kept on lying to all of us. To everyone. And the more we tried to help, the more you pushed us away. You erased us from your life. And now it's our fault that we're not friends?'

'That's not how I remember it,' I scoff.

That's a lie. You know what happened. You pushed them away, just like you're pushing them away now . . .

'You know that's what happened,' Sophia says, her face red with frustration.

I need them out. 'Well, whatever happened back then we're not friends any more. But now you're here at my house. Like vultures.'

'Naomi . . .' Lucy whispers, her eyes shining with shocked tears as they dash back and forth from me to Sophia.

'And what about what Helen did?' I shout.

'Don't drag me into this,' Helen says, her voice cracking.

'Drag you into it? You threw yourself into it. You got into a relationship with my ex-husband.' I turn back to Sophia and Lucy. 'What about that? She was my best friend and she stole my husband. What kind of friend does that? But you haven't discarded her.'

'She didn't steal him, Naomi. He left,' Sophia shouts.

'Oh, my –'

'We know what Helen did was wrong,' Lucy mutters. 'But they both loved you. We all loved you. And after Aiden left – after what happened with Freya – I guess they felt they had lost you . . . the real you. It was wrong of Helen not to tell you but . . . They helped each other. They –'

'I don't need to hear this!' I shout, all my senses turning numb under the full force of my rage. 'I didn't let you into my home to be lectured about my marriage and how it's my fault that my best friend fell in love with my husband. I don't need to hear about what I did. I know what I did. And I don't care if they needed each other.' I turn to Helen, and she stares back at me. 'I needed you, Helen. And you chose him.'

Lucy and Sophia are frozen, their eyes darting between Helen and me, waiting for one of us to fill the ever-expanding silence.

'Naomi,' Helen whispers, 'I know that things will never be the same between us but . . . I need you to know that I love Freya, and I want us to be able to go through this . . . not together but at least side by side. I don't want either of us to feel uncomfortable or be unable to be here for the important things.'

'You mean the press conference?' I whisper, leaning forward to pull a tissue from the box on the table. I blow my nose loudly.

'I just –'

'It wasn't me who told you not to come, Helen. It was Aiden. So, if you have a problem with your husband not wanting you there, you need to discuss that with him. Not me.'

'Well, if you said something to him to make him feel like I shouldn't be there –'

'I didn't say anything to him. Aiden and I don't speak.'

'Don't you?'

My retaliation dies on my lips. What does she mean?

'No, we don't.'

She raises one eyebrow and looks up at the ceiling. Her eyes are watering.

'I really didn't come here to argue with you,' she whispers. 'I would just like to be involved in what's happening. Freya's my stepdaughter and she lives with me. I have a right –'

'No, you don't.'

'I have every right. I look after her, I spend every day with her. Don't you think it kills me not knowing what happened to her? Don't you think I feel sick every second of the day knowing she isn't at home where she's meant to be? I know you think the grief belongs to just you and Aiden but it doesn't.'

'It does! That feeling isn't yours,' I shout, as I stand to

tower over her. 'You can't know what it feels like to lose a child because you don't have one. She's *my* daughter. Mine. Not yours. She'll never be yours!'

'She's more mine than yours and you know it,' she says, her eyes turning cold as she stands to face me. 'That's what you really hate. This isn't about me and Aiden. This is about me being more of a mother to Freya than you've ever been.'

'You two, please . . .' Lucy whimpers, as she cowers in the corner of the sofa.

'You've never been a mother to her,' I say, my voice a low growl. 'You're always away. All you care about is work. You don't really care about her. You just wanted my life: the house, the husband, the child. But you don't really care about any of it, just the image –'

'That isn't fair, Naomi,' Sophia interrupts.

'This has nothing to do with you, Sophia.'

'She's a good mother. And you saying she isn't doesn't make it true.'

'So what am *I*? She's the perfect mother and I'm the monster. The monster Aiden had to run away from. That's what you all think, isn't it? Isn't it?'

'I told Aiden,' Helen says, 'that the safest place for Freya was as far away from you as possible.'

Her words are venom. I can feel them pulsing through my bloodstream, seeping into my system. And Aiden's words, the day he left, echo deep in my heart.

Freya isn't safe with you.

'You stole my life,' I whisper, the words barely escaping my mouth before they're consumed by a sob. My head drops to my chest as my shoulders begin to shake.

'There was nothing left to steal. You had already destroyed it.'

'Helen, that's enough,' Sophia says, as she steps between us.

I lift my head to look at her over Sophia's shoulder – this woman who was once my best friend. There is nothing left of the girl I knew. Nothing left of my funny, supportive, ride-or-die best friend. But she must think the same of me. And the others. I'm a ghost of who I was when they loved me.

'Get out,' I mutter. 'All of you.'

Helen shakes her head and marches from the room. Sophia follows, staring at her feet as she runs after Helen. Lucy hesitates, sniffing loudly, then backs away. 'It didn't have to be like this,' she whispers from the door. 'We just wanted to see if you were okay. You didn't need to push us away again.'

I close my eyes and listen to her footsteps as she runs through the hallway. The door slams behind them.

I stand and puff out my cheeks, the space created filling with air as I hold my breath.

I lash out in a flurry of limbs, kicking over the coffee-table, the still-steaming mugs of tea spilling across the rug, the china shattering into pieces. I grab the closest object to me – the side-table – pull it towards me, and it crashes to the floor. The lamp flickers and extinguishes as it's tugged away from the wall, but the sound of glass breaking brings my rage to a halt.

'Oh, no,' I whisper, as I look down at the smashed frames. They all contain photographs of Freya – memories. All I have left.

I pick up the frame closest to me and loose pieces of glass fall to my feet. My face stares out at me – I am sitting on the ground with my back against the willow tree, Freya cradled in my lap. Aiden took the photograph not long after she was born. He said we needed to capture that memory: me and Freya in my favourite place. It was his idea to move here.

And I know that sometimes – during those times we all have when your mind lingers in the darkness and refuses to step into the light – he wonders if none of it would have happened if we had just stayed in London. If he hadn't brought me back here.

Sometimes I wonder the same.

18

'I think we should move to the farm,' Aiden said, as he stared at the television.

'What?' I looked up at him from where I was lying, my head in his lap, his fingers stroking my hair.

'Well . . . The baby is due in just over a month. There isn't really enough room in the flat –'

'We never planned to leave it,' I muttered, sitting up as fear turned my stomach. 'And the baby's coming so soon.'

'You wouldn't have to lift a finger. I'd do all the packing, or we could hire removal men –'

'There's enough room here.'

'But it doesn't compare to the farm. It's such a great place for a child to grow up.' He ran his hand under my long hair and began to massage the back of my neck, his touch strong and comforting. 'Don't you think? You loved it there.'

Could I really live there again? After everything? After Dad? 'I don't think I can . . .'

'Look, I know it won't be easy. It was their home. And what happened with your dad . . . But you were happy there.'

'But how could I be happy there now? All I can think of is Dad.'

'Your dad loved it and he left it to you. He'd love to know that you lived there, settled, with a family –'

'I know,' I interrupted. And he was right. It's what my

parents would have wanted. Our family had lived there for generations. And it meant so much to my dad. After both my great-grandfather, and eventually my grandfather, died serving in the army, my father was forbidden to join, and instead spent his days tending the farm. It was his life . . . It was mine. And I knew that we should go back there.

But I was scared. And Aiden . . . Aiden loved London, and a move to the country, full of its expansive fields, farmland and small villages, with prying, watchful eyes, was his idea of a nightmare. I just knew it.

'You'll hate it there, though,' I said.

'Well, it will take some getting used to – yes. But I'll do it for you, if it's what you really want.'

His eyes glazed, just for a moment, his usually bright eyes growing dull with a sudden sadness.

'What is it?' I whispered.

'Look, I know your dad dying was the worst possible thing that could happen and I know it hasn't been long but . . . I can't lose you too. And I know that if we get back to the life you loved so much – that your dad loved – it'll be good for you. It'll be a change for me but I don't care. I'll do it for us. For our baby. Think of the life we could have.'

The magic of my childhood played in sepia before my eyes – a blur of long summer days outside, reading, exploring, helping Dad, cooking with Mum, going to the quaint village school where my parents didn't have to worry about inner-city traffic, crime or pollution. Spending day after day with Helen, who lived just down the road . . . An innocent, carefree life.

I reached my hands up to his face and inched forward on the sofa, closing the small gap that separated us, and kissed him.

'Are you sure?' he asked.

I turned my response over in my mouth. It would be hard

to go back, but if he could do it for us, so could I. Aiden was all I had. Him and our baby – I would do it for them. 'Yes.'

'I'll tell the landlord.'

And only two weeks later I walked into the farmhouse, dragging my large grey suitcase behind me.

'Hey, hey – I told you to leave the suitcases, they're too heavy for you,' Aiden said. 'Why don't you just take a look around, make yourself at home again? Leave all the stuff to me and the guys.'

He went back outside to where the removal men were starting to unload the van, and I found myself drawn to the staircase, where hundreds of photos adorned the walls, dressed in dust, trailing up to the rafters. There were photos of my parents, hugging each other tightly; photos of me and Helen as children, our heads close together, blonde and brunette, making funny faces with our gap-toothed smiles; my grandfather in military dress; me and Aiden on our wedding day, our faces lit up with joy.

The last time I had been there, to choose clothes for Dad to be buried in, my body had been paralysed at the foot of the stairs, and I was attacked by memories. But this felt different. They'd be so happy I had come home.

I need to hang some of the baby. They'd like that.

My eyes wandered upwards, following the staircase, until I flinched at the sight of the door at the top. My parents' room. That door didn't need to be opened just yet.

I headed to the console table to my right. I rummaged around in the drawer for the large bunch of keys. Metal clinked against metal as loose keys knocked against each other – countless spares my parents had exchanged with neighbours and friends – until my fingers clenched around the iron ring and I walked to the snug.

My dad's armchair was still positioned in front of the

fireplace, a blanket thrown across the arm. There were still logs in the basket. It was as if life had suddenly stopped one day. Which was the truth, I suppose. One day this house was full of laughter and love, with Dad doing everything in his power to keep the joyful memory of my mother alive, and the next – there was nothing.

Blinking away tears, I put my hand into my jacket pocket, reaching for the burgeoning set of keys and flipping through them. I had forgotten how many there were.

Finally, I slid a brass key into the lock of the French windows and turned the handle – but it didn't open. I pushed against it with my shoulder and it jolted open with a loud creak.

I stepped outside, my footsteps crunching down the pebble path to the orchard. The trees were bursting with fruit, the branches hanging low, green leaves shining in the morning sun. I reached out and pulled off a red apple that looked ready to drop. Rubbing it against my T-shirt, I breathed in deeply, taking in the smell of the countryside: the scent of my childhood. Grass, fresh fruit, the very faint tang of manure, and clear air. Bringing the apple up to my mouth, I took a large bite. Juice burst out and dripped down my chin.

The apple trees began to dissipate, until there was only one here or there, and then there were no more. More grass stretched ahead, and I felt myself pulled forward towards the willow tree and the river. My favourite place.

When I was a little girl, I would read my favourite books over and over again until the pages turned a light brown, as if they had been dipped in tea, and the corners became worn. I would go into the snug and spend ages browsing through the shelves. Then, after taking my time deciding, I would reach up and snatch the chosen one from its slot, run through the French windows and pelt down the path, my feet slamming on the gravel, onto the grass and through the orchard, weaving between the trees until I reached the river. Out of breath, I would sit down with my back against the trunk of the willow, open my book, and fall head first. I'd stay there for hours, losing myself completely, only being jolted back to this world by a touch on my shoulder.

'I've been calling your name,' Mum would say, smiling down at me as I wrenched my eyes from the page. 'How was it?'

'How was what?' I played along.

'Wherever you just disappeared to! The world,' she pointed at the book, 'in there!'

'It was great!' I would scramble to my feet, and we'd walk back to the house together, hand in hand. I continued to hold Mum's hand, even as a teenager.

Especially at the end.

I looked up at the clear blue summer sky. A couple of red kites hovered above the river, the gentle warm wind keeping them afloat, cushioning them from the fall, as they saved the energy in their wings. I lowered myself to the ground with one hand, my other palm resting on my huge bump, and sat down, just like I used to, with my back against the trunk of the willow. The view of the river and the farmland through the overhanging vines offered a comfort I hadn't felt in a while – not since Dad died.

I'm home.

And at that very moment the baby kicked. I gasped and lifted my top to touch the bare skin. My baby was there, just below the surface.

It was a sign, I thought. A sign that, even though grief still rushed through me with every beat of my heart, everything was going to be okay.

I was where I was meant to be.

19

My eyes flutter open as the buzz of voices floats up to the bedroom window from the garden. I drag the duvet off myself and swing my legs out of the bed, my back arched, my eyes still heavy with tiredness.

I hardly slept. I almost flushed my pills down the toilet but I couldn't do it. I couldn't bring myself to take one either, and the argument with Helen wouldn't leave my mind – the words she'd said forced my eyes to stay open in a long, blank stare as I repeated one phrase again and again.

The safest place for Freya was as far away from you as possible.

Is that true? Did just being in this house – in my proximity – put Freya in some kind of danger?

Vomit fills my mouth and I throw myself out of bed and run, hand clamped across my face, to the bathroom. I heave again and again. My throat burns.

Is it over?

When I was pregnant with Freya, I would have given anything for the morning sickness to go away. But this time . . . This time it serves as a reminder. Of everything I have growing inside me. Of everything I have to lose. I have to stay calm until the police leave.

I turn on the tap and splash water on my face and into my mouth. As I brush my teeth, I relish the sight of blood dripping from my mouth into the sink, staining the white porcelain red before being washed away.

I walk back to my room and check the time, but my phone

lights up with a message from Rupert, sent just a few minutes ago.

Are you okay? I didn't hear from you again yesterday. Please let me know you're okay. I'm worried. xxx

I tap the key to respond but loud shouts draw my attention to the window again. I stand and stretch before walking over and looking out of the glass.

It takes a moment to comprehend what I'm seeing, for my brain to synchronize with the events of the past few days.

There are people outside. It looks like hundreds, I can't really tell, but . . . Who are they? They don't look like police. There are young people, in their twenties, and some who are much older, in walking boots and windbreakers. Above all of the hubbub, I can hear Jenning's voice ringing out like a bell, but can't distinguish his words or what he is telling them. I look beyond him to the river and, even though I resist with everything I have, my eyes are drawn upwards to the woods.

Freya is waiting for me. I promised to go back for her . . .

I rush to my wardrobe and pull on a pair of jeans and a thick jumper, then walk quickly out of my room and pelt down the stairs. I need to know what's happening. And I need to keep them away from the bunker. I can't let them find her. I can't let them take her away.

I walk into the kitchen and pause.

People are standing shoulder to shoulder in the snow, all facing Jenning. Listening to him intently. I move to the back door and wait. I want to know what I'm walking into. I need to prepare myself. But I still can't hear what he's saying.

I open the door.

'Naomi.'

I jump at the sound of my name. Kate is standing close to the patio, but instead of looking at Jenning, her eyes are trained on the house. She was waiting for me. I begin to walk towards her in my bare feet but she jogs across the patio to meet me.

'Are you okay?' she asks, as she watches me wrap my arms around myself to brace against the icy wind that is blowing across the river.

'What's going on? Who are all of these people?'

She looks over her shoulder, then walks inside the house and gestures at me to follow her. 'I'm sorry I didn't knock on the door to discuss this with you. We didn't want to wake you, but I was waiting for you to come out. We wanted to get an early start with the volunteers.'

'Volunteers?'

She beams at me, her smile warm and genuine. 'Yes, volunteers. The police have a volunteer task force that we use in cases of missing people. There simply aren't enough resources for police to spare hundreds of officers for a search. So we had a group from the task force, but since the press conference last night, we had so many people come forward and say they want to help. We've had two women – a lady and her daughter – come all the way from the next county.'

I turn back to the door and look out through the glass. 'These people are really all here for Freya?'

'Yes. People want to help. It's when something like this happens that you realize most people are good.'

I glance back at her and she nods at me, smiling in quiet reassurance.

'Can I go out there?'

'Yes, of course.'

I shove my feet inside the boots lying next to the mat and open the door.

'You'll need a coat,' Kate says. 'It's freezing outside.'

'Thank you.' I hoist my heavy winter coat off the peg, and yank it on, zipping it up as I step out and walk across the patio to watch from the grass.

Officers are separating volunteers into sections. They are standing together, tightly knit groups all listening closely to the instructions of the police officer at their helm.

'How many people are there?' I ask, not even looking back to see if Kate is close behind me. I can sense her, hovering at my right shoulder.

'Almost eighty.'

Eighty. Eighty people in addition to the police. Eighty people swarming across the farm, flooding the woods, sniffing out the scent.

They're going to find the bunker.

There's too many of them. So many people all searching for one thing.

You need to stop them.

I rub my hands together. They're red from the cold but sweat is gathering under my hairline, and my chest is clammy under my thick jumper and coat. I look at the sea of people, all readying themselves for the search, and my breath quickens, my heart hammering in my ribcage, faster and faster.

'Naomi?'

I squint at the outline of the person who said my name, prevented from making them out by a shift of cloud and the white winter sun shining behind them. I raise my arm to shield my eyes.

'Detective Jenning,' I say, as his face becomes recognizable.

'I understand that Kate has explained to you about the volunteers.'

'She has. I can't believe this many people have all come to look for Freya.'

He nods. 'The community has gathered around you.'

I don't know what to say – don't know how to react. I stand and watch him, my brain trying to settle on a formation of words, any sentence that may shift the awkwardness.

'What can I do? Can I help?'

'I believe Kate has talked to Aiden and Helen, and they're on their way. You're welcome to join one of the groups and search, but I understand if it's too much for you. It's up to you.'

I can't breathe.

'Okay. Thank you . . .'

My words lodge in my throat and I blink at him in the sun, his image wavering before my eyes – it's like looking out of a window streaming with rain.

'Naomi, are you okay?' Jenning asks.

I try to catch my breath but I can't . . . I can't breathe.

'Naomi?' Kate says, as she places her hand on my lower back, her brow furrowed with concern.

'Kate,' Jenning says. 'Take Ms Williams inside.'

'No . . .' I pant. I need to stay here. I need to know what's happening. 'No, I –'

'It's okay if this is all too much.'

'No, really, I'm okay now.'

My chest is rising and falling quickly, deep breaths rattling into my mouth while only wisps seem to make the journey down into my lungs.

Focus, Naomi. Breathe. You need to know what's happening. You need to do something.

'I'm fine,' I whisper.

'I'll go and get you some water,' Kate says. She turns and walks briskly towards the house.

'Can I borrow you for a minute?' An officer has approached us, and is waiting expectantly for Jenning.

'Are you okay on your own for a moment?' he asks.

'I'm okay now, I promise.'

He walks away and I look down at my shoes.

Don't look at them. Don't think about the number of people –

They're going to find her.

Just concentrate on your boots in the snow –

They're going to find her if you don't do something.

'Mrs Williams?'

Two women are standing several feet away, hesitating, as if they're scared to approach me. One is around my age, while the other is much older, and they're both holding flowers in their arms.

'Hi. Do I . . . do I know you?'

They proceed to walk towards me, but they do so slowly, cautiously.

'We're sorry to disturb you,' the older one says, 'but we wanted to give you these.'

They hand me the flowers. Roses: one bunch red, the other yellow.

'They're beautiful. Thank you.'

'I'm Florence and this is my daughter, Lauren. When we heard your story in the news, we thought it was so devastating, but then they showed images of your farm and I recognized it immediately.'

A tingle vibrates in my chest. Recognized it?

'Are you from around here?'

'No, no, we're not, but my father – Lauren's grandfather – was a child during the war, and he was brought here. To your home.'

I try to swallow, but I can't. My vision blurs. What do they know? Do they know about the bunker?

My eyes dart across to the house, and Kate is walking towards us, holding a glass of water.

'That's amazing,' I whisper, my throat tightening with panic.

Kate is coming.

'Yes, so amazing. He was looked after by your family. Even during the air raids –'

She's getting closer. I need this woman to stop talking.

'And once we realized who you were, I said we had to go and help. That family kept Dad alive throughout the whole war, sheltered him when he needed it the most.'

Kate is so close that her features are clear, her face still set in a worried frown.

'Thank you so much for the flowers and for coming to help. It means so much to me. I'm sorry to do this but I've been feeling a bit faint and should really go back inside.' The words spill out of me, quickly and forcefully, but I can't let Kate near them. I need to get away.

'Of course,' Lauren says. 'We completely understand.'

I turn away, my eyes set on the sanctuary of the house, and walk directly into Kate, the glass of water spilling into the snow.

'Oh, Kate, sorry,' I say, not faltering but continuing my march towards the house. 'I just need to get inside. I feel a bit sick.'

Kate changes direction and walks alongside me, but she glances back at the women. 'No worries, Naomi. Drink what's left of this,' she says, and hands me the glass. 'Sip it. Don't gulp.'

Guilt stabs into my chest. She's so kind. So caring. And she has no idea what I've done. 'Thank you.'

'Who were those women?' she asks.

'Just two of the volunteers. They wanted to give me flowers.'

I push open the back door and put the roses on the counter, next to the bunch Sophia and Lucy brought with them. As I rest my arms on the island, Kate stands by the sink, her back to the window. 'Do you want me to get you anything? Is there anything I can do?' she asks.

I shake my head and look past her out of the window. I can still see those women, running slightly to catch up with their group, who are walking down towards the river.

I need to get the attention away from this search. Away from the farm. Away from the woods.

I glance at the flowers again.

It would be a risk . . .

But what choice do I have?

'Kate?' I say. 'There's something that would help me, actually. I always go and see my parents when I need some peace. I could take some of these flowers – it's a waste for them all to be here. Is that okay?'

She nods. 'Yes, that's fine. Do they live nearby?'

I inhale sharply, the word *live* reverberating around the room. Jenning hasn't told her. And why would he? Of all the countless pieces of information he would have to relay, why would he remember that?

'No. No, they've both passed away.'

She walks towards me, her hands extended pleadingly. 'Oh, I'm sorry – I didn't know.'

'Don't worry. Seriously, it's okay. You weren't to know. I just go to the graveyard whenever I feel . . . When I need their help.'

'Yes, of course. Go. Please feel free to do whatever you need to do.'

'Okay. I won't be long.'

I grab my car keys from the drawer and pick up the roses from Florence and Lauren. I head straight to the front door and close it behind me, pausing to rest for a moment with my back against the solid wood. I inhale deeply through my nose, the breath rattling in my lungs, then exhale, my control so shaky that it emerges in several clouds, like smoke.

I march towards the car and turn on the engine, and as I press on the accelerator it roars back at me.

I don't want to be this person. The person who builds lie upon lie upon lie, the threads overlapping so manically that I can't distinguish one from another or keep them untangled. I don't want to do this. I've been resisting it, trying to keep the untruths contained. But I need to do something. And drastic measures are the only option.

So it's time. Time for one more drastic, desperate lie.

20

I park the car down a lane that runs between two fields on the edge of Montham. The village is tiny, not much larger than a hamlet, with one pub, a post office and a small farm shop. But it has something else. Something vital that I need.

A payphone.

I begin to open the car door but the sound of voices rings up the lane and I sink down in my seat. I can't let anyone see me.

I watch them in the wing mirror: an elderly couple walking slowly towards what would be classified as the centre of the village – the small green with the pub on the corner. She has her hand hooked into the crook of his arm, and he is holding onto it tightly. I slide down further, so that my knees are crumpled together in the footwell, and my head is sideways against the seat.

'It's freezing today, isn't it?' I hear her say.

'Baltic. Let's just do our errands and go home. And then we need to call Bernie and tell him that's the last time we rely on him to drive us anywhere. We'll die a death out here.'

Their voices subside and I climb back onto the seat and watch as their greying heads disappear into the post office. I check the rear-view mirror. There is no one else. The village is quiet, the ageing population keeping to their houses to hide from the cold and the dangers of the snow.

I pull the hood of my coat over my head and step out of the car. I walk quickly, with laser-focus. I just have to reach the payphone, then go back to the car without being seen.

Just get to the payphone.

It's at the end of the road, opposite the post office. I used to come to Montham when I was little, with Mum. My grandparents lived in a house just off the green. I'd visit and they would walk me down to the pond to play and feed the ducks. The payphone is opposite the green, on the road that runs through the village and down to the river.

I can see it. My eyes scan the open space, but there is no one. I lower my head as I walk past the post office, turning my face away so if anyone was to glance out of the window, they would see the back of my hood and nothing more.

Keep going. Nearly there.

Do it for Freya.

I could have gone somewhere busier, somewhere away from the claustrophobia of these minute villages where everyone knows everyone, and a stranger stands out, like a beacon in the night. But I couldn't risk CCTV. The bigger towns, even the ones around here, have surveillance.

I run the last few feet and slam the door behind me, turning to survey the world outside, my cold panting breaths steaming up the glass.

No one saw me. No one.

Now stop delaying and just do it.

I turn towards the phone, but I bend my neck back and rest my head against the door.

I can't believe I'm doing this. If anyone realizes –

You have to do it. They need to focus on something other than the woods. Do you want to be found out? Do you want to lose both your children?

No. That can't happen. I won't let it.

I pick up the receiver and pull out my mobile phone. I have a screen-shot of the number and double-check what I've committed to memory.

I close my eyes and inhale, expelling the breath slowly, my mouth quivering.

My fingers press the numbers rapidly, and I hear the flurry of beeps as the call registers, then the ringing. One ring after another.

'Hello – this is James speaking. Do you have information about a missing person?'

'Yes,' I say, lowering my voice.

'And what information do you have?'

I go to speak but the words falter so I cough instead.

Just breathe. Focus on disguising your voice. Deeper. Raspy.

'I think I saw the little girl from the news,' I say. 'The one who's been all over the papers.'

'Who is it that you think you saw?'

'I think her name is Freya Williams.' I bring up my voice at the end, as if I'm asking a question.

'When do you think you saw her?'

'Early this morning.'

'Can you give me details about where you think you saw her?'

'I was with my son getting petrol, and while he was paying, I looked over at the car filling up next to us, and she was in the back seat.'

'Can you describe the child you saw?'

'She was very little but she wasn't strapped in. She was sitting up in her seat, crying. She had dark brown hair, and I think blue or green eyes. She was too far away to see, but they were definitely light. She was wearing clothes that were too big for her. And she was crying and crying.'

I hold my breath, trying not to let my panic rattle through he phone to be received by him on the other side.

It's nearly over. Just a little bit longer.

'Did you see who the car belonged to?'

'No. I didn't think anything of it at first – I thought she seemed familiar but it didn't click until I got home and looked at the paper. As soon as I saw her picture on the front page, I knew it was her. I'm sure of it.'

'Where was the petrol station?'

'It's a small one on a country road called Boundary Road leading out of Haversham Common.' I pause for a split second, unsure whether to add in the last bit of practised information.

Say it. It's important. Lead them away from the woods.

'It leads to the motorway,' I say.

'And what did the car look like?'

'All I can remember is that it was black. I'm sorry, I didn't focus on the car. As soon as I realized, I wished I had. I'm sorry.'

'Don't apologize. We really appreciate the information. Can I please have your name?'

Shit. I planned the whole story on the drive over, and practised my voice, the exact way I would say the words. But no name.

'My name is . . . Sadie.'

'And your last name, Sadie?'

'Thomas.'

'Okay, thank you, Sadie. Could I possibly take a contact number from you, in case we need any further information?'

I allow several seconds to pass.

'Sadie?'

'I'm sorry, dear, the line isn't very good. I can't hear you.'

'Can I have a contact number for you?'

I pause again. Wait.

'Sadie?'

Wait. Two, three, four . . .

'Pardon? I'm sorry, I don't know if you can hear me any more, but I hope I've been of help. Goodbye.'

I slam my hand down to hang up the phone, cutting off his voice, which was still murmuring out of the receiver.

I lean back against the door, my chest rising and falling rapidly as I'm hit with a burst of adrenalin. My hands are shaking, my teeth beginning to chatter, but my face and neck are clammy.

I raise my hand, push open the door of the payphone, and start to jog, focusing on my car at the other end of the lane. But as I pass the shop, the bell rings, signalling a customer's exit. I stare at the ground as I approach.

Don't look up. Don't stop walking.

They step into my path as they drift out of the shop, and I look up for a second to avoid colliding with them.

It's the couple. The elderly couple from the lane, complaining about Bernie and their risk of dying a death in the cold.

'Oh, beg your pardon. We didn't see you there,' she says.

I pull my hood further forward around my face.

'Good morning,' I mutter, nodding at them politely as I walk away, my feet pounding through the crisp, fluffy snow.

I want to glance over my shoulder but I can't, so instead I walk faster and faster, until my walk turns into a run. I press my keys to unlock the car and throw myself inside, pulling the door behind me. It closes with a heavy thud.

My misty breath pools in the air in front of me, and I look out of the back windscreen. The couple are making their way slowly up towards the car.

I turn on the engine but resist the urge to push the accelerator to the floor and career out of the village. A criminal evading capture. Instead, I pull away slowly, making sure the car doesn't growl and the tyres don't screech.

I check the rear-view mirror, but reflected back at me are my eyes: bloodshot and wild.

The flowers are wet with snow by the time I lay them on the graves. It's only been falling for a few minutes, but it's been long enough for both me and the bouquets to become damp and cold. I arrange them against the headstones, the two side by side.

After I left Montham, I drove the long way to the church. They're buried in a graveyard in the opposite direction from the farm, but I couldn't drive past it to get here – there are police outside and journalists lining the hedgerow. So I drove the back way through the narrow lanes that run through the fields.

It feels wrong to be coming here after what I've done. Would they have reacted in the same way if they'd been forced into my position? Would they be able to understand?

No. Neither of them would comprehend why I would do this. They weren't alive to witness everything that had happened. Everything we went through. All the mistakes I made. If they had been, maybe they would understand me now. But it's probably a blessing that they weren't – that they passed when they did. I wouldn't want them to see me like this. The way I am. The way I was.

I reach out and trace their names with my finger. The stones are cold. Unyielding.

'Is Freya with you?' I whisper.

A child's laugh rings through the air.

I turn my head, squinting to see through the snow that is being tossed about by the wind.

A girl is running towards me down the row of gravestones. She has dark hair and pale skin.

Freya?

She's so close now I can see them . . . Her green eyes.

'Freya?' I whisper.

I hold out my arms. But she doesn't run into them. She comes to a standstill, the smile falling from her face. And an arm comes out of nowhere, from behind, and tugs on her arm.

'Rebecca, come here now,' a woman shouts. 'I told you, we have to leave. It's snowing again.'

That's not my girl's name.

I look at her again. Her eyes aren't green. They're brown.

That's not my girl. Not my baby. Not Freya.

'I'm very sorry,' the woman says, recognition flooding her face. 'Really.'

I nod and she turns away, no longer dragging her daughter by the arm. Now she is holding her hand, stroking her hair as she leads her to the car.

That's what I am now. A stark reminder of what we're so lucky to have but never appreciate – not until they're gone. I'm a warning to hold your child just that little bit tighter. To play with them a bit longer. To watch them closer.

If I'd been more present, had been a better mother, Freya would still be here. She needed me to keep her safe, to protect her, and I didn't. I failed her.

Freya is gone. And it's all my fault.

21

Four years earlier . . .
August

The night we returned home from the hospital, I lay awake listening to Freya's breathing.

In the hospital, the ward had been full of noise and other people, even in the dead of night. But at home the farm was cloaked in eerie quiet. The house made small sounds of its own, creaks and groans, like all old houses. I was used to those. But my body responded to every noise she made. Every snuffle, gasp and cry. Even her movements caused my eyes to fly open, adrenalin flooding through me.

As I lay there her breathing speeded up, until she was almost panting. I held my own breath, afraid to exhale in case I had to jump into action. I was completely still, my muscles tense. Just as I thought there was no way her breathing could accelerate any further, it slowed all the way down to the point at which I couldn't hear it at all.

I sat up quickly and pulled the Moses basket towards the edge of the bed. I tentatively reached out my shaking hand, and placed it squarely on her, her entire torso held in the length of my hand.

Her chest wasn't moving.

'Aiden!' His name left my lips in a high shriek, as I lifted her out of the basket.

'What's wrong?' he murmured.

'She isn't breathing! Help me!'

'What do you mean she isn't breathing?' he said, throwing himself across the bed.

'She stopped breathing! She just stopped –'

A high wail interrupted my frantic words – the cry of a deep sleep, prematurely broken. Freya's arms flailed at the shock of being awake, and her face was screwed up and bright red. My shoulders rose and fell, and I pinched the bridge of my nose as tears of relief sprang to my eyes.

'Naomi, you scared the life out of me.' Aiden's face was white, drained completely of colour.

'I didn't mean to, I thought she wasn't breathing!'

We gaped at each other, eyes wide as our breathing slowed. I expected him to be annoyed, to turn over and go back to sleep. But instead he wrapped his arm around my neck. 'She's fine, sweetheart.'

'I was so scared.'

'I know, but all new parents panic about things like this. Soon you'll stop worrying so much. She's only a day old.'

'I just . . . Aiden, if something happens to me, you'll look after her, won't you?'

'What do you mean?'

'If something happens –'

'Naomi, you're scaring me.' He reached out and cupped my chin in his hand, lowering his head to try to look into my eyes. 'What's going on?'

'I just need to know that if anything ever happened to me, you'd take care of her like I would. I don't want her to be alone.'

'She won't be. Of course I'd look after her, I love her, but you shouldn't be thinking like that. Nothing's going to happen to you. Or her. You're both fine.'

'You won't let anyone take her away from me?'

'Of course not.'

All the questions had come out in a breathless onslaught but I paused for a moment before allowing the final question to spill out of my mouth. 'And you won't take her away from me?'

'Oh, darling,' he said, as he pulled me towards him so that my head was resting against his chest. 'I'll never take her away. She's your daughter. And I love you both. So much.'

'I'm –' I stopped short of completing my sentence.

'You're . . . ?' He nudged me, his thumb rubbing the back of my shoulder.

I'm afraid that I'll always be afraid, I thought. I'm afraid that I'm not meant to do this.

'Nothing.' I looked down and Freya was already drifting back to sleep. 'I'll put her back in her crib.'

I laid her down and tucked her soft cotton blanket down the sides of the mattress, like I'd been taught in the antenatal classes. Tuck them in tightly, ladies, so it won't come loose and cover their face. Risk of cot death. Risk of cot death.

Risk. Of. Death.

I climbed back into bed and kissed Aiden goodnight.

'I'm okay now.' I smiled. 'So silly.'

'It's not silly. I worry too, you know. But being exhausted will make it worse. Just try to go back to sleep.' He turned off the lamp.

I lay quietly, keeping perfectly still, and waited. Waited for the sound of his deep, steady breaths telling me he had fallen asleep.

I never wanted to feel like that again. As if time was slowing down before my very eyes, the entire world taking a deep breath, ready for the fall. For the unbearable feeling of loss. That fraction of a pause at the top of a rollercoaster before you plummet towards the earth.

I had felt it before. When Dad died. I wouldn't make that mistake again.

Never again.

So, by the torch of my phone, I crept out of bed and plucked her from her basket, then quickly climbed back under the duvet. I lowered it to my waist so she wasn't covered – so she wouldn't overheat. But I didn't sleep again that night. Not even for five minutes. Instead I sat with her against my chest, my hand resting against her back so I could feel her breathing against me, matching my own inhales and exhales, secure in the knowledge that she was all right. She was close. She was with me. And only I could keep her safe.

As long as I stayed awake.

22

Why are they all still here?

This isn't what was meant to happen. The police were supposed to have gone, the farm abandoned, to look for her in the big, wide world. And that would have given me time: time to go back to her; time to say a proper goodbye; time to think about what to do. But almost a hundred people are combing the land outside. Searching for her. Not knowing that it's already too late. And I can still see teams of them walking through the snow. Heading towards the woods.

After I got back to the house yesterday, Kate was alone in the garden. All of the police, all of the volunteers were gone – tiny figures in the distance, scattered across the fields and in the woods.

'Are Aiden and Helen here?' I asked.

'Yes, they've gone out with Detective Jenning's group. They're down in the fields on the other side of the river.'

'I want to go.'

I didn't. Part of me wanted to run in the opposite direction, run as fast as I possibly could, until my legs gave out and I could go no further. And the other part – the other part wanted to be here, at the house, watching the woods, staring into the dense mass of trees to the south-east. I need to watch the bunker. I need to know if they're near it, if they find it. I won't be able to do anything but . . . I want to be prepared.

'Naomi, I'm not sure you should go,' Kate said. 'You looked like you were going to faint earlier, and you're still very pale. Why don't you stay here and rest?'

'I should be looking,' I said, in faux-protestation.

'I know you want to help, but there are so many people searching already. What you need to do is look after yourself. That's what's important.'

'If you're sure . . .'

'I am. Go and lie down.'

I nodded reluctantly and shuffled off to the snug. I lay on the sofa, staring out at the woods, ignoring the countless messages from Rupert. Watching the phone ring and ring, his name flashing across the screen. I don't know what to say to him. He wants to give me comfort, and I want to let him – I'm desperate for it – but I don't deserve it. And he doesn't deserve any more lies. I've told him so many.

I'm sorry. I need to be alone. I love you x

My resolve wavered as my finger hovered above the send button. I knew how he would take that message, even with the reassurance of those three words at the end. It would hurt him. But keeping him away is the best thing I can do for him. The kindest, most loving act.

I spent the rest of the day waiting for Kate to tell us. Waiting to hear that there had been a potential sighting. But she didn't say a word. Doesn't she know? But she must: she's central to the investigation. What else do they withhold? What else do they know that they choose not to tell us?

I adjust my position on the sofa, tucking my legs underneath me and drawing my blanket tightly around myself. I'm always so cold, as if the fire inside me, even the tiniest spark, has been snuffed out.

I look up and focus on outside. On the people moving about – the bustling, frenetic energy. But my eyes are drawn to a small figure standing inside the orchard, her hand stretching towards me.

Freya.

No. That isn't her.

I hold my breath and tilt my head to the ceiling.

You're just imagining it. When you look down, she'll have disappeared. Remember: she isn't here any more. She's gone.

I lower my head and my eyes instantly dart back to where she was standing.

I gasp and race to the French windows, pressing my hands against the glass.

She's still there. Still with her hand outstretched, beckoning me to come to her.

I know she isn't there. I know she isn't real. But – what if . . .

She begins to walk out of the orchard and I run. I run out of the snug and into the kitchen, throw on my coat, shove my feet into boots and sprint out of the back door.

I halt my momentum instantly. I almost forgot that the police are here. The volunteers. So many people who seem automatically aware of my presence, even from a distance.

I scan the horizon, looking for her. Has she gone?

Of course she has. She isn't here. You're just tired, so tired. It's your eyes playing tricks. She –

There she is.

I begin to walk through the orchard, towards the river, never taking my eyes off her on the opposite bank. Her image does not waver or recede before my eyes. She is there. And she is watching me. Waiting for me.

My boots are sinking into the snow, all the way up to my shin, and I place my steps carefully to make sure I don't sink too far and allow snow to spill over the rims and down my legs. Even among the noise of all of these people, I can hear the bells of St Michael's ringing, calling people to morning service. People of communion, people of faith.

I cross the bridge, and as I do so, she turns away and begins to walk towards the woods. I trail her blindly as she follows the line of the trees, not focusing on where I'm going, only caring about keeping her in my sight. She stops. I come to a halt and turn around, using the view of the house to ascertain where I am.

'No,' I gasp.

I turn back to stare into the thick copse of trees. Straight ahead, not too far from where I am standing, is the bunker. She has led me straight to it.

You promised you wouldn't leave her here.

She stares at me, her bottom lip quivering, her mouth so red against her pallid skin.

'I'm sorry,' I murmur. 'I can't.'

'Come back, Mummy,' I hear.

I gasp but can't move. I can't do anything. That was her voice – the same soft lilt, the gentle tone.

Why did I leave her? Why did I do this?

'I want to come and get you, but I can't.' I shield my face with my hands. 'I'm sorry.'

The sound of distant voices forces my eyes open.

And just like that – like a candle being blown out by a strong gust of air – she is gone.

She was never there. Just like yesterday, at the church, and before that, in the house: it was all in my mind. But is it my grief conjuring Freya, or my guilt?

She needed me and I wasn't there.

I jump as the heavy thud of footsteps draws closer. A team of volunteers, led by two police officers, is approaching this section of woods from the west. They are further in, but I can see them moving between the trees, their eyes trained on the ground.

Why are they still searching the woods? Why aren't they

focused on the sighting? They're so close to the bunker . . . They could find it today.

Something feels wrong. Different. I shift my weight from side to side, and as my feet sink into the snow I stare down at my boots. The ice underneath me is starting to turn to sludge. The snow is melting. I look up in horror at the sky – no fresh flakes are falling.

'Naomi?'

I turn quickly, my hands flying up in front of my body.

It's Kate – her red hair tucked into a dark grey woolly hat, the tip of her nose crimson from the cold.

'I didn't mean to scare you,' she says.

'I was lost in thought. Sorry.'

'I've been looking for you . . . What are you doing out here?'

'I just needed some fresh air.' The words sound unconvincing to my ear, but she nods sympathetically. Does she really believe everything I say? Or is she just a very good actress? Does she suspect me at all?

'Well, if you could come back to the house, Aiden and Helen are there, and I need to talk to you all.'

'Is something wrong?'

'No, nothing's wrong. It's easiest if I explain to all of you at once.'

We walk side by side towards the river, across the bridge, and through the orchard back to the house.

Is this it? Is she finally going to tell us about the sighting? Or have they already dismissed it as false information?

Maybe someone saw me. I glance at her as we cross the patio, but her exterior is calm, and she smiles.

I step into the house and falter at the sight of Helen sitting at the kitchen table. She has chosen the same seat she always used to sit in when we were little. To the right of the head of the table. I can still see her, the memory clear in my mind: her blonde ringlets clipped back with a bow, her gappy smile, her calling me to sit next to her – 'Namey', she used to call me. We were about eight when she finally managed to say it properly.

Aiden is sitting next to her, at the head of the table. Dad's seat.

'Hi,' I mutter.

'Morning, Naomi,' Aiden says. His face is unshaven still, and his usually large eyes are red and swollen.

'Hi,' Helen says back, her gaze veering to Kate, then back to me.

I go towards the chair one away from Aiden, but Kate is already pulling it out. I can't be stubborn and leave a gap, so I sit down to his left, squeezing through the gap next to his chair to make sure we don't touch. But I'm drawn to him, taking in his sad, watchful eyes. I clasp my hands together – palms clammy, fingertips tingling.

What is he thinking? What does he know?

'Okay, so I have some information for you all,' Kate says, turning in her seat to face us. 'We had a call to the hotline. Someone has said they've seen Freya.'

She waits for an intervention, but Aiden is staring at her in stunned silence and Helen is watching him, refusing to look at anyone else and biting down on her bottom lip. Her trademark tells – she's trying not to cry.

I should say something. 'What do you mean, someone's seen her?'

'They said they were in a petrol station with their son, and saw Freya in the back of a black car.'

'A petrol station? Where?'

'The one on Boundary Road.'

'Boundary Road?' Aiden says, the innocent words imbued

with a singular panic. 'That heads straight to the motorway, doesn't it?' He looks at me for confirmation.

I nod and he brings his hand to his eyes for a second, then lowers it to his mouth.

'So she could be anywhere by now.'

'Well,' Kate says, 'officers are investigating. We're looking at CCTV from the station, conducting interviews –'

'When was this?' he interrupts.

'The call was received yesterday.'

'Yesterday? Why weren't we told? We're the parents – you're meant to tell us these things. Isn't that the point of your job?'

'Aiden, please calm down,' Helen says, her voice cracking as her resolve finally breaks and tears fall from her eyes.

'No, Helen, I'm allowed to be angry,' he says, shrugging her hand off his shoulder. She flinches as if he'd slapped her, and drops her head, staring at the floor as she tries to control her unsteady breathing.

'My daughter is missing,' Aiden continues, 'and you didn't tell us that someone thinks they saw her? Alive? In a car on the way to the fucking motorway?'

'Aiden,' Kate says, 'you have every reason to be upset and angry. But this is our procedure. We don't tell families about sightings straight away because, sadly, when we put out numbers like this, we get a lot of hoaxes. And we don't want to tell you about something for it to end up being a prank. A genuine mistake, okay, but a prank? We wouldn't want any family member to go through that. That's why we didn't tell you until now.'

'So what's changed?' I ask, turning further towards her, so our knees are touching. 'Why are you telling us now? Does this mean it isn't a hoax?'

'We're doing more investigation but we checked the

CCTV of the petrol station at the time the witness told us she was there, and there was a black car with a child in the back. Now, of course, there could be any number of black cars with children inside, but we're tracing the owner of the car and using ANPR – automatic numberplate recognition – to trace where the car went on the motorway.'

An innocent person is being dragged into this. Some innocent man or woman, who was probably filling their car before the school run, is going to be traced and questioned. I never thought . . . I don't know what I thought. I just needed to do something.

Aiden rubs his forehead and frowns – the lines that are etched there burrow deep into his skin. 'Let me get this straight,' he says. 'Someone thinks they've seen Freya and describes the car she was in. You check the CCTV and there is a car that matches the description. But you still have all of these police and volunteers here? Searching the farm? What for? I don't understand why every person you have isn't out there looking for her.'

My head turns from Aiden to Kate.

Yes, Kate – why? Why are they still here?

Kate's face is still calm, but as she speaks, her usual soothing voice is tinged with authority. 'A number of resources have been diverted to investigate the reported sighting. And of course we have people investigating other alleys, but that doesn't mean the search of the farm is put on hold. Until it's concluded we can't be sure that we haven't missed any evidence, and the snow is starting to melt, which might help us. Every second counts –'

'Yes!' Aiden shouts. 'Every second counts! And you're wasting precious time searching the farm when you could be looking for her properly. We all know what you're looking for in the woods – you're looking for a body. You think she's dead. But she could be alive – you have someone saying they've seen her alive – so you need to get out there and do your goddamn job.'

He stares Kate down, seething, like an angry, cornered animal.

'Aiden,' she says.

'I'm sorry.' He hides his face in his hands, his shoulders shaking with silent, suppressed sobs.

I wipe my eyes and glance at Helen, who is staring at him, her lips parted, her face wet with tears.

I face him, my back turned to Kate, and place my hand on his arm. I look back at Helen and her eyes are fixed to it – turning to steel. But I don't care. We are Freya's parents. We were the family, not Helen. Nobody else. Just the three of us.

He looks up from his hands and his jaw is clenched, his face frozen in a pained, muted scream.

I stand up from my chair and lean down so we're face to face. His eyes are searching mine for comfort, like we both did for so many years: seeking reassurance from the other when everything was falling apart.

'It's okay to cry, Aiden,' I whisper. 'I know you're angry. You have every reason to be. But they're doing their job. And we just have to hope, okay?'

'I want her back,' he says, his voice breaking, his eyes fixed on mine.

'I know. Me too. More than anything.'

I reach out my arms and wrap them around him. Helen's eyes widen in shock, but she looks down at her lap, avoiding the spectacle.

He hugs me tightly and as his fingers dig into my back, I hold him closer. We cling to each other: two people trying to stop themselves drowning.

I wish I could ease his pain, but I am the one who caused

it. And everything I did was for nothing. It hasn't halted the search. It has just made it spread, like poison. And it has made Aiden – my Aiden, the one I loved – disappear even further. He is broken.

I would do anything to relieve the pain of her loss for him, even just for a little while. But it will never subside. She'll for ever be his lost little girl. Unless they find her.

And if they find her . . . I'll be dead to him too.

23

A rush of commotion and noise reaches the house on a gust of winter wind. I can't make out what is happening from my view through the porthole window, but a car has turned onto the drive, police lifting the fluorescent tape to allow it access. The crowd of journalists surge towards it as it inches forward, but they're pushed back by the lowering of the tape – the line they cannot cross.

Aiden?

I squint and see a flash of silver. Not Aiden . . .

Rupert.

His car crawls up to the house and into Aiden's space. My stomach turns. Only a few days ago, I watched from this window as Aiden arrived. I ran to the door, my complete and utter joy eliciting a cry of her name. *Freya.* And she galloped towards me, her hair shining in the sun, her eyes bright and alive.

I waver as a sudden burst of dizziness takes hold. I try to steady myself on the glass. The outline of my hand is still there when I push my weight off the window to stand upright. The imprint lasts just a few moments, then begins to fade. When it was cold, Freya used to draw in the condensation that clung to the window of the car. Stick men, smiley faces. Hearts.

Rupert's face appears at the window and he catches my eye, then throws a worried glance over his shoulder, the shouts of the journalists drawing his attention.

I stand behind the door as I pull it open so they won't see

me. Their voices are quieter than I expected, but I hear my name – and hers – in the air.

Naomi. Naomi. Freya. Naomi. Naomi. Naomi. Freya.

'Hi,' he says, flustered. His hair is sticking up at an awkward angle, his ears burning red.

'Hi.'

Both of us are unsure what to say – what the opening gambit should be in this scenario. He comes towards me, arms outstretched. I step into them, trying to shake off the reluctance that has made my shoulders inch towards my ears. I put my arms around his waist, but my clasp is weak. He holds me tighter.

'I know you said you wanted to be alone,' he whispers, his breath hot against my face, 'but I was worried about you. I hate the thought of you being here alone with everything that's going on.'

My hair crinkles noisily against his coat as I nod. I bristle, annoyance making my skin tingle. This is why I didn't want him here. I can't be honest with him about anything – not my migraines, my pills. Or my lies. Nothing.

And I don't want to tell any more lies.

He steps away, releasing me from his arms but keeping hold of my hand. He's clutching a rucksack – instead of wearing it on his back, he's holding it surreptitiously by his side, almost hidden behind his knee.

'Are you planning on staying here?' I try to make it sound like a question, rather than an accusation, but my words fly at him sharply, their edges serrated.

'Only if you want me to,' he answers. Now it's his turn to try to keep his voice steady, but it's tinged with a sort of sadness, his face crestfallen.

I offer him a small smile. 'Of course,' I say.

Now look what you've done . . .

I didn't want to lie.

'Do you want a drink?' I ask, turning towards the kitchen.

He holds up his bag, his eyes shifting up the stairs. 'Where shall I put this?'

'I'll show you later.'

I walk away and grind my teeth at the sound of his bag being placed on the floor. The thud of his footsteps as he trots dutifully after me.

'Wine?' I ask, taking a bottle from the rack behind the door.

'Sure.'

He glances into the snug as he enters the kitchen. He stalls as he takes in the sight of the upturned side-table and his eyes fly back to mine, wide and round in a question.

But I say nothing.

'What happened there?' He cocks his head towards the snug.

'Just an accident,' I say, eyebrows raised, daring him to ask me more questions. But I know he won't.

'Are you okay?'

'Fine.'

I tip the bottle but a faraway beam of torchlight shines in through the window and catches my gaze.

They're still searching outside.

I crane my neck to see better. Lights dart and intertwine in the darkness, and I can see the faint outline of figures progressing south-east. Towards the bunker.

'Naomi!'

'Oh, shit.' I've sloshed wine over the island. It's spreading towards me and dripping off the edge. 'Sorry. I wasn't concentrating.'

'It's okay.' We wipe up the mess and he turns to peer out of the window. 'They're still searching the woods, then?'

'Yes. Kate said that the sighting will be investigated but they still have to complete the search of the farm. Even the woods.'

'It's just so frustrating that it's been snowing. What if they miss something?'

Yes. What if? Until now I've been able to hope that the snow will protect me. That it will have hidden any tracks I made, any evidence of digging I left behind in my rush to get back to the house. But now it has stopped and, hour by hour, what's left of it will melt, uncovering the ground beneath.

'I'm trying to trust them,' I say. 'That they know what they're doing. I just hope . . .'

'What?'

'I just hope they don't find anything in the woods.'

He frowns. 'What do you mean?'

'Well, they're looking for a body. Aren't they? I don't want them to find a body.'

The first truth I've been able to utter.

'Of course not. And they're going to find her. Alive.'

I pour him more wine, concentrating this time on placing the neck of the bottle above the glass.

Don't look outside. Ignore the lights.

He drags the glass towards himself and lifts it to sip, watching me out of the side of his eye.

'Naomi . . .'

'Yes?'

'Do you want a small glass?'

'I can't drink.'

'A small glass will be fine. It might help you –'

'No. I don't want any bloody wine. The baby . . .' The baby is everything.

'I'll make you a tea or something . . .' he mutters, his face ~asing into a forced smile.

He starts to open cupboards one by one, searching for where I keep my mugs. Part of me feels sad for him, that his girlfriend barely deigns to allow him into her house, so much so that he doesn't even know his way around her kitchen. But the other part – the more substantial part – is annoyed. Tired. Terrified.

What if they find the bunker tonight? What if they find Freya?

'Let's just go to bed.'

He looks at the large clock hanging on the wall behind me, lifting his wrist to snatch a glance at the time. 'It's not even seven.'

'I know, but I'm exhausted.'

'Of course. Sorry, of course you are.' He rushes forward and kisses my forehead. He moves his face down, unsure, and kisses me, his lips firm against my own. I will myself to respond, to give him something, but I can't bring myself to do it. My mouth remains still. He steps backwards, his eyes dropping to the floor. He swallows loudly.

'Let's go to bed.'

His footsteps on the stairs vibrate through my body. No other man has ever shared this bed with me. Rupert never stays here. I always go to his. No other man has ever lain beside me in Aiden's place, on his side, their body close to mine. No one.

I stop at my open bedroom door.

The bed is there – the one that was ours. Our marital bed. And, in my mind, so is he.

Aiden is sitting there reading a book, his thick-rimmed glasses pushed down his nose. He is perched on the edge, pulling on his socks, getting ready for work. He is standing in front of me, a cheeky smile on his face as he drops his towel, droplets of water shining on his skin. He is pulling thin sheet over our heads and clambering on top of me as I giggle in delight.

My eyes are drawn to the bedroom window; lights are still criss-crossing their way through the trees.

'I can't do this.'

I turn, my hands holding onto the architrave on either side of the door, shielding the room.

'What?' He looks at me aghast, not understanding the statement. 'You can't do what?'

'This.'

'This . . . Us?'

'No. No . . . just this. You, staying here, overnight. I'm not ready.'

'Naomi . . . We've been together a year now, we're going to have a baby, and I can't stay overnight? Seriously, what the hell is going on? Do you not want to be with me?'

I pause. For the first time since I've known him, there is anger in his voice, frustration swimming in his eyes. A refreshing change from the usual cloying suffocation of his kindness. But I still can't do this.

'I do,' I say. 'I promise I do. I'm just not ready for this.'

'For what? For me sleeping in your room? Just tell the truth. You don't want to be in a relationship. I mean, you don't even refer to me as your boyfriend or your partner, which I know I shouldn't care about, we're not teenagers. But I do care, because I love you, and you're not invested like I am.'

'Because we're different.'

'Different? How? What does that mean?'

'I've been married, Rupert. I've had a child with someone, shared my life with someone –'

'And now he's married to someone else!'

My mouth falls open.

He's never purposely said anything to hurt me before. I am the one with the sharp tongue, who says cutting words and apologizes for them later. Not him . . . Never him.

We stay there, on the precipice, breathless, until Rupert hangs his head.

'I'm sorry,' he whispers, and reaches for me but I cross my arms. He retreats from the door onto the landing. 'I'm so sorry. I didn't mean to. I just got angry.'

'I know.' I want to cry, to scream, but there is nothing. No emotion is forthcoming. 'I knew this was a bad idea.'

'Please. I can't believe I said that with everything that's happening.'

'It's okay.' I uncross my arms and push one of my hands against the frame of the door.

He looks at my arm blocking him from the room. 'I'll go, then,' he says, resigned.

I nod. There is nothing left in me to offer him comfort. I just want to sleep.

'I'll talk to you tomorrow.' The statement leaves his lips as a question – his voice rising in pitch at the end.

I nod again, staring at my toes, which are curled in on themselves, making the muscles in my feet ache.

His footsteps are heavy as he turns and leaves, running down the stairs two at a time and closing the door behind him.

I cross the room to the window. There is nothing but darkness. The lights have gone.

Have they stopped searching for the evening? Have they found something? I wish there was some way of knowing what's happening, but there isn't. I won't know until it's too late. And once the truth is out, I won't be able to force it back underground, no matter how hard I try.

Go to bed.

But I can't take another night of stolen fragments of sleep. I need to be asleep, ignorant and unaware, even if only for a night. I wish I could sleep until it's all over, until the investigation is over: the police gone; the media gone; the constant infection of lies over.

I need a sleeping tablet.

I know the relief will be temporary. The pill will wear off and I'll be dragged back to reality, blinking myself into existence. Realizing what has happened. But even so . . .

I turn away from the window and walk to my bathroom. I run the cold water and tap a tablet into my palm.

Maybe you shouldn't do this.

But I need one.

It all began with these pills.

Knocking it back, I gulp thirstily from the stream of water. Gone.

You shouldn't have done that.

I lift my hand to cover my eyes as regret and anger well to the surface. I hate needing them so much. Why can't I just stop?

Aiden's face, so close to mine, floats into my mind, as clear to me as it was that night – the night we climbed into bed, a few glasses of wine down, sneaking past Freya's room so we wouldn't wake her up. We faced each other, foreheads touching, and within minutes he was asleep. He always fell asleep so quickly: one moment he was wide awake, the next he was gone.

I knew that night would be no different from the ones before it. Another in which I lay like a statue, listening to the sound of Aiden's breathing, my head throbbing from exhaustion but with no respite.

Maybe a paracetamol would help, I thought.

I lifted Aiden's arm from around my waist, tiptoed out of

the room and down the stairs. I walked to the kitchen, looking out at the garden as I passed the window. The outside world seemed to shift and ripple as the clouds floated slowly across the light of the moon. I pulled at the handle of the cupboard under the sink. It opened a couple of centimetres but wouldn't go any further. I sighed, fumbling with the child lock. It snapped open and I reached to the back of the cupboard. I pulled out a box. It was empty. I reached in again and felt another box but could tell by the weight that there was nothing inside. Finally, my fingers clasped a packet, the silver foil crinkling between my fingers.

But it wasn't paracetamol.

It was my sleeping tablets.

I thought Aiden had thrown them all away.

He had sat me down and told me I wasn't taking them because I needed them: I was taking them because I wanted them. And I needed to stop.

He was right. More and more often, the pills had been leaving me with no recollection of the night before, with no memory of our conversations or arguments or moments of happiness. They were leaving me with nothing.

I stared down at the packet and a tingle of temptation ran through me.

I could take one and be asleep within half an hour.

But I had promised Aiden I wouldn't take them again. Not unless I really needed them.

I pushed a tablet against the foil and it popped out into my hands. The turquoise blue of the soluble plastic stood out against my pale skin.

I inspected it, turning it over in my fingers, but shook my head, placing it on the kitchen counter. Don't be stupid, I thought. You don't need them. This does not qualify as 'need'.

I grabbed an empty glass from the sink and filled it with

water. I drank thirstily, my eyes drawn to the small pill resting innocently in the moonlight that shone through the window.

Just this once.

I placed it on my tongue and swallowed. And it was gone.

Aiden opened his eyes as I climbed back into bed. 'Are you okay?'

'Fine.'

'Can't you sleep?'

'I was just thirsty,' I said, holding up the half-empty glass to show him.

'Okay,' he whispered sleepily, as he rolled over. 'Goodnight.'

'Night.'

I pulled the duvet up to my chest and brought the glass to my mouth. I gulped noisily, washing away the lie – and its bitter aftertaste.

Guilt tingles in my stomach as the memory dissolves and I close my eyes. But as I do, my journal creeps into the corners of my mind.

I shake my head. I can't think about my journal. I can't think about all of my secrets that hide within its pages.

I scrub at my teeth and gums. I'm almost used to the sight of blood mixed with the remnants of toothpaste that I spit into the sink. The inside of my mouth is red and sore, the bristles of my toothbrush, splayed from the sheer force of use.

I climb into bed and turn off the light, welcoming the darkness of early evening winter. My hand travels to my left, to the empty space beside me. But yet again, it's as if Aiden is there, the weight of his body causing the mattress to undulate as he turns over, his breathing not quite a snore, but heavy, nonetheless. His arm occasionally flopping over my body, a sleepy kiss in my hair.

Rupert had no chance.

He didn't even get to cross the threshold.

I place my hands firmly on my stomach and close my eyes. I try to envisage the small life growing inside me: how one day, not too far away, that small life will grow into a baby. My child. And I will look after that child. Me. Not anyone else. I won't have another taken away.

But what if it all comes back?

No. It won't.

It could. All that worry. The paranoia, the fear. The —

No. I'm different now. It won't happen again. It can't.

As I drift off to sleep, I imagine my baby — another daughter — with dark hair and green eyes. I hold her close to my chest, her hand gripping my finger, the other opening and closing against my arm.

I love you so much, I say to her. Everything I'm doing is for you. Every dark, foul, nightmarish thing.

All for you.

24

Four years earlier . . .
August

'Oh, Naomi, she's so beautiful,' Helen said, as she looked at Freya in my arms. 'I'm so pleased for you.'

'Thanks, Helly.'

She was the first to visit. Aiden and I had told people we didn't want any visitors for the first week. We just needed to settle into our new lives as a family of three. But I couldn't keep Helen away. Day five she arrived, unannounced. Not even a knock on the door. She let herself in with her spare key as usual.

We sat in the snug and I rested Freya on my chest. Freya yawned, and her eyes began to close as she drifted into another nap. Helen kissed the side of her head and inhaled deeply. 'She smells delicious,' she said. 'Why do babies smell so good?'

'I know,' I murmured. 'She's just gorgeous, isn't she?'

'She really is. And how about you? Are you loving being a mum as much as you thought?'

'I love her more than anything,' I responded. That was the truth. But not necessarily the answer to the question.

Helen narrowed her eyes, assessing me carefully. She knew me too well. 'Are you okay?' she asked.

'What do you mean?'

'I'm just asking if you're okay. You seem –'

'I'm tired, that's all.' I hadn't slept in days. Only snatched moments here and there before fear shook me awake.

'Naomi?'

'Did you say something?'

She reached out and grabbed my hand, squeezing my fingers between hers. 'I said, are you sure?'

'Am I sure of what?'

'That you're okay?'

'Positive.' I smiled at her, but my head was pounding.

'Can I hold her?'

I paused, my brain emptying as panic gripped my body. I needed to hold her. I needed to keep her safe.

'Um . . . She's just fallen asleep so I'll keep hold of her. You could make us some drinks?'

'Okay,' she said casually, as she walked out of the snug and into the kitchen, but I could feel her eyes on me. Watching me closely.

'Aiden?' I shouted. 'Do you want a tea?'

'Ooh, where's the new daddy?' called Helen. 'I need to congratulate him.'

'I'm here,' Aiden said, appearing in the doorway to the kitchen. 'And I'll make the tea. You may congratulate me, Helen, for creating the cutest baby to ever exist.'

'Congratulations, Aiden,' she said, holding her arms out and placing a kiss on his cheek. 'I'm so pleased for both of you.'

'Thanks, Helly.' He beamed.

She returned to the snug and we sat together in silence, both of us staring down at the baby, my vision shifting in and out of focus while Aiden made the drinks. I stroked Freya's dark hair, which was soft and fluffy from her first bath the night before, and she sighed in her sleep.

'So cute,' whispered Helen.

'Here you go, ladies,' Aiden said, placing our two mugs on the table. 'I'll leave you to it. Call me if you need me.' He leaned down and kissed me, his lips so soft against my own, which were still dry from the intense heat of the labour ward.

'Thank you,' I said, watching him leave the room. I stood, my lower back aching, dragged the Moses basket towards me with one hand, then gently lowered Freya inside. I picked up my mug, relishing the feeling of the hot china against my palms. 'It's so nice to have a hot cup of tea. Don't think I've managed to drink one before it's gone cold.' For a moment, I let the smile slip from my face. A crack formed in the façade.

'Is it really hard?' Helen asked, catching my eye as I looked at her through the steam rising from my mug. Her blue gaze was arresting. Demanding. She knew something was wrong.

I sipped my tea, then put it back on the coffee-table. I wanted to tell her. And I knew I needed to tell her. I needed to explain, to tell someone – anyone – that I was feeling out of my depth. That I was pushing my legs against a strong tide that couldn't help but pull me under. That while my head was still out of the water, I was scared I might submerge completely.

But I didn't want her to think I was a bad mother. How could I tell her I was struggling? Good mums don't struggle, I thought. Good mums are naturals: like ducks to water. No drowning.

Is there any such thing? A woman who is so maternal, whose instincts are so impeccably composed, that they are perfectly calibrated with the necessities of motherhood? A mother who never makes mistakes, or wishes she was free, or prays she could be better?

Or are all mothers plagued with a crippling anxiety that they'll never be good enough, and that sooner or later someone will realize the truth? A deep, private fear that, one day, they will make a mistake so terrible that everything they've ever wanted will be stolen away?

How could I tell her that even in the hospital the sight of the midwife holding Freya struck fear through my heart? That the sight of the blue midwives' uniforms and Freya's face nestled against the topsy-turvy time of an upside-down watch sent a thousand questions stampeding through my mind. Were they watching me? Were they making sure I was doing a good job, being a good mother? Was I being a good mother? Good enough? Will I ever be good enough? What will happen if I'm not? Will someone take her away? I couldn't let that happen. Only I could keep her safe.

I forced myself to smile. 'It's hard,' I said, with false openness. 'Tiring more than anything else. But I love her. And she's worth it.'

Helen smiled back at me. 'She sure is. Just promise, if you need anything – anything at all – you'll talk to me.'

'I promise.'

'Good.' She leaned forward and lifted her mug from the table.

'To Freya,' she said.

I raised my own and we chinked our mugs together, and as we sipped, the small gap in my façade was plastered over, blocking out any sliver of true emotion – starving it of sunlight. I had built a wall around myself, brick by brick.

I didn't intend to let anyone pull it down. Not Helen. Not Aiden.

Not even me.

So I would have to put on a show. I would bring out the old Naomi: the confident, playful extrovert.

But she wasn't real.

Not any more.

But even when I wasn't playing make-believe – when I shrugged off the skin of the old me, to reveal the tender, raw skin underneath – there was something else. As if I, like Freya, was reborn, gazing up at an entirely new world, the vivid colours and new sounds assaulting my mind. It was working hard and fast – a flight of ideas – my thoughts constantly running as exhaustion took hold, as if somebody had turned on a tap, and forgotten to turn it off. The usual steady drip, drip, drip of consciousness was now a flood, and no wall or dam, no matter how high or strong, could suppress it.

And all thoughts led back to Freya.

Trees. Leaves. Green. Freya.

Kitchen. Cooking. Relax. Tea. Milk. Freya.

Snug. Books. Read. Words. Discombobulate is my favourite word. Favourite. Freya.

Freya.

Freya.

Freya.

25

It's snowing again. Through the window I can see large grey clouds holding themselves above the tops of the trees, but they look heavy, as if they might fall to the earth, bringing the sky tumbling down with them. Flakes of snow are falling fast and thick. In just a few hours they'll have settled on the ground in a dense blanket. The melting snow could only help the investigation. Maybe this will help me.

The tops of the trees are doused in white, and the ground beneath them will be covered too. A fresh layer of pure snow will conceal the door to the bunker, and Freya within it. And another day will pass when I haven't gone back to her. But as long as she is hidden, she is safe. I won't have to watch her being taken away, like with Dad. She is still here, with me.

My nose is running and I sniff, reaching for a tissue on the bedside table. I wipe my nostrils but a flash of red catches my eye.

Blood.

A nose-bleed.

I hold the tissue around my nose and pinch at the bridge. My head is foggy, and the familiar after-effect of my tablets sends a dizzy wave up and over my head. I close my eyes. Soon it will wear off and the world will fall still.

Just breathe —

Knocking interrupts my thoughts.

Who is that?

What if it's the police? What if they've found her?

My chest tightens. I put aside the tissue and manoeu⁻

myself off the bed, but my legs are achy and unresponsive. As I pull on my dressing gown, the knock rings out again, but it's soft – polite.

Maybe it's Rupert.

Yes – it must be him. He'll want to talk to me. He'll want to make everything better.

I head down the stairs, my feet moving quickly. I pull open the door, my face flushed –

'Good morning, Naomi,' Kate says.

The heat drains from my body, as if someone has pulled the plug from a bath, the steaming water draining quickly downwards. 'Hi,' I say.

'Can I come in?'

'Yes, of course.' I step to the side, pulling the door wide open, and she comes in, tugging off her cream woolly hat, her red hair cascading around her shoulders.

We stand in the hall as she concentrates on taking off her coat, her cheeks and hands pink from the cold. The zip is snagged at the bottom and she wrestles with it, muttering under her breath.

'Would you like tea or coffee?'

'Are you going to make one for yourself?'

'I'll have one if you want one too.'

'Okay, then, a brew would be lovely. Shall I go through to the snug?'

Shit . . .

The snug. It's still littered with broken glass, the coffee-table still upturned, the side-table face down. I was going to sort it out this morning. If she sees it, she'll ask questions. I can hear her footsteps as she follows me, but I peer over my shoulder as we step into the kitchen. She is still looking down, fumbling with the zip, which has caught on the inner fabric of her coat. I dart to the door of the snug and pull it closed, hiding the upturned room from view. The door clicks behind me as her zip finally undoes.

'Stupid thing,' she mutters, looking up at me.

'We can just sit in here,' I say, trying to keep my words from rushing out of my mouth as I gesture at the kitchen table. 'The snug's a bit messy . . . Tea or coffee?' I walk to the sink on the other side of the kitchen, drawing her away from the closed door, and click on the kettle.

'Um, tea, please. Not much of a coffee drinker,' she says, removing her coat and placing it on the back of one of the chairs. 'But I can do it, Naomi.'

'I will. It's good for me to do things, keep my hands busy.'

She nods, her eyes indicating a kind of understanding. 'Sorry for coming so early,' she says. She sits down at the kitchen table, her head turning to the left to continue looking at me. 'I have an update and didn't want to keep you waiting.'

An update. They can't have found her. I would know . . . wouldn't I? There are officers here all the time. But, then, why is she here? What has she got to tell me?

'What kind of update?'

'Maybe you should come and sit down first. Then I'll tell you everything I know.'

They've found her.

Have they taken her away? Have they taken away my daughter without telling me?

The sound of the zip rings in my ears.

The kettle begins to rattle in its holster, steam billowing out of its neck, the usually innocuous noise sounding like a scream.

I clear my throat, coughing loudly. 'Sorry – I've forgotten if you take milk and sugar.'

'Just milk, please.'

I splash milk into both mugs, but some spills. My nails scratch at the wooden countertop. I busy myself by retrieving the teabags from the mugs and throwing them into the sink. I'll clean up later. Whatever it is she knows – that they know – I need to know too.

Placing the steaming tea in front of Kate, I sit down at the table, in the chair directly opposite her, my hands gripping the china.

'So . . .' I meet her eyes, trying to read them. Is there anything there? Something different from her usual kindness? But I see nothing. Nothing except how blue they are, the colour so pale. On another person they could be cold, but on her they are warm. Inviting.

'How are you feeling?' Her eyes narrow, then widen, her eyebrows rising into her fringe as she assesses me.

I shake my head. 'To be honest, I'm not really sure.' She blows on her tea, indicating I should continue. I sigh. 'Scared. Worried . . .'

'I know it's much easier for me to say than it is for you to do, but you need to try to stay positive.'

She doesn't know . . . They haven't found her.

Yet.

A lump forms in the back of my throat and I try to swallow but it remains there, like something's stuck, choking me. 'I'm trying.'

'I know you feel helpless but the team are doing everything they can to find Freya.'

I tighten my grip around my mug, lift it to my lips and sip deeply. The liquid scalds me. Grimacing, I lift my tongue to the roof of my mouth, and can already feel a string of soft skin, loose from the sudden burn. My mug thuds onto the wooden table.

'So, like I said, I've come to give you an update. I've already told Aiden. I called him to ask if he wanted to come to the house so I could tell you together, but he asked me to tell him on the phone. Because of the media. He didn't want to cause a stir.'

It's not about the media. If Aiden really wanted to be here, he'd find a way. The truth is, he doesn't want to be around me. He said he doesn't blame me, but he does – of course he does. How couldn't he?

Maybe he doesn't want to be around me because he suspects I'm not telling the truth. Maybe he's biding his time, waiting until he can figure out what really happened. Waiting to tell them.

My tongue snags on the skin.

'What is it? I thought you said I have to stay positive?'

'And you should. But I do have to tell you that we've concluded the investigations into the sighting that was reported to the hotline.'

My breathing starts to speed up, and I bite the inside of my bottom lip as tears fill my eyes and cling to my lower lash-line. 'And have you found anything?'

'We've looked at the CCTV, asked people who live in the area, gone door to door. We've interviewed the person whose car we traced from the petrol station. That was their son in the car. He was taking him to nursery. We haven't found anything else. We suspect it was a hoax. I know it's upsetting but it happens with every case of a missing person that gets so much publicity.' She reaches for my hand and grips it between hers. Hers are cold and my hairs stand erect. 'You must keep hopeful, though, Naomi. We're still searching the woods, and although it's starting to snow again, the team have found some footprints that were under ice. They lead into the trees so . . . that could be something.'

I blink rapidly and the tears that were hanging from r

lashes are pushed from their ledge. Tears are pooling in the creases around my nose, on top of my lip, and I smear them away. As I do so, more replace them.

The call has achieved nothing. I should have known that one sighting wouldn't suspend the search.

'But the footprints could have been anyone's,' I mutter. 'What if whoever took her has gone miles away –'

'There are officers investigating every possibility, Naomi.'

'What about the river? Have you searched there? I saw people heading that way yesterday morning . . .' They were people I hadn't seen before, clasping large bags, and from the window of the snug, I could just make them out by the bend, the water like a grey ribbon through the snow.

'Officers searched the river the first day, but a specialist team went over it again yesterday. I know you want to hear that we've made progress. But you need to keep the faith. Okay?'

I nod.

What am I doing? Countless people. Specialist teams. All of these officers searching for a little girl who won't ever be found. I could confess. Right this second. Hold up my hands, tell Kate how sorry I am but I was scared – terrified at what they would do if they knew the truth. And once I had lied, it was too late.

A familiar heady wave of nausea washes over me. I can't risk losing this baby. I failed Freya countless times. I can't fail this one too.

Hot tears of guilt and distress pour down my cheeks, and I bury my face in my hands. Kate strokes my arm and makes hushing noises, attempting to offer comfort, whispering that she's sorry and I'll be okay.

To her it must look like sorrow. Worry. Distress. And all of these emotions are flurrying through me as I try to focus on

Kate's sounds of reassurance. But one sends all others shrinking into the background. One emotion that consumes all others. A cloak of darkness blocking out even the faintest shred of light.

Fear.

26

Four years earlier . . .
August

I knelt in front of the graves. Sitting back on my legs, I rested Freya on my thighs, facing them both, and bit down on my bottom lip. I can't cry, I thought. Not today. If I start, I'll never stop.

'Hi, Dad,' I whispered. 'Hi, Mum.'

Freya's fingers, which were wound tightly in a fist, unfurled quickly, just for a second, but it looked almost as if she was waving.

'Say hello to Grandma and Grandpa, Freya.' I rested my chin on her head and gazed at the graves, which looked cold even on that beautiful day. I closed my eyes, and I was there again – in the hall, collapsing to the floor. The house was full of sounds: the paramedics muttering to each other; voices telling me he had passed away; the loud ring of my cries.

I reached out and touched Dad's headstone, tracing my finger along the words. Freya coughed, a loud bark in the silent graveyard, and I turned her quickly towards me, assessing her every movement, listening closely to her breathing. What's wrong with her? I questioned, my mind rocketing towards the most drastic diagnosis. I held her close, my breath quick and unsteady, my hands trembling against her back.

I can't do this.

Crunching footsteps crossed the gravel behind me, until

the sound morphed into thuds as someone stepped onto the grass and came to a standstill behind me.

'You're doing well, love. Remember, I love you.'

It was Dad's voice. Right there, above my head.

'I love you too,' I whispered. 'I need you here. I wish you hadn't left me.'

I turned my head and bent my neck backwards to see his face. But it wasn't his greying beard, salt-and-pepper hair, and brown eyes peering down at me.

It was Aiden.

'Did you hear what I said, darling?' he said, kneeling beside me. 'Would you like some time on your own?'

I frowned at him as grief twisted in my stomach. For a moment he was there – Dad was there – and then he was gone.

'Where . . . ? Um . . . If you don't mind,' I said, as a stabbing pain rushed across the front of my head.

'Of course not. I'll take Freya back to the car.'

'Thanks.'

My eyes darted about the vast graveyard, where rows upon rows of people lay for their final rest. I knew it didn't make sense, but I was searching for him. Searching for his beaming smile and comforting words. But no one was about. Not a soul.

It was just your imagination.

'I really wish I could talk to you both.' My mouth began to waver, so I pressed my knuckles against my lips and squeezed my eyes shut.

'I need your help.' My voice wobbled, barely audible. 'I want to be the best parent I can be. I want to be like you but I feel like . . . I feel like I'm failing. I don't have anyone to talk to. I know I have my friends, and I have Aiden, and he is so supporting and he loves me so much . . . But I'm scared they'll judge me. As a mother . . . As a person. I just don't feel like myself. I don't even remember who I am. If you were here, it would be okay. You'd tell me what to do. I'm scared I'll never be good enough. I'm just not good enough. I'm nothing like you . . .' I sniffed, rubbing my eyes with my knuckles. 'And I'm so tired. So tired. I can't sleep. I'm so scared that something will happen and I won't be there to help her. Please, help me . . .'

I rocked forward and rested my head on the grass. And I cried. For myself. For them.

But mostly for Freya.

I sat up quickly at the sound of twigs breaking behind me. There was no one in the graveyard but I squinted at the woods that line the eastern side of the church.

Someone was there, lurking in the trees.

A woman. She began to approach, holding a large bouquet of flowers. As she got closer, I could see the colour, make out the shape – even imagine the smell. Lilac. Mum's favourite.

I looked up at her face. It was her. Mum. Her auburn hair, but it was long, falling past her shoulders – so different from when she'd died and it was growing back in tufty patches. Her blue eyes.

'Naomi, sweetheart,' she said, as she dropped to her knees and hugged me, her arms squeezing me tight.

'Mum,' I said. 'I miss you –'

'Oh, Naomi, I know you miss her. It must be so hard for you having Freya without her.'

I slowly shrank out of the arms of this person – this person who wasn't my mum. And as she looked me in the eye, the warm deep blue of my mum's gaze transformed into the pale cool blue of Helen's.

'Helen?'

Of course. She brought flowers every year, for Mum's birthday.

'Naomi, what's wrong?' Helen held me by my shoulders, taking in my exhausted face, her eyes searching the graveyard for Aiden. 'Does Aiden have the baby?'

'Yes. He's in the car. I . . .' My words stalled; my throat closed. I threw myself forward into Helen's arms and sobbed, and she held me close, her rhythmic hushing interspersed with reassurances that I was okay.

They had been so real. I could have reached out and touched them.

But they're gone, I thought. You're just exhausted.

'Here,' she said, retrieving the flowers that were still resting on her lap. 'You put them down. She'd like that.'

'Thank you, Helly.'

I balanced the bouquet against my mum's headstone, the flowers grazing the inscription, my eyes heavy as they danced over the words.

'Naomi? Are you okay?'

She can't know, I thought. She can't know that anything is wrong. She can't know that I'm struggling. She can't know that I haven't slept and that exhaustion is constantly looming over me – a vulture, ready to tear me to pieces.

'I'm fine,' I whispered, a reassuring smile plastered across my face, the image of my parents still hanging in the air.

27

'I'm sorry, Ms Williams, I've been told not to let anyone outside.'

I stare at the officer who has blocked my path out of the back door. I peer past him, trying to make sense of his statement, but the scene outside today looks the same as always. A couple of policemen are standing by the fence to the orchard, and I can see a group of volunteers in a field on the other side of the river.

Has something happened?

'What's your name?' I ask.

He is young and his blond hair falls in tufts around his flushed face. 'I'm PC Hennessey, Ms Williams.'

'And why aren't I allowed outside, PC Hennessey?'

He shifts his weight from one foot to the other. 'I wasn't told. I was just told to stop any more volunteers coming through this way.'

'But volunteers wouldn't be coming through the house, would they?'

'I'm not sure –'

'And I'm not a volunteer.'

He crosses his arms, his face turning a deeper shade of red.

I sigh. 'Can I speak to Kate, please?'

He hesitates.

'Kate – Kate Bracken, the FLO. I want to speak to her.'

'Okay,' he says, and walks away, jogging every few steps, as he makes his way to Kate, who is standing by the bridge.

Why wouldn't they let me outside?

A cold sweat begins to tingle across my chest.

Have they found the bunker?

Have they found her?

I click my knuckles as Kate approaches the house, and I keep count as each finger cracks.

Concentrate on the numbers. Don't panic.

'Naomi, is everything okay?' she says, as she steps onto the patio.

I wait for her to reach the door, then lean on the frame. 'That officer who was here before – Hennessey – he said I wasn't allowed outside but he couldn't tell me why. He said something about volunteers.'

'Oh, bless him,' she says, smiling at me as if she's letting me in on a secret. 'I told him the reason, but he's new and he's never worked on this type of case before. He's very nervous. It's your property, you're welcome to come outside if you want to, but we'd prefer just police outside for now. We've had a lot of people crossing and we wanted to do another sweep of the land between the house and the woods.'

'Are you sure?' I ask.

'What do you mean?'

'I mean . . . You haven't found something?'

She reaches out to hold my arm. 'We're just restricting the area for the few hours we have left today.'

I search her face. If she's lying, it's expertly done. 'Okay,' I say, retreating a few steps back into the kitchen. 'You'll let me know straight away if you find something, right?'

'Yes, of course,' she says.

'I'll be upstairs if you need me.'

I watch her turn and leave. Once she reaches the orchard, I run into the hall and fly up the stairs, tripping slightly at the top, but not slowing down in my haste to reach my bedroom window.

I need to see what's happening.

I need to know what they're doing.

I scrape back the strands of hair that have fallen out of my bun and into my eyes. My cheeks are hot to the touch, and my forehead is clammy.

Was she telling the truth? Are they simply restricting that area to police only? Is that all this is? Or are they hiding something?

Am I a suspect?

My eyes fly up to the woods, and I can pinpoint the exact area where the bunker is hidden. But I can't see it from here. It's too far in and the trees are too dense.

I jump as my phone vibrates.

Lucy is calling . . . I can't speak to her. I can't speak to anyone right now.

I jab at the phone, ending the call and throw it onto my bed. I drag the armchair from the corner of the room to the window and sit down, folding my legs beneath me so that I can still see outside.

'Mummy.'

Her voice calls from behind me. I turn my head slowly, preparing myself for a glimpse of her face, her dark hair. But there is nothing.

I breathe in deeply as I turn back to the window, my fingers spread wide on the sill as I try to steady my hands.

I look outside and focus on the police standing by the orchard, deep in discussion. But my eyes are drawn to a shadow by the woods. Dread brews in my chest, my body instantly filling with trepidation as I inch closer to the window, my breath steaming the glass.

Freya is standing at the edge of the woods, her unicorn

pyjamas shining brightly against the snow, Mouse cradled in her arms.

Are they coming for you?

I press my forehead against the window and squeeze my eyes closed.

Don't look. She isn't there.

A minute passes and I open my eyes slowly.

She is gone.

But she has been replaced by a group of police officers, standing in the very spot where the trees meet the fields, all of them staring into the depths of the woods.

My teeth begin to chatter as I dig my nails into the window-sill. I am trapped. There's no way I can know what they know. To be sure of what is the truth and what is a lie.

All I can do is wait.

My body jolts awake and the room is in darkness. My feet are still tucked under my body, but my head has bent at an unnatural angle to rest on the back of the armchair.

How long have I been asleep?

I uncurl my legs and my toes scrunch up in discomfort as sensation returns to my feet. I glance at my watch.

It's nearly 7 p.m.

I stand up and press my nose to the freezing window.

The woods are dark. No criss-crossing of torches near the bunker. No searchlights in the woods. But most nights they've been searching until at least eight. The police have been telling volunteers to go home – *it's too dark and too cold* – but they've insisted on helping until late in the evening.

Why have they stopped? Have they finished?

Or have they found her?

I wrap my arms around my shoulders and rest my chin on my chest. My body begins to rock backwards and forward and my breathing speeds up as panic rushes from my stomach into my throat.

They've found her. That's why the woods are dark. That's why the volunteers are gone. And soon there'll be a knock on the door. And that will be it: even when the evidence proves it was just an accident, I'll never be trusted. I'll lose my baby for ever. I'll lose them both for ever.

I run to the wardrobe, pull out my holdall and stuff clothes inside, not concentrating on what I'm grabbing, not thinking about where I might go. I have no idea. I just need to get out of here.

I dash to my bathroom and grab the packet of pills – which is almost empty – run out and down the stairs, stopping at the bottom to creep across the hallway and peek out of the round window to the front drive.

It's empty. No police car waiting for me. No officers stationed outside.

I walk to the front door and reach for the handle –

And flinch.

What's that noise?

My holdall falls from my hand. I stand still, my muscles completely tense, and listen –

There it is again. Like the sound of banging.

Like a hand on glass.

Someone is knocking on the back door.

Tingles run down my spine, like fingers stroking each and every vertebra.

The police.

It must be them.

But why would they knock on the back door and not the front? Do they think I might run? Are they stationed at the end of the drive, either side of the hedgerow, ready to stop me whichever way I try to escape?

I stand, my body uncurling slowly upwards, and creep to the window by the front door. I can't see anything. No cars. No blue lights. Maybe I imagined –

Bang, bang.

I grab my holdall from the floor and rush to the cupboard. Get rid of it. No one can see that I was ready to leave.

Bang, bang.

There it is again.

I cross the hallway slowly towards the kitchen but stop by the door. Ever so slowly, I inch forward so my feet are just across the threshold. I peer around the edge but I can't see far enough to have a view out of the back door.

I want to run away – just run left out of the snug, into the kitchen, out into the hall, straight up the stairs and into my room, into bed, throw the duvet over my head – until it stops.

Get hold of yourself, Naomi. You're imagining things.

I stride into the kitchen until I'm level with the back door and turn to face it.

A figure has their hood up against the snow, their face almost completely obscured in darkness, but the light from the kitchen is falling on their mouth and jaw.

It's him.

Aiden.

He steps closer, his entire face awash with light as he stares at me through the glass. I hold up one finger – just one moment – and meet his eye as I slide the key into the lock, pull the door towards me and turn the handle at the same time.

I open the door and frown – I can't read his expression. He is breathing heavily, his shoulders moving up and down with exertion, as if he ran here through the snow. But for what?

'Aiden?'

'Hi,' he says.

There is a strange look in his eye, intense and searching. Unease begins to creep down my spine. 'Why have you come to this door?'

He tilts his head towards the front of the house. 'There's still reporters out there.'

My face flushes as his eyes bore into mine.

Does he know? Has he realized I'm lying?

He runs his hand across the stubble on his jawline, something he only ever does when he's nervous. His hair has fallen into his eyes, but he doesn't look away from me. I watch him closely as he bites his bottom lip – a sure sign he has something to say.

'Why are you here?' I ask, my voice quavering with worry. 'What do you want, Aiden?'

He looks down at his feet but then rushes forward, storming towards me, closing the gap between us. I retreat backwards, tripping over my feet, but find my back pressed up against a wall. A thrill runs through me as he grabs my arms by the wrists, pushes them above my head and kisses me, mouth open.

28

He'd sworn this would never happen again. It started a few months ago, in August. He was late collecting Freya and she had fallen asleep on the sofa in the living room at the front of the house. At around eight I heard Aiden's car creeping up the drive. I opened the front door and he was standing with his fist poised in the air, ready to knock.

'I always knew you were psychic,' he said, as his mouth slanted upwards into a wonky grin.

'I was watching out of the window – I didn't want her to be startled by the noise. You know what she's like – if she wakes up and doesn't remember where she is, she'll panic.'

'Good thinking.' He smiled sheepishly at me. 'Can I come in?'

'Oh, sorry. Yes.'

I stepped back and he slid past me into the house. He hadn't been inside since he left. Any time he came to collect Freya after a visit he knocked on the door and waited outside while I got her ready to leave. At first, he would remain silent and no words passed between us, but after a while he began to speak. It was small-talk initially, nothing more, but it developed into jokes and familiarity. The odd kiss on the cheek hello. But then he told me about her. Helen. After that, we regressed to silence.

And in July, they got married.

'Thanks for having her late for me,' he said, as he looked around the hallway. 'I really appreciate it. I couldn't get away at work and –'

'Well, like I said, I'd love to have her overnight –'

'I know, but I'm not ready for that. Not yet. You know how –'

'Well, couldn't your new wife have collected her? Or is she still too scared to face me?'

He clenched his jaw and his mouth set in a stern line. 'Naomi,' he said, but his voice wasn't angry. It sounded sad. Tired.

'Sorry. I know I need to stop doing that. It's not fair on Freya.'

'It's not your fault. I know it was fast – me telling you, the engagement straight away, then the wedding . . .'

'It's okay. To be honest, Aiden, I really don't want to talk about it.'

'Of course, yeah. That's fine. I just – what I'm trying to say is, I understand.'

'I appreciate that. Aiden, I wasn't going to say anything – the last few times I've seen you, I've just ignored it and hoped it would all go away but . . . I'm sorry for what happened. You know . . . the wedding.'

He held up his hands. 'Naomi . . .'

'No, it was wrong of me to turn up like that. I'm a grown-up and I'm so embarrassed. It was just . . . It was a hard day.'

He sighed and looks down at the floor. 'I'm sorry.'

'I am too.'

I turned to get Freya, but I stalled. It would be nice not to be alone for a while, I thought. Just for a little while. Just for one night.

'Have you eaten? I was about to eat. You're welcome to join me before you take her.'

He looked towards the living room, then peered over his shoulder at the door. I could see his brain processing, weighing up the decision.

'What's cooking?' he said, with a wry grin.

'Guess.' I turned to walk to the kitchen.

He sniffed the air as he followed me. 'Oh, my God.' He froze in his tracks, reaching out to hold onto the door frame dramatically. 'I haven't managed to score dinner on lasagne night, have I?'

'You have indeed.' I chuckled. 'Can you open some wine?'

He walked over to the wine rack, and the nostalgia of him in the kitchen, the familiarity of that routine – me serving dinner while he opened a bottle of wine – made my heart tumble into the pit of my stomach.

He poured me a glass, and a small one for himself, as I dished up.

'Do you still not want salad on the side?'

'No, thanks.'

I placed the plates on the table as he set down the glasses, and we sat together as the choreographed pattern of steps into which we had so easily fallen back came to an end.

'Enjoy,' I said, as I lifted my glass to my mouth. But as soon as the words left my lips, and I sipped the wine, the bitter taste of betrayal made me wince.

He left you. You deserved it . . . but he left you. And then he ran off with your best friend. Just because you've both apologized . . . Don't play happy families.

'So, where is she?' I asked.

'Where is she?' he repeated, as he raised his fork to his mouth.

'Helen. Why couldn't she collect Freya?'

He shifted in his chair and looked down at his plate. The skin around his collar flushed pink. 'She's in Saudi. For work.'

She was always away for work. She was the career girl and I was the mother. That was the way it was. The way it always had been, our whole lives – even when we were little girls, I would play with dolls and she would pretend to be an astronaut one day, a teacher the next. Now she was playing the part of Mummy too. But with my daughter.

'Does she still go away a lot?'

'Yeah. About once a month, for a week. Sometimes two. It's . . . it's different.'

'Different from what?'

'From us.'

I met his eye and he didn't look away, instead choosing to stare back at me.

'Yes, but we were in each other's pockets, weren't we?' I said, with a small smile.

'I liked it.'

'Me too.'

He cleared his throat and dropped his gaze to his plate as he began to push the food around with his fork.

'What does Rupert do?' he asked.

'Rupert?'

'Yes. That's his name, right?'

'Um, yes. He's a farmer. He works at the Daley place.'

'It's been a year now, right? You and him?'

'Nine months. It's not that serious, though.'

'Isn't it?'

I shrugged.

He nodded, as if he understood, then leaned forward, over his plate, and scooped a large forkful of lasagne into his mouth, the food puffing out his cheeks. 'It's so bloody good,' he said, and laughed as the tension, hanging above us like a storm, broke.

And I laughed too, until my stomach hurt, and my sides were sore. We had spent so many moments doubled over with the giggles, accidentally spitting out drinks, crying helpless, unadulteratedly happy tears. We had always made each other laugh.

Until we didn't any more. One day, quite suddenly, things stopped being funny.

After we ate, we tidied up – returning to our normal practice. He cleared the plates, I washed them, and he dried.

'Another small one?' I asked him, as I poured more wine.

'I shouldn't really. I've got to drive home.'

'Okay,' I said, and silence fell between us.

'Can I have one of your teas, though?' he asked, his mouth screwed up like a naughty child asking for sweeties.

'Tea?'

'You make the best tea.'

'Do I?'

'You really do.'

'Yeah, your tea's shit, isn't it?'

'It is. You must miss it.'

Our eyes met and he held my gaze, his expression changing as his face turned serious and thoughtful. I didn't look away – I couldn't – and I caught his eyes as they flickered to my mouth.

'Shall we sit in the snug?' he asked, and that feeling – the tingles rushing up my neck – intensified.

'Sure,' I said.

I made the tea and picked up my glass of wine but hesitated as I reached the door to the snug: he was sitting on the sofa, the one facing the fireplace. The fire was crackling in its grate, dying down from when I lit it for Freya. Should I sit next to him? I wondered. Or should I sit somewhere else? Is there any harm in sitting next to him?

I placed his tea on the coffee-table, and moved past him to the armchair.

Don't do anything stupid.

We sat in silence. For a while, as he drank his tea and I sipped my wine, the only sound was the fire as it fought to stay alight, and rain that began to fall and pattered against the windows.

'I miss this house,' Aiden said, as he stared, hypnotized, at the flames, his voice soft and low.

I turned my head to watch him, to stare at his profile, which was lit by warm, dancing light. He looked beautiful. 'Do you?'

He nodded, still mesmerized by the dying fire. He glanced at me, then stood and walked to the fireplace. He pulled a log out of the holder and tossed it in, stoking it gently until flames licked up the sides. He smiled, satisfied.

He walked around the coffee-table slowly, watching me intently. But instead of settling down in the sofa, he walked past his seat and stopped in front of the armchair, his tall frame looming over me.

I looked up at him but was unable to speak. I wanted to ask him what he was doing. I wanted to say that he should get Freya and take her home, but I was bewitched by the look in his eye.

He leaned down and placed his hands on the arms of my chair. Slowly, he moved forward, until our faces were so close, I could feel his breath against my mouth. He sighed and then his lips were on mine, the kiss, strong and urgent.

'Shit,' he said, as he pulled away. 'Shit, I'm sorry.'

'No . . .' I said, but my reactions were slow, inhibited by the shock of what he had done. But as he turned to leave, my body fizzed with energy and I stood quickly and moved around him.

I wrapped my arms around his neck and kissed him. My fingers moved up into his hair and he held my face and shuffled backwards, falling into the chair. I straddled him, and undid his trousers as he undid mine, neither of us breaking the frantic kiss.

After we'd finished – after we both went still, our breath heavy against each other's skin – we went upstairs.

When he left the next morning – Freya happily believing our pre-conceived story that the car had broken down – he said it couldn't happen again. He was married. And I agreed. We said it would have to be the last time. We weren't meant to be together.

Never again.

But it wasn't the last time.

The feeling of Aiden's hands under my top, his fingers on my bare skin, pulls me back into the present and suddenly I'm not thinking. I'm just feeling: my husband, my Aiden.

We frantically kiss and tug at each other's clothes – like clinging to a life-raft in a violent storm. He lifts me up and I wrap my legs around him, my back against the wall, supported by his arms. I gasp at the feeling of having him inside me, inhaling the familiar smell of his skin as he kisses my neck, his stubble rubbing against my collarbone. We move together and our ragged hot breaths are expelled into the fraction of space between us. He is staring at my mouth, and I grip his shoulders as he bites down on his lip.

I want to tell him I love him, I still love him, I have always loved him . . . But instead I focus on this feeling: in this moment, he is mine.

He buries his head in my neck as he moves faster and faster and then stops. As he opens his eyes, his pupils dilate quickly and focus on me. We stare at each other, breathless, and I unwrap my legs from around his body as he lowers me to the floor. He pulls up his trousers and places his hands on the wall on either side of my head, his fingers outstretched. My hands are shaking as I dress myself again, and I watch him as he leans his head on his arm, still trying to catch his breath.

'I'm sorry,' he says. 'I just –'

'Don't be sorry. Please – don't be.'

'I was at the hotel and couldn't stop thinking about Freya and then I just . . .' His voice trails off and he pushes his bunched fists into his eyes.

'You just?' I reach up and uncurl one of his hands into mine. I stroke the soft skin with my thumb: I held this hand for so many years. But then my fingers brush against his wedding ring and I drop it abruptly, like I've been stung.

Don't think about her, Naomi.

I reach out again but this time stroke his cheek, which is rough with stubble. He grabs my hand, but doesn't pull it away. Instead, he holds it against his face, his eyes full of an emotion that I can't quite put my finger on.

'I just . . . Helen had to go back to London for work and yesterday I was alone and just felt . . . so guilty.'

'Guilty?'

'I started thinking that if we were still together . . . If I hadn't left, Freya would still –'

'Don't say it.'

'Freya would still be here.'

There it is.

His words wash over me in a wave too high to jump over, too strong to swim under, and I collapse forward into his chest and sob. Huge, heaving sobs, my whole body shaking. The warm wool of his jumper grows damp as he wraps his arms around me and holds me against his chest, and I cry even harder. His chin rests on my head, and from the tremor in his body I can tell he is crying too.

That was the look in his eye: regret. If only he hadn't left. If only I hadn't been so difficult to live with. If only we had both tried harder, Freya would still be alive.

I murmur into his chest.

He sniffs. 'I didn't hear you.'

I tip my chin upwards. 'I said, it wasn't your fault. None of it was your fault. You left to protect Freya. I was . . . I was a mess.' A fresh stream of tears springs from my eyes. 'I am a mess. I'm so sorry, Aiden.'

He grips me firmly on each arm and gives me a small shake. 'It wasn't your fault – okay? You made mistakes but so did I. I should have been more supportive, more understanding –'

A sob bursts from my mouth and he pulls me back towards him but all I want is to collapse to the floor and sit among the broken pieces of my life. My parents, my husband, my daughter: all shattered into a million irretrievable shards that I will never be able to piece back together. Since I lost my family, life has always been accompanied by a low, dull ache, but since Freya died it's as if a suffocating hand has wrapped its fingers around my heart.

'Naomi?'

I take a second to compose myself. I concentrate on the sensation of his hand stroking my hair, his chin on top of my head.

'Yes?' I whisper, my face pressed sideways against his chest, breathing in his signature smell of Old Spice. But something else is mingling with the scent: something different, but familiar.

Smoke.

He is smoking again. He gave up not long after we met, but I once smelt it on him when Dad died and I became anxious and withdrawn. But I never said a word. We all have ways of coping.

'I just want to say that . . . no matter what happened, you can tell me the truth.'

The fingers squeezing my heart tighten their grip.

He thinks you're lying. I was right: he's suspected me all along.

'What?' I push myself sharply away from him but he holds onto my shoulders.

Panic rises in my chest. How can I lie? Like this – spitting it starkly in his face?

Because you have to.

'You can tell me the truth. If you did something, you can tell –'

'You think I'm lying?'

'I'm not saying –'

'I'm not!'

'I just meant . . . if you left Freya alone for longer than you said or went out without her, or –'

'I didn't. I didn't leave the house.'

'Naomi –'

'Please,' I gasp, as I look up at him. 'Please, believe me. I didn't do anything wrong!'

'Okay, okay, okay. Calm down.' He rubs my shoulder. 'I believe you.'

I let him fold me into his arms and I try to stop my body trembling. He'll be able to feel it.

'I'm sorry,' he says, and the tremor in his voice rumbles in his chest. 'I just want to know where she is.'

I press my lips together, trying to suppress another sob. I can't do this for much longer. I can't keep lying. I don't want this to be my infinity: a life spent keeping track of all my dishonesties. A life of frantically scrambling to maintain the illusion.

Aiden places a kiss on top of my head. 'I'd better go.'

He releases me from his arms and I am a boat cut free from its mooring, adrift on the sea.

'Aiden?'

He pauses, his fingers gripping the frame of the door as he turns his head to look over his shoulder. He's still crying – tracks clearly visible on his fair skin.

'Stay with me?' I ask.

He doesn't say anything. He just continues to gaze at me, his shoulders stooped and low, then turns and steps back into the house, closing the door behind him.

29

I know I should feel guilty. For Rupert. Kind, sweet Rupert. But as I lead Aiden upstairs, to the bed we shared when he was my husband and I was his wife, I feel no guilt. No shame. And as we lie down next to each other, and he draws me into his arms, I am able to forget. I am able to shrug off the years of loss, the thousands of moments of grief and anger and betrayal, and be Naomi again. We are Aiden and Naomi, and I can pretend that Freya is asleep upstairs, safe in her bedroom. In this moment – in my mind – I have my family back.

We are the same. Naomi and Aiden. The same as always.

'Naomi?' He speaks softly, with a question in his voice, as if he is about to tell me a secret.

'Yes?'

He buries his face in the pillow and mumbles something I can't hear.

'I didn't hear you . . .'

He shrugs.

'What did you say?' I stroke his back, trying to coax the secret out of him. He peeks out at me, his eyes so green against the stark white pillow.

'I said . . . I still love you.'

The room is awash with white noise. His mouth is still moving, but I can't hear what he's saying. Instead his *I still love you* replays, over and over. I want to speak, but that same grip of panic tightens around my throat, rendering me speechless.

It doesn't mean anything. He won't leave her. He won't

come back to me and make everything like it was. We can't return to the life we had because everything is changed. Life has changed. We have changed. We are not who we were and we never will be.

But still . . .

'Naomi?' This time, his hand is on my back, his fingers tracing circles that send a shiver shooting up my spine. 'You know that, right?'

Do I? Do I know that? I know that he left because he was pushed, not because he wanted to. I know that he stood by me through everything until he couldn't any more. I know he loved me, more than anyone can reasonably be expected to love a person like me. But still? Still now, after all this time? After everything that has happened?

'I don't,' I whisper, not looking him in the eye but instead tracing the dot-to-dot of moles on his forearm. 'I don't see how that's possible. You . . .'

'I?'

'You left me.'

'I know, but you know why I did that. I did it for Frey–'

'No, not then. This time. You came back to me. You came back but then told me it was over. You ended it for Helen and you broke my heart. You chose her. How can you love me?'

'Well, it's true. I know it shouldn't be but it is. We've put each other through a lot . . . But I love you. I just did what I thought was right.' He tucks the hair that has fallen across my face behind my ear. 'Do you still love me?'

My stomach flips and my hand flies up to cover my eyes, like a coy teenager.

'Do you?'

I shouldn't do this. I shouldn't engage in this conversation. No good can come of it, for him or for me. Not for anyone. To hope for something more will surely only lead to more heartbreak, more grief. The same loss, but all over again. But – just this once – I want to be honest. I want to tell someone the truth. No more lies.

I uncover my face, look him directly in the eye, and nod. I hear him exhale heavily – he was holding his breath. He shuffles closer to me so that we are nose to nose, and kisses me. The kiss is soft, tender, nothing like the fuck-me-now kiss when he threw himself at me through the kitchen door. It's the kiss he used to give me in bed, before saying good-night and falling asleep. Always the same. Even after an argument – even if he was in a foul mood and wanted to ignore me, to hate me – he would kiss me, tell me he loved me, and only then close his eyes.

'I love you, Naomi.' He breathes out the words slowly, each of them a gentle kiss upon my skin, and closes his eyes.

'Come back to us,' I whisper.

He opens his eyes, which are glazed with a question.

'Us?'

The bravery, which I felt so keenly just moments ago, rushes from my body, chased away by a stampede of fear.

'Me. And you . . . Us.'

He sighs, his eyes now stained with sadness. So much has been said. And left unsaid . . . By both of us.

Tell him.

I can't pretend any more. I can't ignore the truth that has been bubbling away in my stomach since I saw the positive sign on the pregnancy test. There are so many lies, but maybe now I can tell the truth about this. About the baby.

The baby isn't Rupert's.

It's Aiden's.

I can't tell him – can I? What if I tell him and nothing changes? What if he chooses her over us?

But what if he doesn't? Maybe this would change everything. He loves me. Maybe this would bring him back, and we could be a family again. Broken, but a family.

That's all I've wanted. That's why I told Rupert the baby was his. Aiden chose Helen and I found out I was pregnant, and Rupert was just so eager for a child of his own, for a family. So I gave him what he wanted. And I hoped I would have a family again.

But it's just another lie. And they both deserve the truth.

So tell him. Tell him about the baby.

'Aiden, I'm pregnant.' I blurt out the words, and his eyes – which had been concentrating on the hand he was trailing up and down my arm – fly up to my face.

'What?'

'I'm pregnant,' I repeat, trying to read his face. His melancholy expression has evaporated but I can't read him. Is that small smile happiness? Confusion? Complete and utter bewilderment? 'Aiden, say something.'

'Does Rupert know?'

'Yes . . . But it isn't his.'

His eyes grow round, wide orbs taking up half of his face, and his eyebrows disappear behind his floppy bed-hair.

'How do you know?'

'I just do . . . The dates aren't right.' He doesn't say anything, just carries on looking at me with that same face, the one I can't read, the small smile and wide eyes. 'Remember that week when he went away?'

He nods.

'Well, that's when it happened.'

'You're sure?'

'Yes,' I mutter. I search his face, looking for a sign, for any clear indication of what he's feeling. But his gaze is fixed at a point just next to where my cheek makes an indent in my pillow.

Please. Please give me some reassurance that I haven't made another huge mistake.

Mistake . . . That's what we said it was the first time it happened. But after the second time I stopped calling it a mistake. And after a while he stopped calling it that too.

Until he ended it.

'Aiden, please talk to me.'

He finally looks at me and his mouth breaks into a grin, his eyes shining with overwhelmed emotion. 'A baby,' he whispers, as he wraps his arms around me, his hands hot on my bare back. 'Our baby.'

I nod, unable to speak.

'We'll figure this out, okay?' he whispers, and I bury my head further into his neck, as if I'm trying to bury my way into his body, under his skin.

He shuffles his face away, just an inch or so, so that his forehead rests on mine.

We'll figure this out.

We lie like that for a while: eyes closed, face to face – an almost perfect moment frozen in time, like we've been transported back to the past, or propelled into the future we didn't get to have. The future we would have had if everything hadn't gone wrong. And then – like we did, night after night for so long – our breathing slows, and we fall asleep.

My body startles awake at the sound of a knock. I frown, trying to place myself back in the present. Aiden is asleep, still facing me, his arm flopped over my waist, his eyelashes fluttering together as he dreams.

I strain my eyes to see my watch: 11:27 p.m.

Who would be knocking at this time?

I look up at the blank white ceiling and the confusion of sleep dissipates – the disjointed pieces stitching themselves together in my mind. The bedroom door is open and, through the large window on the landing, the room is being rhythmically emblazoned with a steady flash of blue.

They're here.

30

'Aiden.' I shake his shoulder roughly. 'Aiden, wake up.'

He rolls onto his back and throws his arm across his face.

'What time is it?' he murmurs.

'The police are here.'

'What?'

He sits up quickly and throws himself off the bed, making his way to the landing in three long strides. The blue lights flash across his face.

They've found her.

We jump at the sound of three further knocks. He turns towards me, his skin shining in the moonlight, which is falling in a bright white shaft through the window.

'Maybe . . . maybe they've found her,' he says, as he pulls his jumper over his head, pushing back his messy hair.

I only nod in response, unable to say anything. Unable to lie – to stoke the hope that has lit inside his heart, only for it to be suffocated all over again. And soon.

I dress myself quickly and follow Aiden out of the room as he rushes downstairs. But as we reach the door he stops and turns abruptly.

'What are we going to tell them?'

'What do you mean?'

'About why I'm here. This can't be the way Helen finds out.'

'I don't know,' I whisper, my eyes fixed on the door.

There are three policemen standing on the other side. Waiting for me.

I can't breathe.

I push past Aiden and place my hand on the door handle.

Inhale . . . Exhale.

I brace myself. Then pull the door open.

Jenning and two policemen look at me.

'Detective Jenning –'

'Naomi –'

'Have you found something?' Aiden interrupts, as he steps out from behind the door. 'Have you found her?'

Jenning falters. His eyes flicker back and forth between us, his eyebrows raised in recognition, but then his mouth sets in a thin, firm line.

'Mr Williams,' he says, nodding at Aiden. 'I didn't expect you to be here. We sent an officer to get you from the Queen's Arms.'

'To get me?' Aiden looks around. 'I came over to keep Naomi company.' He shrugs, all innocence and charm. But then his face turns hard like stone, his eyes, icy and cold. 'Why are you here? Why was someone coming to get me? Have you found her?'

I can't breathe.

Jenning gestures towards one of the policemen, who marches forward to Jenning's side. 'PS Jones, could you please take Mr Williams inside and explain what is happening.'

'I don't want to go inside. Can't you just tell us now? Why do I have to go inside?' Aiden's voice is raised and it echoes up into the night's sky.

The officer – Jones – approaches us, but steps past me and places a reassuring hand on Aiden's shoulder. He tries to usher him inside but Aiden forces him off, with a violent shrug.

'No, no, no. No! I don't want to go inside. I want to know what's going on. Now.' His shoulders rise and fall with the exertion. 'Right now.'

Jenning doesn't move. I can see his brain tick-tick-ticking, trying to figure out what to do next, how best to handle the situation. He breathes in deeply, then sighs.

Please. Not like this.

'Mr Williams. I didn't want to tell you like this and I didn't think you would be here. I'm so sorry, but we found Freya's body in the woods.'

I squeeze my eyes closed. I can't bear to look at Aiden. But I hear the breath leave his body and imagine it floating up to the stars – his last blissful, ignorant breath.

The crunch of steps . . . Someone is approaching. I open my eyes and Jenning is before me, his expression sad and forlorn. Disappointed.

'Naomi Williams, you are being arrested on suspicion of the murder of Freya Williams and for perverting the course of justice –'

'What? Murder? Wait!' Aiden pushes forward, his eyes darting frantically around, unable to focus, unable to understand what is happening. He looks at me – his eyes filled with questions. But there is nothing I can say.

'Naomi?' Aiden shouts.

'You do not have to say anything but . . .'

Jenning's mouth is still moving but I don't follow what he's saying. His words are blurring, morphing into an alien language that I'm unable to process or comprehend, as if someone is dragging their fingers across a record, slowing it down, its melody diluted.

How am I going to explain? How can I make them understand, after all of the lies I've told, all of the steps I've taken to hide the truth? And now everything I've done has made them believe she was killed. And that I was the one who did it.

'Anything you do say may be given in evidence. Do you have anything you wish to say?'

I shake my head.

'Naomi!' Aiden reaches for me but I'm led away. I steal one last look at him over my shoulder and a sharp pain throbs in my heart: his green eyes are wide with shock, his face covered with tears.

For a split second he meets my eye, but only one word reverberates in the frigid winter air between us as they bundle me into the back of the police car.

Murder.

PART THREE

31

The cell is cold. I shiver and wrap my arms around my body, but my hands hold no heat, and my fingers shake against my shoulders. I press my lips together and my bottom lip stings, the skin raw from where I have been chewing it.

When we arrived at the police station, I was taken inside through a back entrance, guided through a winding set of corridors, left, then right, then right again, and as I followed, my thoughts lost themselves in a labyrinth of questions.

What do they know? Why have I been arrested for murder? What evidence do they have? Did they find something I didn't? Do they know something I don't? What do they know, what do they know, what do they know?

My questions came to an abrupt halt as I reached the custody desk. The custody sergeant smiled as he booked me in.

'Now, I know this might sound like a silly question, but how are you feeling right now?' he asked.

I shrugged my shoulders. His eyes glanced down to where my hands were on the counter, my fingers clutching the metal edge. I loosened my grip.

'I'm fine.' I strained to keep my voice steady.

'Do you have any medical issues I need to know about?'

I'm pregnant.

I shook my head.

'Do you have any mental-health issues?'

'No,' I said hurriedly.

'Is there a possibility that you might be pregnant?'

I buried my face in the crook of my arm, which was pressed onto the counter.

'I need you to answer the question.'

I rested my chin on my arm and nodded, looking at the noticeboard behind him.

Now they know.

'How many weeks?'

'It's early. Only ten or so.'

He didn't ask anything else about the pregnancy, just typed notes onto the system and carried on without another thought.

'You are entitled to free legal advice —'

'I don't want a lawyer.'

'You don't have to pay.'

'I know that. I just don't want one.'

'Okay.' He tapped away on his keyboard. The skin under his eyes was dark. I wondered how long he had been on shift – how many people he had processed through this station. How many of them were guilty? And how many of them were innocent? And how many were like me: innocent of what they were accused, but guilty of something altogether different? Something that couldn't be explained and couldn't be forgiven?

'Naomi?' He was looking up at me, eyebrows raised. 'I asked you – can I confirm for a final time that you know why you're here?'

I nodded.

'Can you explain to me what you think you're doing here? In words. Please.'

His fingers were poised, ready to record my answer. I looked up into the harsh white light shining directly above his head and circles flashed before my eyes.

'You think I killed my daughter.'

The words echoed in my ears as he logged my response onto the system.

They think I killed Freya. To him it was just another answer to another standard question. I am just one more cog in the machine. How many people have spent the night in this cell? Thousands? Must be. There is a small stainless-steel toilet in the corner of the room but it doesn't have a cover. The only other object is the bed – a thin blue mat that I'm sitting on, leaning with my back against the rough wall. The cell must have been white once, but it is now a dirty grey. I lean forward, away from the wall.

After they finished booking me in, they asked me to stand against a screen while they took photos of me. A voice asked me to open my mouth, and gloved fingers swabbed the inside of my cheeks. I stood there, staring into the air a foot in front of my face, unable to focus on anything except the over-whelming feeling of dread in the centre of my chest.

They think I killed Freya.

I close my eyes, trying to shut out the image of her face, but in the darkness the edges become sharper: the curve of her Cupid's bow, the curl of her fingers, the tufts of baby hair around her face. I try to shake her image from my mind, but as it disappears, colour seeps into the woods. The trees loom above the open bunker door, the tall trunks soaring up towards the sky, and I am plucked out as if I have shrunk to almost nothing. Invisible fingers drag me upwards and into the branches, screaming. Screaming her name. The bunker door slams shut, sealing Freya inside.

I jump as metal scrapes against metal and the door opens outwards.

'Naomi – it's time for your assessment.' A police officer taps her foot on the linoleum floor. My body doesn't respond and the frequency of her tapping increases. She sighs.

'My assessment?'

She nods but offers no further explanation. It must be a medical assessment. Because I'm pregnant.

I push my body off the bed, dragging the blanket with me as I stand and wrap it around my shoulders.

'Can I bring this with me?'

'Yes, that's fine.'

She leads me to a small room, with a couple of chairs and a desk. A man is sitting in one of the chairs. He stands as he sees me, holding out his hand in greeting.

I extend mine and shake his hesitantly.

What is this? Aren't I meant to be seeing a doctor?

The officer leaves, closing the door behind her.

'Naomi, I'm Matthew. Please, take a seat.'

I sit down and perch on the edge of the chair, my fingers scraping the metal lip of the desk. 'Are you a doctor? I thought I was seeing a doctor. Because of the pregnancy.'

He smiles. 'I'm an FME. A forensic medical examiner. I've been asked to assess you and your mental health.'

My body – which felt as if it was moving all over, each muscle twitching – goes still.

'Mental health?'

'Yes. Please don't be alarmed. I'm just going to ask you a few straightforward questions. It's my job to make sure that it's okay for the police to interview you.'

No. Please not this. Anything but this.

'How are you feeling?'

I shrug. How does he want me to answer that question?

'Okay. How are you feeling about being here? At the police station?'

'I just want to speak to the police and tell them what happened.'

'And do you know what happened?'

'Yes.' I blink rapidly, my eyes watering from being frozen on his face.

'And how do you feel about being arrested? Angry? Sad? Confused?'

'No. I know why I've been arrested. And I'm not angry. I'm . . . numb. I'm just numb.'

He scans my face and turns to face his computer. He taps out a few notes, then swivels back to me. 'You're nearly three months pregnant, is that right?'

'Nearly. Yes.'

'Was your daughter, Freya, your only other pregnancy?'

'Yes. She was my first. This is my second.'

'And how was your mental health when you had Freya?'

I stare at him, my mouth hanging open, unable to respond.

'Did you have any problems during pregnancy?'

'No.'

'No anxiety or depression?'

'Not really depression.'

'Anxicty?'

I nod.

'You were anxious?' he asks.

'Yes.'

'And once you had her, did the anxiety go away? Were you diagnosed with anything?'

My vision blurs. I see myself staring up at the ceiling, night after night, paralysed with fear. The sound of Freya's breathing. The terror. The utter exhaustion.

'I . . . Mostly I just couldn't sleep.'

'Okay,' he says, arching his back, then leaning forward in his chair once more. 'Were you ever prescribed anything to help you sleep?'

Aiden held my hand while the doctor spoke to me for the

first time. Her voice was calming, her sentences measured and judgement-free.

'Yes.'

'What were you given?'

'Zolterol.'

He notes the name on the computer, but his eyebrows rose as I said it.

'And do you still take them now?'

I look down at my lap, and nod. The tiniest movement.

'And do you get any side effects from the Zolterol?'

Mind-numbing migraines. Occasional drowsiness. Nosebleeds. Sections of time that somehow are . . . lost.

'Sometimes. Headaches. Forgetfulness.'

'And – I know this might seem like a stupid question considering what is happening – but how have you been feeling in your pregnancy so far? Similar to how you felt with Freya?'

'I . . . I don't know how to compare them. This . . . hasn't been a normal pregnancy.'

'That's okay,' he says, sighing quietly. He stifles a yawn. 'I'm sorry. Okay, so aside from everything else that's been happening, and I know it's difficult to separate the two, but how would you say your mental health has been so far? How were you feeling before all of this happened?'

'Normal. Apart from needing help to sleep, I've been fine.'

'And how do you feel about being interviewed today?'

'I want to speak to them. I need to tell them what I know.'

And I need to know the truth. I need to understand what happened that night. To know what happened to Freya.

'Well, hopefully we shouldn't be too much longer. I just have a few more questions.'

I slump in my chair. The questions wash over me and my mind isn't here, even as I answer. My mind flits about, from memory to present day to memory, like a trapped bird, flying frantically from wall to window, trying to escape.

I don't want to be in this room. I want to speak to the police and tell the truth. And what I've said in this room has not been wholly accurate. Not quite a lie . . .

But not the whole truth.

32

Four years earlier . . .
August

The sound of a voice echoed in my ears, but it was distant and distorted, as if it was coming to me from outside a dream, in that brief moment between sleeping and waking.

'Naomi!'

Dad?

It was my dad. I wanted to see him, but his face was out of focus. Were my eyes open or closed?

'Naomi, please!'

No. That's not Dad.

It's Aiden.

I tried to blink, to make myself move, but exhaustion was weighing me down, my eyes fixed in place, wide and still.

'Naomi! Give me Freya.'

Freya? Where was Freya?

'Give her to me. Now!'

Hands gripped my shoulders and Aiden's face, centimetres from mine, was suddenly clear. His skin was pale, his hands clammy. He tugged at my arms and I rocked towards him, my head thudding heavily against his chest.

'Let go of her, Naomi. Please! She's crying, let her go!'

Crying? Freya's crying?

Loud shrieks burst into the room, her cries high and unrelenting. I looked down and there she was, my arms wrapped tightly around her, my hands clasping her to me.

How long had we been there? How long had I held her like this, not hearing her cries? Not recognizing her distress?

I released my grip and Aiden scooped her into his arms, swaying from side to side.

'It's okay,' he whispered to her, over and over again. 'I'm here. I'm sorry.'

Eventually his repeated words calmed her, her cries turning to whimpers, until she was lulled to sleep. He walked over to her crib and placed her gently inside, rocking it rhythmically until he was sure she was settled. He turned to me, but watched me from afar, his jaw clenched, his eyes scanning my face as he tried to figure me out.

What hadn't he seen? What hadn't he understood?

He walked to the bed, hesitating for a moment before sitting down next to me. 'Naomi . . . did you hurt her?'

'What? No,' I said, my voice hoarse.

'Are you sure? She was screaming.'

'No, I just . . . We came upstairs for a nap.'

'You couldn't even hear her crying. You've got to sleep, Naomi. You're making yourself ill.'

'No, I'm not. I'm looking after her.'

'Naomi, listen to me. You couldn't hear her crying. She was screaming and you were just holding her against you, staring into space. What if you'd fallen asleep and hurt her? What if I hadn't come home? You could have killed her.'

His voice was ringing in my ears, each of his words an attack.

'You think I'm a bad mother. You don't trust me . . .'

'You're not yourself right now. You need help.'

'No, I don't. I know how to look after her. She's my daughter –'

'She's mine too. I thought you were going to get better,

that it would just pass . . . This is my fault too. I should have realized sooner that you're not coping. I'm going to call the doctor.'

'No, you can't do that.'

'Please listen to me.'

I shook my head from side to side and pressed my hands to my ears, trying to block out his words.

'Naomi, stop. You need help. I know that what happened with your dad scared you, but you can't look after Freya —'

'Stop talking.'

'You can't look after Freya if you're not looking after yourself.'

'Please stop talking —'

'There are people who can help you. I love you but I can't let you hurt her.'

I launched myself at him, my arms flailing, my hands curled into clenched fists that pummelled him relentlessly.

'Naomi, please!' he cried, his words choking him.

He grabbed my arms, forcing them down by my sides, but still I struggled. 'I don't want to hurt you, please, Naomi. Stop.'

He flipped me over so that I was facing away from him, my feet kicking out in retaliation, and he held me there, his arms wrapped around mine, pinning me to the bed. Eventually my screams of anger subsided to low, anguished cries. 'I'm sorry,' I whispered.

He pulled me towards him and I rested my head against his chest. 'Please don't take her away.'

'Darling, I won't,' he said, as he stroked my face, his eyes shining with tears. 'No one is taking her away. But we need to get you help. I promise I'm going to make it all better. Okay?'

I nodded, and he rocked me in his arms, like a small child

who needed protecting. Saving. But within moments, I could no longer hear his words of comfort as the world blurred before my fixed blank stare.

'Naomi, can you look at me, please?'

I lifted my gaze from Freya who was cradled in my arms, and looked towards the voice on the opposite side of the room, but it took several moments for my mind to process what my eyes were seeing.

A woman was sitting on the other side of the desk, her arms resting on the table, a notepad in front of her. Her face was familiar.

'Do you remember me from the other day?'

I began to nod but paused – I couldn't quite place her. Everything was blurry.

'I'm sorry,' I said. 'I don't remember your name.'

'I'm Antonia Ross. I'm a psychiatrist – you were referred to me by the mental-health team. You can call me Toni.'

'Toni,' I whispered. 'Yes, I remember.'

She responded but I couldn't hear her. I blinked slowly, watching her mouth move, waiting for her words to reach me.

'How have you been feeling on the medication?'

'Fine . . . a bit fuzzy. It feels like I can't catch up with what's happening.'

'That's quite normal,' she said, as she scribbled a note, pushing her thick-rimmed glasses up her nose. 'It will take a little while for your body to get used to the dose and then you should feel better. More like yourself.'

More like myself? I thought. But if I'm not myself, who am I? Who is this person?

'Now, last time we were together I explained your diagnosis to you. Do you still understand?'

'Yes.'

'Can you explain it to me?'

I sighed and scratched at the skin on the inside of my elbow, trying to bide my time.

'Naomi, I need you to understand why you've been given the medication. I don't want you to take anything blindly.'

I continued to scratch my arm and avoided her gaze.

'You have a severe anxiety disorder, which is manifesting in obsessive thoughts and causing you to deny yourself sleep. But you need to sleep to be able to look after your daughter. Taking the anxiety medicine isn't enough – you need to take the sleeping medication I prescribed you as well.'

My hand paused. 'I –'

'Aiden told me you haven't been taking it.'

I met her eye but didn't respond, and she leaned back in her chair, clasping her hands together in her lap.

'Why don't you want to take them? You're taking the other medication.'

'I can't sleep.'

'You force yourself to stay awake so that nothing bad will happen to her.'

'Yes. I have to look after her. I have to keep her safe. If I fall asleep anything could happen . . .'

'Remember, this is where it began. With your anxiety. Your fear that something might happen to Freya while you're sleeping. But it's all part of your condition. It's a cycle. And we have to get them both under control: the anxiety and the sleep deprivation.'

Her words trailed away as she waited for a positive response. I shook my head.

'The sleeping tablets are no different from your anxiety medication. They're going to help you. Staying awake all night is not going to help you get better. Staying awake all night won't get you to a place where you and your family can go back to normal. To where Aiden can go back to work. Where you can trust that you *are* a good mother. That's what you want, isn't it?'

I nodded and rested my cheek on top of Freya's head.

'So will you take it tonight?'

Freya lying completely still, not breathing, her lips blue, her skin pale, flashed like lightning before my eyes. A whimper left my lips as I blinked the vision away. 'But something might happen to her.'

'Nothing will happen to her. If she cries, you'll wake up. You're only taking one. And Aiden is there all the time. Okay?'

'Yes.'

'So will you take them? Or shall we have a chat with Aiden?'

'No, I'll take them.'

'And remember: only take one.'

I nodded. 'Just one.'

That night, Aiden and I sat side by side on our bed, and he placed the turquoise pill in my open hand.

'I don't know if —'

'You promised.' He passed me a glass of water. 'Please. Do it for us.' He glanced over to where Freya was asleep in her crib. 'She needs you . . . I need you. I want my Naomi back.'

The weight of his words fell onto my shoulders. Before I could change my mind, I placed the pill on my tongue and gulped the water, forcing it down.

'Sleep now, love,' he said. 'When she wakes up tonight, I can feed her. Just one full night's sleep will make such a difference. Soon you'll feel better.'

I lay down and turned on my side, my eyes fixed on Freya's crib. Aiden moved closer and his arm wrapped around my waist as he placed a kiss on the back of my head. 'I love you,' he whispered into my hair. 'So much.'

I nodded but didn't respond. Instead, I continued to watch Freya, even as my eyes became heavy, even as my breathing began to slow, until finally I could no longer resist. My eyes fluttered closed and she disappeared from sight.

33

The hatch on my cell door opens and an arm reaches in, fingers gripped around a styrofoam cup, its contents steaming.

'Your tea, Naomi,' says the officer.

I get up off the bed and take the cup, the foam squeaking under my grip. 'Thank you,' I say.

He goes to close the hatch.

'Um, wait.' I stand in front of the gap, so he can see me. He looks at me expectantly.

'Um . . . I need to know. Has my boyfriend been told that I'm in custody?'

'What's his name?'

'Rupert Burton-Wells.'

'No, I don't believe so.'

I nod and look down at the cup in my hands. I need to speak to him. I need to tell Rupert the truth. All of it.

'Do you think I could call him?'

He assesses me. 'I'll ask the custody sergeant. Someone will come and let you know.'

'Thank you. I really appreciate it.'

He nods and closes the hatch, and my stomach turns at the metallic scrape of the mechanism as it locks.

'Naomi, you can have your phone call.'

It's a different officer standing at the open door, her hand on her keys. The one from earlier. The woman who took me to be assessed.

I shuffle out of the cell and she leaves the door open

behind me. I follow her, my mind whirring. What am I going to tell Rupert? What should I say? No matter how well I explain myself, no matter how eloquently I portray my state of mind when I did it, he won't understand. He's too good – he would never do something like this, and he couldn't empathize with someone who would.

She leads me to the mirrored phone by the custody desk, explains how it works and stands aside, only a few feet away. I lift it from its hook and it reflects my distorted image back at me. I am unrecognizable.

I hold the receiver to my ear and the ring repeats itself, over and over. Will they let me try again if he doesn't answer or –

'Hello?'

'Rupert.'

'Naomi? What number are you calling from?'

'The police station. Rupert –'

'Has something happened? Have they found Freya?'

I close my eyes and lean my head against the phone booth. 'They've found her . . . She's gone.'

'Oh, Naomi –'

'Rupert, I need you to let me speak. Please.'

I wait. He doesn't interject but his breathing vibrates in my ear.

'I've been arrested.'

'What –'

'They think I killed her,' I speak over him. 'I didn't, I swear.'

He says nothing. Is he still there?

'Rupert – say you believe me.'

'Of course I believe you – I know you'd never hurt her. I can't believe this is happening . . .'

I need to do this quickly, quietly. The custody sergeant is

looking at his screen but I can tell he's listening. I don't want to hurt this man. But I have to.

Do it now.

'But I haven't been honest with you. About me and Freya. Everything about her childhood. About what really happened. I'm sorry.'

'Naomi. I don't understand —'

'I'm so sorry,' I cry. 'I just wanted you to see *me*. Not . . . I'm sorry.'

'Naomi. No matter what's gone on, I love you, okay? Let me help you.'

Be cruel. Be kind.

'The baby isn't yours.'

His breathing hitches. 'You're lying. Tell me you're lying.'

'I'm not. I'm sorry. Just forget me, okay? You can do so much better. You deserve much better.'

I move the phone away from my ear as his confused voice continues to protest loudly. I slam the receiver down. Closing my eyes, I rest my forehead against the cold metal, my breath billowing in my chest.

The custody sergeant is watching me. He heard every word. But they will all know, soon enough.

I'm going to tell the truth. I was scared, and I lied.

Forgive me.

I'm sorry.

34

Jenning fiddles with the recording device on the table next to me. I feel as if it's watching me – waiting: ready to hear whether I will spill my secrets or refuse to speak. No comment, no comment, no comment. Isn't that what criminals say? Metaphorically stick two fingers up to the police and say, *You try to prove it.*

But that isn't me. Once they know the truth about how I found her and hid her, and why I lied, they will understand. Won't they?

What if they don't?

I was seven when I fell through the trapdoor of the bunker. I had lowered myself onto the first rung of the ladder, but my foot slipped and I fell backwards, my stomach soaring upwards away from my body and, for a split second, I felt as if I was frozen, held there by an imaginary force, dangling me in mid-air. But then I plummeted down and landed with a smack on the concrete floor. That's how I feel now, suspended in the sky, waiting for the fall.

Jenning presses the button and it bleeps loudly. A long, dull tone.

'It is three twenty-four a.m. on the twenty-seventh of November. I am Detective Sergeant Jenning and with me is Detective Constable Walker. Naomi, it's my duty to inform you again before the interview begins that you are entitled to a legal representative.'

'I don't want one.' I cross my arms in front of my chest.

I just want this to be over. Let it be done.

'Then we will begin the interview.'

'I have something I want to say before you ask questions.'

The two men look sideways across the desk at each other, then straight back to me.

'Okay,' says Jenning.

I look away from Jenning – the man I've lied to since the beginning, the man who's only been trying to do his job: to find my little girl and bring her home – and my eyes return to the recorder. The red light is on, unblinking. Ready to hear my words.

Speak.

'The day she went missing . . . the day I called the police and said she'd gone missing . . .'

I can't do this.

You have to.

'I lied.'

The words spit out like bullets, fast and unavoidable. Jenning's eyebrows lift, his shock at my acceptance almost palpable. The other officer writes my words down on the page, on the right-hand side of the line dividing the page in two – their questions, my answers: *I lied.*

'But I didn't kill Freya. I woke up, like I said, but she wasn't in her room. So I looked for her upstairs and couldn't find her. But when I went to look downstairs . . .' My voice breaks and I bend my neck back to look up at the ceiling. It feels like I've been keeping this secret for ever. Has it really been only a week? There have been so many lies. All with one explanation. I try to catch my breath, which has become shallow, but my feeble attempts to draw oxygen into my lungs are failing.

'Take your time,' says Walker, obviously deciding that – for dealing with me – honey might be better than vinegar. He is good cop. But Jenning's gaze is cold and unforgiving.

I wipe my nose, which is beginning to run, and focus on the table, rather than on them. That might make it easier.

'When I went to look downstairs, she was there. At the bottom of the stairs. She was dead.'

And with that, my world breaks, a jagged crack running down the very centre of my life. Speaking those words out loud for the first time – *she was dead* – makes it even more crushingly real. To be sitting here, in this interview room, having said those words, and knowing she is probably lying in some mortuary, zipped into a bag . . .

A sob explodes out of me. I've been forcing my lips closed, pressing them together to suppress my cries, but it can't be restrained. I collapse onto the table, my shoulders shaking uncontrollably.

'Naomi,' says Jenning, in a monotone. 'Naomi, we need you to sit up and tell us what happened.'

'Or we can take a break?' says Walker.

I lift my head and catch a look between them before Jenning has a chance to adjust his facial expression. He wants to hear what I have to say. And I want to tell them. I have to tell them. Right now.

'No.' I sniff. 'I want to tell you now.'

They nod.

'When I found her . . . I panicked. I called Aiden to tell him what had happened but I couldn't. I was so scared . . . I was scared of what might happen. I was scared of her being taken away, and before I knew what I was doing I had told him she was missing, that I couldn't find her. And he told me to call the police. And I didn't know how to turn back. I wish I could take it back. I wanted to tell the truth but I couldn't see . . . I didn't know how.'

I blink rapidly, searching for understanding in their faces.

Nothing.

Jenning coughs lightly.

'Did you call the police straight after your phone call with Aiden?'

'Yes.'

'Are you sure?' He taps on the file next to him. 'We have your phone records.'

My eyes search his face, my mind scanning back to the moment I said goodbye to Aiden. I dialled 999, I called –

I didn't call them. I called Rupert.

My breath hitches and I try to swallow but my mouth is dry. Have I made Rupert look guilty too? Do they think he was involved?

'No, I . . . I called Rupert.'

'Why did you call Rupert?'

'I was . . . I was going to ask him for help but I didn't, I swear. He didn't know anything. He was in Bristol. I told him that Freya was missing and he left straight away to come to the farm.'

Jenning sits forward in his seat, his forearms resting on the table.

'Once you called the police – what did you do with Freya?'

His eyebrows are raised as he waits for my response. Walker is watching me too, his pen still above the paper. They already know the answer. They found her. But they want me to say the words. They want me to admit it.

You have to be honest, Naomi.

'I hid her in the bunker in the woods.' I can taste iron in the back of my throat. 'Can I have a tissue, please? I think I'm getting a nose-bleed.'

Walker reaches inside his jacket and retrieves a crumpled one, which he holds out to me. 'It's clean, I promise.'

I take it from him, and dab it against my nostril. Yes – there it is. Spots of blood, bright red, making a pattern like one of those ink-splatter drawings.

'Thank you.'

Jenning waves his hand at me, trying to mask his impatience. 'You can carry on.'

'I hid her in the bunker. I didn't know what else to do. I wasn't thinking clearly.'

'Then what did you do?'

'I came back inside, and tidied everything away. Then I washed my hands.'

'Why?'

I raise my eyebrows at him. Questioning.

'Why did you wash your hands?' he repeats.

'I had dirt on them. You were about to arrive and I didn't want you to see.'

You are disgusting.

'Why did you tell us she had been playing outside? Why not say she had been taken from the house?'

'Because if I said that you'd look for evidence of a break-in . . . and there wasn't any.' I squeeze my eyes shut, shame throbbing through me. It sounds so preconceived.

Jenning leans forward, his hands centimetres from mine. 'Why did you lie, Naomi, if you really thought it was an accident? Accidents happen all the time. More often than you think. More often than reported in the papers. Why lie?'

'Because . . . I know this doesn't make sense, but I was scared of her being taken from me. When my dad died, I watched him being taken from the house. I had to identify him and say goodbye to him in a morgue and I just couldn't stand the thought of having to do that with Freya.' There is no sympathy in his eyes. No glimmer of understanding. 'And I'm pregnant,' I continue. 'I thought the baby would be taken away. I . . . I just panicked.'

Walker scrawls messily across the page, not taking his eyes off me.

Jenning nods. 'That was one piece of information I was surprised to find out. You never mentioned that.'

I need to tell them about why Aiden left. I need to tell them the real reason I was scared I'd lose my baby. My lower lip trembles violently, but I can't bring myself to tell them. I can't do it. The baby will be taken and I'll be alone. Two children, gone: one dead, one lost.

'It was an accident,' I repeat. 'Please believe me.'

'You know what you're saying you did constitutes an offence?'

'Yes.'

'Wasting police time . . . Preventing a proper burial. Perverting the course of justice . . .'

'Yes.'

'See – do you want to know what I think? I think you're clever. I think you've had this whole story planned out in case we found her. And I think you're admitting to all of this to try to avoid the real offence you committed.'

'Murder?' I gasp. 'I didn't kill her – I would never harm my child. It was an accident. She fell.'

It must have been an accident. It must have been. Anything else is unthinkable.

He leans back in his seat, a smug, cocky look on his face. Self-assured. As if he is keeping a secret that will change everything.

'Well, like in all cases when we find a body, Naomi, the pathologist conducts an investigation. We asked them to do an emergency one, quick turnaround. And do you know what they said?'

He picks up a piece of paper that until now was lying innocently on top of his file. He slides it across the table and the words blur before coming into focus. I scan them hastily until I stumble upon the final paragraph – the conclusion. I read the words, my brain failing to understand their meaning.

I read them again.

I slowly look up at the officers, both watching me – waiting for my reaction.

Please, no. It can't be.

'Do you understand now why we don't believe you?' He pulls the paper back towards him, files it away.

'Freya's death was not an accident.'

35

It wasn't an accident.

Somebody did this.

I put her to bed and the following morning she was at the bottom of the stairs. She fell. She must have. But the pathologist . . .

Clear evidence of a non-accidental death.

That's what the report says. Non-accidental death. And a whole report leading up to those words explaining the evidence that supports the conclusion. Like a science experiment in school: hypothesis, investigation, evidence, results, conclusion. But I don't understand the evidence. I can't understand the outcome. It isn't possible. It has to have been an accident.

'It was an accident.' I scratch my arm, and it stings. Jenning's eyes swivel to watch me and I remove my hand, place it on my lap.

'Naomi, I want you to listen carefully, okay? There is clear evidence that someone was involved in the death of your daughter – she might have fallen, but it was not an accident. Lying more is not going to help you.'

'I'm not lying.'

'Naomi,' Walker interrupts. 'At this juncture, I'm going to ask you again if you would like a lawyer.'

Asking for a lawyer now will make you look guilty.

'No.'

'Are you sure?'

'I don't need a lawyer. I'm telling the truth. I didn't kill her. I just tried to keep her safe.'

'Okay.' He nods at Jenning.

Jenning opens his file and places several pieces of paper face down on the table. But I can see that there are colour images on the other side.

I close my eyes. 'I don't want to see those.'

'We need to ask you questions about them —'

'I don't want to see photos.'

'Naomi, you don't have to look at them if you don't want to, but we have to ask you questions about them,' says Walker, his voice firm. No more softly-softly. 'Okay?'

I keep my eyes closed but I can hear the sound of pages being turned over, the gentle flap as they are placed the right way up, images exposed. I squeeze my eyes closed so tightly it feels as if my head is going to implode.

Jenning speaks to the recorder. 'I am showing the accused a photograph of the hands of the deceased.'

I shake my head violently from side to side.

Don't look, don't look, don't look.

'Naomi, what does that look like to you?' He pauses. 'Naomi . . . you said this was an accident. You need to look so you can give us an explanation.'

I open my eyes but look at my hands, which are clasped together on my lap, gripping the tissue stained with blood. I slowly raise my eyes to the table, and then to the photograph, intending to take a quick glance, just brief enough to understand what they're trying to show me, but once my eyes fall on the image, I'm unable to look away.

Each image shows a close-up of one of her tiny hands, the fingers curled over. Jenning jabs his pen on each page in turn, directing my gaze towards her wrists.

'What do you think that is?'

I can't help but lean in closely, the photograph so close to my face, the page ripples each time I exhale.

The photos show each wrist from both angles. Palm up and palm down. On both arms are deep purple bruises, wrapped around her wrists, like matching bracelets, each dappled with different hues of blue and purple.

'Bruises . . . She's bruised,' I whisper.

The fingermarks are clear. Someone grabbed her so tightly that it bruised. Someone hurt her.

'Did you notice these bruises when you put her to bed?'

Her loud, joyous laugh as we played in the bath floods my ears. There wasn't a single mark on her.

'No. I didn't.'

He turns over another photograph. I can see the shape of Freya's lower lip, the gentle slope of her chin. Along her jaw there are several purple imprints.

'What do you think those marks are?'

'Br-bruises.'

'What do you think caused them?'

I know the answer but I can't say it. I can't let the words leave my mind because, if I do, what happened to Freya will be real.

'It must be from when she fell.'

'Be honest, Naomi. What do those marks look like?' He stares at me with a challenging glare.

'Fingers.'

'Yes. The grip of a hand around each wrist. Did you do that to her?'

'No!'

'Did you grab her face?'

'No, I promise.'

He picks up the pathologist's report again, and turns the pages.

'Page three of the pathologist's report details "an injury to the back of the head which is not consistent with a fall but rather with blunt-force trauma". Do you know what that means?'

I do, but I shake my head – I can't say those words. I won't. Someone hurt my baby.

'Blunt-force trauma,' Jenning continues, 'means that the injury to the back of Freya's head was caused by it being struck by something with force. Can you explain how she would have got such an injury?'

I shake my head, unable to speak.

'Now, when you were booked into the station, we took photographs of you.'

'Yes.'

'Take a look at these.'

He flips over two more pieces of paper, but they are not the photos of me that I expected, head to shoulders, like the mugshots of celebrities you see in the papers. One is a photo of my arm . . . The other the back of my neck. When did they take those? I hadn't been concentrating on what was happening, I couldn't focus on anything except the word 'murder', replaying over and over again in my mind.

'What's that on your arm?' He moves his fingers across the photograph, over my forearm, from the elbow down towards the wrist.

I squint at the photo, absorbing the image, then look away, but my right hand begins to tremble.

'What is that on your arm?'

'A scratch.'

'And here on the back of your neck?'

'A scratch.'

He nods, his lips pursed as if something sour is coating his tongue, acrid and bitter. 'A scratch,' he repeats. 'And it doesn't look fresh. It's healed but it must have been quite nasty when it first happened.'

'I . . . It's just a habit. I do it all the time. I do it in my sleep . . .'

Silence fills the room but the noise inside my mind is deafening. My thoughts are screaming at me, shouting to be heard. Telling me to run.

'I didn't do this.'

'Didn't you?'

'No! No, no, no, no, no, no, no. No.'

I'm shivering but the room is stifling – so hot, the air unbreathable.

I can't breathe.

All of the oxygen has been sucked from the room: it's an airless vacuum and I can't escape. I gasp, but it's futile: my throat is closing as panic tightens its grip of my body.

'Naomi?' Walker rushes and kneels at my side, his hand on my shoulder. 'Naomi? Lean forward. I think you're having a panic attack. Just lean forward, put your head between your knees and breathe.'

Someone killed my daughter while I was sleeping.

I grasp at his arm, raking his jacket with my fingers, the material crumpling under my grip.

'I can't –'

Someone killed my daughter while I was sleeping.

'You can. Listen to me: breathe in. Slowly. Okay, good. Now, breathe out. Slowly does it. Okay, again. Breathe in . . . Breathe out . . .'

My breathing is evening out under the direction of his calm, firm voice. My pulse, while still unnaturally fast, begins to slow. I pull at the high neck of my jumper. My chest is drenched with sweat.

Breathe in.

Breathe out.

I meet his eyes and his wrinkled brow relaxes.

Someone killed my daughter while I was sleeping.

'Better?' he asks.

I nod. Then turn my head away from him, and vomit loudly onto the lino floor.

Was that someone me?

36

They took me back to my cell. Gave me a cup of tea. Asked me if I wanted to see a medical professional. I told them, no, it was a panic attack, I'd be fine. I just want to get the interview over with. The cup of tea is still in my cell, going cold.

I need to know what happened. Someone hurt my child, and because of my stupidity, because of my lie . . . they're going to get away with it.

And I've made myself look like the culprit.

Maybe you are . . .

I close my eyes, my brows knitting together as I try to summon the image of her bedroom at the very moment I said goodnight and closed the door. Had anything changed the following day? Did I miss something that would have helped me, would have made me realize it wasn't an accident at all?

I frown as the image wavers in my mind, the details murky. Something wasn't right when I went up there and whispered her name into the empty space. And it wasn't just that feeling – the feeling of dread lingering in the corners of the room. It was something else.

A small detail shifts into focus and my eyes spring open as I finally see what I've missed all this time.

Her bag.

Her bag had moved.

When I dressed her for bed, I put it by the wardrobe. But the next day when I went to get some of her clothes for Jenning, I tripped over it . . . It was by her bed.

And her door . . .

Her door was open. I closed it when I said goodnight, the click of the lock loud in the expanse of the landing. But when I went looking for her, it was ajar.

Who opened it? Did I go into her room? Why would I go in there once she was already asleep? Why? Why would I go back to her?

Why can't I remember?

Did you hurt her?

I resist the urge to clap my hands over my ears as Aiden's words from all those years ago chatter at the front of my skull, as if his voice is inside my head.

I didn't hurt her. I couldn't.

I wouldn't.

'Naomi – are you ready to begin again?' says Jenning.

'Yes.'

He flips over another photograph – but in this image Freya is alive. She is standing in front of her bookshelf, grinning like the Cheshire Cat as she looks up at her beloved *Alice in Wonderland.*

'Did you take this photo?'

'Yes.'

'When did you take it?'

'The night before she . . . The night before I found her. Before I got her ready for bed.'

He reaches his hand down the side of his chair, pulls up a plastic bag, and puts it on the table in front of me.

'Are these the clothes Freya is wearing in that photograph?'

I clench my jaw, and reach out for the bag, but hesitate just as my fingers graze the plastic. 'Can I touch it?'

'You can touch the bag,' says Walker.

I pick up the bag, and it crinkles in my hands as I squint at the miniature garments inside. Her striped cable-knit jumper, white alternating with rainbow colours. Her blue denim dungarees, slightly frayed at the knees from where she fell over at Aiden's house, on the patio in their tiny garden. He told me he'd tried to throw them away, but she'd said he couldn't. I want to tear the bag open, press the clothes to my face, and scream into the material.

'Yes . . . That's what she was wearing.'

He extends his arm down the side of his chair again, and retrieves another plastic bag. I pinch the skin on the inside of my arm.

'Can you please confirm that these are the clothes you told us Freya was wearing last?' says Jenning.

'Yes.'

'But you admit now that she was actually wearing these clothes?' He holds up the first bag in mid-air, almost shaking it at me.

'Yes.'

'Why did you lie?'

'Because I didn't want you to find her. I'd already lied about her being missing. I'd already hidden her. I didn't want you to find her.'

He cocks his head from side to side, as if he's assessing my words, but disbelief is painted on his face, clear as a picture. Walker finishes writing but carries on looking down at the paper, pen poised.

'This is a photo we have taken from your house,' Jenning continues. He places an evidence bag in front of me containing a framed photo. The frame is mirrored – it sits in a collection on the console table in the hall. 'Can you take a look at the photo, please?'

I pick up the bag, stretching the plastic taut so that I can see through it to the photograph inside. It's me and

Freya, just a few months ago, at the end of the summer. I'm crouching down beside her and her arms are wrapped around my neck.

We're standing in the hall. On the rug. The rug I hid in the bunker with her.

'The rug in that photograph was in the bunker with Freya. Did you put it there?'

'Yes.'

'Why?'

'Because she was on top of it when I found her. I thought if I left it there you might find something.'

'Why did you use the bunker?'

My eyes dance between them, confused by the sudden change of subject.

'I don't understand the question.' I scratch my cheek – the skin is hot.

'Why did you choose to hide her in the bunker?'

'I've told you this already. I didn't want you to find her. And I had to act quickly ... It was the only place I could think of.'

'That bunker isn't on any official documents, is it?'

'No ... They were a secret in the Second World War. There are loads of them, hidden all over the country.'

'And you actively kept the bunker a secret too.'

'How do you mean?'

'We assume that Aiden doesn't know about the bunker. Otherwise he would have mentioned it.'

I sniff. My lip quivers. 'No, he doesn't know.'

A little voice creeps into my head. *Someone else knew.*

'How did you find –'

'How long were you together?' he says, cutting me off. He asks the question lightly, but he knows what he's doing. He has buried the knife deep in my heart – and is beginning to twist.

'Over five years.'

'And he lived in the farmhouse for how long?'

'A year and a half, give or take.'

'So five years together, over a year in that house, and you never told him about the bunker?'

'There was no reason to,' I stammer. 'It never came up.'

'It never came up in conversation during the five years you were together?'

'It was somewhere that was important to me and my dad. When he died, I stopped talking about it. It was just too hard to speak about, so I never brought it up.'

'Are you sure?'

'Yes.' I glare at him. 'Why are you asking me about the bunker? I've admitted I took her there.'

'We're just asking you questions. This interview is your chance to tell us your version of ev—'

'And I have. I am. I'm telling you the truth.'

He taps his finger on the table, his eyes scanning the pile of documents next to him. 'Before I carry on,' he says, 'is there anything else you did during the investigation that you want to tell us about?'

The sighting.

Do they know it was me? Have they realized it wasn't a hoax – a teenager with too much time on their hands – but, rather, it was me, trying to steer them away from the woods?

Should I tell them? It will only make me look more guilty. *But you swore you would tell the truth.*

'Yes,' I say, before I can stop myself. 'I . . . I made the phone call. The call saying that Freya had been seen in the back of a car.'

Jenning pauses, and sighs wearily. Walker stares at me, then glances sideways at Jenning, his eyes wide with surprise.

They didn't know.

'Why did you do that?' Jenning asks, his voice giving nothing away.

'The searches were getting closer to the bunker. I thought that if I made you think she was being moved out of the area, you'd leave the farm.'

'And did you realize the amount of police time and resource that would have to be diverted to investigate your lie?'

'I . . . Yes.' My cheeks flush, and the heat of shame spreads down the back of my neck.

Jenning pauses, scratches his cheek, and the sound of his nails against stubble makes my skin crawl. I bite down on my back teeth, hard.

'Okay. Let's move on. Why did Aiden leave you?'

'Pardon?' I balk.

'Why did he leave you? It's a simple question.'

Walker's pen scratches away on the paper, the noise amplified.

'He just left. He wasn't happy . . . We weren't happy.'

'Well, that's strange, because look . . .' He opens a file and drops an array of photographs in front of me. I try to focus, but the images of my life – my family – blur together in a kaleidoscope of memories.

Freya's first birth–

Aiden's thirtieth –

A picnic in Regent's Pa–

The first time we took Freya swimm–

My brain scrambles as it tries to assess and reject the images it is receiving, but Jenning picks out one photo, and places it in front of me.

But this one is not printed on a piece of paper. It is an actual photo, six by four, one edge slightly worn from age.

Freya is a toddler, snuggled in Aiden's arms, and Aiden is gripping my waist, our faces all set in jaw-breaking smiles. The day before he left . . .

That photo wasn't on my phone. I deleted it.

'Where did you get that?' I say, under my breath.

'As you can see, we have photos of you as a family. Look.' He jabs his finger on the photo in the centre of my face. 'Look – this one was taken the day before Aiden left. Would you agree that you both look very happy?'

'Where did you get that photo?' I repeat, trying to increase my voice in volume, but it sounds dull in the small confines of the room.

'Answer the question, Naomi.'

Where did they get that photo?

'Naomi.'

I nodded.

'Answer out loud, please.'

'Yes – I agree.'

'Does Aiden look unhappy?'

'No.'

'But you said before that he left because he was unhappy. But we have a family photo taken the day before he left and he looks like the happiest man on earth. So, why did he leave? What happened to make him leave so suddenly?'

'Where did you get that photo?'

'Why did he leave?' he parrots back at me. 'We can play this game for hours, if you want, going round and round asking the same questions.'

'There was an accident.' I spit the words out viciously, almost snarling, my shoulders rising up to my ears.

I hang my head. Why am I taking this out on them? None of this is their fault. It's all mine, it always has been. I wipe my nose with the blood-stained tissue.

'What happened?' Jenning repeats in a flat monotone, his stare blank as he waits for me to answer.

'There was an accident.' I say again.

'Did Freya get hurt?'

'Pardon?' My breath catches in my throat.

'Did Freya get hurt?'

And that's when I realize.

They know everything.

37

Three years earlier . . .
December

The room veered from side to side as I opened my eyes, like a boat rocking on violent seas. I stretched out my limbs – there was so much room without Aiden in the bed. He had left the day before for a work trip and I had spent the rest of the day wishing he would come back. Freya hadn't been herself – she wouldn't stop crying, even though I did everything I could think of to comfort her, keep her entertained, make sure she was happy. But once I put her to bed, my head was throbbing, fingers tightening around my temples, so I decided to take my tablets and go to sleep.

I raised my eyebrows, stretching them as far up my face as I could, trying to focus on the window, anything to make the room come to a standstill. Finally, the view beyond the window settled into place and I lay back in the bed, my arm slung above my head.

The view through the glass was so beautiful – the tops of the green trees were visible and the sky was such a pale blue it was almost white. But something wasn't right about it, like a photograph on the wall, hanging at an angle or slightly off-centre. And then it clicked.

The sky shouldn't be blue. It should be dark outside.

I sat up and reached for my phone: it was 10:47 a.m.

'Freya?' I shouted, as I flung myself out of bed, my body thudding to the floor as my fuzzy mind tried to coordinate my movements. I ran across the hallway, not fully comprehending that the house was silent – no sounds of a one-year-old who had been left in her cot for hours – and pulled open her door, which slammed into the wall.

Her cot was empty.

'Freya?' I screamed, as I spun in circles.

I ran down the stairs, barely breathing, glancing into the empty dining room before running a loop though the kitchen to the snug, then to the living room and back out into the hall. She wasn't there.

'Freya!'

I flew back up the stairs and into her room. My eyes darted around, trying to make sense of her empty cot.

Where is she? Did someone come and take her?

I need to call the police.

I inhaled deeply, trying to slow my quick, uneven breaths. But as I made my way to leave her room, the wardrobe door caught my eye: it was ajar.

I approached it slowly, my arm extended, and yanked it open.

The hangers were bare, unclothed and swinging gently on the rail. All of Freya's things had been removed.

'No . . .'

I returned to the cot – her favourite toy was gone. The grey mouse with soft fuzzy fur: she loved passing its tail between her fingers as she drank her milk, until her eyes drifted and closed.

And then I saw it. I hadn't noticed it before, camouflaged as it was on her white sheet. Lying there, in the centre of her mattress, was a piece of paper. The light shining through the window made it almost transparent, and Aiden's scrawled words were visible: like looking through a ghost.

I reached out a shaking hand and picked it up, but I

couldn't bring myself to turn it over. I whispered to myself, trying to convince myself to read the words set out on the page – refusing to do so wouldn't change the situation I had caused. Hesitating wouldn't change what was written.

I flipped it over and my eyes consumed his words quickly – as quickly as he had written them, his usually neat writing sloppy – swallowing them whole, my stomach sinking with the weight of each sentence.

Freya's arm is broken, she fell out of her cot. I'm taking her to the hospital and then taking her back to my old flat. I won't tell them what happened – but I will if you try to take her back.
She's not safe with you.

The paper crumpled in my hand as my fist closed around it, the words disintegrating on the page.

She broke her arm – she must have been so scared. She would usually wake up at 7 a.m. and call for us, her voice floating across the landing and into our room. But I didn't hear her. Did she shout when she realized no one was coming? Scream? Cry? Or did she just take action, try to swing her leg over the bars before tipping over the top and –

My hands gripped the edge of the cot and I rocked forward, my mouth open in an inaudible cry.

No – don't break down. You can get him to bring her back. She's yours. He can't just take her away.

I reached our bedroom and clambered across the bed, then grabbed my phone, tapping in Aiden's name within seconds. I pressed the phone to my ear, and the faint thrum of my heartbeat pulsed rhythmically against the screen.

It rang. And rang. And rang. Then –

Voicemail.

I hung up. And instantly dialled again.

It rang, and rang, the tone sending the sickly feeling of panic skyrocketing into my chest.

Voicemail.

'Aiden, answer the phone,' I shouted.

I opened a message and frantically tapped on the keys, my desperate words filling the screen.

Aiden, please. I know that you're angry with me. I know that you don't want to talk to me and you have every reason to be furious, but she's my daughter too. You can't just take her. Please come back and we can talk. I love you both so much. Please call me.

I hit send and gripped the phone even tighter, hanging onto it like a lifeline.

Please call me back. Call me back, call me back, call me back. Please, Aiden.

The minutes ticked past, and the phone didn't ring. I needed to do something to make him call. And I knew Aiden – the only way to make him speak was to make him snap. To force him to retaliate.

I can't believe you just left me there. What if I had overdosed? Don't you care about me? Don't you love me?

I hesitated before hitting send – I didn't want to infuriate him, but there was nothing else I could do. At least then I would have him on the phone and I could try to get him to listen. To let me explain.

Three minutes later, his name lit up my phone. I took a deep breath, then lifted the phone to my ear, and answered. 'Aiden –'

'How dare you? Seriously, Naomi, how dare you bloody say that to me?'

'Aiden, please listen!'

'No, I won't. You listen to me. I knew straight away that

you'd only taken two. It was a brand-new box, you left it on the side. Remember, when you were taking these pills because you actually needed them, I used to help you. Have you forgotten that it was me who made sure you listened to Toni and only took one? It was me who helped you stop taking them when you were getting addicted, when you couldn't remember what day it was or what we did the night before. Or have I been a fool this whole time and you never actually stopped taking them?'

'No, I –'

'Please don't lie to me, Naomi.'

'I tried.'

His breath shook in my ear as he took in my words. 'You tried?'

'Yes.'

'You never stopped taking them.'

'I did –'

'For how long?'

'I . . . A – a week or so.'

'I can't believe you did this.'

'Aiden, please – I'm sorry –'

'Why did you take two?' he says, a rasp in his words. 'How long have you been taking two?'

'I didn't mean to. I thought I only took one –'

'But how long have you been taking two?'

'Sometimes one doesn't help.'

'You're unbelievable.'

'Aiden, please listen.'

'Nothing you say can explain this. I get that it was hard for you – you were ill and you needed them. And I always supported you. I tried my best to look after you. But you've been so much better. It's been ten months since you came off your anxiety medicine. You don't need the sleeping pills any more.'

'I do need them. I can't function without them.'

'I don't believe that. I don't believe you . . . If you'd just talked to me, I could have helped you. I've only ever wanted to help you. You could have talked to me. Or if not me, your friends, Helen . . . But you've been lying this whole time.' He stopped, his frantic, angry breaths loud in my ear. 'You've broken my heart.'

'Aiden!' I cried. 'I'm sorry. Please come home – I love you.'

'No, I can't. I can't trust you any more. I can't look at you the same way. You didn't have to see Freya, lying there. She was screaming, Naomi – her nappy was soaked through and she was holding her arm and trying to get off the floor. I . . .' His words died, his tears preventing him from finishing his sentence.

'But you can't just take her. Aiden, she's my daughter, she needs to be at home with me –'

'No, she needs to be where she's safe. And that's with me. I can't trust you to look after her any more. I can't trust that you won't . . . Did you hurt her?'

'Hurt her? Aiden, I know taking the pills again was wrong and I shouldn't have lied to you, I should have talked to you, but it was an accident. She fell trying to get out of her cot –'

'How do I know that for sure? What if she's been like that all night? Can you remember anything about last night after you took the pills?'

'No, but you know me, Aiden. You know how much I love her. I would never hurt her, you know that!'

'I'm not sure any more. I thought I knew you but clearly I don't.'

'Aiden –'

'Listen.' He lowered his voice even further, his words coming out in whispered mutters. 'I've told the hospital she fell off the bottom step and landed on her arm. I don't need social workers coming into my life and monitoring how I look after my daughter when I haven't done anything wrong. But if you try to take her back, I'll tell everyone what you did. I'll do everything in my power to keep her with me because that's where she's safe. And I'll let you see her, but only with me there. Do you understand?'

'Yes,' I whispered. 'Aiden, I —'

'I've got to go.'

The dial-tone blared out of the speaker, its dull note underscoring my shock as I took in the ruined remnants of my life. No husband. No daughter. Just my mistakes and utter devastation.

We could never go back to before. To the time where he hadn't taken her away — to when we were a family. When I was a mother in his eyes, not a monster. His best friend. Someone he could trust, not someone he had to arm himself against, to protect himself and our daughter.

That night, once I was no longer able to cry, and a heavy numbness had devoured me, I sat downstairs in front of the fire and stared at the Christmas tree. Just the week before, Freya's eyes had been round with amazement the first time she saw it. The previous Christmas — her first — she was just a baby, only four months old. But this time was different. She had reached out to touch the spiky branches, giggling as she batted at the bright shapes of the ornaments. Aiden had lifted her, pretending to balance her at its pinnacle. Our angel at the top of the tree. She had smiled — her grin making me want to both laugh and cry hysterically, my world felt so full.

But now she was gone. The house was empty and quiet, and the tree watched me as it stood forlorn and alone in the corner of the snug.

I curled up on the sofa, unable to sleep in our bed without

Aiden, and stayed awake until the fire died in the grate. Then I reached for the packet of pills on the coffee-table and stared at the two tablets that popped out into my open palm. I hesitated.

Don't do it, I thought. I shouldn't do this.

You've already lost everything. What harm can they do now?

I opened my mouth, placed them on my tongue — and swallowed.

38

My eyes are shut, my head hanging down so that my chin is touching my chest, my nails scraping the palm of my hand.

'Are you going to answer the question, Naomi?' Walker asks.

'I can't,' I murmur.

'We have evidence that he came home from a work trip and found Freya with a broken arm and you passed out on your bed. Is that correct?'

'She fell.'

'Were you taking sleeping pills every night?'

I nod.

'Answer the question out loud, please.'

'Yes.'

'Why were you taking them?'

I shake my head, resisting the urge to bring my hands up to my ears, like a child trying to block out unwanted taunts.

'And you're still taking them now.'

'Yes.'

'Would you describe yourself as an addict? Would you now?'

'It was an accident,' I repeat robotically.

'And yet you say that Freya's death was an accident too. And we know that isn't the case. That's two very convenient accidents when your daughter was alone in your custody.'

'I would never hurt her.'

'But she did get hurt, didn't she?'

'Please believe me, I would never hurt her. I would never even think about hurting her.'

'Never?'

'Of course not. I love her.'

He collapses back in his chair and massages his neck, fingers creating deep wrinkles in his skin. For the first time, I catch a glint of a wedding ring, shining in the light. What does his wife think of him being a detective? Does she mind that she is alone in the middle of the night? Does she wish he was at home with her instead of at work? Or does she appreciate him for it, reassuring herself that, yes, he might work every hour of the day and never be home but he's a good man?

Is goodness all that matters?

My right hand moves automatically to my own rings. The diamond is dull – it hasn't been cleaned in years – yet it's still there, trying desperately to shine. The wedding ring – a plain band – sits proudly underneath it, the metal scratched. I click my fingers one by one, and try to breathe slowly, but the air catches in my chest, like when you swallow something the wrong way.

'We contacted your GP – a Dr Galbraith?' Jenning says, and his words ring in my ears. My body jerks like I've been stung, and he raises his eyebrows at me. 'She referred us to an Antonia Ross. We have your medical records.'

And there it is – the moment I think I knew was coming all along. The moment of silence, that reflective pause, before the sky tears open and the storm begins.

They know.

But how much do they know?

It's as if they have everything: as if they have all the pieces of my life and have been slotting them together – building their story. My story.

And that's when I notice it. It has been sitting there all along, under the files of evidence and paperwork. Hiding in plain sight. How did I not recognize the worn leather of the spine? How the pages are visibly curved from years of my fingers leafing their way through the entries?

My journal.

Jenning coughs and I meet his steady gaze.

'Tell us about your breakdown.'

39

The room is blurry, as if I am underwater, the world morphing and shifting before my eyes. I grip the edge of the table, my nails digging into its metal rim, but I am unable to stop it rocking. I'm unable to steady myself.

Focus on one spot. Yes – concentrate on something, anything, on the tap, tap, tap of Walker's pen against the pad of paper, but . . . I can't. My diary pulls my unwilling gaze towards it, and as much as I want to, I can't look away.

They know.

Have they always known?

Jenning places the journal in front of me, and presses his finger onto the plastic surrounding it, protecting it from contamination.

'Do you know what this is?' he asks, his voice almost a growl.

I could deny it. Say I have no idea what it is – make them prove it. But they would prove it eventually. More lies aren't going to help me. Only the truth can do that.

'Yes.'

'What is it?'

'It's my journal,' I whisper.

How did they find it?

'You're going to have to speak up,' Walker says, pointing his pen at the recorder. 'It needs to be able to hear you.'

'Sorry.'

Jenning leans forward, his forearms encircling the evidence in front of him.

'Can you confirm that the entries in this journal,' he waves his hand in the air, 'were written by you?'

'Yes,' I mutter, but I clear my throat as Walker raises his eyebrows, gesturing again with his pen. 'Yes, I wrote them.'

My admission is received – loud and clear.

'Why did you write them?' Jenning says.

How do I explain this? How can I possibly explain that those pages saved my life? My mind was poisoning itself, and it was those pages that helped me seek out the truth: a ray of hope in the darkness of so many lies.

But they were a short-term saviour. I still lost Freya – in the end.

'I wrote them because . . . my psychiatrist thought that writing down everything that had happened since Freya was born would help me get better. That it would help me separate what was real from what my anxiety was making real.'

'You told us that you never thought of hurting Freya.'

'I didn't, I swear. I would never hurt her. I was selfish and, yes, I made mistakes, but I loved her.' My voice cracks, as if I am breaking open, shattering into pieces. 'I love her.'

He opens an ugly brown paper file, containing a single sheet of paper. A photocopy . . .

A page from my journal. He slides the copy across the table and my handwriting glares back at me. But this is not my usual neat, upright script – instead, the letters are large, and slanting to the right across the page, as if they were racing to commit themselves to paper, my hand not working fast enough for my mind. They are like looking through the innermost thoughts of a stranger. Me, but absolutely not me – not who I actually am. Not really. Just the desperate explanations of my troubled mind, trying to make sense of itself.

He prods his finger onto the paper. I want to wrap my

hand around it, bend it back and shout at him that, if he does that one more time, I will break it off.

But I don't. I just wait.

'If you could please read that page for us, Naomi,' he says, removing his finger and stretching his arms above his head, his back clicking as he stifles a yawn.

I yawn, my body unintentionally echoing Jenning's actions back at him in mutual exhaustion. But I need to focus. I begin to read but falter at the first line.

I tried to forget that I ever even wrote this. As soon as I did, I wanted to rip it out, erase it from my history, as if it had never existed, but I stopped myself as my hand grasped at the paper, which crumpled beneath my fingers. I smoothed out the page – this journal is a reminder of who I am, I thought. And who I am not. These words will never be true.

I am not a monster.

I scan the words, but my mind is one word ahead each time, already filling in the blanks.

Toni says I'm getting better but I still can't sleep without the pills. I try – but I lie awake, watching the clock as the hours of night click onwards to morning. I need them . . . What if I always need them? Even years from now, when you are no longer a baby, will I lie awake, my mind refusing to give in to sleep, unless I swallow those two little pills? Dulling my ever whirring mind into submission? Compliance by coma.

But if I am caged, then so is Freya. In here. With me.

Maybe she would be better off without me. Maybe she would be better, kinder, greater, if it was just her and Aiden, and I was gone.

But he can't take her away. He promised he wouldn't. And I won't let him – I'd rather die. And if that happened, no one would be here to look after her. Only I can keep her safe.

I would just have to take her with me. Both of us together. Alone – but together. I wouldn't need to tell anyone. We could just go to the bunker.

It would be quick. No one would know. And they would never find us.

'Finished?' Jenning asks.

I try to nod, but my head feels heavy – I can barely lift my chin, which is falling towards my chest. Instead, I shove the piece of paper away from me and it skitters across the table. I don't want it anywhere near me.

'Ms Williams has read the diary entry,' Walker says to the recorder.

'Did you write that, Naomi?'

I try to speak but the words won't form. 'I – I – I . . .'

'You said you wrote the journal. The handwriting is the same . . . Naomi!' He raises his voice and I jump, a rabbit startled by a gun-shot. 'Look at me. Did you write this?' He labours over each word, his voice sharp and staccato.

'Yes.'

'So when you told us you have never thought about hurting Freya, were you lying?'

'No!'

'It says it there, plain as day: "I'd rather die. I would have to take her with me. We could just go to the bunker. It would be quick. No one would know. And they would never find us."'

'I was still ill. I was struggling.'

'Struggling how?'

'With the sleeping pills. I didn't want to take them. I've never wanted to take them. But I had to and I felt like a prisoner. I wanted a way out, but that was just a way for me to vent, to get rid of bad thoughts. I suffered with intrusive thoughts. I never would have done it.'

'We're not so sure.' His eyes search my face and I shake my head. 'Because your daughter is dead. And somebody killed her. You admit that you hid her in the bunker. The very bunker you never told your husband about and you said you would take her to in this.' He slams his fist down on the page. He immediately averts his gaze, and ever so slightly shakes his head.

He shouldn't have done that . . . He shouldn't have lost his temper. As he uncurls his fist and moves his hand away, it is shaking. He breathes in deeply, and pauses, but as he releases his breath, his next question billows out. No reprieve.

'We have evidence that you once tried to take Freya from Aiden. Is that correct?'

The wedding . . . How do they know about the wedding?

Helen. I can still see the look on her face when she noticed me outside the church, Freya hoisted around my waist. The disbelief. The anger.

'Tried to take her?'

'From Mr Williams's wedding. To Helen Williams. In July of this year. We have a statement that says you turned up at their wedding and tried to take her. Is that correct?'

'Who made a statement? Was it Helen? Did Helen tell you that?'

'Did you?'

'Yes, I went to the wedding.'

'Did you try to take Freya?'

'I went to the church . . . and, yes, I tried to take her home with me.'

'Were you going to hurt her?'

'No. My husband – ex-husband – the man I loved had just married someone else, my best friend, and I couldn't bear to see my daughter there with them. That was my family, not hers. So I tried to take her. I don't know what I was thinking,

I would never be able to keep her, but I wasn't going to hurt her.'

'Exactly. You were never going to be able to keep her. You knew, because of the "accident", because of the reason Aiden left you, you were never going to get your daughter back. And, as you've just said, you couldn't bear to see this other woman imposing herself into your family. You didn't want to be replaced. Is that correct?'

'No, you're twisting my words.'

'Did you want to punish Aiden?'

'No.' I am overwhelmed with a sudden desperate need to cry. I pinch the skin on the inside of my arm.

'Tell us about the affair.'

I sit up, so suddenly that my back arches slightly, like someone has stabbed me in the spine, the blade disappearing up to the hilt.

'We have evidence that you had an affair with Aiden – correct?'

Who told them about the affair?

Aiden?

This can't be the way she finds out.

That's what he said – only a few hours ago. Aiden would never admit to the affair now. He didn't want her to find out this way. And that was before . . . before I was arrested for murder, at a time when a door had been cracked open to expose a sliver of a future with me. With our baby. But that door has been slammed shut. And as much as I hate to admit it, he won't want to lose us both. He'll have lost everything.

So how do they know? There's no one else.

Unless she knew all along. What if she found out? We were always so careful but what if . . .

Helen's face appears in my mind – the day she came to the

house with Lucy and Sophia – the look of disbelief in her eyes when I said Aiden and I didn't talk.

Don't you? she had asked. But it was a statement, not a question.

I cover my eyes with my hands, pressing the heel of each palm into the socket.

'Naomi, answer the question.'

'Yes, okay? Is that what you want? But this has got nothing to do with Freya!'

'When did it begin?'

'In August.'

'Before Freya died, when was the last time you and Aiden were sexually intimate?'

I shake my head, slowly at first, but then, faster and faster, my neck aching as I try to block out his questions.

'When was the last time you slept together before Freya died?'

'Towards the end of October.'

Aiden moves before my eyes, his pale skin in the dim light of the bedside lamp, his body warm against my own, his green eyes filled with a stubborn kind of sadness.

'And last night when we arrested you, Aiden was at your house. Had you slept together?'

'Yes.'

I don't mean to answer the question but it flies towards me so quickly that I fire the truth back with equal speed, each of us rallying back to the other.

Stop answering these questions.

'So the entire time you want us to believe that you were mourning the accidental death of your daughter, while keeping her death a secret, you've been continuing an affair with your ex-husband.'

'No, that's not right.'

'You've been able to continue this affair because you aren't mourning at all. You killed her, didn't you?'

Don't answer.

'We weren't continuing anything – he had ended it!'

Jenning had been poised to propel his next question at me – but the interrogation dies on his lips, which split into a small, satisfied smile. Walker looks up from his notebook, his expression mirroring Jenning's own.

You've played right into their hands.

'When did he do that?' Jenning asks.

You've given them a motive.

'The end of October. He came over to the house and said it was over. But . . . I accepted it. I swear.'

Walker is looking sideways at Jenning, who has leaned back in his chair and is focusing on the ceiling. I can almost hear his thoughts as they brim and bubble to the surface. He rolls his neck in a circle, then tugs at his collar, pulling it away from his throat.

'So . . .' he says '. . . you and Aiden had an affair from around August to the end of October when he ended it. When did you ask for the overnight stay?'

Please don't ask me that. Please don't make me tell you.

'When did you ask to have Freya overnight?'

'The night before she stayed over,' I gasp.

'Is it correct that this was the first time Aiden agreed to let Freya stay with you since you separated?'

I nod and a sob that has been trapped in my chest frees itself in a violent cough.

'What did you do to make him let you have her overnight at such short notice?'

Don't answer that question.

'Answer the question, Naomi.'

'I told him I would tell Helen about the affair.'

'So he agreed that you could have her overnight?'

'Yes.'

'And the following morning she was dead.'

'Yes, but I didn't kill her. I wouldn't do that. Why would I do that?'

'Did you do it to punish Aiden? For not wanting to be with you any more?'

'No!'

How is this happening? Everything – every little detail of what has happened from Freya's birth to now – has fallen into place to condemn me.

'If you didn't do it, who did?' he continues. 'Who was it then?'

'I don't know!' I cry.

'Did you do it on purpose?'

'No, it wasn't me!'

'Have you had another breakdown?'

'No, I haven't – there's nothing wrong with me any more.'

'Then who was it?'

'I don't know. But it wasn't me.'

I collapse my head into my hands and tears drip onto the table, my face blurred in the brushed-metal surface.

This can't be happening. This isn't happening. It's all in my mind. It must be . . . It must be.

'Do you have anything else you would like to say?' Walker asks.

I don't respond – can't respond. Instead, I watch my morphed reflection. Everything is changed. My whole life – our whole history – has tilted on its axis. Skewed.

Jenning murmurs something in the direction of the recorder and jabs the off button, the red light turning black. Their chairs scrape as they push them back to stand up. I turn my head and watch as Walker's feet circumnavigate the table.

'Can you stand now, Naomi? We need to take you back to your cell.' Walker touches my shoulder but I am limp like a rag-doll. I can't move.

'Naomi? Go with DC Walker, please,' Jenning says.

My legs obey and I find myself standing as Walker holds my arm.

'The officer outside will take you back to your cell now, okay?'

Jenning watches as I shuffle along next to Walker, moving towards the door.

'Wait.' I pull against him, trying to release my arm from his grip. 'Wait, wait, wait, wait.'

'Don't struggle, Naomi.'

'I'm not struggling, it's just . . .'

If I let these words leave my mouth, my guilt will cement itself completely in their minds. But I can't do this on my own.

Say it. You have to say it. It's already gone too far.

'Yes?' he asks, his foot tapping on the floor impatiently.

'Can I speak to a lawyer? Please.'

40

The tap in my cell is dripping, and the sound of the water reverberating against the metal sends a soft plinking sound around the small room, oddly comforting as it marks each second in the absence of a clock. They took away my watch.

I don't know how long it's been since they told me they would call a duty solicitor, but an officer walked me back to my cell, my feet dragging slowly across the floor, my shoes shuffling along the corridor – my body running only on adrenalin.

'Try to sleep,' she said. 'You must be knackered.'

I lay down on the bed and covered myself with the thin blanket, pulling it up to my chin, and tucked each side under my body.

But I haven't slept.

Bruises on her wrists . . . An injury to the back of her head . . . A scratch on your arm . . . You never told Aiden where the bunker was . . . Did you do it to punish Aiden? Are you sure you never wanted to hurt her?

Am I sure?

I wrote those words, the words on the page saying I would take her with me. That it would be quick. But I was ill. That was just my frustration pouring onto the page, the blank pages simply a vessel to fill with all of my negative emotions, a place to lock away my intrusive thoughts. But what if, ever since then, that seed has taken root in my mind? Poisoning the soil.

Why didn't I tell Aiden about the bunker? Jenning thinks I intended to do this all along, that it was my secret I kept buried within me, as deep inside my heart as the bunker's concrete walls are buried beneath the earth. But it isn't true. Nothing would make me hurt her. Not Aiden leaving me. Not anxiety. I'm sure of it.

You've been sure before, though.

My fist flies sideways into the wall. The pain shoots up my arm and I cry out. The wall is stained with a smatter of blood, my knuckles, sliced open. I push myself to sitting and lean back, pressing my stinging fist into the blanket.

Drip, drip, drip.

The tap is still dripping, but the sink moves in and out of focus as my weary eyes droop closed and almost instantly fly open.

I can't sleep now . . . I need to figure this out. They think I killed Freya.

Maybe you did.

No. No. No, I didn't. I didn't. That's not true.

True? But you haven't told them the truth . . . Not all of it. You've seen her.

The hallucinations.

At first I thought seeing Freya at the bottom of the drive was my grief. But then I saw her outside the window. And at the graveyard. Then, again, at the farm.

Was my mind convincing me that the impossible was real? Like before, when I saw Mum and Dad? I can still remember now how my skin tingled – an icy chill on that warm summer's day – the first time I saw them in the graveyard. It can't be, I had thought. But they were there, as clear as the cloudless sky behind them. And that was how it felt when I saw Freya. She was so alive as she trudged through the snow.

And the journal is all that I have . . . Toni told me I should try to write down as much as I could about every day leading up to my diagnosis, and I tried. 'Is this everything?' she asked me, as she flipped through the pages.

'Yes,' I responded. Everything I can remember I recall in forensic detail, but everything else is just blank space. Completely empty, as if those days never happened.

And what if that's the truth of it all? What if the hours between putting Freya to bed and waking the following morning are just blank space? My mind choosing to erase what it would rather not remember. It's done it before. Maybe it's done it again . . .

I hang my head between my knees, forcing my fingernails into my temples.

All the evidence is there. The evidence says that I killed her. My heart is sure that I didn't, couldn't. Never.

But my mind does not trust me . . . It doesn't trust itself. It has already proved that it is the ultimate deceiver, a conjuror of cheap tricks and illusions.

But my daughter trusted me.

And I loved her. More than any other person. She wasn't a weapon for me to wield against Aiden, to upturn his perfect world. She was *the* world – my world. She was everything.

There must be another explanation.

How did the police find the bunker? On their own? The snow was so thick, I really believed they might not find it. But they must have done. Only my parents knew about it – anyone else who was connected to it died long ago, its existence dying with them, one of those quirks of time passing. A buried piece of history. A relic of my childhood, lost alone in my imagination.

But you weren't always alone.

The room sways and I close my eyes. I straighten my back, and lean against the filthy wall, trying to process what my subconscious tried to tell me in the interview, trying to fully understand the memory that has clawed its way out of the dirt, gasping as it breaks through the surface to the world above.

I took Helen to the bunker. Just once – only a few days before I broke my leg and Dad closed it off for good. She didn't like it. She was always a bit of a princess, unwilling to dirty her dress, or ruffle her hair, which fell in ringlets back then. I never took her back. But she knew.

She told them where the bunker was. She told them about the affair.

And she must have told them about my journal. She knew about the hiding place: it wasn't concealed when we were little – the spare bed was against the other wall and we used the cupboard as a space to hide our secret treasures.

She must have suspected I wasn't telling the truth and told police about the bunker. Does she really believe I would kill Freya?

Unless . . .

Did Helen do this?

How could she have? The doors were locked, no sign of a break-in. And would she hurt Freya to punish me and Aiden? The Helen I knew – the Helen who was my best friend – would never be able to do something like that. But I also never believed she would begin a relationship with my estranged husband. Never believed she would betray me for him. But do we ever really know what a person is capable of?

I press my fists together and rest my chin on my hands, my open knuckles burning beneath the weight of my head, my thoughts racing.

Either Helen – once my oldest friend, my greatest confidante, Freya's stepmother – did this . . . or I did. Either Helen did this to get revenge, or I did it without even knowing.

But how can I find out what really happened? Will I ever know the truth?

Was it her?

Or me?

41

'Wake up. Your lawyer is here,' says a voice from the door.

I wasn't sleeping: my eyes were merely shut, the lids moving rapidly as the evidence against me – and her – ran like an old film on a projector against the black space behind my eyes. I roll onto my side and sit up. The officer is standing by the door, which has swung open, its metal spine exposed.

'Quickly now,' she says.

She leaves the door open behind me and moves ahead, turning her back as she squeezes past me, then down the tight corridor, and I shuffle behind her obediently. There are no windows, no indication of the possible time of day. Just the dim row of cells, and the reception area shining yellow with artificial light.

'What time is it?' I croak.

She flicks her wrist, forcing her sleeve to move up her arm to expose her watch. 'Just gone half past ten.'

Hours have passed. I couldn't tell, as I sat lost in my thoughts in the cell, whether minutes had ticked by or days. Sixty seconds equal a minute, sixty minutes equal an hour, twenty-four hours in a day. A week has passed since Freya died. Almost two hundred hours. So much . . . yet so little. If I close my eyes and reach out my hand, I can imagine her hair running through my fingers, her head against my stomach as she grips my legs in a hug. But it is also as if she was never here – only as a figment of my imagination, the memories already fracturing in my mind. They say time heals. But no amount of time will ever stitch together the gaping wound left by her loss. A thousand lifetimes could pass and I would still be left breathless at the realization that she is gone.

'Here you go,' says the officer, gruffly.

I have been following blindly, but she has led me into a small room, with a table big enough for two chairs, a petite woman, with cropped brown hair and slight features, like a pixie, sitting in one. She stands as I enter and holds out her hand.

'Naomi Williams?' She smiles, and I can't decide whether that is appropriate, or whether her face should remain sombre, passive.

'Yes.' I reach out and grip her hand, but her handshake takes me by surprise. It's limp, and there's no movement.

'I'm Olivia Poulter but, please, call me Olivia.'

'Hello.' I glance over my shoulder at the officer, who nods at Olivia and closes the door.

'Please, sit down. I know this must be frightening.' Her voice is very soft, and her tone is as if she is speaking to a child, a vulnerable one who needs to be coddled. I sit in the chair and watch as she laboriously lines up her notepad, pen and stack of papers in lines, perfectly parallel to the edge of the table.

'Right,' she says, her voice just louder than a whisper. 'I know you must be very concerned with what's happening, but I want to reassure you that I'm here on your behalf and it's my job to represent your interests as if they were my own.' Her words are like molasses as they trickle at a painfully slow rate from her mouth. I want to shake her, make her words fall loose faster, more freely, but I sit patiently, my fingers cking at the loose skin around my nails, which are bitten vn, short and ragged.

know what you said in interview and I've seen the

evidence they've shown you. Is there anything else you want to tell me about what happened?'

'I don't know . . . I don't know what else to say. I told them everything.'

Tell her about Helen.

'I –'

'You understand that I'm here for you and you alone,' she interrupts. 'You can tell me the truth.'

'The truth?'

She doesn't believe me.

'Yes.'

'You don't believe what I said?'

The words emerge as a whisper but I want to shout at her, reach across the table and grip her hands between mine, shake her shoulders and make her believe me. If I can't believe in me, I just need one person who will.

'I didn't say that, Naomi. But there are inconsistencies in your evidence and you have admitted to lying on multiple occasions, which may not reflect well on your capacity to tell the truth at trial. The prosecution will simply say, "If she lied about X, how can you believe her when she says Y?"'

'But it's the truth. It's what happened.'

'Now, I'm just playing devil's advocate here – that's something I have to do – but what if you were being honest in your interview, but your version of events isn't the truth? What if your version of events is just what you *believe* happened?'

'I don't understand,' I say.

I want her to say the words. I want her to look me in the eye and say the words.

What if it was me?

'I understand that you're pregnant,' she says, changing subject as she aimlessly flips through the file in front of

'Yes.'

'And when you suffered from severe anxiety disorder you felt anxious, paranoid?'

'Yes.'

'And when you were very sleep-deprived you suffered with hallucinations?'

I nod.

'Have you felt like that recently? Have you had any hallucinations?'

'I . . .'

She looks up from her notebook, her pen poised over the page, ready to document my confession. She narrows her eyes as the space between us expands – a canyon of quiet making her appear as if she is on the horizon of my vision, rather than two feet away, just across the table.

'Naomi?'

Can she use evidence of hallucinations against me? Can she represent me if she believes I'm guilty?

Do I have any say in this at all?

My hand, which is covering my mouth, begins to shake. I bring it down to my lap and bite my lip, forcing the bitter truth to stay in my mouth. But I said I would tell the truth – that I wouldn't lie. Couldn't lie.

'I've seen . . .'

'Yes?' She presses the tip of her pen onto the page, and a tiny dot of black ink stains the white paper.

'I've seen Freya. A few times. But I know she isn't real. I understand that she's dead.'

Dead. The word shatters as it collides with the floor.

Look at the pen. Just watch the pen as it glides across the page – don't think about Freya. Just concentrate on the ink it leaves its marks. Like footprints on snow, frozen in perpetuity.

'I'm not losing my mind,' I whisper.

'I don't think you are. And by their questioning, the police clearly don't think you are. Also, the FME who saw you when you first came in cleared you as fit to be interviewed. I have your mental-health assessment here.' She taps her pen against the file. 'You lied about your disorder, but he says here that, and I quote, "There is no evidence of suffering from a mental-health disorder that would result in her being unable to be interviewed".'

'Standard practice,' I mutter.

'It isn't standard practice to be mentally assessed, Naomi.' She shakes her head. 'They wanted to make sure you were fit to be interviewed so that anything you said would stand at trial. They also wanted to get you to dismiss the defence of having some kind of psychological breakdown. They asked you outright and you categorically said no, which ties into their story. Their version of events is that you did this on purpose. That this was a premeditated act to get revenge on your ex-husband for ending your affair. And that's the case they will run at trial.'

Her eyes widen, round and owl-like, as she waits for my response, but I don't say a word.

The facts don't lie. I had an affair with my ex-husband. He ended it and I blackmailed him into letting me have our daughter overnight. The next day she was dead and I lied about it. I hid her in a bunker that only I know about. I gave them the wrong clothes to mislead the dogs. I have scratches on my arms that I can't explain away as an innocent habit. I've neglected her before. And I've thought about hurting her before – my thoughts documented in black and white in my handwriting. But that isn't what happened. That isn't the trut'

It can't be.

'Now, what we need to think about isn't what their ca

but what your case is. If you get charged, what are you going to say in court? What is our case?'

I need to tell her about Helen. Her knowledge of the affair and the bunker. But what if she doesn't believe me? I can already tell – I can feel it pouring from her – that she thinks it was me. That I had some kind of mental collapse. That I snapped. Telling her about Helen will only make that worse. The crazed woman driven to murder by jealousy, blaming the new wife. And what if I'm wrong? What if – after all of this – it was actually me who did it?

'I don't know what I believe any more. I was so sure but . . .'

'But?'

'I'm so tired. And so sad. I just want this to all go away.'

'We can make this all go away, but you have to decide what you want to do.'

'So what can I do? Tell me what I should do.'

'I can tell you your options and there aren't many.' She holds up her hand, raising one immaculately manicured finger. 'One. You can plead guilty to the charge, which will be murder among others. That would mean a mandatory life sentence. But you say you didn't murder your daughter, which eliminates that.' She pauses, scanning my face.

'Two.' Another polished finger. 'You plead not guilty, tell your version of events to the jury, just as you told them in your interview, and hope that that gives them enough doubt that they can't convict you. Remember – the prosecution have to prove their case. You don't have to prove anything.'

A trial. I'll have to relive everything, recount the entirety f what I did to hide what happened, everything from my 't – my anxiety, my addiction, the times I failed as a her, over and over again – to a room full of strangers.

'I can't do that,' I say, as my chest tightens.

'Try to keep calm.' She reaches out to touch my arm. 'You don't need to decide yet.'

I look down, concentrating on the rise and fall of my chest, willing oxygen to fill my lungs. 'I can't admit something I can't remember.'

'But is it a possibility that your mind has simply blocked it out?'

'I don't know. I want to say no. But . . . I don't know. I can't be sure. So – yes, I suppose.'

'The FME noted in his report that you said a side effect of your sleeping tablets is that you sometimes forget periods of time?'

I nod.

'And you took a sleeping tablet the night it happened?'

'Yes.'

'Okay.' She inhales deeply and sighs, tapping her pen against the page. She hesitates for a moment, before looking me in the eye. What doesn't she want to say?

'The only other option is we try to prove manslaughter by diminished responsibility.'

'What does that mean?'

'That you did kill your daughter, but when you did so you were not in control of your actions. But that will be difficult as we have a mental-health assessment that says you are currently fine, and it's hard to prove your past mental state. Especially as in your interview you insisted there was no chance that you had suffered a mental breakdown.'

'If it goes to trial on a murder charge . . . do you think I'll be found guilty?'

'Jury trials are unpredictable. And, sadly, juries are ma of humans, and humans are predisposed to react emot ally to certain cases. And the police are building a s case. The scratches on you are one piece of the puzzle. You hid Freya's body. Add to that the fact that you lied to the police and deliberately misled them, and that there's no evidence of a break-in. Your version of events means that someone else has to have done it.'

Tell her about Helen.

'I –'

I can't. There's no evidence against her, nothing I can point at to show that she did this. There's nothing but my suspicions. And my suspicions count for nothing.

'If I go to prison . . . what will happen to the baby?'

She releases a breath slowly, as if she is preparing herself, or me, for the answer.

'That depends on the sentence. You would have to be released before the baby turned eighteen months old. If you get more than three years, it is likely they will take the baby away and put it with a foster carer. Unless there is another family member who can take parental responsibility.'

'I don't have any family members. No siblings. And my parents are dead.'

'The child's father? The police have said you have a partner . . . Rupert?'

'He isn't the father.'

'Oh.' She searches my face for the answer. I see the instant it clicks – it's all too visible on her face. 'How can you be sure?'

I meet her eyes across the table. 'The timings don't work.'

'Does he know?'

'I told him earlier . . . On the phone.'

The sound of his confused voice, tainted with sorrow, ⸱oes just behind my shoulder. As if he is there in the room, I am shattering his world all over again. My vision blurs ⸱ tears come. There's nothing left.

'And does Mr Williams know?'

'Yes.'

'And what does he think?'

'He was happy,' I mutter. 'But . . . I'm sure now he's just concerned. He'll want to make sure the baby is okay. That he can protect this one.' I close my eyes, and they flicker rapidly, the sensitive skin at the corners stinging so keenly it's as if it will tear away from itself, like tissue paper. 'I did all of this to keep my baby. The lies, the secrets, hiding Freya . . . I put myself through it because I was scared that if I told the truth I would lose them both. If I'm found guilty, whatever the charge is – murder, manslaughter – my baby will be taken from me. Right?'

I watch as her face transforms into a mask, tinged only with pity as she nods back at me.

'Yes – I'm so sorry, Naomi.'

'Please, don't be. The baby will be better off with Aiden anyway. It's my fault . . . I wanted this baby so much. And when I saw Freya at the bottom of those stairs, desperation just took over. Please . . .'

I falter as that begging word leaves my lips. I need to swallow, but the stone that has been sitting heavy in my stomach has risen to the back of my throat, and a sudden gust of anguish flurries up through my body. Olivia clutches my hands between hers, hushing me gently. 'It isn't over yet, Naomi.'

'But it is. Of course it is – no one will ever believe me.'

No one ever will. And I don't deserve to be believed. That's the true irony. I have submerged myself in lies. I am guilty of that. Guilty of being a bad mother, guilty of black mailing and neglecting and betraying. I did so much to le the police away from the truth and towards a lie. Te them she was missing. Giving them the wrong cl

Making sure to say that she was taken from outside because there would be no evidence of a break-in.

No evidence of a break-in.

No evidence of a break-in. Those words – said by both Jenning and Olivia – keep hovering just above the surface of my mind but I'm unable to reach out and grasp them. Grasp their significance. But they niggle away, like the voice of a toddler, repeating the same statement over and over until they are finally acknowledged.

There must be evidence of someone coming into the house. No evidence whatsoever . . . That would make sense for my lie – the alternative reality I created for everyone that she had been snatched from outside. And it would make sense if Freya's death was a tragic accident, a fall in the night. But it wasn't. Someone did this. And if it wasn't me, surely there would be evidence of that. A forced lock. A broken window-pane I'd missed. There was nothing.

It was me. It must have been.

Except . . .

'Bye, Namey!'

Helen's voice rings in my ears, childlike and sweet, and I watch as she is led down the drive by her parents, holding their hands on either side. She looks back at me as I wave goodbye. 'Love you!'

I gasp as I finally break through the surface, emerging from the darkness and into the light, the reason those words have been taunting me making sense at last.

There was no evidence of a break-in. But that doesn't mean it was me because . . .

I'm not the only one who has a key.

'Wait . . .'

sit up, poker-straight. Olivia – who until now has sat
ly, her eyes trained on my face – startles.

'What's wrong?' she asks, her voice hitching upwards even higher.

'You told me that for my defence to hold water, it has to have been someone else who killed Freya.'

'Yes, I did, but –'

'Helen has a key.'

'Pardon?'

'I need to speak to Detective Jenning.'

'Wait – Naomi. What do you mean, Helen has a key?' Olivia asks, leaning towards me.

'Ever since I moved into my own place, she's always had one. We were best friends, she came and went from mine and I did the same at hers. When we moved back to the farm, I gave her a key. I think I even mentioned it in my journal. When I found out she was with Aiden, she gave it back to me but I forgot about . . . I forgot about the key they gave her parents.'

'They?'

Olivia is watching me expectantly, her eyebrows raised high into her long fringe.

'My parents. They gave Helen's parents a key when we were little, just in case. She must have got it from them. She told the police I tried to take Freya from the wedding, she knew about my mental health, about where I had hidden the journal. She's the only other person who knew about the bunker. And she knew about the affair. Surely that's a motive. She killed Freya and now she's trying to make me look guilty.'

'Do you really think she's capable of doing something like that?'

'It was her. It must have been her . . . Because if it wasn' her, it was me. And it can't have been me. She was r baby.'

'I know you don't want to believe you did this, Naor

'Please,' I interrupt, reaching out to grasp her hand, imploring her to understand. 'Please. It must have been her.'

She scratches her eyebrow, her cheeks puffing out as she briefly holds her breath.

'Okay. I'll ask for someone to go and get him. And he will have to look into anything that could lead the investigation away from you.'

I nod furiously.

She stands quickly and pulls the door open.

'Excuse me, can we have an officer here, please?' she calls into the corridor.

She drums her fingers on the door frame as she turns at the sound of footsteps coming from the other direction.

'Yes?' a voice says from the other side of the door.

'Can we please speak to Detective Jenning? My client has some information she believes is important.'

'I'll go and get him. It'll be a few minutes – I think he's upstairs.'

I hear the person retreat back up the corridor and Olivia steps back into the room, closing the door behind her.

We wait, my eyes darting from her blank face to the clock on the wall, its hand juddering around its face.

Where is he? I need to speak to him. I need to convince him of what she has done. My words have condemned me. But maybe they can also absolve me. I just need him to listen.

My body jolts as the door swings open, as if an electric current has been plugged into my veins. I rush to my feet, the chair smacking against the back of my knees.

'Detective Jenning, I have something I need to tell –'

'Naomi,' Jenning says, holding out his hand, the gesture stopping me short. 'We have some more questions for you. Come with me, please.'

'My client has information for you that you are under a

313

duty to investigate. Information that points to a different person being involved in Freya's death,' Olivia says, her voice dripping with authority – her gentle attitude disappearing completely. 'What are your questions concerning?'

Jenning's eyes bore into me, his anger visible beneath the surface.

'New evidence.'

42

My eyes are drawn to Jenning's movements as he prepares the recorder on the table, his fingers moving stealthily over the buttons, but I flinch at the feeling of Olivia's hand pressing down firmly on my thigh under the table. Her fingers squeeze. My leg bounces up and down beneath her fingers, nervous energy spilling out of me. She looks at me sideways. Calm down, her eyes say silently. I force my legs into stillness, pressing the soles of my feet into the floor. But I begin to move my hands, picking at a ragged piece of skin on my index finger.

What have they found? What new evidence? What do they know?

Calm down, Naomi.

My body tenses at the long beep. Alerting the room that it's recording. Listening. Waiting for a confession.

What if my suspicions of Helen are just further acts of denial? My mind simply refusing to accept what it has done.

I breathe in sharply as I pull more skin loose and watch as a drop of blood pools around my cuticle.

'Interview of Naomi Williams commenced at eleven seventeen a.m. My name is Detective Sergeant Jenning and I am accompanied by Detective Constable Walker. Also present is Olivia Poulter, Ms Williams's solicitor, who has been instructed since the last interview was terminated at six twenty-three a.m.'

Olivia crosses her legs, her pen poised over her notebook he waits for Jenning to begin.

'You don't have to answer any of the questions, Naomi,' she had said, after Jenning had come to get me. She had ushered him outside, saying she needed some time with her client. I balked. I am somebody's client. 'We don't know what evidence they've found so my advice to you is to say, "No comment." If they ask you a question that goes against your version of events, don't argue with them or try to give an explanation, just stay quiet. "No comment." Understand?'

I had nodded at her. But what if they tell me something that clicks the pieces into place? What if the wall collapses and everything comes rushing forward?

'Naomi.'

The room comes into sharp focus. Jenning is leaning towards me, his forearms pressing into the table, closing the space between us. His eyes are red. Exhaustion doesn't suit him.

'I'm sorry,' I whisper. 'I didn't hear the question.'

How many times have I done that now? Disappeared into the far recesses of my mind only to be jolted out by an intruder to find that I have missed a whole segment of my life. What if that's what happened?

'I asked you to tell me about your relationship with Mr Williams's wife. Helen.'

It was her.

Olivia switches legs, this time the right crossing over the left, and my eyes dart sideways to meet hers. She nods.

'She was my best friend. Ever since we were little.'

'But now she is married to your ex-husband.'

'Yes.'

'And what do you know about her relationship with Freya'

Her relationship with Freya. Cold fingers trace their v up my spine, the hairs on the back of my neck standir attention. Warning me. She betrayed me once. And now she has done this. How didn't I see it? How did I not realize?

'She did this, didn't she?' I say. The taste of metal hits the back of my throat, dull and tinny. Another nose-bleed. I press my knuckle to my nostril, but my finger is not tinged with red.

'I'm asking the questions, Naomi,' Jenning says, as he sniffs loudly, then lets out a loud sigh. 'What kind of relationship did Helen have with Freya?'

'They lived in the same house. Freya used to talk about her quite a lot. She liked her. But I can't tell you what kind of relationship they had . . . I wasn't there. You should ask Aiden. Or Helen.'

He leans back in his chair and I watch the muscles in his cheeks move as he tenses his jaw. As if he is swilling liquid around his mouth, mulling over his next question, unsure of what to ask. Or simply pausing for effect.

'You believe that Helen did this?'

'Yes.'

'Because of the affair?'

'Yes.'

He smiles – no, not a smile, a smirk. Wonky and wry. Like he is withholding his own secret.

'What makes you think that?'

'Because I know Helen. And she was willing to betray me to have Aiden for herself. She wouldn't have liked me taking him back.'

'She could have just stayed. Swept it under the carpet like so many people do. She loves him, doesn't she?'

'She –'

Olivia interrupts me, holding her hand in front of me, like a parent stopping a child launching themselves into a busy

'Excuse me, but how is my client meant to answer

questions about the feelings and thoughts of another person? And what relevance does this have to the investigation of murder? If you could please make whatever disclosure you have, or I will be advising my client to go no comment.' She looks at me sternly.

'It's relevant, Ms Poulter, and the disclosure is forthcoming. And it's up to your client whether she goes no comment, and seeing as she's been so open to asking questions so far, she may wish to continue to do so. Naomi – it's up to you whether you answer this question, okay? Do you think Helen would stay with Aiden because she loves him?'

'She's stubborn. And proud. Wilful. I don't think she would just stay.'

'Would you?'

'Me?'

'After everything you've been through, you continued to have an affair with your ex-husband. Would you stay with him? Through anything?'

'Don't answer that, Naomi,' Olivia says, her voice low and sharp.

My eyes flicker back and forth from Olivia to Jenning. Her face is grave, instructing me to remain quiet. His – open and eyebrows raised – is willing me to answer.

'Yes. I love him. I'd do anything for him.'

He begins to write, and I can see my words hanging upside down – my declaration of love suspended on the page. *Anything*. He finishes and fixes his gaze on me, the smirk of a few moments ago ironed out into a straight-set grimace. That look sends another gust of cold up my spine.

'What explanation did Aiden give you for being in the house that night?'

I pause, my mind whirring.

'Aiden? For being in the house? I don't understand .

'Why did you lie for him?'

I shake my head, my hands covering my mouth. I turn my eyes to Olivia and she tilts her head and nods.

'No comment.'

Please, no.

'What did he say to you to explain what had happened? What did he tell you to get you to lie for him?'

I close my eyes tightly, but tears drip down my face and roll off my chin onto my hands.

'No comment.'

Please. Anything but this . . .

Jenning opens his file and passes Olivia a piece of paper. She bites her lip as her eyes scan the information, but then she settles on something and her gaze becomes still. Her brow furrows but she doesn't look up from the page. She simply places it on the table in front of me.

Jenning raises his eyebrows and I stare back at him, my eyes and cheeks burning.

'Did you help Aiden hide the death of your daughter?'

On the paper are flight details. Two seats booked from London Gatwick to Abu Dhabi on 20 November at 5:40 a.m.

The passengers: Freya and Aiden Williams.

I look up from the page, my eyes darting from Jenning to Walker searching for an explanation. They stare back at me, waiting for my response.

'I don't underst—'

Flights booked for Freya and Aiden. No evidence of a break-in. Helen has a key.

No. It can't be.

He was trying to take her away.

43

No.

No, no, no, no, no.

My head is shaking from side to side, left to right, left to right, and my teeth chatter as if the room's temperature has plummeted. I have lost control of my body. I've lost control of my mind. I must have done, because the words on the page cannot be true. The words coming out of Jenning's mouth, slow and gruff – Aiden has been arrested – cannot be true.

There was no evidence of a break-in. And his wife has a key.

No.

Why would he do this? Why would he want to take her away from me? Was he going to leave and never come back?

There must be an explanation. He couldn't do something like this. He would never hurt her. He loved her. A love that was so pure he left me – the person he cared about most in the world – to protect her. It can't have been Aiden.

Not my Aiden.

'Did you know that Aiden was trying to take Freya away?' Jenning says.

What did he say? All movement comes to a halt – my body hitting the brakes.

They still think I'm guilty.

'Did I know?' I mutter, the words sounding foreign and strange.

'Were you trying to stop him taking her and somethi͙ went wrong?'

'No!'

'Were you helping each other when you hid Freya?'

'No! I told you – I've told the truth. I've been telling the truth this whole time.'

I *have* been telling the truth, and I almost believed – they almost made me believe – that I had done this. If it hadn't been for Helen – the affair, the bunker, the key – I would have been sure it was me. I would have crumbled. Broken. Aiden has known the truth this whole time.

How could he do this?

'You say you've told the truth. And we've never doubted you hid Freya, that you lied about her being missing, gave us false evidence to lead us away from what you had done. But the part we doubt is the why.'

'Why would Aiden do this?' The words splutter out of me – half cry, half cough.

'We're not asking about Aiden. We're asking about you. What happened that night? Why did you hide Freya?'

A rush of blood floods my face. In his eyes I am stained with guilt, and nothing I say, no evidence to the contrary, can wash away that stain. I am the jealousy-fuelled ex-wife with a history of mental-health problems. And not just any mental-health problems. Post-natal. The kind that is covered in the papers when a mother kills their child. The kind that isn't talked about. The kind that leaves a mark. The stain. This man will never believe me.

'I've told you,' I start to speak slowly, but my heart is racing and my words begin to gallop towards him, furious and quick. 'I didn't want to lose my baby. I knew, I just knew, that if I told the truth, that I'd found her at the bottom of the stairs, everyone would believe I had done it. And the baby would be taken away. And look! You've proved my point. ou thought I was guilty. And even now, when you have the evidence that someone else was involved, you still don't believe what I've told you. If Aiden got into my house to take my daughter away from me, why the fuck would I lie for him?'

We lock eyes. Two battering rams standing their ground. I refuse to look away.

I can't let him win.

Olivia places her hand on my back, her palm firm between my shoulder blades. I had forgotten she was there, but I look at her now and know what she wants me to do. She doesn't need to say it. It's what she has wanted me to do all along. Just one glance and it's as if she is screaming the words in my ears.

Keep your mouth shut.

'Did you see Aiden at your house in the early hours of the twentieth of November?'

'No.'

I can feel Olivia's eyes on me, her gaze fixed to the side of my face.

'What reason did he give you for being in the house?'

'I –'

Olivia's hand shifts to my shoulder and squeezes.

'No comment,' I whisper.

'Was there a struggle?'

'No. No comment.'

'Did you hide Freya together?'

'No comment.'

'Did Aiden ask you to help him hide Freya?'

I lick my lips, anger seething through me. 'No comment.'

'When he asked you to help him, why didn't you call the police?'

'No comment.'

'Why did you lie for him?'

'No comment.'

'Was it because you love him?'

'No comment.'

'Because you wanted him back?'

'No comment.'

'Because this would be your secret?'

'Stop it, stop it, stop it!' I scream.

Silence engulfs the room. I can feel the tingle of all of their eyes on me, waiting for me to do something. Say something.

I look up and around at the three of them before meeting Jenning's eye.

Say something.

'I'm sorry,' I whisper, even though it is a lie. 'But please don't ask me any more questions. I don't know anything else except . . .'

'Except?' Jenning says, as Olivia sighs. I must be her most disappointing client yet.

'I didn't help Aiden. If I'd known about this, I would have told the truth. But . . . he would never hurt her on purpose. There must be some explanation . . . Are you questioning Helen?'

'Helen was not involved, Naomi,' he retorts. 'Think about what you're saying. There was no ticket booked for her. And –'

'But she knew about the affair, she was angry. What if she did this and she's trying to get the blame put on me and Aiden –'

'It was Aiden who told us about the affair.'

What?

'But . . . but she knew about the bunker. That's how you found Freya.'

'No –'

'Detective Jenning,' Olivia interrupts. 'I'm already minded to report you for the aggressive and leading manner of your questioning. If you have disclosures to make, I'll need to see the evidence.'

'No, she didn't tell us,' Jenning continues, ignoring Olivia completely, his eyes fixed on me. 'A dog had strongly signalled near the area but there was no other evidence. However, a third party then gave us intelligence about the bunker and we decided to excavate the area.'

A third party?

The volunteers. Those two women who knew about the house.

Jenning sighs and reaches up to rub the back of his neck, before jolting it swiftly to one side. It clicks. 'Helen hasn't given us evidence against you, Naomi. She's given us evidence against Aiden. She is why he's been arrested.'

My brain stalls, unable to process the information. Helen has given the police evidence against Aiden?

'Helen hasn't been giving you evidence against me?'

'No. She's the one who found out about the flights. She found a payment and looked into it. And she's also told us that Aiden kept a spare key to your house, and it's missing.'

'Aiden kept a key to my house?'

'Yes. Police are searching their house and Aiden's room at the Queen's Arms. I want you to listen carefully to what I'm about to tell you.'

My mind is swimming, Jenning's voice small and echoing, like he is speaking to me from the bottom of a gorge.

Aiden kept a key, Aiden kept a key, Aiden kept a –

'It's Aiden who has been giving us evidence against you.'

These words hit me aggressively, his voice suddenly loud and distinct, his message a punch to the chest.

Aiden?

I close my eyes as Jenning carries on speaking and the many fragments of my shattered heart splinter.

'He's been giving the police evidence from the moment you were arrested. He told us about the affair. He told us about the wedding. He helped us find your journal and told us about why he left. He's in an interview room right now, and his story is that he booked the flights but changed his mind. That he has no idea where the key is, that he lost it a long time ago. He's still trying to blame you. And without more evidence, we don't have anything else against him. So if you helped him hide Freya, you need to tell us. Stop trying to protect him and tell us what you know.'

He's still trying to blame you.

How could I be so stupid? So blind? He told them everything.

'I – I don't know what else I can say. I didn't do anything,' I cry. 'I don't know anything about what Aiden did. I wish I could tell you I saw him that night but I was sleeping. I swear.'

Why would he do this? Would he make me look guilty to save himself – is it as simple as that? Self-preservation is a human instinct. But so is love . . . Isn't it?

I look at Jenning, and beyond the anger, his eyes are awash with some kind of sadness. Pity, maybe. But looks can be deceiving. And we have all been deceived.

But who will they believe?

Aiden? Or me?

The sound of a knock jolts through the room.

'Sergeant? There's something you should see.' The voice of an officer leaks in through the small gap in the door.

'What is it?' Jenning says, sticking his head out.

I strain to hear – to pick out words from their mutterings – but the officer's whispers are quiet. Gasps in a roaring ocean.

'You stay here.'

The door clicks shut behind him.

I close my eyes and my head rolls backwards, my neck aching with the weight.

How could he do this? And how could he hurt her?

The image of Aiden cradling Freya against his chest creeps across my vision. Her tiny body just small enough for him to hold her with one hand. His skin white against her pink cheek. I can hear her giggling as he chases her around the kitchen, speeding up until her unsteady toddle destabilizes her and she lands with a soft plop on her nappy. I can see the ferocious look in his eyes as he tells me he'll always want her to have a relationship with her mother, but if he has to protect her, he will. He only ever wanted to look after her. And he did – he went over and above, more than most fathers ever have to.

I open my eyes and blink against the harsh light. The blank white ceiling is suspended above me, a patch of damp invading the room from the corner, its dark brown fingers spreading inwards. Like Aiden's hands wrapped around our daughter's wrists.

44

The door clicks open. I look up at the clock on the wall – over an hour has passed in that room. One small room, and an hour's worth of silence.

I sit up quickly, my body alert with a rush of adrenalin, but it isn't Jenning entering the room, his gait purposeful and assured. Or Walker. It is Kate. Kate – with her warm eyes and slow, careful approach.

What is she doing here? Where's Jenning?

Kate moves to the place opposite me. She is holding several loose sheets of paper, and as she sits down, her eyes are as kind as ever, but her hands . . . Her hands are shaking.

'Hi, Naomi,' she says. Her voice is soft, just those two simple words imbued with such understanding. But what is she doing here?

'Where's Jenning?'

'I –'

'You haven't turned on the recorder,' Olivia interrupts, turning her head purposefully towards it, her eyebrows raised.

Kate breathes in slowly through her nose. Her mouth twitches.

What is on those pages?

'Ms Poulter, apologies for not introducing myself straight away. I am DC Kate Bracken and I've been the family liaison officer for Naomi and Mr Williams.' She leans across the able to Olivia, her hand extended.

Olivia grasps it and shakes it, with far more power than

when she first shook mine. 'Pleasure,' Olivia says. 'I'd appreciate if you could update us on what is happening. DS Jenning left the room quite abruptly and hasn't returned.'

'I understand. And if you don't mind, I'll talk to Naomi directly.'

Olivia nods, her eyes darting back and forth between us. Kate turns to face me, and places her clasped hands in the centre of the table, inches from my own.

'Naomi, I need you to understand that I'm not interviewing you. I'm here as your family liaison officer. I'm here to talk to you as Freya's mother. Not as a suspect.'

My breathing is shallow and slow, and the room shifts out of balance.

Not as a suspect?

I focus on Kate, on her warm, sad eyes. She reaches across the table and rests her hand on mine.

'Sergeant Jenning told you that Helen said Aiden kept a spare key to your house,' she says.

'Yes.'

'A team was sent to search his house in London but officers were also sent to search his room at the Queen's Arms.'

I hold my breath. I want to force the words out of her quickly – I need to hear her say it – but I also want to close my ears or clamp my hand over her mouth. Just a few more moments when I can pretend there has been some kind of mistake.

'Officers at the Queen's Arms found the key in the glove compartment of Aiden's car. We asked him about it in interview and –'

'What has he said?' Anger churns in my stomach as I imagine his countless ways of explaining the key's presence. Countless ways of turning the blame against me.

'He confessed, Naomi.'

'Confessed?'

'Aiden's been charged.'

'With what?' I say, my voice loud – almost a shout.

'Manslaughter.'

Manslaughter?

But she was a little girl. Just a little girl.

'Please, no,' I cry.

'I'm sorry, Naomi.'

'I thought there must have been some mistake, some explanation –'

'I know.'

'I feel sick –'

I stand up, and my chair falls backwards behind me, hitting the floor with a metallic clang. I lift my hands to the base of my throat –

I can't breathe, I feel sick, I need air.

My breath is trapped in my chest – a butterfly in a bell jar, beating its gossamer wings, desperate to escape. The sound of my frantic gasps is dulled as I double over and sink to the floor.

Kate kneels in front of me, her face close to mine. 'Breathe, Naomi,' she says, as she takes my hand. 'I'm so sorry, but you need to know what happened that night.'

Kate is a blur, the bright white lights illuminating her from behind, but I lock onto her face.

Breathe, Naomi. Focus on what she is saying. Breathe.

'Naomi, are you okay?' Olivia asks, her hand on my shoulder. 'Do you need to see a doctor?'

'No! I need to know what happened.' I search Kate's face for the answers. I need answers. 'What happened?'

'Naomi, listen,' Kate says. 'There's something we want to how you. It's somewhat unorthodox, and might be criti-zed but I – at least – think you deserve to see it.'

'What are you going to show her?' Olivia asks, her voice tinged with concern.

Kate's eyes don't leave my face as she responds. 'Footage of Aiden's interview,' she says.

'She shouldn't be seeing that,' Olivia says, shaking her head, her top teeth peeking out of her open mouth.

Kate lets go of my hands and retrieves the sheets of paper from the seat behind her and sets them in front of Olivia, pointing at the signatures on the page, her index finger almost white from the pressure.

'Aiden and his solicitor have both signed statements of consent for this footage to be shown to Naomi. And his solicitor will sit with us when we show you.' She turns away from Olivia, and the stern sheen covering her eyes disappears, revealing her usual gleam of caring. 'Aiden wanted to talk to you himself – he begged us to let him explain to you face to face – but, of course, that isn't allowed.'

'Why? Why did he do this?'

'Come with me. It'll be the easiest way for you to understand what actually happened. And why. I'm so sorry, Naomi.'

Pity pours from her in a flood. No one should feel sorry for me. No one should pity me. Pity for the woman who was so in love that she couldn't see, couldn't hear, or even feel, how terribly wrong everything had gone. Sadness for the mother who has lost even more than she could ever have realized.

I want to stand, to go with her, but I can't get my legs to take my weight. I want to move but my body won't listen.

Manslaughter, manslaughter, manslaughter.

'I just need a second,' I say.

'Do you want me to stay with you or would you rather be alone?'

'Alone, please. Sorry.'

'Don't apologize,' she says, as she stands and leaves.

I try to look at the statements but the words – too small to read from where they lie in the centre of the table – swim across the page. All I can make out is Aiden's signature: the large swirling A, followed by the inscrutable 'Williams' beside it.

Olivia places her hand on my knee. 'Are you all right?'

'I need some water. I feel a bit dizzy.'

She rushes to her bag in the corner of the room, then thrusts a bottle into my hands. I scrabble with the lid, my hands not doing what they're supposed to do. I can't even open a fucking bottle.

'Here, let me.' She opens it and hands it back to me. I gulp, even though the water is lukewarm and stale. The bottle crackles as I suck all the air out of it, and the plastic crumples in my hands. I pull my mouth away and gasp.

'Better?'

'Yes. Thank you.'

'Of course. Are you ready?'

'Just one more minute.'

I want to wait. Just a few more minutes in this space and time where I have not been told the whole truth. Where the words he has said in his interview have no power over me. Before my life – once again – transforms.

I close my eyes and see his face. His green eyes. That knowing smile.

My body floods with emotion, but instead of an intricate cobweb of different feelings, there is only one. Unadulterated. Not sadness. Not fondness. Not even love.

My body is seething with anger.

Roaring with rage.

I want to scream. I want to kick holes in the walls of this room, overturn the table and throw down the chairs. If he is still here, in a cell in this building, I want him to know. I want him to hear what he has done.

But my anger is overcome by one thought. *Freya. I need to know. I need to know what he did to you.*

'Can you come with me?' I ask.

'Of course,' Olivia says, as if it is her choice, not her job.

Only a number of hours ago I couldn't stand this woman and her slow, condescending voice. But now she is all I have. Just her. And, for once, I need her to treat me like a child. I need her to wrap me in cotton wool and be there when I hear the truth. Because, however painful this will be, I need to know.

Aiden's face is paused on the screen.

'Are you ready?' Kate asks.

I nod, not taking my eyes off his face. They are stinging, my eyes watering in their desperation to blink, but then the image judders to life. He shifts in his seat and rolls his neck in a wide circle, his hair touching the base, then his chin touching the top of his chest. If the sound was clearer, I'd be able to hear the bones clicking. This is my Aiden. The Aiden I have known for so long. And so well. But . . . I don't know him at all.

'I don't think I can do this.'

Kate taps the keyboard and the image pauses again, Aiden's chin still dropped to his chest.

'You can,' she says. 'You need to hear what he has to say.'

I look up at the ceiling, hold my breath and then release, like I was taught. I lower my gaze and glance at Aiden's solicitor, who is sitting several seats away on my right: he has a notebook on his lap and a pen gripped between his fingers, but his eyes are closed, his expression pained. Turning m head, I avoid the screen until the very last moment. But then there it is. Aiden's face.

'I'm ready.'

Kate taps again, and Aiden rolls his neck in a circle.

'Aiden,' the voice of a disembodied police officer says, out of sight of the camera, although I can see her leg. 'We are recommencing your interview at eleven twenty-two a.m. I am Detective Constable Lauren Sharp and I am accompanied by Detective Sergeant Andrew Webb. We have some further questions to ask you. Are you happy to continue?'

'Yes.' He crosses his arms and sits up straight, fully occupying his space.

'Aiden, you previously stated that you booked the flights for the twentieth of November, but very quickly realized that it was a bad idea and you shouldn't do it. Is that correct?'

'Yes.'

'And that's why you deleted all the evidence of the booking.'

'Yes . . . I know it looks wrong, but I swear, as soon as I'd done it, I changed my mind.'

'If you had gone through with it, how were you planning on getting Freya?'

'Like I said, I didn't think it through. It was a stupid mistake.'

'Did you have any way of getting into Naomi Williams's house?'

Aiden lifts his hand to his jaw, fingers partially covering his mouth. 'No,' he says, voice confident and assured.

'Are you sure?'

'Yes. I had no intention of actually getting those flights. That's why I deleted the booking. It was an impulsive action because I was angry. That's all.'

He is utterly convincing.

A hand slides across the table and places a piece of paper in front of him. I squint at the screen, trying to make out the image, but I can't see it.

'Aiden, take a look at this.'

Aiden gawps at the photo, lifting it from the table so that it is close to his face. His hands are shaking.

'The pathologist has taken a more in-depth look at the bruises on Freya's face since her first report. At first the report simply noted the bruising, but didn't give any detail about the hand that caused it or any other details. However, we now know that whoever did this is most likely left-handed and grabbed Freya's face from the front. We know this because the hand is flipped – the thumbmark is at the bottom. Do you see that?'

I bite down on the inside of my bottom lip as my teeth begin to chatter.

'I . . .' His words disappear, but he nods.

'Did you do this to your daughter, Aiden?'

He stares agape, still looking at the image, the paper trembling in his hands.

'No comment.'

'No comment? Are you sure?'

'No, I . . . I didn't do that.'

'Are you left- or right-handed, Aiden?'

Aiden looks across to his solicitor, his eyes round and startled.

'No comment.'

'It's an easy question to answer. Are you left-handed, or right?'

Aiden is left-handed.

'Left. But I didn't do that.'

'So who did? Naomi?'

'I don't . . . No comment.'

'She's right-handed, isn't she?'

'No comment.'

A hand reaches across and takes the photo from Aiden. After a moment, another evidence bag is placed on the table.

I gasp, lifting my hand to my mouth as I take in the bag's contents.

Mouse. Freya's favourite toy.

'Do you know what that is, Aiden?'

Aiden's face has fallen, his jaw tight and clenched. He reaches out to touch the bag, but withdraws his fingers the moment they graze the plastic, as if it has burned him.

'Aiden?' the officer repeats. 'What is that?'

'It's . . . it's Mouse,' he whispers. 'Freya's toy.'

'Mouse was with Freya's body when we found her. Naomi admits taking Mouse with Freya's body to the bunker. When was the last time you saw this toy?'

Aiden's mouth quivers.

'I – I don't know.'

'Did Freya have Mouse with her when she died?'

'I don't know.'

There is a pause. Aiden sniffs repeatedly, his breathing loud in the silence.

'This morning we interviewed your wife.'

Aiden falls silent and still, his eyebrows raised. Did he know then? Did he know what she had done? Or did he never suspect that she would turn away from him?

'She told us that you kept a spare key to Naomi Williams's house. Just in case. And we searched through your belongings at the Queen's Arms, including your car, and found . . .' an evidence bag is placed in front of Aiden '. . . this.'

Aiden looks down at the bag, then back at the officer, his ow furrowed.

'What is that, Aiden?'

'A . . . a key.'

'Whose key is that?'

'I . . . I don't know,' he says, feigning confidence, but his voice breaks.

'Well, we checked, and it's a key to your ex-wife's house. A key you just told us didn't exist. Why did you lie about having a key to Naomi's house?'

'I . . . I didn't,' he mutters.

'Are you sure? This is your chance to give us an explanation for why you lied.'

Aiden's eyes dart off-camera.

'No comment.'

'This key was in your glove compartment. Did you hide it there after going into the house?'

'I . . . I . . . No.'

'Did you let yourself in using this key?'

'No, please, listen to me –'

'Did you hurt Freya?'

Aiden doesn't answer but covers his face with his hands as he lets free a juddering cry.

'Aiden, did you –'

'I can't do this.'

'You can't do what?'

'I'm sorry.'

'Why are you sorry, Aiden? Did you hurt Freya?'

'I didn't mean to!'

The room falls silent. Aiden leans backwards and stares up at the ceiling, his eyes wide and full of anguish, as cries rack his body.

'Can I have a moment with my client?' his solicitor asks.

'Of course.'

The screen turns black.

'What's happ–'

Kate nods and directs her gaze towards the screen. It judders back to life and Aiden is in the same seat, in the same clothes, the same ungroomed hair and stubble but – he is changed.

Aiden lowers his right hand from his mouth and begins to chew the skin on his left thumb. I can feel his nerves, his anxiety, through the screen. His eyes are puffy and red, but his mouth is set in a straight, resolute line. He holds his hands together on his lap. The room on the screen and the room I am in overflow with silence. Two rooms waiting with bated breath.

'It is eleven fifty-four a.m.,' the officer says, her voice low in anticipation. 'Aiden Williams, your legal representative has told us that you wish to give a full account of what happened in the early hours of the twentieth of November. Is that correct?'

'Yes,' Aiden whispers.

'Go ahead.'

'In August, Naomi and I began an affair . . .' He stops speaking.

'Carry on,' says the voice of the officer.

'In September, I received a job offer in the UAE. I said I wanted to go but my wife said we couldn't. She said we couldn't leave because of Naomi, and that Freya needed to see her mum. That she couldn't do that to Naomi. I brought it up in conversation with Naomi once, nothing specific, just asked how would she feel if we had to move abroad for my work, just to gauge how she would react and . . . she didn't react well.'

I didn't. And he promised me he would never take her away.

'In October I decided to end the affair. I knew that we ̄eded to get away from Naomi, and get away from everything that had happened. So, I ended it and tried again to convince Helen that we should leave and go to the UAE.'

'When you say, "that we should leave", you mean leave without telling anyone?'

'Yes.'

'You understand that what you planned on doing is a criminal offence?'

'Yes . . .' He pinches his nose, his eyes screwed shut.

'And what did your wife say?'

'She said, no way. She couldn't do that to Naomi.'

Helen refused to take Freya away.

'You and Naomi had an affair,' the officer says, continuing her questions. 'And this wasn't a stranger. She used to be your wife. There must have been some feelings involved. So why did you choose to end the affair and try to convince Helen to leave with you rather than staying with Naomi?'

Aiden sits up in his chair, straightening his back, which until now has been curled over, as if heavy weights were bearing down on his shoulders.

'Naomi's and my relationship has been complicated. It only ended because I felt like I had to protect Freya. It wasn't because I stopped loving her. And the affair . . . it was wrong. I know it was wrong, but no matter what has happened between us, it's been hard to distinguish between the Naomi that I despise and the woman I fell in love with. But Helen . . . Helen has been there. She was there for me and she was there for Freya. She looked after Freya every day. She was the constant in both our lives. I couldn't leave her for a woman like Naomi. I love Naomi, but I would never be able to trust her again. So I did what I thought I had to do to keep my family together. Me, Freya and Helen.'

His family.

In his eyes, his family does not include me. But whe

338

told him about the baby, he seemed happy. Hopeful. Was that real? Had his feelings changed? Or was he acting? Did he actually love me again? Or was it his way of controlling me – making sure I believed he would never betray me? Making sure I would protect him.

'Let's move on,' the officer says. 'What happened leading up to the twentieth of November?'

'At the end of October, I ended the affair. I should have ended it earlier but, like I said, it's complicated with me and Naomi. She took it better than I thought she would. You know, I thought . . . I thought she would get angry. Cry. But after that she just went quiet. I didn't hear from her at all. We didn't speak when I dropped Freya off. And then on the eighteenth she asked me if she could have Freya overnight the following day. When I said no, she said she would tell Helen about the affair if I didn't let her. So I said yes.'

'Then what happened?'

'I went home and Helen was packing her bags to go to an overnight work event. I tried to speak to her about going away but we got into an argument. She told me she didn't want to speak about it again and she left.'

'So what did you do?'

'I . . .' Aiden lifts his hand and pulls on his bottom lip, then wipes his eyes with the back of his hand. 'I decided to leave without Helen. I got angry that she didn't understand, and angry that Naomi had backed me into a corner. I felt trapped . . . So I decided I would take Freya and leave.'

'Is that when you booked the tickets?'

He nods, sniffing loudly.

'Helen was away that night so I booked the tickets for a ~ht in the early hours. Then I got my copy of the key to mi's house. The one I kept after we separated. I thought about calling Naomi and making an excuse to collect Freya, but I was afraid of what Naomi might do.'

He lowers his head and pulls on his wedding band, sliding it on and off his finger.

He was going to leave Helen. He was going to leave us both – take Freya, and run.

'Carry on,' the officer says, jolting Aiden out of his thoughts as he firmly pushes his ring back onto his finger. 'What happened that night?'

'At just gone one in the morning on the twentieth, I got to Naomi's house.'

I'm going to be sick.

I close my eyes, but as I do, the house appears, whirring and juddering into life.

'I entered the house at around one fifteen. I knew that Naomi would be sleeping. But I checked her sleeping tablets to make sure.'

'Then what did you do?'

'I went from the bathroom to Freya's room. I thought I'd just wake her gently and tell her she needed to be quiet and we had to go, but . . .'

His voice breaks and I open my eyes. He is hanging his head, his shoulders shaking as he begins to cry.

'But?'

'But that isn't what happened.'

I squeeze my eyes shut again. I don't want to hear what happened. I don't want to imagine what happened. But Freya's bedroom emerges once again, materializing in the darkness.

'Freya woke up quite suddenly. She's afraid of the dark and petrified of strangers. She didn't know who I was. She was scared. She tried to shuffle away from me but I reached to try to comfort her.'

He stops again and I open one eye to squint at the screen. His hand is raised to his face, pinching his nose, as he takes deep breaths in and out. Trying to regain control.

'Do you need some time?' the officer asks him.

'No. I need to do this now.'

'Okay. So – slowly take us through what happened next.'

'She panicked and ran. She tripped on the rug and then ran onto the landing. I tried to pull her back. She was running towards Naomi's room so I tried to grab her and she lashed out. She dug her nails into my wrists. She was thrashing about, scratching as hard as she could, so I held onto both of her wrists. I didn't realize I was hurting her . . .'

Bracelets of purple bruises snaking around both of her tiny wrists – I'll never forget that image.

'I kept on saying, "It's Daddy, it's Daddy", but she began to scream. She was frightened, she's always been so frightened of everything. Ever since she was little. I tried to pull her towards me so she could see my face but she wouldn't stop screaming. So . . .' He shields his face with both hands, his head shaking from side to side.

'So?'

'I covered her mouth. I tried to calm her down but she just wouldn't stop struggling. I shook her. Just once – I didn't mean to be rough, I've never been rough with her, but I was so scared of Naomi waking up. I told her to stop it, but she wouldn't listen. But when I shook her, her head hit the corner of the banister. And then she threw her weight backwards to try to get away from me and I . . .'

His head collapses into his hands and his shoulders are shaking as a low, shuddering cry comes from deep within 'm.

'And I let go. I didn't realize how close we were to the top he stairs. And she just tumbled down them, over and over again. She just kept going down, down, down, until she hit the bottom.'

He stops speaking, and the officer remains silent. All that can be heard is the slight static of the camera, as its ever-seeing eye captures this confession.

Aiden sits back in his chair, and his face is pale, tears visible even on camera.

'I think I went into shock. I remember thinking, She's okay, I'll get her rucksack and Mouse, then pick her up and we can go. I don't remember what I did with her bag. I think I picked it up and dropped it. My hands just . . . wouldn't stop shaking.'

He closes his eyes and I can almost see what he's seeing, the same image I'm confronted with every time I close my eyes. Freya at the foot of the stairs.

'When I got to her, I tried to wake her up. I tried but . . . she was gone. I knew straight away and . . . I just panicked. I didn't know what to do. I dropped Mouse and ran. I'm so sorry.'

He left her.

'And you hid the key in the glove compartment?'

'I . . .' His eyes are darting from left to right. 'I thought I put it back in the house, in the drawer. I was sure . . . But I wasn't thinking. I must have panicked and put it in the car.'

'What did you think would happen when Naomi woke up?'

'That she'd think Freya had woken up in the night and fallen. I thought she'd call me or an ambulance or the police. When she phoned, that's what I thought she was going to say. I never expected her to lie. And then it was too late. I had to lie too.'

'Why did you give us information that would support th⌐ investigation's suspicions that Naomi killed Freya?'

I look at the screen. He shakes his head, pulls at his co⌐

I do not blink. I do not allow my gaze to veer away from his face but watch intently, waiting for his excuses. Why did he do this? Why did he try to blame me?

'The baby,' he whispers. 'Just before the police arrived at the house to arrest Naomi, she told me she was pregnant. And the baby was mine. I love Naomi – I do. I told her I did, and that was the truth. But I don't trust her. And once I knew that Freya had been found, I thought it would be better . . . I thought it would be better for her to be blamed and for me to have the baby.'

He leans forward, his head in his hands, and descends into sobs. As he rocks back and forth, he cries out the same two words, over and over again.

I'm sorry.

45

Kate pushes a button on the keyboard and the screen turns black. I stand, pushing myself to my feet, my nails scratching at the worn metal of the table.

'Naomi?' Olivia says. 'Maybe you should stay seated.'

'I just need to move,' I say. The sound of my voice surprises me. It is quiet, calm.

I walk out from behind the table towards the door.

Aiden killed our daughter.

My hands curl into fists at my sides and I begin to pace the short length of the room.

He may not have meant to – but he did. It was his fault.

I stop and lean my forehead against the wall, try to focus on how it feels rough against my skin, the smell of damp lingering on its surface.

He knew. He knew this whole time and he lied.

But isn't that what you did?

'No. That's not the same.'

'Pardon?' says Kate.

I didn't mean to say that out loud.

It's not the same. I thought she had fallen. I didn't know what had happened and I thought I would lose the only thing I had left. He knew the truth and he stayed silent. He let me tell my lie.

I shake my head, knowing that, soon, I'll no longer be able to control the burgeoning storm crackling and roaring inside my chest. Count to five. One, two, three –

He tried to take her from me. He killed her. And if Helen hadn't come forward, he would have let me take the blame.

My rage bursts out of me, like thunder. I pound my fists into the wall, over and over again, and my feet kick forward. I scream. An inhuman howl, like a dying animal. The same noise that broke out of me when I first found her. And now I have to lose her all over again.

My knuckles begin to bleed but I carry on hitting the wall. No one tries to stop me. No one tries to calm me down. And I don't want them to. I continue to scream until my screams subside into sobs, and I'm so exhausted that I collapse to the floor – a crumpled piece of paper, discarded without a second thought.

'Naomi?'

I open my eyes, but they're raw and small. I don't know how long I've been here, but I look up at Jenning and Walker standing above me, their faces patient. Expectant.

'Where's Olivia?' I croak, my throat sore.

'I'm right here, Naomi,' she says, peering out from behind Walker. 'Would you like some water? You should have some water.'

She kneels down next to me and hands me a small plastic cup. My hand quivers as I lift it to my mouth, and she steadies it, tilting it forward to let me drink. I sip gratefully.

My mind and body are numb. Whatever happens now, I won't feel it. It won't hurt. I feel as if every nerve in my body has been stripped of feeling. Not so long ago, I was searing with pain and anger but now . . . There is nothing. Nothing at all.

'Am I going to be charged now?'

'Yes,' he says. 'We need to take you to the front desk.'

'Okay.' I nod, unable to respond in any other way.

I am numb. I march behind them, my head low, through the maze of corridors towards the front desk. And with each step I think only of Freya.

'Can you stand there, please?' says Walker, pointing to the floor by the desk. I step forward, planting my feet into the floor as firmly as I can, preparing myself to hear them reel off my crimes. Jenning and Walker take a couple of steps back, flanking me on either side.

Olivia shifts into sight. 'Are you okay?' she whispers, squeezing my shoulder. Her mascara has smudged beneath her lower lashes, her pixie hair – which had been so chic and smooth when I first saw her – is now askew. This can't have been what she expected when her phone rang in the darkness.

I nod at her and turn back to the officer sitting on the other side of the desk, behind his computer. The one who is going to charge me.

'Naomi Williams, you are being charged with the offences of preventing a lawful burial and perverting the course of justice.' His voice is dull. A blaring monotone. As if he is reading items off a shopping list. 'The details of those offences are that from the twentieth of November of this year, you concealed the death of your daughter Freya Williams and misled the police into conducting a missing persons investigation. Do you have anything to say in response to these charges?'

I shake my head. What can I say?

'Naomi Williams,' the officer behind the desk continues, 'you are being remanded into custody as we have substantial grounds to believe that you will fail to attend if you are released on bail. The officer will escort you to your cell and you will be taken to the magistrates' court tomorrow for your first hearing.'

346

'Wait – I won't run. I promise. Please, can I go home?' My eyes dart frantically from officer to officer, settling on Jenning – the only one not avoiding my desperate gaze.

'Believe me, Naomi, we aren't doing this to punish you,' he says. 'But I know how much you want to keep your baby. And we can't take the risk that you'll abscond.'

A female officer steps out from behind the desk, and holds me by my elbow. Olivia steps towards me.

'Naomi, I'll see you tomorrow morning, okay?' she says. 'At the magistrates' court. I'll come down to the cells.'

I nod blankly. I am unable to feel anything, or even comprehend how I should be feeling. A ghost. Nothing more.

The officer nudges me and my feet begin to move. One foot in front of the other. Left, right. Left, right. A door slams. I turn and notice she is no longer holding onto my arm. I am in a cell and the door is closed. Solid metal. Impenetrable. I revolve slowly: this cell is exactly the same as the one I was in before, except the toilet, with its exposed bowl of scratched metal, is in the opposite corner. The bed against the opposite wall. A reverse image.

I am a reverse image. Everything is the same as it was this time yesterday. But everything is changed. Last night I was telling Aiden I loved him. Asking him to come back to me and the baby. He told me he loved me. And maybe he did – does. But not enough. Never enough to trust me with our child. Never enough to choose me over himself.

And then there's Helen. Yesterday she was nothing except the woman who took my husband. The best friend who betrayed me. And now if it wasn't for her – for her evidence – would have taken the blame. And everyone would have eved I did this. Even me.

I'm never going home again. I'm going to be kept in a cell until I plead guilty. And I *will* plead guilty.

Then I will go to prison.

And then they will take my baby.

46

Five weeks later

'All rise,' calls the clerk, as she opens the door to the side of the court. The judge enters and everyone stands, the movement almost synchronized. The courtroom is full, our barristers in the front row, and in the row behind them, Jenning, Walker and Kate sit sombrely, in formal clothes, files of evidence on the desks in front of them, just in case.

At the very back of the room, barricaded behind a wall of glass and manned by a guard, Aiden and I sit, separated only by a security guard on the chair between us. To the left of the room, is a public gallery. And it is full. I haven't looked at the news – I've tried to avoid the TV in prison, going back to my cell if anyone changes the channel and the image of newsreaders lights up the screen – but everyone talks. And some prisoners get the paper. It's been all over the national press. Front pages and leading stories, even in the lead-up to Christmas and New Year. The mother who lied about her daughter being missing. The mother who hid her child's body. The father who caused it. I saw a front-page headline before I could avoid it: columns of writing and a large photo of my face. *Mother or monster?*

I search the gallery for Rupert. I told him not to come, but I can't help looking for him. He isn't here.

My eyes dart around the courtroom, but everyone is used on the judge, their heads turned away from us.

Except for one person, craning her neck to look over her shoulder, her blue eyes fixed on me.

Helen.

'Good morning,' says the judge, as he nods at each barrister. He settles into his large chair, the leather squeaking slightly as he adjusts his robes. 'You may be seated.'

I sit down, my eyes fixed on the judge. Under his wig he has grey hair, which is turning white, and a friendly face. Kind.

Please, let him be kind.

'Your Honour,' the clerk says, 'first on your list is the case of the Crown against Aiden Williams and Naomi Williams.'

'Yes,' he says, opening the file in front of him. 'Let's begin.'

'Aiden Williams, please stand,' the clerk says.

Aiden stands, and I can hear his breathing, heavy and quick.

'Aiden Williams, you have been charged with involuntary manslaughter, attempted child abduction and perverting the course of justice. On the charge of manslaughter, how do you plead?'

The word 'manslaughter' reverberates around the large courtroom. The press are all frozen in their seats, waiting for his response. The clerk's voice is professional, devoid of emotion. She must hear stories like ours all the time. I wonder how difficult it is to maintain the cool distance that she seems to have. Or does each case – each time she says 'manslaughter' or 'murder' – stay with her? Will this story stay with her or will she wake up tomorrow and reset like a machine?

Will she remember Freya?

I turn my head just the smallest fraction. Until this moment, I haven't looked at him. I couldn't allow myself to do so. Even at the magistrates' court, the day after

350

were charged, I refused to glance his way. Even when I could feel his eyes on my face. Even when he whispered my name.

But now I allow myself to look. I want to see his face when he says it.

'Guilty,' he mutters.

My hands begin to shake. He'd said he was going to plead guilty. But Olivia warned me that he might change his mind. That his barrister would advise him to fight it, that he could argue it was a horrible accident and that he'd had no idea he was putting Freya in danger when he entered my house in the dead of night and tried to take her.

'On the charge of attempted child abduction, how do you plead?'

He glances across at me, his green eyes shining with tears. 'Guilty.'

'And on the charge of perverting the course of justice, how do you plead?'

'Guilty.'

'You may be seated.'

He collapses into the hard, plastic chair, and rocks forward, until his head is leaning against the glass.

I close my eyes and wait for my name.

'Naomi Williams.'

I stand quickly. The press all turn their heads to watch me, lifting their faces from their notebooks, their scrawled notes in shorthand.

'You have been charged with preventing a lawful burial and perverting the course of justice,' the clerk says. 'On the count of preventing a lawful burial, how do you plead?'

I mull the word around in my mouth for a moment, see how it tastes, before spitting it out. 'Guilty,' I say. It tastes bitter. But no more foul than I deserve.

'And on the charge of perverting the course of justice?'

'Guilty.'

'You may be seated.'

I sit down and exhale deeply.

What now?

The judge sits up straight, and peers over his glasses at the front bench of barristers.

'I've read all of the papers, but before we move onto mitigation, could I please have a run-down of the facts, Mr de Courcy?'

From where I am sitting in the dock, I can see only the prosecutor's back, but his black gown falls off his shoulder as he stands to give the judge his helping of *the facts*. The gown is worn, the material frayed and thin at the edges, and he makes no effort to straighten it. He starts to speak and I try to shut out his words. I've heard the details so many times that it is as if I was there. I have played it over and over again in my mind. It's as if a narrator, omniscient and eerily distant, whispers Aiden's horrors in my ear. And, in reality, I was there. I was in the house, comatose in its silence, just across the landing.

Asleep.

I disappear into my thoughts, only faintly aware of each of our barristers standing in turn, putting forward our cases, our personal circumstances. Our mitigation. As if anything could mitigate what has happened.

I don't want to focus on my barrister explaining my history of anxiety and how it led to my reliance on sleeping tablets. Or how the reliance on sleeping tablets led to Aiden leaving with Freya. How my past caused the sequence of events that led us here, to this very courtroom.

And I don't want to see the look in the judge's eyes when my barrister asks for a low sentence so that I may have a chance to keep my baby. When he explains how my love for my children led to the lie in the first place.

The sound of knocking sends me spiralling out of my thoughts. It is my barrister, his fist poised gently against the divide. He gestures at me to move to the section of the dock where there is a gap between two panels of glass.

'Sorry, Naomi,' he whispers, 'the judge has asked how many weeks pregnant you are. Olivia wasn't sure whether it was thirteen or fourteen and he wants to know exactly.'

'I'm fourteen weeks on Monday.'

'Thank you,' he says. He strides back to his bench, his robe billowing behind him.

'Your Honour, Ms Williams is fourteen weeks pregnant on Monday,' he says, his voice projecting around the large room. 'As you can surmise from the events that have taken place, what Ms Williams wants more than anything is to have the opportunity to keep this child. Not to have to suffer the loss of this one too. She understands that she made a terrible decision to lie, but she did so out of desperation. Everything she did was born out of a mother's desperate need not to have her children taken away. I would ask that you take that into consideration in your sentencing decision. Unless I can assist any further, those are my submissions.'

'No, nothing further,' the judge says. 'I will return to my chambers for consideration.' He turns his gaze to the dock, his eyes assessing both of us in turn. 'Given the nature of these offences and the sentences you are likely to receive, I will not delay sentencing to receive reports. I will sentence you both today. But you will be taken back to your cells.'

He stands and the clerk gets to her feet.

'All rise,' she commands, and I stand, with Aiden, with the police and the press and the lawyers and the onlookers, and vatch as the man who will decide the rest of my life, walks ɔwn from his podium and leaves the court.

*

'All rise,' the clerk announces.

The buzzing courtroom quietens again as the clerk stands, announcing the return of the judge.

He nods at the lawyers and some people in the gallery sit down, but I remain standing. Olivia told me to stand until I was told to sit down. And I don't want to do anything to upset this man. Not this man – the man who will decide my future. I have spent the past month trying to condition myself, preparing myself for the fact that prison is where I'm going to stay. But going to prison isn't what I'm afraid of. The real fear – the type of fear that swells in the very bottom of the barrel of your stomach and sloshes over the rim, making you sick – is for how long. Will I keep this baby? Or will they be taken too?

I instinctively press my hand to the bottom of my stomach, where a small, neat bump has emerged. This baby has started to show much earlier than Freya did. I think I heard once that this is normal for second babies.

Second babies . . . My second baby, not yet here, still growing inside me. My first baby – gone.

Aiden shifts his weight, and the sound of his suit jacket – which now hangs limply off his thin frame – sparking static against his leg, is the loudest sound in the large room. Mine and Aiden's bodies are the perfect reflection of each other: the left hand gripping the right behind our backs; one leg tucked behind the other.

'You may be seated,' the judge says, gesturing to the courtroom, his hand flapping limply. 'You two, please remain standing while you are sentenced.'

Tears sting the corners of my eyes, and my nostrils flare in an attempt to stop them but I fail. They burn.

'I have read the evidence and heard the detailed histo and facts of this case,' the judge says, in a solemn barito

354

have been a judge in the Crown Court for almost fifteen years and this case, surrounding the death of a young child, is the most tragic I have heard in my tenure. I can only hope that a case such as this one never comes before me again. Nor that any child has to suffer as she did at the hands of one of her own parents.'

Suffer. She suffered. And I wasn't there to help her. To kiss it better or make it go away.

A sniff interrupts the stark hush of the small dock and I glance at Aiden. He is crying too.

'Aiden Williams, you have been a kind and loving father. You looked after your daughter as her primary caregiver from when she was sixteen months old. I understand from your mitigation that, until these events took place, you have always done what is best for her and protected her with every ounce of your being. But for selfish reasons you decided to attempt to commit the unlawful act of removing her from her mother. This unlawful act ultimately led to her death. While I fully understand and accept that you in no way meant to harm your daughter, she did come to harm, and died because of your actions. Your actions are further aggravated because of what you did post your daughter's death. You decided to leave her there. You left her there to try to rid yourself of any blame in what had happened. You left her there knowing that her mother would have to find her.'

I flinch.

'And when she found her and lied, saying that she had gone missing, you still did not come forward and expose the truth. You did not do this as you did not want to reveal what you had done.'

Aiden's cries are no longer silent but explode out of him erratic sobs. He tips forward and rests his head against glass.

'Naomi Williams, I understand the pain you must have gone through in finding your daughter the way that you did. I also understand your medical history, and the history between you and your daughter that led you to fear you could lose your unborn child. But that pain and that fear do not excuse the fact that you fed the world a lie. You misled the police, and to your knowledge at the time of your actions, you misled your daughter's father. Furthermore, you hid your daughter's body and actively misled the police in their investigation.'

Please let it be over soon.

'It is sometimes easy to forget the vulnerability of the children in our care. It is easy to forget their complete and utter reliance on us to look after them. It is easy for feuding parents to forget that their child can so quickly become collateral damage. And this is a case of the death of a child born out of the actions of that child's parents. Parents who used blackmail and deceit to destroy the other, however unwittingly. But instead you destroyed the future of your child. I only hope that you are both now ready to let each other go.'

He pauses.

It is coming.

Don't hold your breath, Naomi. Keep breathing.

'Aiden Williams, I take into account your early guilty plea, your previous good character and mitigation. For the offences of involuntary manslaughter, attempted child abduction and perverting the course of justice, I sentence you to ten years' imprisonment.'

I sneak another sideways glance at Aiden. He looks straight ahead and nods, but his face crumples and tears continue to stream down his face.

'Naomi Williams.'

I nod at him, my eyes imploring.

Please, please, please. Please let me keep my baby.

'I take into account your early guilty plea, your previous good character and your mitigating circumstances. For the offences of preventing a lawful burial and perverting the course of justice, I sentence you –'

Breathe, Naomi.

'– to three years' imprisonment.'

Three years. What does that mean?

I search for Olivia, and she turns in her seat, giving me a reassuring nod.

'The baby?' I mouth, then press my lips together, my nerves humming.

'Naomi Williams,' the judge says, and the low murmur that had begun to swell in the public gallery quietens once more, 'I understand that you will be anxious about what will happen to your child while you are in prison.'

I nod.

Can this really be true? Is she really mine?

'It is not my job or my duty to advise you, but as you have been sentenced to three years' imprisonment, and you will be released at the halfway point, it is likely that you will be released before your child is eighteen months old. Your keeping your child is dependent on your being given a space in a prison's mother-and-baby unit, but I'm sure that your legal representative and social services, who are present here in the courtroom, will do all they can to ensure that you and your child are not separated. Please, Ms Williams, work with social services, not against them. They are here to help you.'

'I will,' I say, pushing my hand against the glass in front of me, reaching out to this man who has shown kindness. 'Thank you.'

'I will rise,' the judge says.

'Court rise,' says the clerk.

Everyone stands, moving together, eyes forward, but Helen turns to look at us. Her long blonde hair falls over her black blazer, her blue eyes brimming with emotion.

The gate behind us clangs open and other guards appear, ready to take us down to the cells. An officer grasps Aiden's arm but he turns so that he is facing me as he backs through the door. I shouldn't look at him, but I can't help it. I need to look at him one last time: this man I loved. This man I hate.

I capture just a snapshot of those eyes before he disappears through the gate.

I turn back to the courtroom, my eyes searching for Helen, but her seat has been abandoned. I scan the room frantically and a flash of blonde hair catches my attention – she is enveloped by people as they exit through the doors at the back of the court, jostled gently by the tide of onlookers.

'Helen!' I bang my hand on the glass as I shout her name.

She jumps and turns to look at the dock.

Our eyes meet.

She was my best friend. And after everything that happened, everything we both did – she saved me. She has lost everything and she did it for me. She did it for Freya.

'Thank you,' I say, barely able to whisper the words.

She nods, and for a brief moment we are bound together, like we always were. Like we always will be.

The other guard, the female one, nudges me gently. 'Come on, love,' I think I hear her say. I take one last look around, then turn from the courtroom – from the real world – into the arms of custody.

It is over.

And my baby is staying with me.

Epilogue

Elisia looks up from her toys as birds fly overhead, and she watches as they land on the river.

'Do you like the birds, darling?' I ask. I'm sitting with my back against the willow and she is sitting on a blanket surrounded with toys. Toys that belonged to Freya when she was a baby.

I look out across the water. The fields are still empty, but I have talked to John about having some of his cows – he has more than he can manage now he is nearing retirement. I've picked the apples from the orchard – I won't allow them to fall and rot. This farm is my home. And I'm going to look after it. Treasure it. I've filled the house with photographs. Now Freya's smiling face is accompanied by photographs of my parents. There are even some of me. And countless photos of Elisia.

They let us take photos in the mother-and-baby unit. I constantly snapped away on the shared camera, not wanting to miss a single second of Elisia's first year, knowing that all the photos I was capturing would be sent to me when I was released into the real world: an electronic bundle of memories. And the memories aren't all bad. I focus on the positive 'n each one, rather than the negative. Even though there was prison officer outside the door, Elisia was born safely in a spital – the same hospital as Freya. Even though we

359

returned to a prison, the unit was full of other mothers and there was a playroom full of toys. And even though I had to follow a prison regime, there were people who cared, people who helped me. I don't need the pills any more. And Elisia and I got to stay together.

Other women aren't so lucky. In another life – another judge or another social worker – I wouldn't have been so lucky either. Someone was looking after me, making sure I didn't lose this baby too.

Maybe it was Freya.

'Elisia, be careful, sweetie.' I chuckle as she tries to stand – lifting her bum in the air and pushing off with her hands. She topples over, giggling as she lands on the blanket.

'You silly-billy.' I laugh. 'Try again.'

She was born on 9 July. Freya would almost have been five: old enough to be a brilliant big sister, young enough that they would have played together eventually. She would have looked out for her baby sister as they grew up. Protected her.

Every day I wish I could have done the same for her.

I need to go to the shops – I'm planning a party for Elisia's birthday next week. A couple of the mums I met in the unit are coming, and I'm going to make a cake. We'll sing.

Freya loved singing.

I lean my head back against the tree and clench my fists, inhaling deeply. It's so hard not to think about her. So difficult for every thought not to connect back to her in some way. Especially now that I'm home. The farm holds so many memories, good and bad, and it's difficult to separate the two. People have suggested that I leave, move on, start afresh – but I can't do that. This was Freya's home. All of my connections to her are here, and if I leave, the bad memories might start to dissipate, but the good will also disappear don't want that. I want to remember her as she was – my shining little girl.

I just have to remember what Maria taught me. Maria – my social worker from the unit, a Greek lady whose care swung from soft words to brutal honesty and back – always told me: remember Freya. Honour Freya. But do not dwell. Do not wallow. Do not let anger consume you.

I can always feel when it's happening. When the rage begins to bubble away, I'll reach boiling point and explode, if I don't stop myself. Anything can trigger it: a man with green eyes, a child clutching a toy. Something so small, but I want to scream, and it takes all of my willpower and all of my determination not to let my fury take over.

But I'm getting there. A huge part of that arrived this morning. Closure. I opened it slowly, savouring the feeling. It slid out of the envelope and I opened the maroon passport at the identification page. This is my beginning. My new beginning with my old name.

Naomi Jackson.

I am no longer tied to him.

I try not to think about him at all. I try not to focus on what will happen when he's released from prison and wants to see Elisia, but instead concentrate on taking small but significant steps towards a life where I'm in control. Where I know what I'm capable of being without him. That I'm enough. My last name is just one of those many, many steps, but I know that I will get there eventually. Eventually, his hold over me will begin to fade – like a bruise, deep and purple, which yellows over time and eventually disappears – and I will move on. But it will take time. He was the biggest part of my life, in the best and worst way. He gave me Freya.

And he took her away.

I draw my legs up to my chest and rest my head on my

knees, my eyes peering over the top so that Elisia is still in sight.

Sometimes I wish I could forget. I wish I could rid my mind of the memory of Aiden's laugh, the way it felt when his hand rested on the nape of my neck; the fullness of my heart when he caught my gaze in his. It was love. Real love. But life – complicated, confusing, tragic life – interfered. Tore us apart in a way we never wanted. In a way that might not have happened if we had made different decisions.

I have tried not to think about Rupert as well. I've tried to forgive myself for what I did to him, and everything I put him through. A few days after I was released, I passed Harriet Daley, whom Rupert used to work with. She told me he has moved to Oxfordshire. He's engaged and his fiancée is pregnant. I'm happy for him. It's what he always wanted but I could never give him.

'Elisia, come here,' I call. 'Come to Mummy.'

She turns unsteadily towards me and begins to take tentative steps in my direction. I kneel, holding out my hands towards her as she falls into my arms. I lift her high above my head and she shrieks, then wraps her arms around my neck.

'I love you,' I whisper, into her dark hair. Hair just like Freya's.

When she was born – when the midwife handed her to me – Freya appeared. She was all I could see. She was there in the way Elisia brought her hands up to her face to cover her eyes as she slept. Her small pouty lips. The blue eyes that slowly darkened to green. Freya was always present. And the guilt tore me in two. How could I be a mother to my baby when my daughter was gone? How could I do it? But over time I have realized: Elisia is here, and Freya is not. And while losing Freya still feels like drowning, her sister needs me. And for her, I must keep fighting. It's hard to accept, but there's no other way through. It has to be done.

Of course I still struggle to sleep.

In the unit, there was always noise. There were other mothers and their children, babies crying, screaming, wanting to be fed, shouting for attention. But it wasn't just the noise that kept me awake. It was the fear.

When Freya was born the seed of fear planted itself in my mind, and the anxiety watered it, nourished it, allowed it to bloom. They gave me the pills and the pills made me sleep. But then I couldn't sleep without them. So I lost her and Aiden. And, like a self-fulfilling prophecy I was powerless to stop, my worst fear – the fear I had held in my heart since the first time I held her in my arms – came true.

I couldn't help Freya. I couldn't save her.

Asleep, I was useless.

Asleep, I was no mother at all.

I look at my watch. It's 12:15 p.m.

She should be here soon.

I turn to look away from the river and towards the house. I scan the building, from left to right, listening for the sound of footsteps. A rhythmic thud on wood turns my gaze to the bridge over the river and –

There. There she is.

Helen.

Her blonde hair has been cut short, the chin-length bob accentuating her cheekbones. She smiles as she sees me looking over and raises her hand in a hesitant wave. I stand up, scoop Elisia onto my hip and walk through the knee-length grass towards her. We come to a standstill beneath the shadow of the willow.

'Hi,' she whispers, her bottom lip trembling.

'Hi.'

When I was released, I called her, not knowing whether she would answer or even have the same number, but then I heard her voice – the same voice, from my childhood, saying my name. I don't know what she is to me any more, where we fall on the vast spectrum that our relationship has traversed, but I want her to meet Elisia. She needs to see what she has saved.

'This is Elisia,' I say, as Elisia looks away from Helen to point at a group of ducks that are swimming down the river.

'Is she . . .' Helen says, a question lingering in her voice. 'Sorry. I've just got here and I'm already blurting out –'

'No . . . Ask what you wanted to ask.'

'Is she . . . Williams?'

'Jackson.'

She nods at me, understanding. 'Elisia?' Elisia turns at the sound of her name.

Helen's eyes grow wide. 'She looks just like . . .' Her words disappear as she squeezes her eyes shut and several tears escape through her lashes.

'Just like Freya.'

She presses her lips together and sniffs. 'Can I hold her?'

'Of course.'

'Will she mind?'

'No, she's super-friendly.' I smile at her encouragingly. 'Say hi, Elisia.'

Elisia holds up her hand and bats it wildly, her fingers flapping up and down. 'Hi,' she shouts.

'Oh, wow! That's a big voice.' Helen laughs. She places a large shopper she's carrying on the ground and reaches out her arms. Elisia leans over, happy to be held by a stranger. She grew up around an ever-changing group of women. In the unit she watched people leave only to be replaced by someone else. Another face for her to look at, another voice for her to listen to. Another person to play with.

'I brought you something,' Helen says. 'Well, a couple of things.'

She hands Elisia back to me and I place her on the ground. She stands up unsteadily, then waddles off towards her toys. When I look back at Helen, she's holding a small cake, covered with pink icing, a single silver candle in the centre.

'I didn't know what your plans are for Elisia's birthday but I wanted to make her something.'

'Thank you,' I say, smiling. 'Not like you to bake.'

'Oh, I know. I'm trying to get better at this kind of stuff.' She laughs, then pulls something else from her bag. A small rose bush, its branches empty apart from a few little white buds, just beginning to bloom.

'This is for Freya. I thought you could plant it somewhere and it would be a nice way to remember her. You don't have to plant it if you don't want to.'

'I love it.'

She holds it out to me, arm extended.

'Thank you.'

'You're welcome. She loved roses, didn't she?'

I smile, my heart feeling as if it's about to burst. 'Yes. Because of . . . because of Alice.'

We plant the rose by the bend in the river, where I'll be able to see it from the snug. The sound of the gentle breeze whistles through the woods and a bird calls, its song beautiful and sweet. We lower the plant into the ground and pack down the soil, our hands moving together. Helen's left hand is bare except for a silver ring on the index finger. I look down at my own hand. The rings that had been there for so many years, indented into my skin, are gone. I asked a prison officer to cut them off and she obliged. I thought I'd feel sad. But I didn't. I felt free.

'Thank you, Helen.'

'You're welcome.' She sits down on the ground, lifts Elisia onto her lap and kisses the back of her head. I sink down beside her.

Say it. Say the words you've wanted to say for the past eighteen months. Tell her.

'Thank you for what you did. I –'

'Naomi, you don't need to thank me.'

'I do. I really do. Because if it wasn't for what you did, I could have gone to prison for a long time. I would have lost Elisia. And without her . . .'

'Please, don't cry, Naomi. It's okay.'

I flinch as she places her arm around my shoulders, but she grips tightly. 'Everything's okay now,' she says, as she lets go. 'You're home.'

Ask her. You need to ask.

'Helen?'

'Yes?'

'Why did you go looking for evidence against Aiden?' I blurt it out before I can change my mind. 'I'd been arrested, all the evidence was pointing towards me.'

She turns her face to the sky and the sun shines down on her as she blinks into the light. 'When the police asked me how I found the bank statements, I said I was checking another account but . . .'

'But?'

'But I was actually looking for proof of something else.'

'Proof of what?'

'The affair.' She lowers her face and our eyes meet.

'When did you find out?'

'One day in September. We were dropping Freya at your

366

house for a visit but he was telling you that we had to collect her early for my mum's birthday. I stayed in the car but you said something and it made me suspect.'

'Said something to Aiden?'

'Yes. You were getting upset and he told you he had to leave. You whispered two words. *Just stay* . . . I tried to excuse it, I tried to come up with a reason for it, but I couldn't. So I started looking through his phone. I couldn't find anything, he was always so careful, so one day I followed him. All the way to your house.'

'Why . . .' I stare at her in disbelief. 'Why didn't you –'

'Why didn't I, what? Why didn't I leave?' She shrugs half-heartedly, her eyes dull. 'I loved him, Naomi. I didn't want to give him up. I'd sacrificed so much to be with him. Our friendship . . . I had to believe I hadn't made a terrible mistake.'

I understand completely. We understand each other, in our own little ways.

'So the night you found the flight payment you were looking for proof? Why?'

'The night you were arrested I called Aiden's mobile but he didn't answer. I must have called ten times but . . . nothing. So I called Kate to find out if something had happened but she said she hadn't seen him. I called the Queen's Arms and asked to speak to him in his room but he wasn't there. And that was when I knew he was with you.'

'I'm –'

'You don't need to say anything. We're past that now.' She looks at the ground, her fingers picking blades of grass and flicking them aside. 'I'd thought it was over. I'd seen a message come through. In October. You asked him why he was ending it. He had no idea that I saw it and he deleted it as soon as he read it, of course. But I thought it was over. So when I realized you were together that night, I started looking through his things to see if it had ever ended in the first place.'

'It did. He ended it. That night was –'

'A one-off?' Her eyes shine with hurt as she meets my gaze.

I nod.

'Anyway . . . That was when I saw the payment. I started looking through his emails but there was nothing. So I called the airline and they sent through the details. We had argued about moving away for so long . . . I couldn't believe he would do it without me. That he would leave me. I didn't know what to do . . . But then Kate came to the house and told me they'd found Freya. She said you'd been arrested and were being questioned. And then I remembered the key . . . I didn't want to believe it but . . . I just knew. I knew it was him.'

The cold grip of fury squeezes in my chest. And I can see it there too, in Helen's eyes. Grief might be like a fire, roaring and burning out of control, but slowly, gradually, it dissipates, becoming more manageable. Always there but smouldering beneath the surface. Flickering gently. But anger and betrayal don't burn: they freeze. They freeze solid around your heart and never melt away.

But Helen understands. We are bound together by fury and betrayal and love. We always will be.

'Shall we go inside and do the cake?' I ask.

'Sure.'

I stand up and lift Elisia onto my hip, then Helen and I walk side by side to the house, our legs swishing through the long grass of the orchard.

We settle in the snug, kneeling around the coffee-table. I light the candle and Elisia's eyes grow large and round. She squeals in delight as we sing, her chubby hands clapping along to the words.

We lean forward and I blow out the candle.

'One thing I'll never understand,' I say, choosing my words carefully. 'Aiden is so controlled. He doesn't make mistakes, he never has. But . . . the key. He said he thought he'd put it back, but he didn't. He was hiding his most horrific secret, but he left the key in his car that whole time. If he'd just put it back where it belonged . . .'

She picks up the knife and slides it into the cake, portioning out a perfect slice. I wait for her to say something, but she stays silent.

'It's so unlike him,' I whisper.

She looks up, fixing me with her gaze.

'Yes.' She raises one eyebrow as she hands me the plated slice, a glint in her sparkling blue eyes. 'Completely unlike him.'

I look out to the woods as her words sink in. The trees, heavy with green, shine brightly in the gold light of afternoon and my eyes follow the line of the river as it snakes towards the house.

Helen is still watching me, her cool eyes burning, waiting for a response. I meet her eyes and smile, before looking down at Elisia.

I am home.

My gaze is drawn back to the outside world. The farm, the river, the orchard. The woods. But my eyes come to rest on Freya's rose.

Sleep well, darling girl.

Sleep well.

Acknowledgements

As a child I spent hours upon hours in bookshops, browsing through the shelves, lost in the worlds and characters that writers had created. To be writing acknowledgments for my own novel is something I never imagined I would get to do, and I am forever grateful to every person who helped me bring this book to life, and to every person who has supported me.

Firstly, thank you to my agent, the wonderful Kate Burke. Thank you for plucking me out of your slush pile and helping me hone my story for submission. I'm so happy to have you on my team. Thanks also to James Pusey, Hanna Murrell, Sian Ellis-Martin, Ane Reason, Lizzy Attree, Daisy Way and the rest of the team at Blake Friedmann.

To the inimitable team at Michael Joseph. Your enthusiasm and passion for *When They Find Her* was truly overwhelming and I knew straightaway that my book and I were in the safest, most imaginative hands. Thanks to Vicky Photiou, Laura Nicol, Madeleine Woodfield, Amy Baxter, Laura Marlow, Deirdre O'Connell, Christina Ellicott, Rachel Myers, Louise Blakemore, Nick Lowndes, Hazel Orme and Beth O'Rafferty. Thanks to Lauren Wakefield for the stunning cover which captures the book in the most perfect way. And thanks to the rest of the team at Michael Joseph who read my novel when it first landed on my editor's desk.

That, of course, brings me to my editor. Clio, I can't think of anything more I could want from the champion of my book. Thank you for helping me turn *When They Find Her* into something I am so proud of, and for your excitement and passion at every stage. I'm incredibly proud to be your first acquisition for Penguin Michael Joseph.

Thank you to the teachers who always encouraged my love for writing and intensified my love for literature: Mr McClean, Mrs Cottman and Ms Miller – you made school a time of joy and inspiration.

I have been overwhelmed by the writing community who, in an industry that could be rife with competition and jealousy, have been so supportive. Thanks to Emma Albrighton and Natalie Dawn for all of your support since we first met at Winchester. And thank you to the VWG: an incredible group of ridiculously talented writers who have become my friends and confidants.

Thanks to my friends Lauren, Jess, Rick, Pam, Jas, Karen and Natasha, for enduring hours of me talking about writing and books, and for celebrating with me along the way.

Thanks to my friend Andy Summers, for always being there to answer my questions on police procedure. I know that there are still many inaccuracies in this book, Andy, and I apologize: it's for artistic purposes, I promise.

To my family. I am completely indebted to you all for your enduring love and support. My siblings: Eva, thank you for teaching me to be strong and determined; Kyriacos, thank you for nurturing my imagination from such a young age – I blame you for how dark this book is.

Mum and Dad, I owe everything I am and everything I have to you. Thank you for encouraging my reading obsession and for always supporting me. This book is yours.

To my children, Christiana and Jacob, you are my constant source of inspiration. You are my whole world.

And finally, Daniel. Thank you for being my partner: in parenthood and in life. Thank you for building our life with me. And thank you for always believing.

Reading Group Questions

1. In *When They Find Her*, Lia Middleton makes the reader an accomplice as they're party to Naomi's lie from the beginning. How did this impact your reading experience?

2. Do you think Naomi could have admitted to her lie early on in the novel? If so, is there a particular turning point in the novel where Naomi goes too far and can't possibly tell the police what really happened?

3. Did you feel sympathy towards Naomi throughout the novel? If your sympathy grew or waned, when and why was that?

4. How do you think you would have handled the situation Naomi's friends found themselves in when Helen and Aiden got together?

5. How did you respond to Aiden's character at different points of the story?

6. How did you feel the setting added to the story and tension? Do you think it's important that the story is set during the winter?

7. How did you feel about the depiction of parenthood in *When They Find Her*?

8. Is there anyone who you think Naomi should have confided in about what really happened to Freya? If so, who? Rupert, Kate, Aiden? Or somebody else?

9. *When They Find Her* explores a number of issues which can feel taboo in society – including mental health, struggles within motherhood and addiction. How did you find Middleton's treatment of these subjects?

10. How did you feel about the ending? Did you see any elements of the resolution coming?

He just wanted a decent book to read ...

Not too much to ask, is it? It was in 1935 when Allen Lane, Managing Director of Bodley Head Publishers, stood on a platform at Exeter railway station looking for something good to read on his journey back to London. His choice was limited to popular magazines and poor-quality paperbacks – the same choice faced every day by the vast majority of readers, few of whom could afford hardbacks. Lane's disappointment and subsequent anger at the range of books generally available led him to found a company – and change the world.

'We believed in the existence in this country of a vast reading public for intelligent books at a low price, and staked everything on it'
Sir Allen Lane, 1902–1970, founder of Penguin Books

The quality paperback had arrived – and not just in bookshops. Lane was adamant that his Penguins should appear in chain stores and tobacconists, and should cost no more than a packet of cigarettes.

Reading habits (and cigarette prices) have changed since 1935, but Penguin still believes in publishing the best books for everybody to enjoy. We still believe that good design costs no more than bad design, and we still believe that quality books published passionately and responsibly make the world a better place.

So wherever you see the little bird – whether it's on a piece of prize-winning literary fiction or a celebrity autobiography, political tour de force or historical masterpiece, a serial-killer thriller, reference book, world classic or a piece of pure escapism – you can bet that it represents the very best that the genre has to offer.

Whatever you like to read – trust Penguin.